Terror in

At first Rikard thought that Droagn was suffering hallucinations. Then he saw giant lizards with eight legs moving among the rubble. Rikard found it hard to be frightened by them, though their intent was all too obvious. He was numbed by the Tathas effect, and kept slipping back into mental darkness . . .

"Kitah bley!" Droagn shouted. Rikard felt the dim edges of the psychic blast which Droagn *projected* against the creatures, but they weren't intelligent enough to be affected.

Rikard finally became aware that he was in danger. He drew his gun and closed the connection to the implants in his hand, arm and brain. But the effect of the time dilation thus produced was bizarre, dreamlike, nightmarish.

The monsters were closing. Rikard missed his shot. He was dumbfounded. He had never missed before when he was wired into his range finder. He fired again.

And missed . . .

Critical Raves for Allen L. Wold's Previous Novels

"Unique and lively. . . hair-raising and thought-provoking . . . absorbing."
—*Fantasy Newsletter*

"A remarkably expansive imagination . . . highly recommended."
—*Library Journal*

"Engrossing . . . gives your wonderbone a good tingle."
—*Milwaukee Journal*

"Plenty of excitement . . . entertaining . . . offers escapist, wish fulfillment adventure."
—*Publishers Weekly*

Also by Allen L. Wold

Jewels of the Dragon
Crown of the Serpent

LAIR OF THE CYCLOPS

ALLEN L. WOLD

WARNER BOOKS

A Time Warner Company

WARNER BOOKS EDITION

Questar® is a registered trademark of Warner Books, Inc.

Cover design by Don Puckey
Cover illustration by Richard Hescox

Warner Books, Inc.
666 Fifth Avenue
New York, NY 10103

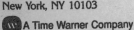 A Time Warner Company

Printed in the United States of America

First Printing: January, 1992

10 9 8 7 6 5 4 3 2 1

The galaxy is full of life, but it is not evenly distributed. Some areas are teeming with it. Elsewhere the stars are almost devoid of worlds suitable for the development or maintenance of life. Except in scale, it is no different from conditions on a life-bearing planet, which has frozen polar regions, desiccated deserts, mountains with too little air, sea bottoms with too much pressure. That portion of the great spiral arm in which the Federation lies is one of those that is dense with life, with sentience, both native and colonized.

It is natural for people of different physical form or cultural origin to be somewhat in conflict with each other. Where cultures are very different, this conflict is less—they are not competing for the same things. Where they are very similar, the friction is often great, since each wants and values what the other has. It is much the same with physiology. Two humanoid races will on the one hand understand each other better than if one were a carnivorous arachnoid and the other a herbivorous mamalochordate, but on the other hand, those species that are different are not in competition, and neither views the other as prey or predator.

—1—

In those areas where intellect, and cultural integrity, proved strong, the differing species and cultures learned to get along somehow, though not without their wars and struggles. Where a culture was immature, or an intellect incomplete, a species usually died, exterminated by its adversaries. In the time of the Federation, most star nations were stable, and genocidal conflict was confined to only those systems where new species were first emerging into starflight, and then only if older and wiser people could not prevent the slaughter.

The Federation, however, was exceptional even so. It had far less than its share of troubles, compared with the other star nations. There was crime, of course, but that is a personal and individual aberration. There were governmental, philosophical, and artistic differences, of course, but they seldom caused any overt violence. Tolerance between differing species was extremely high in the Federation, and even similar and hence competing cultures tended to try to find some compromise to their mutual benefit. Some scholars speculated that it was the continuing influence of the M'Kade, whose advent some thousand standard years ago had brought about the current form of government known as the Federation, which was responsible for this enviable condition; others that it was something intrinsic in the stars themselves, similar to that which promoted life in the first place.

There were exceptions, of course. Frequently conflicts arose between peoples who were so similar to each other that an outsider couldn't have told the difference. Sometimes war broke out within a single culture, which fought with itself far more bitterly than it ever had with anybody else. But these were the exceptions, and in other star nations were both more common and more violent. In large, the Federation was the epitome of peaceful coexistence.

Trokarion

1

In the pitch-darkness a blinding spark of white light appeared, at about head level, slicing down, leaving behind it an intensely glowing wormtrail of molten stone and metal. A second cutting torch began working at the same point as the first, slicing horizontally. As the two spots of fire moved, the cuts behind them cooled and dimmed, but still light shone through from the illuminated chamber beyond.

The first torch finished its long downward stroke and started to cut across the bottom, just as the second torch turned its corner and started down the other side. The first torch finished and winked out just before the second met it. The cut panel fell into the darkness with a shattering crash.

Two furry beings, clutching cutting torches, filled most of the impromptu doorway, silhouetted by the light from the chamber behind them. Their bodies were spherical, with no apparent heads. Four dog legs radiated from the lower portion of their bodies, and there were two arms, one on either side of the upper portion. They began to stow their equipment into carrying cases, sitting on the stone floor behind them, which cases also held their power packs, attached to the wands by heavy cables.

They wore no clothes, only a simple harness over their thick fur, a harness that supported pouches in lieu of pockets. The fur of one was black, of the other mahogany. Their bare dog feet each ended in two huge yellow talons, easily eight centimeters long, and their hands, working with the precision of long practice, had two fingers and one thumb, almost as formidably taloned as their feet.

The area in which they worked, illuminated by unseen lamps off to the right, was made of crudely dressed stone, and looked like nothing so much as a pre-steam-age sewer. Shadows shifted, greatly elongated, on the wall behind the two workers. There were other people present.

When the cutting torches were properly packed the two workers helped each other set the heavy cases onto their backs, hooked on to studs on their harnesses, right behind the heavily lidded, half-dome eyes that bulged up through the fur on the top of their spherical bodies. The eyes were green, as big as a Human fist, with round black pupils. Their mouths were twenty-centimeter-long gashes, just forward of and below the eyes, thickly lipped, and with fangs ten centimeters long projecting in a downward curve from each corner.

The black-furred one stepped away from the doorway for a moment and came back with two powerful battery lamps and handed one to the mahogany-furred being. The space behind them did not grow appreciably darker, there were other lamps in the care of the people behind them.

The two shone the lamps into the darkness. The room now revealed was only four or five meters on a side, and completely bare. The material of the walls—stone? plastic? concrete?—was blackened as if by great heat, and irregularly corrugated as if compressed by great pressure. The wall through which the two furry, spherical beings had cut was the most distorted, especially near the ceiling that sloped down there, tinged with white along the join, and streaked with dark, grainy iridescent colors where the chemical composition of the structural material had been transformed by the heat.

After only a moment's hesitation the two workers stepped through the newly cut portal and to either side, set down their lamps so that they illuminated the larger portion of the chamber, and began moving aside the rubble of the fallen section of wall. As they worked, a shadow separated itself from the others cast on the primitive stone wall beyond the opening, and a Human stepped up to the new threshold and stood watching.

He was taller than average by some centimeters, slender, and he moved with an easy grace, indeed seemed graceful even when he was standing still. He was not exactly handsome, but then it was hard to tell with the bizarre helmet that covered his head and the left side of his face down to his chin. Over his left eye was a camera turret, the wide-angle lense now in place, the focus working almost silently, controlled by direct neuro-connections. The ear on that side was covered by a microphone complex, with precision-close, general-surround, and directional long-range mikes, chosen at the wearer's option, just like the camera lenses. A smaller mike curved around from his cheek to just in front of his mouth.

He was dressed in leathers and so, in spite of the recording helmet, couldn't be mistaken for a mere reporter. These unusual clothes consisted of a well-fitting pseudo-leather jacket—perhaps a bit long below the belt, with fancy stitching across the shoulders—and leather pants, snug but supple, tucked into calf-high boots, all of a rich tan color. He also wore heavy gauntleted gloves, of the same make and design, and on his hip there was a holster, in which snuggled the heaviest caliber revolver made in the Federation, the usually illegal, six-shot, .75 megatron. Not a reporter's weapon at all.

The shadows behind him moved again, and another figure came to the portal, humanoid in appearance but with movements that were simultaneously fluid and clumsy, suggesting otherwise. Its clothing was a loose-fitting gray jacket and full-cut trousers that seemed designed to conceal its form and hence its species. Its head was wrapped in gray, as was its face. Goggles covered its eyes, and a translating vocalizer covered the area where its mouth and nose might be expected to be.

"The stories would appear to be true," it said. Its tone was completely neutral, completely mechanical, with no hint of what kind of vocal apparatus might have produced it, though its pitch suggested a masculine gender.

"Of course they are," said another of the four-legged, spherical furry beings, who had come up to stand behind the gray-clad humanoid. His fur was a dark brick color, his eyes slightly more yellow than those of the two workers, and unlike them his black leather harness supported, along with the power pack and such, a holstered pistol, pen recorder, communications equipment, and other things the nature and purpose of which could not be immediately determined by the casual observer. He pushed his way past the gray one as if he didn't want to touch him, but stopped short behind the tall Human who was still recording every inch of this small chamber. The workers finished clearing the rubble, picked up their lamps, and stood on either side of the opening as if awaiting further instructions.

The tall man stepped forward first, followed and flanked by the gray one and the Kelarine supervisor, whose heavy toe talons clicked harshly on the heat-distorted floor as he walked. Then the portal behind them was darkened as a gigantic figure moved into the opening.

Its torso, bronze and green and deep blue, was, from top shoulder to waist, almost as tall as the individual in loose gray standing in front of it. A thick neck supported a head that was both wolflike and snakelike, with small bat ears set high on either side, domed eyes, and fangs that extended well below his lower jaw. On his head he wore a crownlike device, a circlet of black metal with curved spikes just in front of his tall, pointed ears.

He had four arms, one pair above the other, each longer than an average Human is tall, longer even than the man in leather. One huge hand carried a large case by straps, another held a device as big as a chain saw but without the chain of teeth and with a grip that fit his hand perfectly. In a third hand he carried a tapering staff, some two and a half meters long, with a knob at one end and a blunt point at the other, and in his fourth was a special lamp that shone with the light of wavelengths subtly different from those of the other lamps, less yellow and more blue and red at the same time, as if his eyes had evolved under a bizarrely different sun. And below his waist he had not legs but meter after meter of thick serpentine coils, bigger around than a Kelarin, extending back beyond the portal and out of sight.

"What do you think, Droagn," the man said, though he didn't look around.

ˉI can't tell,ˉ the creature *projected*. He did not vocalize, but used a special kind of telepathy that was comprehensible by all present, though the language he used had not been heard in this part of the galaxy for over fifty thousand years. ˉEven if this were Ahmear work, there's nothing left to prove it.ˉ

If the Kelarine supervisor had been a bit fastidious about getting too near the gray-clad humanoid, he was absolutely wary of the serpentine Ahmear. His ancestors had known the Ahmear, before that species had left this part of the galaxy so many aeons ago, and not all of the stories and legends that had been passed down were of the kind to instill confidence in the presence of this being, a freak survivor, unique within the Federation or any other star nation with which the Federation had general communication.

So the Kelarin kept well to one side as Droagn slid through the portal to join the others—or at least most of him did.

The two Kelarine workers moved across the room as the

three came in, and when Droagn was fully within, two other Kelarins, one black, the other a pale terra-cotta with amber shading, came to the hole in the wall, carrying a variety of equipment and the last two lamps. In other circumstances they might have been considered tough characters who could take care of themselves and were equal to whatever situation in which they might find themselves. But keeping company with the Ahmear, a creature from their past thought mythical by most and demonic by some, made them more than a little cautious. They kept well clear of Droagn's slightly twitching tail tip.

There was no door set into the archway on the far side of the room, and only blackness beyond. The two lead Kelarins carried their lamps toward it while the tall Human followed gracefully behind. It was he who gave direction to the group, though without speaking, and the rest of his party accommodated him as they followed.

The next chamber was larger than the first, just as empty, just as discolored and distorted. "*Gh'a-vaan ge'shlathik,*" the Ahmear said, actually vocalized, as he came through the arch.

The man turned and looked up at him, surprised by this revelation of his companion's excitement. "What was that again?"

"Sorry," Droagn answered, "I just said, 'This really feels weird.'"

"That's what I thought you said," the man replied, and turned back to his recording.

He was thorough in his work, but even the most complete recording of an empty chamber cannot take long. The only thing to see here, opposite this open portal, was a closed door, twisted and warped by the same volcanic heat that had distorted everything else. The two Kelarins with the cutting torches did not need spoken instructions. They went to the doorway and started setting up their equipment again.

But Droagn just snorted and slithered toward them. They quickly backed out of his way, their green eyes glittering overlarge in the reflected light of their lamps. The Ahmear put down his own lamp and the strap-bound case, pressed his two huge upper hands against the door, and pushed. The material of the door was a lot more fragile than it had appeared, weakened by heat and time, so that it crumbled with his first effort. Droagn coiled back and let the hired workers clear the rubble.

Beyond was a broad corridor, going to right and left. It was twisted and warped, as if the underlying structure of the building had suffered far more damage than was suggested by what they had so far seen.

The two workers shone their lamps, one in each direction. The tall man, with the gray-clad humanoid beside him, looked first down to the right. Some meters away a tongue of solidified lava protruded into the hall from what had once been a doorway. Beyond it another intrusion had been forced through a narrow crack in the wall. Farther on the shadows were too dark to tell.

To the left were other, similar intrusions. The black stone was frothy, streaked with white, sometimes half cutting off the corridor, and one tongue of lava dripped down from a gap in the ceiling, like some petrified theatrical curtain.

The Ahmear pushed through the door and paused a moment, looking first one way, then the other, while the tall man on his right, and the gray one on his left, waited patiently. "That way," he *projected* at last, pointing to the right. "The other way around is more direct, but the corridor is completely blocked off past the first turn." There was no visible clue as to how he came by this information.

There were other volcanic intrusions in the corridor past the first two, but nothing else. If there had once been any floor covering, or wall covering, or furniture, or decorations, they had either been removed, or destroyed by the heat that had so warped and distorted the structure. Even so, the tall man recorded every step of the way, though he made his steps long and did not pause except once to duck under a tongue of black-foamed rock, its edges sharper than knives.

They came to a corner where the corridor turned to the left. There was less plastic deformation, but they still found intrusions and lava tongues from cracks in wall and ceiling, and once they came to a massive intrusion, from a doorway, that nearly closed off the corridor altogether.

Just past the second corner, on the inner side of the square that they were traversing, they came to an exceptionally large double door, set into a somewhat more elaborate jamb than normal, and here the leading workmen paused. Droagn came forward and put his huge hands against it to push it open, but this time the doors did not crumble or break. The Kelarins moved with a bit of a swagger as once again they set up their torches and started to cut. This time, however, they were working with security steel and not just structural materials and volcanic tuff.

At last the heavy doors fell away with a great crash and slid down a broad, steep ramp, which lay immediately beyond.

"It looks good, Rikard," the Ahmear said to the man. He gestured toward the floor of the ramp. "Too coarse a texture for feet or wheels or sliders, but just right for 'snake bellies.'"

Rikard and Droagn stepped aside to allow the Kelarins to precede them down the ramp, but the workers held back, talking quietly among themselves. The terra-cotta one noticed Rikard looking at them, nudged the supervisor, and they all fell silent. Then the supervisor stepped up to Rikard.

"This is as far as we go," he said. "We're already way beyond our depth." A thick pink tongue flickered around his white fangs.

Rikard, taller than the Kelarin by a full head, just looked at him a moment. "That wasn't the deal, Kath Harin," he said.

"We've shown you into the ruins," Kath Harin said. "We can't give you any more guidance."

"You can carry the equipment. That's what you're being paid for too."

"Yeah, and it's enough for slog-work like that, and even enough for keeping Msr. Tail here company"—he flickered his huge yellow eyes at Droagn—"but just barely. But it's not enough for us to go down there." He jabbed at the doorway with a heavily clawed finger.

"If these ruins are authentic," the gray-clad humanoid said with his flat mechanical voice, "then what is there to be afraid of? This city has been buried for fifty thousand years."

"We had a deal," Rikard said to Kath Harin. "Ten kay apiece, down and out. If you won't come down, there'll be no pay coming out."

˜And the sooner we go down,˜ Droagn *projected*, ˜the sooner we'll *be* out. Let's do it.˜

The Kelarin paid no attention to him but looked at the tall Human instead. "Hell, Braeth, you owe us for what we've done so far anyway." He reached out a clawed hand, as if expecting coins to be dropped into it. The talons glinted in the light, long and strong and sharp enough to rip a man in half with one stroke.

Rikard Braeth's only response was to reach up with his left hand and carefully remove the optical helmet. His right hand, gloved and gauntleted, hung negligently by the butt of the heavy pistol on his hip. His face, now that it could be seen, was not homely, and was quite young—he was only thirty-one, given a Human life span of some two hundred years. His expression was bland, and his voice was neither loud nor soft as he said, "If I order a car and you deliver only the engine, you don't get paid until I get the rest. How do you want it?"

˜Take it easy,˜ Droagn *projected*. He reached out one hand and gently placed it on Rikard's shoulder. The ends of his fingers came almost halfway down the man's chest. ˜I'm supposed to play the heavy, you just make the decisions.˜

Rikard looked up at him and snorted. "You can be heavy if you want," he said. He watched the Kelarins. They had lost some of their fragile bravado. "I just don't have much patience with people who claim to be such tough dudes and then quail at the sight of a dark ramp." He gazed calmly at the Kelarine supervisor as he spoke.

Kath Harin lowered his clawed hand. He glanced at the gray humanoid, who was silent. The goggles the gray one wore revealed nothing, not even at what he was looking. The supervisor's tongue flickered once, then he went back to his crew, and they spoke quietly together for a few moments. Then he turned back to Rikard.

"Look," he said, "we signed on for one kind of job; this is turning out to be something different, a lot more dangerous than what we bargained for. The deal is this, we quit now or you double the rate."

Rikard snorted again, disgusted this time. He stared at the brick-red supervisor until Kath Harin could no longer meet his gaze. "All right," Rikard said, "twenty kay apiece. But no more chickenfooting, or you get nothing."

The four workers bobbed in the way that was their equivalent of a nod. "All right," Kath Harin said. "But you've got the heavy artillery. Be ready to use it if you have to."

Rikard's only response was to put his recording helmet back in place.

They went down, the two Kelarine workers in the lead with their lights, then Rikard Braeth flanked by the gray one and Kath Harin, then Droagn, and well back the other two workers with their own lamps. The textured floor of the ramp was canted from side to side, the walls were twisted, and in some places there were cracks running through the surface. But aside from that it was an easy descent.

There was no sound, except for their own footfalls or the equivalent; no smell, of mold or rot or char or even mustiness; no color, other than a multitude of shades of gray, no iridescent heat discoloration as they'd found above; no movement to the air.

The descending ramp turned one full circle, then leveled

off where a door was set into the outside wall. They did not pause here.

"Notice the lack of dust," the figure in gray said.

"What about it?" Rikard asked.

"It means that everything was removed from this place either immediately before or immediately after it was buried. I am impressed that the materials used in construction haven't decomposed more than they have. This must indeed be Ahmear architecture, rather than that produced by a physically similar species."

"Of course it's Ahmear," Kath Harin said. "Everybody knows that."

"I don't," Droagn *projected*. "This place is too big. In my time we didn't build cities, just private residences and the occasional orbiting station. We like to be roomy, of course, but— He reached up to touch the black metal circlet with its projecting spikes that sat on his head. "This place is at least a hundred times bigger than any chateau I've ever known." It was the circlet that enhanced his natural telepathic abilities and gave him an extended *sensing* of the place they were exploring.

"Only a hundred?" Rikard asked. If this had been a Human city it could easily have accommodated fifty thousand people.

"Maybe two hundred," Droagn said.

They went down the ramp, level after level, until it ended, thirty floors below, in a roughly circular chamber, with nine doors around the sides. All the doors were closed. The floor here was nearly level. The walls showed no compression or burning.

"Are we at the bottom?" Rikard asked Droagn.

The Ahmear's dome eyes seemed to gaze through the walls. He turned his head, the light glinted off the points of the spikes on the circlet he wore. "Nowhere near," he said at last. "We'll have to find another ramp."

"So which way do we go?" Rikard asked.

"Lots of options," Droagn said. He tapped the black

crown on his head with a finger. With it he could feel the difference between rock and air for quite a distance. He pointed to the fourth door on the left from the ramp. ˜I'd guess that's our best bet.˜

Rikard adjusted the recording helmet, scanned the chamber one last time, then waited as the Kelarine workmen, taking their cue, went to the indicated door and started opening it. It was not fused shut, so a few moments' work with prybars did the trick. Beyond was a broad corridor. The party resumed their previous formation and entered.

˜The ceilings are right, though,˜ Droagn said to Rikard. They were four meters above the floor. ˜A comfortable height for an Ahmear.˜ His own head rose to three meters above his serpentine lower body. ˜For a private dwelling, that is.˜

There were widely spaced doors along the corridor, but Rikard did not pause. The rooms beyond the doors were spacious by Human standards, cozy in Ahmear terms, and all completely empty. Those on the left had windows, now completely darkened by volcanic scoria and pumice.

The corridor went on for three hundred meters or so and then came to a tee. Droagn gestured and they turned to the right.

"This is older than fifty thousand years," the gray one said as they proceeded down the slightly narrower branch.

"Well of course, Msr. Grayshard," Kath Harin said, "it would have to be, wouldn't it, for it to have been buried by a volcano that is well known to have gone off fifty-one thousand three hundred and twenty-one years ago."

"Indeed," Grayshard said. "That is to say, I believe this place to be more than one hundred thousand years old."

"How can you tell?" Rikard asked.

"There's something in the flavor of the dust."

"This dust's got no smell," one of the black Kelarins protested.

"That is my point," Grayshard answered.

The corridor ended in an arch, beyond which was a large

chamber, its ceiling eight meters high. Their footfalls and talon clatters echoed in the open space, and the light of the lamps, broad-beam as it was, showed the far wall only dimly. There were two doors on either side of the arch. There were five doors in each of the other walls, more or less evenly spaced.

Droagn concentrated again, extending his senses through the black circlet, then directed them to the fourth door in the right-hand wall. Beyond was another, much smaller chamber, with one door in each of the other walls, and a ceiling once again only four meters from the floor.

After that it was a maze of rooms, chambers, short connecting hallways, and more rooms. They proceeded more slowly now as Droagn tried to find them the best way. It was a job for which the circlet he wore, a device called the Prime, and once thought to be the oldest pre-Federation artifact in existence, was not truly intended.

"You're going by more than just 'feel,'" Rikard said to him once.

"I'm assuming that this was indeed built by Ahmear, and applying logic. That doesn't always work, of course. What if you found yourself in ruins built by Humans even five thousand years ago, a different culture, a different people. Could you predict what each empty room might be, or where each empty corridor might lead?"

"If it were as empty as this," Rikard said, "I'm not even sure I could tell it was Human."

"Exactly," Droagn replied.

"But I'd know it wasn't built by Atreef, or Belshpaer."

At last they came to another door, massive and double, but when Droagn pushed the panels aside, all they found beyond it was the top of an elevator shaft.

Droagn turned to look back the way they had come. "I'm not sure," he *projected*, "but I think there's an opening between floors that way."

They went back around the corner and entered the first door on their left, toward the outside of the structure. The room was perfectly empty, with lava-sealed windows opposite them and a door to the right. They went through the door into another room like the first, but with two doors in the direction they wanted to go. Droagn directed them through the one on the left, near the outside of the building.

This opened into a relatively narrow corridor, barely wide enough for two Ahmear—or four Humans—side by side, with occasional doors on the inside wall, and no windows outside. Every forty to sixty meters or so the outer wall had cracked, and congealed tongues of black bubbly lava projected partway into the corridor, sometimes only a few centimeters, less often farther.

Rikard had not consciously counted paces before, but it seemed to him that they had gone a lot farther back along this outside corridor than they had come on the inner one from the ramp. He was about to mention this to Droagn when the lamps picked out the end of the corridor just ahead.

There was a single doorway, at the end. It opened at a touch, into a chamber that was much larger than any they had yet entered, and far more distorted. The outside walls had buckled almost completely and were heavily corrugated, half melted. The floor and ceiling actually met in two places, and the rest of the floor sagged down in a shallow depression that matched the sagging ceiling.

Here and there in this room, for the first time, were low piles of ash and char. Grayshard went over to the nearest of these and knelt in a strange way that implied that his knees worked differently from a Human's. He reached out one gloved hand and poked a finger into the centimeter-high pile of dust, spread out like a thick smear across the slanting and buckled floor. "A complex of organic materials," he said. He moved his finger elsewhere. "Plastic or wood, I can't tell which." He stood, a flowing movement that still seemed clumsy, and went to another pile that differed only in being slightly more granular, and poked his finger into it. "This is much the same.

"This room," he said as he stood, "was so badly burned that there was nothing left to take away. If the inhabitants had evacuated before the disaster, they would have cleared this room too. That it was not, that the furnishings were left to burn to ash, conveys to me that the emptiness elsewhere was due to later salvage."

"If there *was* anything to salvage," Rikard said.

"Oh, there would have been. Or it would have been left as strews of dust, as it was here."

"I take it that's our exit," Rikard said. He pointed to a fused doorway on the far side of the room, near the inner wall.

The two Kelarins with the cutting torches went over to it and unpacked their equipment. But instead of cutting through the door itself, Droagn had them make a new opening just beside it, where the material of the wall was a bit less melted and distorted.

Beyond was another, smaller chamber, with lots of ash and char, in smears and mounds, some of which were rather substantial, but all situated more toward the inner wall. At the outer wall the ceiling nearly met the floor.

On the far side of this room there was yet another door, and this time the workmen cut through it. And there, at last, was another ramp, leading down into silent darkness. This one was broad and shallow, as if intended for ceremonial rather than strictly functional use.

They followed the ramp around seven full circles, descending seven levels as they did so, and then it ended in a large open space with the feel of a lobby or an antechamber to it. There were doors and open arches in the other five walls, and even as they came off the ramp, from each door and arch came strange creatures, huge and spherical and covered with thick fur, nearly black above and shading to tan below, shambling on six legs, each with two heavily clawed toes.

They resembled the Kelarins as a bear resembles a Human, half again as tall and far bulkier. Huge eyes projected upward from the forward top of their bodies, and their mouths, at the front, were gaping slashes nearly thirty centimeters across, filled with a grotesque array of huge fangs. Shadows bobbled wildly as the Kelarine lamp-holders recoiled in near paralytic surprise and terror. The creatures, in turn, seemed confused by the light, and milled around the outer edges of the room.

"A pod of fathak," Kath Harin choked.

The last two Kelarins began to back up the ramp as more of the fathak came in, pressing those who had first entered. The terra-cotta workman dropped his equipment, except for the lamp, and ran. The other three workmen followed in short order.

Rikard held his place, though the darkening of the chamber, lit now only by Droagn's blue-red lamp, encouraged the fathak to surge forward. Grayshard drew his gun, while Droagn put down the case and the lamp so that he could brandish the staff and the chain-sawlike thing. Kath Harin had drawn his own gun, and seemed undecided, whether to stay and fight or follow his vanished crew.

"They do seem to be hungry," Droagn *projected* softly.

That was enough for Kath Harin. He turned and bolted up the now-dark ramp.

"Wait," Rikard called to him.

"You wait," Kath Harin's receding voice called back. "And keep your money!"

In the light of Droagn's lamp the thirty or so fathak moved more comfortably now, more determinedly, concentrating their attention on the three remaining adventurers. At last Rikard let his gloved right hand rest on the butt of his megatron. As he drew the weapon a pad of special mesh on the palm of his glove closed a circuit between a scarcovered implant on the palm of his hand and the contact on the butt of the gun. His perception of time slowed, by a factor of ten.

At the same time, concentric rings appeared, floating in his sight, in his uncovered right eye, and a small red spot, low and off to the side, showed where a bullet from his gun, if it were fired at that moment, would strike. The automatic ranging device, implanted in his head and arm and hand, compensated for the distance and motion of the fathak in focus at the center of the concentric rings. It showed him where to aim—no elevation at this range, no lead since the motion was directly toward him. As the red spot entered the innermost concentric circle, centered between the fathak's eyes, he squeezed the trigger.

He started to choose a new target even as the bullet left the gun, its flat arc taking it, almost visible to his speeded-up senses, unerringly to the point where he had aimed. He picked and shot five more fathak with a physical speed that almost matched his subjective perceptions, imparted by the complex circuitry that involved not only his hand, eye, glove, and gun, but other circuitry in his brain and body as well.

As he was firing Grayshard wielded his own peculiar weapon, of a type and shape unknown in the Federation, a micropulse laser that fired multiple bolts of extremely brief duration. Each pulse was weaker than that produced by a Federation gun, but in a hundredth of a second a thousand of them pulsed out, and the fathak that was its target crumpled and charred.

At the same time Droagn wielded his chain-saw weapon, a forceblade in fact, an energy sword that added two meters to his reach. The body of the weapon was its generator, while the blade was its wave guide. Though it weighed nearly fifteen kilograms, he wielded it like a foil. It simply cut the fathak in half.

When Rikard's gun was empty he rocked it back in his hand to break the connection and return to normal time. As he had fired, with his left hand he had extracted a full clip from the cartridge pouch at his belt, and he now reloaded in one smooth motion. He had accounted for six of the fathak, Grayshard had downed four, and Droagn five.

Now he just watched as Grayshard fired again, and in real time the laser seemed like a shotgun, or a machine gun in its effect. Hundreds of tiny holes opened up in the body of the fathak in front of him, many of them penetrated dozens of times by succeeding microbolts. The creature fell and slid forward, stopped by the carcasses in front of it. At the same time Droagn swung to the side, the forceblade crackled, his reach took the end of the weapon over the stacked corpses in front of him to slice yet another bearlike monster from side to side.

The rest of the fathak tried to stop, but those behind piled into those in front, who in turn were piling up on the bodies of those slain. Rikard and his companions held their fire. The next three seconds seemed interminable as the beasts at last came to a complete stop, then began to run away. Another moment and, except for the dead, the three adventurers were alone again.

Rikard holstered his reloaded gun and went to the foot of the ramp. There was no sign of light from above. "Kath Harin," he called. "It's all over, come on down." There was no answer, no sound of talons on the floor.

"They're out of my range," Droagn said. The power was off on his forceblade, and the only light in the chamber came from his lamp, still on the floor.

"We can't carry all this stuff." Rikard surveyed the equipment the Kelarins had left behind. He hoisted one of the cutting torches onto his shoulder. He pointed to a leather case with a carrying strap. "Can you take that?" he asked Grayshard.

"I'll try." It weighed only about four and a half kilograms, but it threw him badly off balance.

Droagn picked up his lamp, tucked the big case and his staff under that arm, and with the other two arms picked up a number of the heavier bundles.

"Which way do we go?" Grayshard said.

Droagn paused a moment in concentration, then turned to the archway immediately to the right of the foot of the ramp. "This takes us back inside."

They left the chamber, no longer empty, stinking with

blood and burned flesh. Since Droagn had the only light, he led the way.

There were frequent ramps, though they seldom descended more than three levels at a time. The thin layer of dust on the floor became minutely thicker with each level down, until at last they left obvious prints in a coating of ash that was perhaps as much as a millimeter in depth. There were more drifts of ash in the few rooms and chambers through which they passed. As they went deeper these became thicker, coarser, subtly colored varying shades of gray and dark brown and dirty white.

Then, an hour after the fathak attack, the nature of the place changed. Here there were large expanses of open floor, the ceiling was supported by free-standing columns, and the outer wall was almost completely window, though it was dark with the compacted volcanic ash.

Smaller chambers were set in clusters which formed broad columns or short partitions, which served to divide the larger spaces into distinct areas. The whole level had the feeling of being at ground level, though there were at least two similar levels below. Droagn got his bearings, then they started in toward the middle of the structure.

They left the area by a covered concourse, passed through another lobby with what might have been shops along some walls, and through another concourse, fractured and with intrusions of lava that had penetrated the deep layer of ash above. They went through a smaller lobby, a glassed-in balcony, a tubular passage that once had hung suspended, perhaps over gardens. On the other side was a glassed-in balcony adjoining another small lobby, with balconies on all four sides. From there Droagn led them down ramps into the service cellars.

Here they followed a corridor with pipes and machinery and cables along the ceiling to another lobby on that same level. From there they followed a broad, darkened concourse that ended in a very small lobby.

"You still think this is a chateau?" Rikard said.

"Something like. There was one group of us, a culture called the Lambeza, who did in fact establish larger, shared communities wherever they were. They didn't wander around as much and . . ." He stopped, put down some of the stuff he was carrying, reached up, and, grasping the circlet by one of its projecting spikes, took off the Prime with one hand and massaged his scalp where it rubbed against the metal band with another.

"There weren't very many of them," he went on, "and they didn't live on many worlds, but they were fairly stable, and so everybody else sort of looked on them as record keepers and the like." He bent his head as if he were giving Rikard a sidelong glance. "Just exactly the kind of people you like to deal with. If this were a Tomiro townhouse, or a Rohmaiik chateau, there'd be nothing for you to find. Oh, maybe a small personal library, but what can you learn from a few best-sellers. No, if you're going to find anything interesting, it would have to be in a Lambeza residence. At the most there'd be three or four hundred families here. They were different. But then, they didn't survive into my own time.''

The far side of the small lobby in which they stood was all windows, fractured and crazed, bowed inward by the pressure of lava and ash. There were other, similar lobbies to either side. The one to the right turned a corner in the direction they wanted to go.

On the third side of the square they turned away toward the center of the ruins, but shortly found their route completely blocked. There was no covered concourse, no readily accessible cellars, and no side passages within the reach of Droagn's Prime. Only a lava-sealed window.

Droagn put down all the equipment he was carrying, and Rikard knelt to unpack the cutting wand. Droagn took the wand, which looked like a pencil in his huge hand, and quickly cut through the wall just below the ceiling, then down to the floor on either side of the door frame. By the time he and Rikard packed the cutter back in its case the metal had cooled.

Droagn gripped the cut edge on the right side up near the top and pulled back. The material of the frame bent toward him, then an uncut spot gave way and the whole panel ripped inward.

The surface of the scoria and pumice stone, where it had pressed against the window, was as smooth as the window itself had once been. Droagn picked up his staff and, thrusting it like a spear, struck against the black glasslike material with the blunt end. When it struck, the power of the blow, not inconsiderable in itself, was magnified by the staff and converted into a succession of vibrating shock waves. The volcanic stone shattered.

He struck again, and again, boring a tunnel. After about fifteen meters they came to another window, which they broke through into yet another small lobbylike chamber.

Beyond this there were only cellars. They passed through two fairly large rooms, then a long service corridor with side rooms, some of which showed signs of having been stripped of built-in equipment. At the end was a narrow service ramp, going up one full circle to a door that opened easily into a little alcove on the side of a large open space, with what looked like sales counters along one wall, and a complete window wall opposite the ramp, with an open portal beyond to a walkway, covered by transparent glazing, that crossed over a once-open space.

They hurried through the once-suspended passage. It went on for twenty meters and ended in another open area, subtly different from the first.

There was color here, or the remnants of color, darkened by heat and time. Columns supported a ceiling two levels overhead, around which were balconies. In the wall opposite the windows were a series of broad, shallow alcoves, each with an elaborate, wide, double bifold door, geometrically ornamented. On either side broad corridors went off into the darkness, with counters on the inside walls, more arches farther on.

Droagn slid off to the right, to another series of alcoves up the broad corridor from the doors, and Rikard and Grayshard followed. In each of these alcoves, as wide as the others but about three times as deep, were three elevated floor sections, each of them shaped somewhat like a comma, with the "tail" starting at the floor and rising to the "head," which was nearly a meter above it. They had once been covered with some kind of material, the texture of which was almost visible though now it was no more than fine ash.

Droagn slithered around to one of the commas and lay on it, his torso elevated, his serpentine lower body comfortably curling down the tail and then around the whole "couch" two and a half times. ˜Get a couple friends,˜ he said, ˜and sit around and chat before the show begins.˜

Grayshard shone the light around the walls of the alcove. "Look at that."

It was a niche, within reach of the couch opposite that on which Droagn reclined, in which rested a small object. Droagn took it down.

˜Just a cup,˜ he said. He held it out to his two friends. Lamplight glinted off the crystalline facets. It had a foot and a short stem. It looked not much different from any number of other wineglasses Rikard had seen, except for its capacity, which was about a liter. ˜Just my size.˜

Grayshard had backed out of the alcove, and was shining the lamp onto the wall over the archway. "And this," he said.

Rikard and Droagn went out to look. There was a plaque set into the wall above the center of the alcove arch. It might have been bronze or some similar metal. It was deeply inscribed. But whatever language it might have been, it was like nothing any of them had ever seen before. And on either side of the text, placed as if to hold it up, were the graven figures of two beings exactly like Endark Droagn.

2

Rikard's camera eye had the whole scene recorded. Even if nothing else were found, the figures carved over the doorway would prove the Ahmear origin of these ruins, and his reputation—his other, academic reputation —would be assured.

"I think it's time we went inside," he said. His voice was surprisingly calm and even. But he could feel himself grinning.

They went to the nearest of the large, decorative bifold doors. Rikard stood for a moment, contemplating the carved panels. It was all abstract work, and subtly different from anything else with which he was acquainted.

On Rikard's right Endark Droagn coiled on his long, serpentine body. His hands were working as if he wanted to push the doors open. To Rikard's left and a bit back was Grayshard, silent, motionless.

Though there were other Ahmear ruins on Trokarion, they had only recently been recognized as such, and all were mere fragments. The only other Ahmear artifact in the known galaxy was the Prime, which Droagn, the only living Ahmear in the known galaxy, now wore. And here, today, they had found a cup, a bas-relief, and these doors at least. The archaeological, historical, cultural worth of what might be found beyond made Rikard's chest tight and his hands clench.

To calm himself he turned his attention to his recording helmet and became consciously aware of its readouts, subtly superimposed over the external image in his left eye. He raised an eyebrow to adjust the color scale to compensate for the hues from Droagn's lamp, increased sensitivity down to half a lux, and increased the depth of field so that he wouldn't have to constantly change focus. Inertial compensators kept the helmet level, and kept his head movements slow and smooth. There was not much to record in the way of sound, so he kept the mikes set to 360-surround and set the volume high, but not so high that it picked up his or Droagn's heartbeat, or that the sound of footfalls would be unpleasantly loud.

"Okay," he said.

Droagn put his huge hands on the ornately curved levers of the door latches, pressed down, pushed to either side, and the panels folded in on themselves and away. He held the lamp so that it was just above Rikard's head, and together, with Grayshard close behind, they entered a huge, vaulted and columned space that the lamp was barely able to illuminate.

Between the columns, and as far as the light could reach, were statues, mostly life-size set on daises, and all Ahmear. Other serpentine sentients there might once have been, but a Human can tell the difference between his own species and another, and Droagn knew, too, that these were representations of his own people.

It was a long time before Rikard remembered to breathe. Though they could see only a portion of this great chamber, there was more within their view than in many smaller local museums Rikard had visited. Coffee table books could be published, art and archaeological monographs certainly would be published, even news services off-planet would report this find.

Yet this was not their objective. But since they still had to cross this hall of statues, Rikard was determined to make the most of the opportunity. He recorded everything.

Most of the statues were of a single Ahmear, in poses that suggested that they were being commemorated by the sculpture. At the base of each dais was a plaque, engraved in the same unknown language as that over the arch outside in the hall. A few were multiple figures, and these were usually

reduced in scale, but not always. One set of three fig\
was represented fully three times life-size.

There were a few statues with rather more dramatic
poses, arms upraised, or rearing high on their coiled tails, or
representing some abstract idea rather than a specific person. Some of these were only twenty or thirty centimeters
high, on pedestals that brought them up to what, for an
Ahmear, was a comfortable viewing level—about eye level
for a Human. Rikard was sorely tempted to take one or two
of them. Aside from their historical value and great age,
they were marvelous works of art. But now, he knew, was
not the time to collect, that would be on their way back out.

The hall was large, and there were an awful lot of statues,
and they saw only those nearest them as they crossed the
dark, echoing space. They were placed not at random but
according to some system, not exactly chronological but,
Droagn guessed, more cultural or spatial, though not exactly
that either. The aesthetics of the people who had built this
place had been lost with them.

Most of the Ahmear notables represented by statues wore
nothing other than their scales, but quite a few wore
harnesses, similar in function if not in design to Droagn's. It
was a matter of providing pockets and a place to hang things
rather than a need for warmth.

Or modesty. An Ahmear's genitals were carried inside the
body and didn't need to be concealed. But in one section the
figures were actually wearing clothes, shirts or vests or open
jackets, though they wore aprons or short skirts rather than
pants.

In another place there were several Ahmear wearing
armor—and armor designed to cover a serpent was very
complicated indeed. Some of it was the equivalent of
pregunpowder armor used by all but the most pacifistic of
species, but a few pieces were of the more modern powered
kind, such as worn by heavy-duty police or local military
forces. There were still other figures who wore, or carried,

other items of apparel, the nature and function of which was less obvious.

It was difficult for Rikard to pass by so quickly. He would gladly have spent hours if not days here, going from object to object, learning as much as he could about each one.

Most of the statues were made of bronze, marble, petroplastics, and other materials that could stand unchanged forever. But some had been made of less permanent materials, such as wood perhaps, or the softer plastics. Perhaps there had once been moisture in this place, or maybe it had been the heat, or possibly even some bacteria or mites had survived to feed on the more organic substances, because some of the daises held only piles of crumbling rubble, and some of them nothing at all.

At last the light from Droagn's lamp reached the far wall. They hurried now, and as they neared the far side of the room they could see, off to their left, the arch of another doorway, fully as large as the one by which they had entered. There were no other doors to either side, though the lamp did not reach into the corners of this great museum room. That simplified their choices for them.

The room beyond was, if anything, larger than the first. That this was a serious museum and not just a hall of commemoratives was now apparent, since the objects contained in the wall alcoves adjacent to the door, on daises and pedestals elsewhere in the room, and in settings simulating normal use, were all items of furniture. Most were crumbled beyond recognition, but there were enough left in a sufficient state of preservation to be more than tantalizing.

One piece, for example, looked like an oversize chair, though how an Ahmear could sit in it was not at all obvious. Droagn dared not try it out, as it was far too fragile. Another was a couch, much like the built-in ones out in the foyer, but both more luxurious, with now collapsed and powdering leather, and less functional, due to the highly carved wooden rails and posts, now split and shrunken.

"This is all very old," Droagn said.

"That's fairly obvious," Rikard commented dryly.

˜No, I mean, it would have been old in my time.˜

"At least twenty-five thousand years older," Grayshard said.

˜I mean *old*,˜ Droagn *projected*, vocalizing a growl at the same time. ˜I took some art history classes when I was in school—it was required—and I'm trying to remember . . . it's the pedestals, that's what it is, each one unique. The Lambeza stopped using that display method, ah, about two million years ago.˜

"It can't be *that* old," Rikard protested.

˜Of course it can, we've been around a lot longer than that. If only *some* pieces were displayed that way, then you might say that they were leftovers in a modern museum, but since every damn thing has its own special base, then that's the way this museum was set up.˜

There were obvious tables, cabinets, belly cushions as Droagn called them, some almost intact, others identifiable though collapsed under their own weight. The original intent had been to demonstrate differences in style, exemplary forms, variations in material, cultural influence. Even in its current state there was much that could be learned, though it would take scholars several centuries just to sort it out, especially without Ahmear help.

Elsewhere there were objects that, while apparently of Ahmear manufacture, were totally incomprehensible, even to Droagn. There was a thing like a very narrow toy top, balanced on a circular foot, with several niches around its widest part. There was what might have been a child's slide—even Ahmear children liked to slide—except for the transverse slots and the seven spikes projecting straight up from the sloping surface.

In spite of the size of this display area, they passed through quickly. Rikard was becoming saturated. It was not easy to maintain a high level of interest when almost everything was both unrecognizable and in a state of ruin and decay.

Again there was a single large doorway on the far side of
the hall, not quite so large as the first two, and beyond it
was a wide corridor. The walls were a succession of shallow
alcoves set about a meter above the floor.

This was sculpture of a more decorative nature. There
were statuettes, plaques, carvings in stone of various kinds,
castings in bronze and other metals, work in permanent
plastics and ceramics. Rikard recorded as many as he could,
but to have done every piece justice would cost hours. He
could only hurry past and pause when something special
caught his attention.

Such as a half-meter-tall statuette in what might have
been silver, it was so black and corroded, of an erotically
entwined pair.

"Which is the male and which the female?" Rikard
asked Droagn.

¯If you can't tell, you don't need to know. ¯

Another might have been carved out of wood, but only
the preservative matrix was left, the original material long
since flaked away, a bust of some personage, whose features
could still be made out in spite of being only a sponge of
plastic fibers.

One fine piece was carved out of crystal, in the shape of
an animal that Grayshard thought was native to this world
but now extinct, long and lean with six legs and an arching
neck and flowing tail.

On one pedestal was a pile of rust in which lay a few
gemstones, large and brilliant and elaborately cut.

Farther on they came to a sword-wielding warrior, with
three shields, carved out of what might have been ivory.

Not far from that was a perfectly preserved bronze,
untarnished due to a plastic coating, commemorating an
event with two Ahmear shaking hands. Behind them was a
stylized starship, in forced perspective. On a plaque below
the figures was a text in a different alphabet from that on the
others they'd seen.

There was a centauroid figure carved out of green stone,

like jade, more feline than equine. There was a blown-crystal representation of a Taarshome, except that it was supposed to be lit up. There was a series of plastic representations, one-tenth size but in natural color, of Kelarins in various dramatic poses.

There were small sculptures of animals, some native, some exotic. There were more representations of Ahmear and Kelarins, and of a few other species as well, but no Humans. There were a few abstracts, mostly of mixed media, some of them partially collapsed as the wood or leather or nondurable plastic gave way to time, desiccation, and even here the heat of the volcano.

Each of the objects had its own pedestal, within its shallow alcove, and each pedestal was unique. Some few of these also had inscriptions on plaques. ˜Notice the cartouches, ˜ Droagn said. ˜This is very old Lambeza. ˜

"Can you read any of the languages?" Rikard asked.

˜I can't even read the alphabets. ˜

The treasure was too vast for them to take it all in. But even Rikard's quickest glances were recorded, and could produce a few good still images of each object.

The corridor ended at last, in a broad but simple double door. Beyond was a gallery, very long but not much wider than the corridor. At first Rikard thought that it was empty, but he soon realized that the irregular pattern on the walls was in fact the remains of frames. This had been a picture gallery, but at this end at least most of the pictures had crumbled away. A hostile environment for fifty thousand years had destroyed every canvas, leaving only the frames, and sometimes not even those.

A few pictures did remain, but the first three they passed were so darkened that they were black. Rikard paused for a few seconds by each to get a broad-spectrum recording, in case something could be made of it later.

The fourth intact picture was different. It was indeed a painting, rather than a photograph, and very dark, but something of the subject could be told. There were trees, or perhaps clouds, and some kind of ruined structure, and several Ahmear standing around talking with some humanoid race, with animals like large dogs and featherless birds standing near, as if pets. Rikard almost touched the canvas, but Grayshard stopped him. "I can smell it from here," he said. "If you sneeze on it, it will shatter." Rikard backed away, took a few more seconds of recording, and they passed on.

About one percent of what had once hung in this gallery remained, four out of five as merely black patches within crumbling frames, the remainder as barely visible pictures. Rikard recorded what he could, and even Droagn was excited, but Grayshard reminded them that they were not at liberty to dawdle. "Where we have come in," he said, "others can follow."

"But nobody has," Rikard said, "in all this time."

"They had no reason to. But when Kath Harin and his crew get to the surface, if they haven't done so already, they'll have reason, if only to get paid after all."

The gallery came to an end at last, but instead of passing into the next chamber, Droagn paused in the archway connecting and put his hand on the side panel. ˜A service door, I think.˜ He pushed. Nothing happened.

"Here it is," Rikard said. He touched a small raised plate at one side. The door opened, and they went through.

On the other side was a narrow and rather steep ramp going down. The surface was more strongly corrugated to accommodate the steeper pitch, but even so it was tricky for Rikard and Grayshard. They went down what might have been two levels, and at the bottom was another door, with a much more obvious latch plate. Beyond that were the cellars.

These were similar to the below-level areas they'd been through before, but were much better preserved. They had been more strongly built in the first place, and being farther from the volcanic heat had suffered less thermal damage.

It was a maze. In any living city this would have been of

little or no interest to Rikard and his companions, but down here were surviving mechanisms from the Ahmear's time, technology that, though perhaps in large part not different except in detail from that now used by one or more other peoples in the Federation, was in some cases unique. More prosaic, perhaps, than the Prime, a sophisticated communications device once intended to link individuals and coordinate their actions in time of conflict. But Ahmear, nonetheless. And almost all of it valuable in a historical if not a technological sense. Rikard recorded on the fly as they went.

Droagn found another ramp, and they descended another level. Now they were well below the original ground, where power, water, waste, and air-conditioning equipment were kept. Below this, if there were anything at all, it would be deep wells, or geothermal systems. And if that were all, then Rikard's job was done. He could just start back up, record what he could, pick up a few trophies, and go home and start writing his monographs.

They had traversed nearly the whole of this subcellar when they came to an alcove in which was set a much heavier door than any they had encountered before. Droagn probed beyond it with the psychic enhancement of the Prime.

¯There's a ramp going down, but I can't tell much more than that. The walls are too dense.¯

"Then this is what we want," Rikard said. "Let me have that green case."

Rikard opened the case, and from it took tools that resembled the cutting torches the Kelarins had used, but more compact, and heavier, and without connecting cables. The power was an integral part. He attached a triggering device, the cutting points with an optic shield at the end, shoulder strap and hand grips, and last a fuel cell of nearly eight liters capacity. When he triggered the mechanism there was a crack, and a spark of light that was bearable only when seen through the nearly opaque shield and that reflected brilliantly off the wall in front of them.

To get the same power legally would have required a generator the size of a truck. The police usually assumed, if they found one in private hands, that it could only be used for cutting open safes and the like.

Rikard set the torch to the latch plate, but ten minutes of concentrated burning produced not even a mark. He tried the hinge side of the door, but accomplished nothing there either.

"What the hell did they make this out of?" he snapped as he turned off the torch.

˜I think they call it multicollapsed alloy,˜ Droagn said. ˜If it's any consolation, that means this is the right place.˜

"So how do we get through? Can you work the lock?"

Droagn lowered himself so that his dome eyes were level with the latch plate. He ran his fingers lightly over it. It was cool to the touch in spite of the torch. He put his ear to it and tapped near it with a knuckle. Then he put his face in his hands and tilted his head so that the horns of the Prime nearly touched the latch, and concentrated for a long moment.

˜It's mechanical,˜ he said at last, ˜but I have no idea how it works.˜

Grayshard said, "May I try?"

˜Be my guest.˜ Droagn moved back from the door.

Grayshard stepped up to it and held out his left hand, palm raised, just inches from the latch plate. He did not touch the door with his gloved hand. Instead, a thin bundle of red-tipped white fibers extended from between the glove and the sleeve of his jacket, the end dividing and redividing until the individual fibers were too small to be seen. So small that they could penetrate between the door and the jamb. There was a pause. The bundle of off-white fibers twitched. Then there was a click, and the door swung open.

Rikard packed away his useless cutting torch. Droagn gripped the latch of the now unlocked door with all four hands and pulled back. The muscles on his shoulders bunched as he braced himself on his semi-extended lower body, and with the faintest of raspings the door swung outward toward him.

The blue-red lamp illuminated a small antechamber beyond, from which a ramp descended in a straight line instead of a spiral. They gathered up their equipment and went down.

After about fifty meters the ramp came to a landing, turned one hundred eighty degrees, then descended farther. A little later they emerged from the wall of a broad, high corridor, three meters above the floor. The corridor extended to right and left beyond the reach of the light, but on either side as far as they could see were large doorways, spaced maybe twenty meters apart, heavily framed, and closed with very solid-looking doors.

Grayshard went to the nearest door opposite the ramp. He brought his hand up to within a few centimeters of the latch plate, and once again the bundle of red-tipped fibers extruded from between his glove and sleeve and penetrated the lock. There was a soft click. He gripped the latch handle, and even under his feeble pulling, the door swung open.

The room beyond was spacious by Human standards, even considering the Ahmear proportions. Past an entrance-way was no museum display, but an actual Ahmear residence, abandoned intact. Couches similar to those they had seen outside the museum stood on the floor. There were low tables, shelves against the walls, a console that looked like nothing so much as a home entertainment center. There were what might have been magazines on one of the tables, a cup of some kind on another.

Adjacent to the living room was a dining room/kitchen combination. Scaled to Humans, it would have been considered too large for efficient use. Droagn opened several cabinets. Those holding utensils, dinnerware, appliances, were all but unchanged by time. Where food had been kept were now only piles of dust, though here and there a container stood intact. There was no bad smell. Beyond the kitchen was a laundry.

They went back through the living room to a large bedroom with a bathing alcove. Ahmear beds were low to the floor, and this one, big enough for maybe three adults, looked like it had once held a fluid-filled mattress. There were smaller "chairs," a thing that might have served as a dresser, but no clothes. A light harness hung on one of the chairs. There was no art. The bathing alcove, besides a closable shower/tub arrangement, contained typical Ahmear sanitary facilities—a trench in the floor that had once been padded—and what Droagn said was a polishing and coloring cabinet.

There were few personal possessions. ¨But then, there wouldn't be,¨ Droagn said. ¨This is a tiny place, for emergency use only. And it *was* being used. And then they left, all of a sudden.¨ He fingered the harness, which crumbled to the floor.

"I don't get the feeling of panicked flight," Rikard said.

¨I don't either. It feels more like they just left and never came back. Caught outside when the volcano hit. Something like that.¨

The next apartment was not identical with the first. The living area was smaller, the dining area was larger, and there were two bedrooms sharing a single bath. There were books here—electronic devices now dead—and the remains of a meal on the table. In the second, smaller bedroom were what Droagn identified as toys, for a child equivalent to a Human of about six years of age. Not having had any children, he didn't know for sure.

They left the apartment and Droagn turned his attention to the Prime. After a moment he pointed to the right, back the way they had come.

All the doors had symbols on them, the equivalent of room numbers. There were three symbols in each case, which looked to Rikard like base sixteen—which made sense, since an Ahmear had three fingers and a thumb on each of four hands. When the nature of these symbol sets changed, from three digits to two digits and a third symbol of a different type, Droagn had Grayshard open the door.

This was not another residence, but a room full of machinery. They walked to the back of the chamber. Some of the machinery was out in the open on shelves, brackets, or pedestals, some of it was behind transparent or louvered or opaque panels. Droagn touched buttons and flipped switches, which made Rikard nervous, though nothing happened.

As they came back toward the entrance Droagn opened a panel on the right, which proved to be a cover for an access hatch, which opened into the next chamber. It was just big enough for Droagn to fit through. Rikard and Grayshard followed.

If the first chamber had seemed mechanical in nature, this one seemed more electronic, and yet that wasn't exactly right either. Some of the devices were freestanding, some were enclosed. Some were in clear view, others concealed. Some were connected to others, or to a kind of network, others appeared to be isolated. And set down casually on a console, the purpose of which nobody cared to guess, they found a black metal circlet, similar to the Prime that Droagn wore, but with shorter spikes that were tipped with knobs instead of being pointed.

˝It's a Subordinate,˝ Droagn said. He took off the Prime and put on the other circlet. ˝It doesn't work—no, wait a minute . . . ˝ He looked at the Prime in his lower right hand. ˝It would work, if I could wear the Prime at the same time.˝ He handed the Subordinate device to Rikard.

Rikard had worn the Prime once, but had not been able to make any use of it. Still, he tried on the Sub while Droagn put the Prime back on his own head. That is, he held the Sub in place at the top of his head, to keep it from slipping down onto his shoulders. He could just barely feel, in the back of his head—or maybe in his sinuses—a tiny tickle, and Droagn's words, as if spoken from a great distance away, *Can you hear me?*

"Sort of," Rikard said. He took the device off and

handed it back. Droagn slipped it up on his upper left arm, where it fit almost like a bracelet around his equivalent of biceps.

They went back out to the main corridor. Droagn concentrated through the Prime, scratched at the Sub where it encircled his arm, and looked first to the right, up the corridor in the way they were going, then left, the way they had come. "The residences are that way, the mechanical is this way. Administrative should be back there, and the place we're looking for should be at this end of the corridor."

They could just see the end wall in the light of his red-blue lamp. The last room on the right proved to hold plumbing, but the one on the left opened onto a small lobby, and beyond that what appeared to be a miniature version of the museum above. The room was only two hundred by two hundred meters, though there were arches at the back and to the right that led to other chambers.

It held furniture, sculptures, sample machinery, paintings, bits of everything. Only here, instead of a dais for each object, everything stood on benches and tables, close together, with only the narrowest—in Ahmear terms—of aisles between.

Some of the objects seemed to be broken. Others were obviously very fragile. There were a few duplicates, as well, and there were glassed-in cases, which were locked, which contained a few small sculptures and devices that Rikard guessed were just too valuable to leave upstairs.

And here, unlike everywhere else, the climate was controlled, or at least once had been. Here was no dust, paper and fabric were still intact. There was an antiseptic if dead scent to the air.

There were statues, paintings, strange devices that might still have been operational. Here were the objects that the citizens of this lost city wanted to make sure would survive an emergency.

Droagn put down the case he'd been carrying and Rikard knelt to open it. He thumbed the catches on either side and it split in half. He raised the top half and let it open all the way back to the floor.

The inside appeared to be solid, but in the middle of each of the two newly exposed surfaces was another catch, recessed into the interior cover. Rikard thumbed them simultaneously and the case split in two once more, in the other direction this time. Rikard opened the two sides away from each other, so that now the case was twice as wide and twice as long and a quarter as deep as it had originally been.

And again, the inside was covered by panels. Rikard undid four more recessed latches, in the middle corners of the panels, and one by one opened them. The space beneath them was very dark, and something about it made his eyes dance, though he'd opened this case many times before.

"All right," he said, "you hand the stuff to me."

Droagn had put everything else down by this time, and Grayshard had already gone off to select a few of the smaller items. The two of them worked as if they had rehearsed, picking out those pieces that were intact, strong enough to be carried, and unique.

They brought sculptures, crystalware, silver objects, mechanical devices, small paintings removed from their frames, booklike things. Rikard remained kneeling in front of the case, took each object in turn, and put it down into the darkness of the case, leaning forward as if it projected down through the floor for half a meter or more, and reaching back under the edges.

The case was a lot bigger inside than it was outside, and could contain up to ten times its normal closed volume. It was, in fact, the outer frame of a four-dimensional storage device. They were hard to come by, very expensive, and one as small as this was illegal, since it could so easily be used for smuggling—as indeed this one had been used on numerous occasions.

Rikard packed the art objects away as methodically as his two companions selected them. Droagn also picked out a few items, pieces of jewelry mostly, such as pendants on chains and finger rings and buckles for his harness, that he could just wear.

The case was beginning to fill up, but by now Grayshard and Droagn were selecting items from the far sides of this large room. And then Droagn called out, *"Kah-ta'yahh!"*

˜We've got something here,˜ he *projected*.

"What is it?" Rikard called back.

Droagn was holding a small sculpture of an Ahmear, a boxlike shape in black and gold, and a coil of chain, but his fourth hand was gingerly touching the Prime on his head. ˜Power,˜ he said. ˜Not too far from here.˜

Rikard got to his feet. "We have visitors?"

˜No, it's in the walls.˜

Grayshard, carrying a crystal dagger shape in one hand and his micropulse laser in the other, moved in his flowing, clumsy way toward Droagn. "Emergency backup power."

˜Probably,˜ Droagn said.

"So where is it coming from?" Rikard asked.

˜The other side of this wall.˜

"There's a door over that way," Grayshard pointed. They put the artworks down and went to it.

It was a small service exit. It opened easily and beyond was a corridor, narrow and featureless except for a few cryptic symbols on the wall. There were no other doors until the other end, perhaps a hundred meters away, where there were more of the strange symbols.

They entered a chamber, lined with strange panels, each with a dimly glowing dot or bar or other symbol. Opposite the door was an arch, and through that they could see another, similar chamber. There was another chamber beyond that, and another, as far as Droagn's light could reach. Each of the chambers was more or less the same, sometimes slightly larger or smaller, or more square or more rectangular, but all of them with the panels with their glowing telltales.

They went through four chambers, slowly, and stopped at the fifth. There were at least as many more beyond.

˜I think this is a library, ˜ Droagn said. ˜Rather primitive, but still under power. ˜

Grayshard reached up to one of the panels. His gloved fingers brushed lightly along the edges. "Nuclear batteries," he said. "They're almost dead, maybe another ten or fifteen thousand years of life left."

Droagn looked closely at one of the panels. Then he touched the glowing spot in the middle of it. A concealed aperture opened and something very much like one of the electronic books they'd seen in the outer room slid out. He held it in one hand and touched the spot again. Nothing happened.

He opened the covers of the book. There were no pages. The inside surfaces were white, and glowed very faintly. ˜Each one a separate title. Lavish display of wealth, up there, in the city. This equipment would have cost a fortune. Printed books would be a lot cheaper, but look. ˜ He touched a corner of the opened cover. The page on the right formed an image, characters in an unreadable alphabet, an obvious title page. Droagn touched corners, stroked edges. The "pages" changed. Mostly they were text, once a table of some kind, mostly on just the right-hand surface, sometimes across both surfaces. Once he got a kind of command line at the bottom, but he couldn't bring it back a second time.

"So you'd consult the librarian," Grayshard said, "and check out your own electronic copy."

˜Exactly. These would be the classics. ˜ He closed the book, turned it over. The cover was plain. He opened it up, upside down, and turned it on again. The text appeared right side up. He closed it again and looked at the spine. A row of small symbols was etched into the surface.

"You've handled books like this before," Rikard said.

˜Once or twice. ˜ The inner surfaces of the book began to fade. The characters disappeared, and then the surfaces went dark. ˜You can get a couple million words into one of these. Actually, the ones I saw were sort of miniature libraries in themselves. This could be the equivalent of an encyclopedia. You can recharge it of course. That's part of what this place is all about. ¯ He tapped the panels. ¯On full charge it should last, oh, upward of a year. ¯

"We've got to take a few of these," Rikard said.

¯Absolutely. But which ones?¯

"Does it matter?" Grayshard said. "Take random samples."

"I guess we'll have to. How far does this place go?" Rikard peered on down the sequence of chambers. "Let's go see, and get our samples on the way back."

The library in fact extended only twenty-five chambers in all. In the last one Rikard, following Droagn's instructions, took out a book and opened it. The alphabet used in this one was different from the first.

¯Far more recent, ¯ Droagn said, ¯no more than a half a million years old, I'd guess. That's Tashique, a dead language in my time. ¯

They worked their way back toward the entrance. In each chamber, each of them selected a book. Droagn carried those Grayshard picked out. At first, Rikard wanted to open each one, for just the few moments that its power remained, but Grayshard urged him to just bring them along.

But there was no stopping him when they got back to the first chamber. The panels here were oversize, as were the books they produced. Rikard opened one, and it was filled with graphics. Not exactly art, nor electronics diagrams, nor business charts, but something else. The color faded and the images faded and the surfaces went dark before he could begin to get a grasp of it.

¯I think we'll take a couple more of these, ¯ Droagn said. ¯You pick them out, I'll take these to the case. ¯ He relieved Rikard of his burden of books and went back to where the case was lying, still open, on the far side of the museum workroom.

"Just be quick about it," Grayshard insisted.

"What are you so nervous about," Rikard asked as he looked at another volume. It was an art book, and he'd seen some of the paintings up in the gallery above, so he put it back.

"Kath Harin," Grayshard said.

Rikard hurried. He had to just go by guess and hunch. These oversize volumes were designed to show their graphics to their best advantage, so they were quite large and rather heavy. He put back two out of three, but when Droagn returned he'd selected a dozen of the electronic volumes.

"Let's go," Grayshard insisted.

Rikard turned in place, so frustrated to have to leave so soon. It wasn't like he would get another chance to come down here again. His finger punched a lit symbol almost at random, and a large volume slid out.

He opened it, and stopped. The image that came up on the fifth press of his thumb was of a ruin, a photograph of some old building weathered by time and the elements. And a ruin like none he'd ever seen before.

"It's archaeology," he said.

"So take it," Grayshard said, and gently pushed him out the door.

Now Rikard hurried too. The more time they spent down there, the more time Kath Harin had to think about being cheated and plan some kind of retribution.

As quickly as he could he packed the books into the case. It nearly filled it. Then he closed it back up and hefted it. It weighed little more than it had empty, though it moved sluggishly. The weight was compensated for, but it still had inertia.

"All right," he said to Grayshard. "I'm ready."

"Then let's go."

From one of the other cases Droagn was carrying, Rikard took a cross-shaped object with a thickened intersection. He stretched out the telescoping legs of the cross until he could set his 4D box down on it with the ends of the cross just projecting beyond the sides of the case. Then he took a small remote control, pressed the ON button, and the carrier

rose up about twelve centimeters. Droagn picked up the rest
of the equipment, Grayshard took the remote from Rikard,
and they left the reserve museum with the gravity float
following behind them.

They moved at a slow walking speed, and now had no
interest in their surroundings whatsoever. It was all Rikard
could do, in fact, to keep from running and shouting. He
was already composing his acceptance speech for when the
Society of Local Historians gave him the prize for prehistory
research.

They came to the ramp and started up. They followed
their own prints back through the power generators, water
pumps, waste recyclers, air conditioners. But when they got
to the top of the ramp at the next level, Droagn paused.

¨We're not alone,¨ he *projected*. He put down the equipment he carried.

"I told you Kath Harin would come back," Grayshard
said. He pocketed the remote and drew his micropulse.

¨No, not Kelarins. Humans.¨

"Damn," Rikard said. There were few enough Humans
on Trokarion, so if there were Humans down here, they
weren't just locals who'd wandered in by mistake.

"Shall I *project*?" Grayshard asked, referring not to the
kind of one-way telepathy Endark Droagn exercised as his
normal mode of communication but to a peculiar ability of
his species, the Vaashka, to emit a kind of psychic scream
enhanced by a chemical substance natural to them. The
result was, usually, stark terror and panic in those within
range.

"I'm not shielded," Rikard answered.

¨Then it's my turn,¨ Droagn said.

They were in a semi-open space, the ramp behind them,
arches ahead and on either side. There were conduits, ducts,
large electronics panels here and there, more of them in the
chambers beyond. Droagn looked first one way, then the
other.

And then a woman's voice said, quietly but distinctly, "Just freeze."

3

Rikard's right hand was centimeters from the butt of his gun. Grayshard's micropulse was pointed vaguely at the ceiling. Droagn held only his staff. And then Rikard felt the edges of an Ahmear psychic attack, as Droagn *yelled*, a directed telepathic shout guaranteed to stun anyone within a hundred meters or more.

But at the same moment several figures, carrying laser rifles and wearing helmets with reflecting faceplates, stepped into view from either side. They were not affected by Droagn's *projection* at all.

"Nice try," the voice came again, from one of the archways directly ahead of them. A moment later, even as other armed figures came from the sides and ahead, a woman appeared, dressed much as Rikard was, carrying her helmet under her arm. She wore dark brown leather pants and a waist-length jacket, black calf-high boots and belt, with a 10mm unitron pistol in a black holster on each hip. Her hair was short and dark, with a touch of gray at the temples—Rikard guessed her to be not yet a century old. She was above average height, though still shorter than Rikard, with an athletic build and graceful movements. She was attractive, but her face was hard.

"And if *you* try anything, Vaashka," she said, "I'll just blow you away."

Grayshard slowly lowered his weapon and set it back into its holster. All eyes were on him. And then Droagn's staff twisted in the air. One of the woman's companions fired, and the blue bolt of the laser struck the staff just above Droagn's hand. It went spinning out of his grip. The woman said nothing, but looked up at Droagn with a soft-hard smile. Droagn let himself relax, and smiled back at her.

The woman didn't seem to object to all the sharp teeth showing, and if her companions did they didn't show it. There were some two dozen of them, both men and women. Rikard wouldn't have time to even grip the butt of his pistol, let alone draw it. He slowly raised his hands.

The woman in charge made a slight motion with her head, and six of her minions slung their rifles over their shoulders and came up to Rikard and Grayshard and Droagn, and quickly and expertly relieved them of their weapons. They also kicked the equipment Droagn had dropped out of the way, and dragged the case Grayshard had been driving off to one side. One of the six held out her empty hand, palm up, in front of Grayshard. He said nothing, but after a moment handed the gravity float's remote control to her. The woman watched, a faint smile on her face.

"You got down here awfully quickly," Rikard said to her.

"We took our time," the woman said.

"Did Kath Harin hire you before we came down?"

"I have nothing to do with him."

"I'm sure. He wanted to cover his desertion, take whatever we found, and he hired you to do it for him."

The woman just smiled, quietly self-satisfied. Rikard could see in her eyes that she was reading him even as he was trying to read her. And this woman was good. He smiled a bit himself.

Her smile broadened. "I've been following you for some time, Rikard Braeth," she said.

"Indeed. I'm flattered."

"Because of my attentions? Why not. You're getting quite a reputation for yourself."

"That's not necessarily a good thing."

"I agree. Which is why you'll not have heard of me. I prefer to keep out of the public view."

"So who are you then?"

"My name is Karyl Toerson. Mean anything to you?"

"Nothing at all."

"Good enough." She made a gesture with her right hand. Three of her minions stepped forward and took the black case with the microcutter, Droagn's red-blue lamp, and Rikard's recording helmet. They did not bother with anything else.

Toerson gave no further orders. Her people moved as if they had rehearsed. They split into three groups, one taking the lead, another guarding the rear, and the third with Toerson, Rikard and his companions, and the equipment in the middle. Rikard needed no instruction either. He went along with his guards.

"Why have you been following me?" he asked Toerson after a moment.

"You get into interesting places. And you find interesting things."

"You seem more than capable of doing the same yourself."

"Perhaps I lack a little something that you have," Toerson said. "I don't feel comfortable searching public records."

They went on in silence for a way, through the maze of the cellars to the steep ramp with its corrugated floor, and up that to the gallery.

"So what happens now?" Rikard asked.

"We go somewhere for a while, until I can clean this place out."

"Everything?"

"Most of it."

"And what about me?"

"You and your friends will be my guests until I'm finished here. Then I'll give you back what's yours and let you go."

"And how long do you figure that will take?"

"I don't really care." She turned to him and smiled.

Even though she was three times his age, he should have found her appealing, but something about her put him off . . . terrified him.

They passed through the corridor of decorative sculptures, through the hall of furnishings, then into the commemorative hall.

"Aren't you going to get any of this?" Rikard asked.

"Aside from what you have there," she gestured to the 4D case, "no. Right now I just want to get you out of here and to where I know you'll be safe. Then I can loot this place at my leisure, and not worry that you'll bring troops down here. The government up in New Darkon has known about this ruin since before their little civil war began, and they've done nothing about it for two hundred years. Of course, they don't know *what* was in it, or they'd have sealed it off, war or no. Serves them right if I take everything."

They came out into the high foyer, with the bas-reliefs over the alcoves. Two of Toerson's people closed the double bifold doors behind them. They went through the once-suspended walkway, the large open area with the sales counters, into the alcove and up the narrow service ramp to the upper-level cellars and the lobby beyond.

"Why don't you just kill me and get it over with?" Rikard asked.

"Because I'm not the only one who knows where you are, and if you suddenly show up dead, somebody will come looking for me, and I'd rather not hassle with that."

"But you're going to keep me locked up for an indefinite period."

"Sure. Just a hundred days or so."

They went back through lobbies, covered concourses, service corridors, up ramps, through tubular passages, up the lobby levels, up more ramps, and at last to the large six-sided chamber where the fathak had attacked. The bodies still lay there. The place was beginning to stink.

"How long do you think you can keep me?" Rikard asked quietly.

"I'm not going to fool with you," Toerson told him. "I'd rather not kill you, because it would hassle me, but if *you* hassle me, I will."

Rikard offered no trouble during the ascent, nor did his companions. Toerson had the upper hand now, but it might not always be that way.

They went up the tower, up the broad shallow ramp, through the chambers where the floor and ceiling met, past the open elevator shaft, through the maze of rooms and hallways. At last they came to the circular chamber at the base of the last long ramp to the top.

But instead of going up, they headed toward the door opposite the one by which they had entered.

"You didn't come down this way?" Rikard asked.

"This is only one of four towers," Toerson said. "You came in at the one under the old theater on Rebank Street. But there's too much fighting going on in that neighborhood for my taste. You're not the only one who can check the records, even though I don't like to do it. I found another tower had been run into when they laid the sewers out in the Wildercroft development. It's a lot quieter out there, and not really that far away from here."

They went through a series of chambers, completely empty except for the thinnest film of dust, until they came to the outer wall of the tower, where windows now blocked by lava shone black with white streaks through it. They turned left into the next chamber, and there, instead of one of the windows, was an opening in the outer wall. Beyond was a circular tube with a flat floor, once transparent but now crazed, twisted, charred black and white. It was wide enough for two Ahmear, so they could proceed four abreast.

It had once hung suspended between the great corner towers, though now it was completely encased by solidified lava. There were no breaches in the distorted glazing, but the tube dipped, rose, twisted, and in one place the side walls nearly came together. Droagn had to squeeze to get through.

At one time this tube would have been a shortcut from tower to tower. At that time the view must have been spectacular, with the city below them and the countryside spread around. Now it was just a long, narrow, dark tube, which seemed to go on for an awfully long time. Perhaps there had been a beltway in here back then, but if so it had been removed or destroyed along with everything else.

At last they came to the other tower, but the first chamber they entered was the most distorted Rikard had seen. The walls were all corrugated, the ceiling dipped low on either side and in the middle so that Droagn could not ''stand'' up straight, and the floor tilted precariously to the left. Opposite the entrance from the tube was a doorway, which Toerson's people had cut through.

They passed through several other chambers, through doors that had been cut through or cut around. Rikard wondered where all the equipment was. Perhaps there had been others in the party who had done this work and then left when Toerson had found Rikard's tracks.

There were many intrusions here, even in some of the inner chambers. In some cases they were just thin curtains or strings, in others the lava half filled a room, or blocked most of a corridor and had been cut away.

They came to the far side of the tower and there took a ramp up one level. It was so distorted that sometimes it was hard to tell what had been floor and what wall. The floating 4D case got stuck once or twice here, as the gravity float was a simple warehouse tool and had never been intended for this kind of work.

At the top of the ramp they went through a door into a room, and from there out another door onto what had once been an observation deck. There was no glazing at all, and yet there was a bubble in the lava, which left most of the deck free.

From the sides of this bubble there were several small

tubes going off in different directions. There was also a rather large natural tube going down, the origin of the bubble in which they now stood. Directly ahead of them, halfway up the side of the bubble on a sort of a ledge, was another, larger tube, angling up. The leaders of the group were already starting up the slope toward this tube, making use of footholds that they'd cut into the black lava when they'd come in.

But before they could reach the ledge, a head and torso very much like Droagn's, though smaller, came out of the larger tube, followed immediately by two more. Similar figures appeared in each of the other, smaller tubes. Rikard just had time to see that they, like his friend, had four arms apiece, and serpentine bodies below the waist, and then stone-tipped spears were flying through the air.

The armor Toerson's people wore should have been proof against the spears, but two of the men had taken their faceplates off and went down when they were hit in the face, and a third spear found a chink between a woman's helmet and her shoulder.

The snake men moved so fast that only a few of the Human defenders could get off a shot before they were overwhelmed and had to fight hand to hand. Toerson, with Rikard, Droagn, and Grayshard in the middle group, was pushed back toward the gaping hole in the floor of the bubble. The attackers gave way on that side, and before the Humans realized their danger a woman was pushed in. She fell screaming for a long time. There was no sound of impact.

Human legs are better than snake bellies when push comes to shove, and encouraged by this incident, the crowd of humans started to inch back toward the escape route. But before they could make much progress the snake men suddenly thrust in from the sides and another man went staggering over the edge of the hole into the darkness.

Toerson shouted orders. Her people yielded suddenly on one side and thrust strongly on the other, toward a side passage. The press threatened to crush Grayshard but Droagn protected him from the worst of the crowding as the beleaguered Humans pushed through the surrounding snake men and entered the largest of the side tunnels.

The surface of the tunnel was frothy stone, alternating with glossy streaks, mostly black but occasionally striped with white, reflecting the light of the lamps and sparkling around them. At least they had to defend from only one side, and while those continued to struggle hand to hand, those immediately behind them were at last able to bring their rifles to bear in the manner in which they had been intended. There was a brief volley of laser shots, and the hissing crackle of blistering flesh as the bolts struck at point-blank range. The snake men fell back out of the tunnel, and for a moment the fight paused.

"Where does this thing go?" Toerson demanded. A couple of her people went to find out.

A rock the size of Rikard's head hit the floor a few meters in front of him and bounced up to strike one of Toerson's people in the face. The woman went down without a cry, the rock wedged into her helmet. There were one or two panic shots, then a second rock came zinging in, hit the ground at a flat angle, and broke in two. One half smashed into the ceiling, but the other half hit a man in the center of his chest and folded him up like a newspaper.

And then a wave of snake men plunged into the tunnel, each brandishing a kind of javelin in one hand and carrying more in their other hands. They threw the javelins even as the Humans opened fire. But these light weapons could do no damage, and the laser shots decimated their front ranks. Those behind threw as fast as they could, and went down almost as fast under the concentrated laser fire. Then the snake men broke and they retreated, losing more of their number even as they did so. Aside from the two Humans who had been hit by the rocks, which were supposed to have been only a distraction, there were no other casualties.

"Against the walls," Toerson ordered. Even as she spoke

a rock whistled into the tunnel, struck the floor near the middle, and spanged off down the tube. A moment later another rock came in, struck the floor a little farther down the tunnel, then zinged off into the darkness.

"Now move back," Toerson said. "Fast!"

They did so until they came to one of the rock missiles, where they met the two scouts coming back.

"It gets narrower after a while," one of the men said, "and then I don't know."

"We couldn't see very far," the other said, "but there weren't any tracks. I'd guess it was a dead end."

˜You should know,˜ Droagn *projected*, ˜that they are gathering up there in the bubble. They have more catapults like the one that threw the rocks. ˜

Those who still wore their helmets could not receive Droagn's telepathic communication, but Toerson and one or two others could. Toerson stared at Droagn in surprise, then forced herself to regain her composure. "And back the other way?" she asked.

˜It's empty. It's not a dead end. ˜

"How many catapults do they have?" She quickly accepted Droagn's method of communication.

˜I think six. Like crossbows, not slings. ˜

"And they can bounce those rocks around corners. Maybe we'd better keep on following this tube and see where it leads us."

The two scouts preceded the party down the tube, while the last five fighters covered their rear. Rikard, Droagn, and Grayshard stayed in the center of the group, still under guard. Toerson joined them, nonchalant at first, then she looked sideways up at Droagn, at the Prime, at the Subordinate on his arm. Her face gave no hint of her thoughts.

"I thought you were unique," she said to him. "Those 'people' back there, they look like they might be relatives of yours."

Droagn flashed her one of his carnivorous smiles. ˜So it would seem. ˜

"There were Ahmear here fifty thousand years ago," Rikard said. "What else could they be but the descendants of the last few families who didn't escape the volcano?"

"And they've been down here all this time," Toerson said incredulously, "without causing even *legends* up on the surface?"

"Maybe," Grayshard said, almost as a non sequitur, "it was they, and not the Kelarins, who scavenged the top levels."

"Living off canned food until they found some way to provide for themselves," Toerson said. "I don't believe it."

"You don't have to," Droagn said.

The tube did narrow after a short ways, but then broadened again a bit farther on. There were no signs of passage other than the footprints of the scouts on the floor.

"Are they following us?" Toerson asked Droagn.

"Not yet," he said. "But then, I can reach back only a hundred meters or so."

They came to a three-way branching, and on Droagn's suggestion took the tube on the left. After sixty meters or so the tube began to slant upward, at first just gently, then more sharply, until they were climbing a fifteen-degree slope. It got gradually broader, and then leveled off where, suddenly on the walls, were the marks of tools. They slowed, and the lights showed that the tube ahead was more and more worked.

"It would appear," Grayshard said, "that we've come to the outskirts of a colony."

"There's somebody coming behind us," one of the rear guard called out.

"Then let's move it," Toerson said.

They hurried forward. The walls of the tube became almost completely artificial, carved smooth, with here and there some ornamentation taking advantage of a change of color in the frothy rock. The tube turned into a corridor, with alcoves on either side, and this turned into an arcade, with a second level above supported on columns carved out of the living pumice. Without needing orders, ten of the eighteen surviving fighters started looking through arches and into chambers.

"This place looks good," one of the women called from an arch on the far side of the larger space. Toerson hurried to inspect. Rikard's guards did not relax their vigilance.

Toerson reappeared in the arch at once. "Let's move it," she said. Her people responded quickly, bringing Rikard, Grayshard, Droagn, and what remained of their equipment along with them.

There was no other entrance to the chamber beyond the arch. It was rough-hewn, with boulders and piles of rubble scattered on the floor. Toerson directed Rikard and his companions to move toward the back, while the rest of her people took up sheltered positions near the front, between the largest of the rock piles and the left-hand wall.

"Here they come," Droagn warned. Two seconds later the broad archway was filled with snake men, throwing spears, javelins, and stone-headed battle-axes. Toerson's troops opened fire, the front line withered, and the attack stopped. The surviving snake men hurried back out of sight, and several of Toerson's people stood from their rocky shelter, to get a parting shot, but were met by a hail of deadly accurate arrows.

Five of her people were slain. Two arrows hit Grayshard, who fell to the floor of the chamber, and three more hit Rikard, and he too fell, though the arrows just bounced off the combined armor of his leathers and underlying meshmail. The battle acquired a desperate feel, as Humans and snake men exchanged laser fire for arrows.

Droagn lowered himself beside Rikard, and pointed to a shallow recess in the right-hand wall, shielded from the others by a shoulder-high pile of debris. Rikard nodded, touched Grayshard, and quietly the three moved into it. Grayshard did not seem hampered by the two arrows sticking into him. From the recess it was a clear path to the archway—except for the cross fire.

"What's the plan?" Rikard asked quietly.

˜I've been trying to talk with them," Droagn said, ˜and they can hear me, I think. We're not the same people anymore.˜

"What can you possibly be saying to them?" Rikard asked, astonished.

˜'Get away from here, leave us alone.'˜

Then the snake men began throwing stones that, because of their greater mass, succeeded in knocking one or two defenders down, and smashed one of the lasers to pieces. Toerson and her people became too busy defending themselves to worry about their prisoners anymore.

˜I'm going to try something different,˜ Droagn *projected* to Rikard. He concentrated for a moment, directing his thought at the snake men. And then there was a pause in their attack.

˜Now,˜ Droagn said, and started toward the archway. Rikard and Grayshard had perforce to follow. And just as they got to where Toerson could see them, the snake men launched a withering volley of rocks, forcing her and her surviving people to keep down out of sight.

Rikard, Grayshard, and Droagn ducked around the corner of the archway. They were safe from Toerson for the moment, but now they were surrounded by snake men who, though smaller than Droagn, were still formidable, and who coiled tensely around them, their weapons held at the ready. They carried small smoking lamps, made of some translucent material and stone, which cast only a minimal light.

Droagn raised himself up, and stared around at them, and after a bit the snake men began to cower. A dozen of the snake men gathered around Rikard's party and, leaving the others to deal with Toerson, escorted them away from the arch back the way they had come.

When they came to where the two-level arcade became a simple corridor, Rikard called a halt. "I want my gun back," he said to Droagn, "and the case too, if we can get it."

˜I'll see what I can do,˜ Droagn said. He turned away

from Rikard, crossed his lower arms, raised his upper ones, and froze. The snake men gathered around him.

For a long moment Droagn and the snake men just looked at each other. Then one of the snake men, who seemed to be something of a leader, raised a hand and turned toward several of his—her?—companions, four of whom went off toward the sounds of distant fighting. They waited for a long moment, then there was a sudden and furious sound of lasers crackling, and the chatter of Toerson's unitron pistols going off.

"What the hell's happening?" Rikard asked.

˜Just what it sounded like,˜ Droagn said. ˜Our four friends appear to be unhurt. They're just at the limit of my reach.˜

"Why don't you give that to the 'sergeant' there," Rikard said. He jabbed at the Sub on Droagn's arm and pointed to the leader of the snake men. "Maybe it would help."

Droagn snorted in disgust, then took the Sub off and handed it to the snake man, who looked at it dubiously, then put it on.

And for a moment stood enraptured. The other snake men watched, at first apprehensive, but the "sergeant" must have reassured them, because they turned back to Droagn, more obsequious than before. And then the other four snake men came back, with Rikard's 4D case, his megatron and re-cording helmet, Grayshard's laser, and Droagn's lamp and forceblade.

˜Now let's get out of here,˜ Droagn said, to the snake men as well as to Rikard and Grayshard, and they hurried off toward Toerson's entrance route.

They paused when they got to the bubble. "We don't know where that comes out," Rikard said as he looked up at the hole high in the bubble wall.

"It's got to be more direct than going back down and up again the way we came," Grayshard told him. "And look." He pointed at the lamps the snake men carried. Wisps of smoke were blowing away from Toerson's exit. "We're not that far from the surface."

Droagn spoke with the snake men once more. The "sergeant" offered him the Sub, but Droagn gestured that he should keep it. Then he and Rikard and Grayshard climbed up the side of the bubble to the exit tube. It narrowed after a while, became steeper, then leveled off again, and all at once came to a natural chamber, the far side of which was an ancient Kelarine stone wall that had been recently breached.

They passed through the opening into a chamber with irregular and uneven stone floors, and with stone columns supporting simple barrel arches. There were footprints on the floor where Toerson and her people had come in, but otherwise the stones were covered with a half-damp muck. There was no illumination other than Droagn's lamp. Along one side wall were some rotting crates and barrels, but nothing else.

They went out through a sagging wooden door and followed the footprints through similar chambers until they came to stone stairs going up. The small room at the top was noticeably newer, and opened onto an ancient service underground, about the same age as that by which Rikard and his companions had entered, with sewers, water, and other services, now mostly unused. It was about a thousand years newer than the previous work.

Even here the ground was slick, and the footprints Toerson had left were fading, in spite of their great number. Here there were rats and other creatures, whose trails obscured those of the descending Humans, but there was enough of a trail left to follow, along stone sewers to brick sewers to concrete sewers to a manhole shaft that went up by way of a ladder.

Rikard and Grayshard climbed, Droagn just lifted himself up on his tail and squeezed through after them into newer service ways, made of plastic composites and mostly pretty clean all things considered, with service lights every hundred meters or so. There was no real trail anymore, as this place, though many hundreds of years old, was well used. Droagn *felt* for a way, and they went along the sewer until they came to a shaft that went up into an enclosed space and not, as they had expected, into the street. The shaft was a municipal service entrance in the cellar of a private building.

The city above them was in a state of revolution, and had been for two centuries, and they ran a real risk of getting caught either by loyalist soldiers or rebel forces. And they had no idea where in the city they were—except that it was someplace called the Wildercroft development—or where that might be relative to their planned escape.

There were windows high in the walls, and Droagn reached up to look out. ˝It's night out there,˝ he said.

The door was not locked from the inside, so they went out into a corridor going right and left, with a stair going up directly across from them. At the top they came to a back foyer, with a corridor to the left that led into the main part of the building, an elevator opposite the stairs, and double glass doors to the right.

They went out into the middle of a side street. There were streetlights shining at the corners, some buildings were lit up nearby, but there was fortunately no traffic at the moment. They went to the corner to read the street sign, and looked it up on the map that Grayshard produced. A car came by. The driver was startled by Droagn's appearance and sped off. Otherwise the night was silent, and they heard no gunfire.

"Here we are." Rikard pointed at an intersection on the map. "And here's where we went down." He jabbed at another place, not that far away. Grayshard put the map away while Rikard put on his recording helmet again, and spoke into it, giving instructions to the vehicle they'd left waiting. It would take some moments for it to arrive on automatic. There was nothing to do now but wait.

"This has been too easy," Grayshard said in his emotionless, mechanical voice.

"I feel the same way," Rikard said.

He kept his hand on the floating case of trophies. The longer they stood there, the more he began to think that it was awfully quiet for a city in the middle of a civil war. And then they heard the hum of a floater come to a stop, out of sight around a corner a block away. The engine of the unseen car did not shut off.

˜They could be just letting somebody off,˜ Droagn said. ˜Or picking them up.˜

"Not likely at this hour of the morning," Grayshard said.

Then from another corner came the hum of two more vehicles. They also stopped and idled, not quite inaudible in the night.

"I think we're in for trouble," Rikard said.

The weapons they carried were all illegal. They would be assumed to be belligerents by whichever side caught them.

"Let's be discreet," Grayshard suggested, so they went back to the building from which they had come, but the door was locked from the outside. Grayshard went up to pick the lock, while Rikard and Droagn kept watch.

There came the sound of a heavy-duty engine from up the street, and from well above it, but this time it did not stop. The floater making the noise came to the lamp-lit intersection and slowly passed through. It was a military vessel, a troop van.

Grayshard came away from the door before its spotlight struck them. "It's electrical," he whispered, "I can't open it."

The troop van stopped now, and the other three floaters came into view, lightweight carriers with light weapons and stunners. Then there was another sound, and yet a fifth floater came up the street, heavier than those on the ground, smaller than the one in the air. It looked like a command vehicle. The other floaters hesitated. This new one settled to the curb next to Rikard and his companions and the back door opened.

Rikard looked at the troop van and light armored floaters. They waited. He kept his hands well away from his side as he stepped into the open door of the command floater. Grayshard followed immediately, then Droagn entered, pushing the floating case in front of him.

The door closed behind them. Rikard stepped forward and sat in the empty driver's seat, took the controls, and they slowly drifted away. The military vehicles behind them started to follow as an escort.

But as they passed the two light floaters ahead of them, one of the Kelarine drivers looked over, saw Rikard at the controls, realized they'd been fooled, and spoke into a mike. Rikard just grinned, stomped on the overdrive, and the floater, equipped like a command car should be, streaked up past the buildings and into the night. He cut on the jets, and they were away.

"The hell with the hotel," he said, "let's get out of here."

Mensenear

Mensenear is a Federation world, in a system near the border with the Abogarn Hegemony. It is an important commercial world, populated mostly by Humans but with a substantial minority of other species. Most of these come from the Federation but a few originate in the Hegemony. This multispecies nature is especially true in Mensenear's larger cities, of which Three Rivers is the most important. It is here that most extraplanetary commerce takes place, where foreign, extraplanetary, and extra-Federal legations have their offices. Thus it is not unusual to see beings of a variety of forms, and each form from a variety of cultures, not only in the shuttleports but in the streets, hotels, and even restaurants.

Rikard drew no undo attention, being Human and, here, wearing clothes more or less of the same style as a typical Federation traveler. His leathers would have been too out-landish, and would have drawn the attention of the police, who recognized that such clothes were usually worn by those adventurers called Gestae. He still wore the meshmail underneath, just as a precaution, but his gun was carefully packed away in an extradimensional compartment in one of his smaller bags.

Grayshard, still swathed in his concealing robes, hood, and goggles, did not get even a curious glance. Though his attire was atypical for this world, it was no stranger than might often be seen near the starport. And while he appeared humanoid, his movements were too obviously unhuman, and so, as an alien, he was allowed greater liberty of dress.

But Endark Droagn was strange, even for a sophisticated and multispecies city like this. No other race in Three Rivers was as big as he, none were in the least serpentine, and though there were several sentients with four or more arms, they were not so decidedly muscular. And they wore clothes, not just the harness that served Droagn as a place to hang his pockets. He drew a lot of unwanted attention, and it was with some relief that the three found themselves at last on their way up to their hotel suite at the top of the city, with only four professionally uncurious service people to handle their luggage, including Rikard's large 4D trophy case.

It was a long ride up, even on a limited service elevator. Rikard and Grayshard sat in comfortable chairs, a low table with a vase of flowers between them. Droagn coiled in the middle of the floor. The bellhops, three men and a woman, stood by the doors with the luggage on three floats. There was no sense of movement, but a large display to the left of the wide double door showed interesting symbolic pictures as they passed each group of floors. When, after not quite two minutes, the picture showed a stylized skyline, the door opened and they got out.

The lobby, tastefully and expensively decorated and furnished, was rather small, only some six by six meters. Opposite the elevator was the main entrance, a double door of wood panels, plain but perfectly stained and finished. To the left was an open closet. Immediately beside the elevator to the left was a service door, almost unnoticeable in its plainness. And to the right, a double glass door opened onto a balcony that overlooked the city. There were several comfortable chairs, low tables in the corners, and plants in elegant pots and containers, some on the floor, some on wrought metal stands.

One of the hotel men opened the front door for them and stood to one side as Rikard and his companions went into a large, well-furnished, and rather formal parlor. Windows on the right overlooked the same balcony as the lobby. There was a formal dining room across from the entrance, large enough to seat a dozen people. There was a closed double door to the left and a bathroom beside the lobby entrance. The furnishings, compared to the lobby, were as a wealthy collector's living room might be, compared to an average person's supplied from the mass market. It was absolutely unostentatious, and overwhelming in its taste and quality. Rikard tried to pretend that he was used to such things.

The other bellhops brought in the luggage, and the man who had let them in offered to help unpack.

"Thank you," Rikard said, "but that won't be necessary. We have special needs that only we know how to take care of."

The chief bellhop inclined his head, and they left the floaters in the middle of the parlor.

The double doors opposite the windows led into a rather less formally furnished living room, with a windowed el to the right at the far end. Opposite the parlor door was a broad hallway that led to the bedroom suites. Droagn took the largest of the three, which was barely big enough, while Rikard and Grayshard, in the smaller suites, felt like they were rattling around.

At the back of the hall was a foyer, with glass doors on two sides that gave access to a patio in the corner of the building and the balcony that surrounded the apartment on three sides. From there they could see the whole city below them, though clouds obscured part of their view, and they were high enough so that some stars showed, even at midday. There was no smog, and the temperature, though cool, was well regulated.

Rikard went back to his room and took out his gun and holster, which he slung over his shoulder, and his gloves, which he tucked into his belt, and another device, the size and shape of a small computer. He flipped down the front panel, which contained a keyboard and trackball, revealing a complex graphics screen. He turned it on and the device floated by itself, just above waist level.

The screen was blank at first. He touched a couple keys and an image formed, showing a 3D wire-frame picture of the room and everything in it, including himself, and everything just behind the walls. Using the trackball he rotated the image, then tipped it to look at the ceiling. There was a red spot, on the ceiling, right over the bed.

He brought up a bull's-eye cursor, selected the red spot, and a secondary window opened on the screen with a data readout. It was a sonic bug, probably just a standard hotel security and safety device. Rather than try to remove it Rikard took another small object from one of his cases, with the appearance of a pocket radio, as which, in fact, it could function if need be. He put it down on the nightstand by the bed, then brought the security monitor over. He selected both the bug spot and the camouflage device, selected commands from pull-down menus to focus the radio's signal on the bug. He turned the radio on and, watching the security monitor, said, "This is a really great room."

Dialogues on the screen told him that the bug had picked up his words, as it was supposed to. He then whispered, "I like it a lot." A marquee on the screen reported that an alternate message had been sent, and a window opened to show the text, "It reminds me of home," which was what the radio had tight-beamed directly to the bug, overriding Rikard's whispered words. Whenever he spoke in a normal voice, the bug would hear, but anything said below a certain level would be covered by something innocuous, delivered at the same effective volume. It could produce as many different voices as there were people speaking.

Satisfied, he took the security monitor over to the comcon, jacked it into the optional headset, and ran through another check, using trackball, menus, and keyboard. The screen showed a complex diagram that changed with every instruction. As far as he could tell the whole system was secure, but just to be safe he got another device from his electronics case and plugged it into the phone instead of the headset. Now, if anybody were to use any indirect form of tapping, he would know, and would be able to provide cover when he needed to.

He did a general scan of the other rooms in his suite, especially the bathroom, but found nothing else. Then he went down the hallway, scanning as he went, and knocked at Grayshard's door. There was no answer so he went in. He found another sonic bug over the bed, which he left alone, and then went across to Droagn's door. It was ajar, so he went in, scanning the entrance and closet as he did so. After all, someone such as he, viewed by many as a criminal, could not hope to continually slip through the cracks of the law without taking certain precautions.

The sitting room was clean, but the bedroom was a shambles. Droagn had moved all the furniture up against the walls. He had the mattresses off the beds and onto the floor, to make a space big enough for him to lie on, but it didn't look like it was going to work. ˉWhat are you finding?ˉ he asked.

"That you've made a mess of things," Rikard said. He showed Droagn the display on the security monitor. Droagn saw the red spot of the sonic bug and nodded.

ˉDo you suppose they'd send up some extra mattresses?ˉ he asked, and waved one hand at the comcon.

"Call and find out," Rikard suggested, making an OK sign with his hand as he did so.

ˉI can't,ˉ Droagn said. ˉI can't *speak* the language.ˉ

And of course the bug couldn't pick up his *projecting*

either—though other, more sophisticated devices might. Rikard ran through a whole new series of tests, while Droagn recited a simple childhood poem, about swallowing rats, over and over again. Nothing showed. Rikard gave the OK sign again. "I'll do it for you," he said, and using Droagn's comcon, he did so.

"They'll be a few minutes," he said when he hung up. "Kind of make this look neat, will you?" Droagn bared his fangs, and Rikard went into the living room.

Grayshard was sitting on a sofa, glancing through a hard-copy magazine. He looked as though he'd been dropped onto the sofa from a great height, kind of bent in the wrong places and sagging the way no Human could sag. Rikard did a scan, found no bugs. Those in the bedrooms were probably a safety precaution against night accidents.

"Can I take off my clothes?" Grayshard asked.

"They're going to be bringing some extra mattresses up for Droagn. Can you wait a bit?"

Grayshard sagged a little lower and turned a page.

Rikard took his security monitor through a smaller, personal dining room into the kitchen, through the formal dining room and parlor into the lobby, then through the bathroom that served both the parlor and the living room. Everything was clean, even the little bar off the living room. He turned off the monitor, set it down on the counter, and checked out the stock.

Before he could choose anything the door chimed. It was the mattresses, six of them carried on a float directed by three staff. They were a bit apprehensive when they saw the holstered gun that was still hanging from Rikard's shoulder, and left the mattresses in the lobby. Rikard went to tell Droagn, then chose a local beer from the cooler in the bar and watched as Droagn carried all six mattresses under his lower arms back to his room.

"Now may I undress?" Grayshard asked.

Rikard sipped his beer. "Want something to eat?" he asked in return.

"Very much so. Will we have to send out?"

"Probably."

Just then Droagn came back from his room carrying a number of objects. By the parlor door he stood a kind of walking stick. On a table by the dining-room door he put an inverted teardrop of crystal. On the counter in the bar he put a thing made of three chrome rings at right angles with spikes projecting from the intersections. ˜How's that?˜ he asked.

"Just fine," Rikard said. Each of the items was a special weapon, which Rikard had had built to Droagn's specifications, and had modified so that he, Droagn, or Grayshard could each use them with equal ease. He took the holster from his shoulder and hung it, with the gloves, in plain sight on the back of a chair in front of a desk that stood in the window el. "But somehow I don't think we're going to need them."

"It never hurts to be safe," Grayshard said. "If we're going to order, let's do it please. I'd like to get out of this rig."

"Let's see what we've got here first," Rikard said. He went into the kitchen and checked out the stocks. There was light snack food and beverages in plenty, but he was hungry, and there was nothing to satisfy either Grayshard or Droagn. He dropped his empty beer into the cycler and opened another from the refrigerator. "Any preferences?" he called to the other two as he punched room service on the kitchen comcon.

˜They haven't got it,˜ Droagn said. Grayshard said nothing.

Ordering his own meal was easy, but it took some discussion before room service understood what he wanted for his companions. By then he was into his third beer and beginning to unwind a bit. When he went into the living room Grayshard was still slumped on the sofa, and Droagn was coiled on the floor by the el.

˜If I don't get fed soon,˜ he said, ˜I'll eat a bellhop.˜

"Can they serve me?" Grayshard asked. "I would rather not have any more canned rations."

"I think so," Rikard said, "but they didn't sound like they liked it."

He sat down by the living-room comcon, which was conveniently located next to the bar. He took an LCD card from his shirt pocket, turned it on, skipped through several screens until he came to the number he wanted, then made a call.

"This is Jack Begin," he said when his call was answered. "I'd like to speak to Msr. Nevile Beneking, please."

"*I'm sorry,*" the person on the other end said, "*but Msr. Beneking can't be reached at this time.*"

"I was given this number," Rikard said. "I was told that he would be interested in 'refound commodities.' "

"*I see. Just a moment please.*" Rikard waited. "*You may try this number.*" The voice gave it to him. Rikard noted it on his LCD card.

He punched the new number. Droagn uncoiled and went into the bar. The call was answered. "I'd like to speak with Msr. Nevile Beneking, please," Rikard said.

"*I'm sorry, Msr. Beneking does not wish to be disturbed.*"

"Forgive me for intruding," Rikard said, "but I have merchandise for sale, in which I'm sure Msr. Beneking would be interested. Would you please give him that message, and my number?"

"*Msr. Beneking does not usually respond to phone solicitations.*"

"I'm sure," Rikard said, "but remember the guy who came off the Tschagan station? The one with four arms? Well I have some more of his things, tell Msr. Beneking that."

"*Very well,*" the voice said, with very little enthusiasm, and Rikard broke the connection.

He sipped his beer. Droagn came out of the bar with a pitcher of water from which he sipped without a glass—it was about the right size for him—and coiled in the middle of the floor, looking at Rikard. Grayshard twitched. The comcon rang. Rikard smiled and answered.

"Msr. Begin," the woman on the other end said, *"I represent Msr. Beneking, returning his call. Where can we talk?"*

The front door rang. Grayshard pulled himself together—literally—and went to answer it.

"I'd be glad to talk anywhere," Rikard said into the comcon, "just so long as I can guarantee security."

Two service people came through the living room with a cart, under Grayshard's supervision, and began to set up in the smaller dining room.

"We appreciate your concern," the agent told him. *"Is it possible to see some of this fellow's merchandise?"*

"Of course," Rikard said, "that's why I called." Aromas began to drift from the dining room, some mouth-watering, others less so. "I'm most concerned that a proper buyer be found."

"Msr. Beneking is very good at that. Perhaps you can give me an indication as to the kinds of refound commodities you have for sale."

"Sculptures," Rikard said as the two service people, looking rather pale, left the dining room. "Paintings, a few. Books."

"Books, did you say?"

"Yes, electronic. I don't have the right equipment to read them, they're very old, but I've seen a few pages." Droagn went into the dining room with Grayshard.

"I'm sure Msr. Beneking can arrange to have translators ready. How much material are we speaking of?"

"Enough to make it worth both our whiles. Where and when can we meet?"

"The Museum of Natural History, Alien Environments entrance. How about three this afternoon?"

"Okay," Rikard said. "I was just about to have lunch." Then he listened a while longer as the agent gave him explicit instructions. Then he disconnected and went to join his companions.

The table was set, and Droagn and Grayshard were waiting for him. Rikard had a steak, baked yellow topers, fresh green telins, and a salad. At Droagn's place was a very large slab of very red meat, very fresh and still bleeding, and a bowl of assorted fruit. In front of Grayshard was a tureen from which the less pleasant smells were coming. It contained a frothy mass, rather grayish brown, slightly bubbling.

"Now may I undress?" Grayshard asked.

"We've got a couple hours," Rikard told him. "Make yourself comfortable."

Grayshard unbuckled his jacket and the swathings around his head. Inside was a dense mass of white fibers, like coarse horsehair, writhing and red-tipped, hanging in the basket frame that formed his body. Great bundles of fibers went down the arms and legs of his disguise. As the jacket fell aside, clusters of fibers twitched at joints and connections, so that the metallic skeleton became rigid. He kept only the vocalizer. He had no limbs, though bundles of fibers could serve, if weakly, in their place. There were no organs, no top or bottom, just a huge naked myceleum, massing nearly as much as a Human. Grayshard pulled himself out of his now self-standing disguise and dropped to the floor, then slithered across it to the chair he'd chosen and into it. He immersed several thousand fiber ends into the mass of fermenting material in the tureen and started to absorb it. "Not bad," he said through his vocalizer. "Were you able to get ahold of the dealer?"

"It's all set up," Rikard said.

"Do we take the whole case? Droagn asked.

"Might as well," Rikard said, "but we'll go fully armed."

"They may disarm us," Grayshard said. Absorbing nutrients in no way interfered with his speech.

"I'm sure they will," Rikard said, "but you just keep your jacket loose."

Grayshard waved a few red-tipped tentacles in the air.

After the meal and a short rest they took the trophy case down to the hotel lobby where a uniformed man met them without surprise or comment and conducted them to the street, where a large limousine van with vaguely official markings was waiting in the porte cochere. Rikard and Grayshard sat behind the driver's seat, and there was plenty of room in back for Droagn and the case.

They drove away from the hotel, along busy but uncrowded streets lined with buildings not nearly so tall, past several parks into a kind of enclave in the heart of the city. Behind a screen of ornamental shrubbery, trees, and immaculate lawns was the museum, immense though not tall, sprawling in all directions. There were lots of vehicles in the main parking lot, but they went around to the side.

Rikard and Grayshard got out, their weapons unconcealed. The driver stayed at the wheel. The back opened and Droagn slid out. Some of the museum's visitors stopped to stare at him. Rikard and Grayshard paid no attention to anybody. Droagn pulled out the heavy case, which wobbled on its floater. Rikard turned toward the steps leading up to the columned portico, Droagn followed pulling the case, and Grayshard came behind, operating the controls that enabled it to accommodate the stairs. At the top Rikard opened the glass doors and let them precede him into the large lobby.

It was like any good museum lobby. There were information desks, souvenir desks, signs to the shop, several specimen displays of large alien life forms, columns supporting balconies at two levels, corridors going off to right and left and ahead on either side of a broad stair to the mezzanine below the first balcony. There were plenty of visitors, of a variety of species and cultures. Many of them paused to stare at Droagn.

There were also security guards, who watched them enter with some visible apprehension. One of them came over. "I suggest you check your luggage," she said. She gestured at the floating case but was looking at the gun on Rikard's hip, and her expression revealed that she knew Rikard for the Gesta he was.

"I'm here to see Msr. Nevile Beneking," Rikard said. He made no move or gesture.

"I see." The guard glanced over her shoulder at her colleagues. "Very well then, you know the way?"

"We do," Rikard said, and again preceded the party up to the mezzanine. At the top was a broad corridor that led deep into the building, lined with doors on either side. It ended at an elaborately ornamented double door. Without pausing Rikard led them through it.

The room they entered was a highly decorated antechamber, which might have been used for official gatherings and such. There were benches, chairs, low tables, a bar now folded away, and doors ahead and to the right. There were mounted examples of several exotic creatures, mostly water dwellers, floating above pedestals. Against the high ceiling was another creature, but whether its habitat was air or water Rikard could not say. There was nobody present, though near the entrance there was a discreet desk where visitors might be greeted. To the left, behind this desk, was a small service door. Obeying the instructions he had been given by comcon, Rikard went to this one and opened it.

But he hesitated before entering the long corridor beyond. He could see unconcealed spy eyes in several places along its length, and seams where security doors could suddenly close. There was only a single door at the far end, which didn't look special but which would be almost impervious even to a blaster bolt.

After a moment he took a breath, stepped into the corridor, then stopped. A mechanical voice spoke from the ceiling above him.

"Msr. Jack Begin," it said. "You must leave your weapons here." A panel in the wall beside him opened. He did not hesitate this time but took off his holster and placed it on the shelf thus revealed, and put his gloves, which he had been carrying in his belt, beside it.

He stepped forward again. "Okay," the voice said. "Next please."

Droagn was immediately behind Rikard. He pushed the case into the corridor. "I can't read that," the voice said from the speaker. "You'll have to leave it outside."

"It's a 4D case," Rikard said. "It's got all our merchandise. If you don't want it here, where can I show it?"

After a moment the voice said, "Bring it in."

Droagn pushed it farther forward and came in behind it as Rikard moved out of the way. The voice from the speaker said, "Please remove your harness." Droagn did so and placed it on the shelf next to Rikard's gun and gloves. Then Grayshard came in and without being told put down his laser.

"Can you move without that support frame?" the voice asked.

"Do you really want me to?" Grayshard asked back.

"Perhaps not, but I hope you'll forgive us for taking further precautions when you enter."

"I'd do the same," Rikard said.

"Please continue," the voice told them, and they went toward the door at the far end of the corridor.

The door opened as they neared and they entered a plain room with a large desk, several chairs, and three people standing in the middle, talking to each other. One had his back to the door, while the other two, a man and a woman, each half faced it.

"Now you understand, Msr. Beneking," the man whose face Rikard could see was saying, "that we get first choice in this matter." He paid no attention to Rikard as he came in.

Beneking murmured something in response.

"It's the least you can do for us," the woman said. "We've gone to considerable trouble for you on short notice." She, too, ignored Rikard and Grayshard, who was right behind him.

"I understand completely," Beneking said. "I *want* you to have first pick, that's why I asked you to help me."

Then Rikard's 4D case came floating in, the man glanced at it, then Droagn came into view, and the man's eyes widened. So did the woman's, as behind Rikard Droagn reared up to his full height. Beneking turned to see what was happening, and now it was Rikard's turn to stop and stare. "Nevile Beneking" was, in fact, his uncle, Gawin Malvrone.

"Good God!" Rikard and his uncle said, all but simultaneously. For an instant Rikard didn't know what to do. It had been a long time since he'd seen his mother's brother. But a smile began to dawn on Gawin's face, and he let his feelings dictate. He and his uncle stepped toward each other, and greeted each other with a strong hug.

"Rikard," Gawin said. He stepped back but held Rikard's shoulders. "How are you?" He was nearly as tall as his nephew.

"I'm fine, Uncle Gawin, how are you?"

"Very well, very well indeed."

"It's been fifteen years since I've seen you, Uncle Gawin."

"That long?"

"When you came to Mother's funeral."

"Ah, yes." He let his arms fall. The expression on his face hinted not at grief but at guilt. "And I'm sorry. Your grandfather strictly forbade my visiting you again."

There was nothing for Rikard to say. His mother had been cast out of her family when she'd married Rikard's father.

"I understand you found your father at last," Gawin said after a pause.

"Yes. For a few moments. We, ah, got everything straight before he died."

"I'm glad. And you've been taking after him in a way."

"Now what gives you that idea?"

"I've been following some of your exploits," Gawin said with a wry twist to his mouth, "not all of them admirable."

"I'm doing what I can," Rikard said. "Maybe this particular 'exploit' will get me the academic standing I've been looking for."

"Maybe it will. I can hardly wait to see what you brought—Msr. Jack Begin."

He and Rikard laughed, and became aware once again of the rest of the world around them.

The other two Humans were standing well back, rather surprised at what they had heard, and looking a bit dubious about continuing. Droagn and Grayshard just waited. Gawin Malvrone's attention was once again drawn to Droagn, who was used to that sort of thing and not used to being ignored at all.

"Uncle Gawin," Rikard said. "May I present my friend Endark Droagn, an Ahmear. He survived twenty-five thousand years in stasis as a prisoner of the Tschagan. And this is Grayshard, a Vaashka here on, ah, special assignment."

"Pleased to meet you both," Gawin said. "As I have been keeping track of my nephew's adventures, so I have heard much about you." He then introduced the other two Humans, who were Alfard Mitchelle and Larnie Browen, directors of the museum, who had arranged this secure meeting place.

"Now let's get down to business," Mitchelle said. "Whoever you really are. Do you have things to show us, Msr., ah, Begin?"

"I most certainly do." Grayshard, using the control box, settled the big case down to the floor.

"And you are in fact in the market for art objects, Msr., ah, Beneking?"

"I am."

"Very well then."

Browen moved closer. "Let's see what you brought," she told Rikard.

Rikard opened the case, while his uncle and the two

directors watched in fascination. Then he began to take things out of the case, one by one. He handed them to his uncle—all the sculptures, crystalware, silver objects, mechanical devices, small paintings, booklike things. With each item the other three Humans became simultaneously more excited and more constrained. Their breathing became slow, deep, irregular, their faces beaded with sweat, their movements were slow and tense and tight. Gawin handed the objects to Mitchelle, who handed them in turn to Browen, who put them down first on the desk, then on the chairs, then on the floor around the desk.

"How did you *get* all this?" Browen asked at one point.

"I have Droagn to thank for that," Rikard said. "He saw the reference in *The Journal of Pre-Federal Studies*, and recognized the site for what it was."

"I mean, how did you deal with the government of Trokarion? They're having a war there, aren't they?"

"Not all of Trokarion, just Elsepreth. It's a rather unimportant country really, and mostly *because* of their silly civil war. Basically, I didn't deal with them at all."

"You mean you stole all this?"

⁻The only people,⁻ Droagn *projected*, which made everybody stop for a moment in surprise, ⁻who could be said to *not* steal this stuff, are my people—and I sort of acted as their representative.⁻

". . . ah, I see," Browen said.

"Try not to make them jump so," Rikard said to Droagn. "They might drop something."

"But," Mitchelle said, "you had to go through Elsepreth territory to get to the site."

"I did. Should I take it back?"

"No. No . . . no."

"Good."

He kept on taking things out. Gawin Malvrone, Alfard Mitchelle, and Larnie Browen looked each item over, but were so overwhelmed that they spent only a moment with each in turn, and at last the three just withdrew to the windows, from which they stared back at the haphazard collection of art and artifact. Rikard felt good about it.

"Now we come to the books," Rikard said, and he started lifting them out, one by one, and piled them on the floor beside the case. "You want to take a look at these," he said when the case was empty. He stood and took the top one from the pile and held it out to them. "They need to be recharged, though."

"Right," Browen said, "no problem. I think." She took the book, turned it over in her hands, opened it—it still carried a residual charge—looked at a page or two before it went dark, examined the spine, the edges. "No problem at all," she said again, and moved a statue of two Ahmear amorously entwined—or something like that—aside on the top of the desk so she could activate the comcon. She spoke briefly into it. A few moments later a chime sounded over the door. She spoke into the comcon again, "Just leave it there," then went out into the corridor. She came back almost at once with an electronics cart, which she plugged into a wall receptacle. Then she took the Ahmear book and fit it between a complex of clips and busses. A small red light came on, and after a while it turned green. She took the book out of the device and opened it again.

"Fully charged," she said. She handed it to Mitchelle, and put another one in the clips.

It took a long time to charge them all. Rikard, Grayshard, and Droagn were as fascinated with the contents as the other three. Mitchelle had supper sent in. But at last everybody began to overload—except possibly Grayshard—and Browen served drinks from the private bar as they sat and stared at the treasure.

Gawin still held one of the books open in his lap. Occasionally he "flipped" a page. "I can't get a fair price for the books," he said, shaking his head. "There is no fair price for something like this."

"I know," Rikard said. "Just do the best you can." He sipped his drink, a smoky malted whiskey called Croich, with a peculiar flavor that few people besides himself liked. He had been surprised when Browen offered it to him.

"So what do we pick?" Mitchelle asked Browen.

"God, do we have to decide tonight?"

"Not at all," Rikard said. "I'll leave everything with 'Msr. Beneking' here—I think I can trust him—and you can deal with him at your leisure, or his."

"That really would make things a lot easier," Gawin said.

"And this is only a fraction of what's at the site," Rikard reminded them. "A proper expedition needs to be sent there, with all their documents in order, to collect and preserve everything else. Of course, if you do that, the value of these things will drop drastically."

"Dollar value is not what's at stake here," Browen said. "Besides, even under the best of circumstances, it would be decades before anything more could be removed."

They sat silent a moment. Without looking up from his book Gawin said, "You might be interested to know that the site on Trokarion has been reported to the news bureaus, and the authorities in Elsepreth have been pressured into doing something to preserve it, in spite of their civil war."

"Indeed," Mitchelle said. "If the existence of the site becomes common knowledge, the value of these objects could in fact increase."

"It could," Gawin said. He glanced up at Rikard. "There's more," he said. "A special force of Federation police has been assembled and sent to Trokarion to assure the safety of the site." His eyes met Rikard's squarely. His expression was quite serious. "The commander of this force is to report directly to a certain Brigadier Leonid Polski."

"Ha!" Rikard said.

It was a name he knew well. Years ago, when he'd started his career as an adventurer, Polski, then just a colonel, had become his friend and mentor. It had been Polski who'd helped him find his father, who'd later brought him into the brain pirates business, through which he'd met Grayshard and Endark Droagn. But there had been a woman, once Polski's friend, then Rikard's, and she'd gone back to Polski. And Rikard and Polski were on opposite sides of the law, more or less.

Gawin was still looking at Rikard. Mitchelle and Browen, sensing that something was going on, were quiet. "Brigadier Polski has been quoted as saying," Gawin said, "that the opening of the Ahmear city has to have been done by either Rikard Braeth or Darcy Glemtide."

"He said that?" Rikard said after a pause. "That means she's no longer with him."

"So it would seem, at least on a regular basis."

"But she hasn't come looking for me, either." He sat silent for a long moment. "How do you hear all this stuff?"

"I subscribe to a news service, and keep a repeater with me all the time." He reached up and took a small crescent shape from behind his left ear. "The master is over there," he said, nodding toward a small briefcase beside the desk.

"That must cost a bundle," Rikard said as he struggled with his thoughts.

"It does, but it's worth it."

"Does your news service say anything about anybody else being there besides me?" Rikard asked.

"No," Gawin said. "Was there?"

"She was a Gesta, I could tell. She ambushed me, and nearly got away with the treasure. She had a lot of people with her, and she scared me."

Gawin put the repeater crescent back behind his ear and listened a moment. "There's no mention of any party being there after you left—which doesn't mean that they weren't, especially if she was one of your kind." He looked up at Rikard again. "Do you know who it was?"

"Somebody named Karyl Toerson."

Gawin looked surprised. "There's been no mention of anybody by that name," he said.

"Maybe she didn't get out," Rikard said. "There were Ahmear down there too, or at least the decadent descendants of Ahmear, and they ambushed us in turn." Mitchelle and Browen were more than surprised by this news. "We were able to get away, with Droagn's help, but we left Toerson down there."

"Then maybe she's dead," Gawin said.

Rikard looked at his uncle closely. There was something in his expression that hinted at more than a casual interest. "You've heard the name before," he said.

"I knew her once, long ago. You had every reason to be afraid of her, but I thought she had died long before now."

"Apparently not. Is there any mention of Ahmear-like beings down there?"

"No." He stared off into middle space. "For what it's worth. If she survived this long, I wouldn't count on her having died now. She's too tough."

"How did you know her?"

Gawin ran his hand across his mouth. "I'd be careful if I were you," he said. "Maybe those Ahmear people did her in, but maybe they didn't. If she shows up again, don't try to reason with her, and don't trust anything she says. Just get away. She's twisted, and evil."

"That was the feeling I got," Rikard said. "Gestae can read each other, and she's one of that kind that gives us a bad name."

"Not," Mitchelle said, "that you really need any help."

Rikard looked at the man, who was speaking in all seriousness, but he felt the mood break. "We do our best," he said wryly.

Gawin stood and put the Ahmear book down on the stack. He got his briefcase and took out the repeater master. It looked just like a small, portable comcon. He touched a few buttons and stared at the screen. "I've not been sitting idle," he said. "I've gotten responses from three of my associates. Considerable interest has been expressed by a number of reputable people, mostly universities and museums. The artworks will all be well studied and available for public viewing." He put the master down on the desk. "The books will be more of a problem, though, finding just the right place for them, since they'll all need to be translated. I've a number of places in mind, which not only are good at that sort of thing, but which also communicate with each other." He looked at Droagn. "I don't suppose I could interest you in helping out."

"There's nothing I can do for you," Droagn said. "I don't know those languages any better than you do. I can speak with you because my form of telepathy works that way, but written language is something else. I can't read anything I've seen in any of the books."

"That's too bad," Gawin said. "But even untranslated, I'm going to try to see that copies of the books are made available to the public. Or at least some of the better picture books."

"That suits me just fine," Rikard said. "And I guess that just about wraps things up."

"Except for the matter of payment," Gawin said.

"Certainly. I'm not going to haggle with you, Uncle Gawin. I'll open an account here in Three Rivers, and you make the deposit."

"I haven't made you an offer yet."

"It doesn't matter. I'm not poor, Uncle Gawin. Besides, I like to have various accounts in various places—in case of emergencies."

"Of course. I'm flattered that you trust me."

"Msr. Nevile Beneking," Rikard said, "has a very good reputation among the Gestae of my acquaintance. That's why I came to you instead of anybody else."

Gawin nodded, pleased at the compliment. "Then I suggest a drink to close the deal."

There was general agreement to that. And shortly afterward Mitchelle and Browen had some trusted members of the museum staff come in and pack most of the things away. Gawin asked permission to stay a while longer, to look at a few of the electronic books some more, and Rikard, Grayshard, and Droagn decided to stay with him.

They made themselves comfortable, but rather than look at old books, Rikard and Gawin got involved in family reminiscences. Rikard knew little about his mother's family, nothing about his father's, and Gawin was not too communicative, so mostly what they talked about was Rikard's childhood on Pelgrane, how his father had gone off looking for one last fortune and not come back, how his mother had grieved and died, how Rikard had found his father at last and lost him again, almost immediately, this time forever, to a murderer's gun. Rikard found that he, too, had things to be reticent about, the fortune that his father had found after all and which Rikard now had, his relationship with Darcy Glemtide and how that had ended, some few of his exploits that had less to do with historical "research" and more with just plain raising hell.

Endark Droagn joined in the conversation as he could. He sympathized with Rikard's position, and could understand it. Grayshard said little, but did not seem bored. He never did.

It got late, and conversation wound down. "I wish I could see you more often," Rikard said to his uncle.

Gawin fiddled with his drink, and for a moment would not meet Rikard's eyes. "There's a lot about your mother's family you don't know," he said at last.

"I know that Grandfather and Grandmother hated my father, and never much cared for me."

"That situation has not improved," Gawin said. "And it's completely unjustified, as far as I'm concerned. Maybe it's about time we did something about it."

"Such as?"

"Father strongly disapproves of what I do for a living," Gawin said wryly, "and does not know I do it. You will have to be discreet. If he finds out, he can cause me considerable trouble that, being the supposedly grown-up person I am, I would find more than just unpleasant, but intolerable."

"I have no idea what you're talking about."

"I know. But family secrets have been kept too long. Why don't you come visit me, on Malvrone."

"I'd like to do that. What came first, the planet or the family?"

"No one remembers. Or cares. Will you come?"

"I will. When?"

"Give me about fifty, sixty days to clear this business up."

"All right. That will give me a chance to turn in a monograph or two. Maybe this whole business will impress Grandfather a bit, don't you think?"

"It might, but I wouldn't count on it."

"How about money? Mother always said her family had more titles than wealth. Does he need any help? Would he accept it from me?"

"It would not be a good idea to offer," Gawin said. He seemed oddly disturbed by the suggestion. "I think your first idea is the better one, emphasize your career as a scholar and a historian. Father doesn't keep track of these things much. He's fastidious about propriety, that's at the root of the problem."

"I can be very circumspect when I have to," Rikard reassured him. "I do have all the credentials I need. I publish quite regularly, you know."

"Yes," Gawin said, "I do."

"It's getting late," Grayshard said quietly. It was the first time he'd spoken in several hours.

"It is that," Droagn said. "Let's bring this business to a close and get some sleep. We don't want to be here when the staff comes in the morning."

"You're right," Rikard said, and he pulled himself to his feet. "I'd just like to take one more look at that archaeology book." He walked over to the desk where it lay. Droagn sighed. Rikard opened it and stared at what he assumed was the title page.

The book was an artwork in itself. Though they had been able to recharge this and the other books, there were no other objects exactly like them anywhere in the Federation. Rikard touched the corner of the screen and flipped through a few pages. Gawin came over to look, and Droagn did too, standing behind them and looking down over their heads.

The book was heavily illustrated, with photos, renderings, graphs and charts, and diagrams. There was extensive text as well, in body, sidebar, caption, and special in-text notes. It dealt with sites that were archaeological treasures at least a million years ago, if not more, and so were incredibly ancient now. If any of the sites illustrated could be found they would be of immense value, dating as they did from the time long before the ascent of Humans.

Rikard turned the pages, just skimming, but now and then he paused to look at one of the illustrations more closely. Many of them dealt with Ahmear sites, but as many more dealt with other races, such as the octopoid Rel-Geneth, the humanoid Drovish, the centaurian Charvon, the arachnoid Ratash—and the Kelarins, of course—all of which, except the Kelarins, Rikard recognized and knew to be extinct. Most of the pictures were originals, but a few, by their slightly reduced quality, seemed to be reproductions of much older pictures, and were obviously so, as when the older picture was an actual photograph or holograph instead of the current technology of the book.

"We've got to go," Grayshard said softly from behind them.

"In a moment," Rikard said. He turned more pages, and then Gawin stopped him.

"Look there," he said.

Rikard looked at the picture more closely. The site illustrated was that of a certain kind of ruin, and the peculiar structure that Gawin was pointing to was simply in the background behind it. "There's something about that..." Gawin said, then picked up his portable comcon and searched quickly through several screens of text. "That's it," he said at last. "I knew I'd seen something like that before." He showed his comcon to Rikard.

On the screen, in the background of a picture, was the image of a conical mountain of white stone. "That's on Dannon's Keep," Gawin said. The slightly twisted cone on his comcon was greatly eroded, while the one in the Ahmear book was whole and its spiral form more obvious, but they were apparently the same kind of formation, altered by a million years or more of weathering.

"I was there on, ah, business," Gawin said. "I saw these things, took a picture. Nobody could tell me what they were, except that they were metamorphic limestone. It's a rather peculiar geological structure, and there were no explanations as to how it was formed, but there are a number of them in various places around the world, and nobody was much interested in them. But if what I saw was the same as these things here"—he jabbed his finger at the Ahmear illustration again—"then they're not natural after all." The cones in the Ahmear book, despite their unfamiliarity, were obviously artificial structures.

"I've never seen anything like it before," Rikard said. "I can identify the major architectural forms of every major culture of any starfaring species in the Federation, but not this." He felt a thrill of excitement run through him. He looked up at Droagn. "Could that possibly be of Ahmear origin?" he asked.

"No way. I'm not an historian, but for what it's worth, I've never seen anything like it either."

They turned a couple of pages, and there was another illustration, with the unweathered cone in the background. This one was clearer, and comparing it to the picture Gawin had brought up on his comcon, it was obvious that the two were the same thing.

"Not marble mountains after all," Gawin said, "but the eroded remains of some kind of building."

"And if that's true," Rikard said, "they must belong to a species so far undocumented." He felt himself grinning. Precoursor history was his favorite. "But who were they?"

Gawin typed codes into his comcon, but the only message

that came on the screen was, "No records of any such architecture."

"It was something your people knew about," Rikard said to Droagn.

ˉMy species,ˉ Droagn said, ˉbut not my people. This is all ancient history to me too.ˉ

"I've got to check this out," Rikard said. "Maybe it's nothing, but if it's what I think it is, my reputation is made." He looked at Gawin. "'Historian discovers hitherto unknown sentient species.' Would that impress Grandfather?"

"It would impress anybody," Gawin said, "but your grandfather isn't just anybody."

"I've got to give it a try. You need fifty, sixty days. I can get to Dannon's Keep and back by then. If it's a false lead, I'll at least have done something interesting with my time."

"I guess it wouldn't hurt to try," Gawin concurred.

Dannon's Keep

1

The Federation and many of the surrounding star nations, such as the Abogarn Hegemony and the Anarchy of Raas, are dominated by Humans—by virtue of their numbers rather than their great age or superior technology. Many of the other intelligent species are also starfaring, but many are not.

The Zapets of Dannon's Keep are an example of the latter. They are humanoid and highly technological, and in some ways they are superior to the average Federation culture. But they never developed a star drive, and have no desire to explore the stars. Their world is well within the Federation, and they are fully aware of the Federation surrounding them, but pay it no attention and have no interest in it. They permit visitors, and being humanoid have little difficulty with most of them.

And so it was when Rikard and his companions arrived. The facilities at the system jumpslot were minimal, as was the station orbiting Dannon's Keep itself. A Federal agent cautioned them about being on a non-Federal world, and then they took the shuttle down to the surface. During the brief descent they could see the gemlike cities among the fields and forests. The farms were checkerboarded with wilderness and parklands. There were few small communities in those parts of the world where the dominant cultures existed, and few large cities elsewhere. They landed at Vergemal, one of the three cities with a spaceport. The ground staff was half Human, and a quarter other alien.

The rest were Zapets. They were as tall as Rikard, on the average, adapted to their slightly cooler, darker world, with huge eyes, soft fur the color of sunset covering their entire bodies and faces, long narrow noses, large ears, and hands with fingers twice as long as a Human's. Despite their fur they wore clothing, and boots or shoes on feet that more resembled a long-toed dog's than a Human's.

The city of Vergemal was typical, mostly vertical and densely built, dimly lit by Human standards but well ventilated and with plenty of interior open spaces for all that, and highly ornamented, even in the most functional areas.

Accommodations for off-worlders were not easy to come by. Within the spaceport, nobody needed rooms for more than four or five days, and out in the city they were not accustomed to dealing with anyone but themselves. But at last Rikard located a garage, for Droagn, with facilities appended for himself and Grayshard, which suited them just fine.

Rikard and his companions caused considerable attention as they found their way around, looking for someone who could help them locate the mysterious architecture in Gawin's pictures and the Ahmear book. The university was of no help, nor was the Federal bureau of parks and land management. But then Rikard tried the largest tourist bureau in the city, and though they were not really prepared to help alien visitors, the director did recognize the eroded cones, calling them volcanically modified sedimentary extrusions, and was even able to tell them that the ones in the picture were located in the forested region of an underdeveloped country called Laka Chuka.

Having solved that problem, they next had to obtain a vehicle, special equipment, and supplies. Rikard had taken it for granted that he could get whatever he wanted here, as he had everywhere else, but such was not the case. The Zapets just didn't know how to deal with them. It took them more than ten local days to equip themselves, and not only at greater cost, but at the complete loss of any anonymity they might have hoped for.

But at last they were able to head for Laka Chuka. It was a three-day trip by air truck, even with no stops. They passed out of the region of high culture and big cities, and headed south into the dense forests. There were occasional small towns, then only villages, then nothing but trees. The truck's navigation panel had no entry for their destination, so they had to go on direction and coordinates alone.

Two hours after passing the last village they flew over small areas within the forest that had been clear-cut. Each was only a few hectares in extent, and there were other, similar areas where new trees were growing up. In another place they saw where a section of the forest had been thinned, but not cleared, and in another area it appeared as though only selected mature trees had been removed.

This part of Laka Chuka was home to a people called the Una Tlim. They were considered primitive by the sophisticated city dwellers to the north. They made their living by tree culture, and provided much of the more civilized world with lumber. They were a proud and independent people, divided into innumerable communities who fought among themselves for land rights, and were, as far as Rikard knew, totally unfamiliar with off-worlders.

It was midafternoon of the third day when they saw something on the horizon ahead of them. As they neared it proved to be the white, eroded cones, apparently the ones in Gawin's photo, though they were approaching from a slightly different angle. Rikard couldn't help but wonder what his uncle had been doing in this part of the country when he'd taken the pictures.

The cones were hundreds of meters tall, steeply angled, with nearly pointed tops, their sides grooved and notched and ridged. Together they formed an equilateral triangle, sticking up out of the dense forest. There was no place to land.

They went back a few kilometers to a clear-cut section they'd passed by and set down. The trees had been removed very recently, and the stumps were still damp. The brush had been collected into several piles around the perimeter of the clearing and the ground smoothed over. These people took good care of their forests.

They loaded their equipment on four industrial-grade floaters. There was lots of room left over, just in case they wanted to bring anything back. Now they faced the prospect of a hike through the forest, pulling and pushing the floaters along with them. They would have to clear a trail as they went, but dared not damage any trees, lest they arouse the antagonism of the Una Tlim.

Before they could get under way, the Una Tlim themselves showed up. They were somewhat more solidly built than the Zapets of the city, their fur was rather paler, and though the city folk considered them primitive, they carried high-powered rifles and laser woodcutting tools. They did not seem happy to see Rikard and his companions, especially Droagn.

In anticipation of such an encounter Rikard had come equipped with vocal translators, the use of which rather startled the locals, but which enabled them to negotiate their assistance, though not without considerable haggling over what work was to be done, what price was to be paid, and what precautions Rikard's party had to take to avoid damaging the trees. What he wound up with was four Una Tlim and a leader, whose name was something like Oakly, and whose primary duty, it seemed, was to keep Rikard out of trouble.

The trip was uneventful, and they camped that evening near the base of one of the white marble cones. The trees grew right up to the base, and the undergrowth a little way up it. The Una Tlim made their camp in tents, which each one carried, while Rikard set up a larger shelter, under Oakly's guidance, where he and Grayshard and Droagn could sleep. The Una Tlim built a fire, and they were all as sociable as they could be. They did not share food.

Rikard slept well that night, until Droagn roused him, halfway between midnight and morning. ˝We've got company,˝ Droagn said. ˝More Zapets, and they're sneaking through the trees.˝

Rikard dressed quickly, buckled on his holster, and left Droagn and Grayshard in the shelter while he went to talk to the Una Tlim leader.

"I was hoping," Oakly said, "but it was not to be. We have left our own territory, so near were we to the border, and these others think we have come to steal their trees."

"So what do we do?" Rikard asked.

"Get up onto the mountain, so that they can see that we mean no harm."

When Rikard got back to Droagn and Grayshard, they had already taken down the shelter and stowed it on its floater. Their five Una Tlim porters joined them almost at once, and they quickly moved to the base of the cone, only a dozen meters away. But even as they started up the steep, detritus-covered slope, there were shots from behind them, and one of the porters fell.

Their position was indefensible, but they did what they could. Oakly and the three remaining porters fought bravely, Grayshard's micropulse laser was effective—the darkness didn't bother him much—but Rikard and Droagn could not see any targets, and just fired into the trees at random.

And then it was all over. Their porters lay dead, their attackers, whom they never saw, fled into the forest.

"Let's wait for daylight," Rikard suggested. "It's going to be tricky enough to climb this thing when we can see."

Dawn was not too far off, and they were not disturbed the rest of the night. Droagn kept watch. When the sky above them began to brighten, and the top of the cone turned bright red in the rays of the rising sun, they put the essential equipment on one floater and left the rest and started up.

The surface of the cone, past the layer of forest detritus, was as white up close as it had seemed at a distance. The weathered marble was corrugated, rough, and though the slope was steep it was relatively easy to climb, at least for Rikard, as there were plenty of handholds and footholds. Grayshard managed fairly well, unburdened as he was. Droagn found it a bit tricky, especially since he had the greater burden of pulling the float while Rikard managed the lifting controls.

When they got to the height of the treetops Rikard put on his recording helmet, scanned the horizon, took a close-up of the surface of the cone, and spoke into the mike. "This is marble, metamorphosed limestone. In nature it would be from sedimentary shell deposits, in this case, who knows."

"Perhaps," Grayshard said, "the structure was organically grown, then fused."

Rikard stared at him. "Grown? By what?"

"Domesticated coral perhaps."

"I've never heard of anything like that," Rikard said. "Besides, coral needs an ocean and this was grown on dry land."

˜It's been done before,˜ Droagn *projected*, and Rikard automatically vocalized for the sake of the recording. ˜There used to be a people we called Kapanosians, sort of like hairy birds with long legs. They had domesticated a kind of a mollusk that produced excessive amounts of shell when properly fed and stimulated. They'd put these snails into molds, grow a structural piece of calcium carbonate, then use other snails to weld the pieces together. Weirdest damn architecture you ever saw.˜

"I'll just bet," Rikard said.

They continued climbing, and using a variety of optical

enhancers, they scanned the corrugated and eroded surface for any sign of an entry, but found none. Rikard added his commentary to the recording as appropriate.

The higher they went, the more the surface was worn away, and if the outer walls were thin enough, they might eventually find a place where the weather had broken through for them. From the pictures in the Ahmear text, it had seemed that there might be an entrance of some kind associated with a projecting shelf and vertical ridge, but if there had been such a structural feature on this cone, a million and more years of erosion had erased any traces of it. Nor could Droagn, using his Prime, detect any hollows within.

But at last they could climb no farther. They were halfway to the top, and the surface offered no more purchase. They clung as best they could to the side of the cone while Rikard took a stonecutter from one of the boxes on the floater. After the expedition into the Ahmear ruins he'd decided that such a specialized tool was worth bringing along, and so it proved. With it he was easily able to chip holds and corrugations in the smooth stone. And this revealed that the nature of the material of the cone changed subtly a few centimeters below the surface.

They worked their way, more slowly now, upward to where the going became easier again, where the surface became split and fractured. Now it was Droagn's turn to pause. ˉIt is hollow,ˉ he said, ˉbut it's a long way in.ˉ

"Does it get closer to the surface anywhere?" Rikard asked.

ˉIt's hard to tell. The cracks here complicate the image.ˉ

They moved farther upward, until once again Droagn, using his Prime to probe into the cone, suggested they pause. ˉI think we can cut through here,ˉ he said. ˉThe space inside can't be more than four or five meters in.ˉ

Rikard got out another stonecutter for Droagn and they set to work while Grayshard kept watch. They first cut themselves secure footholds and belly-holds, then started to make a large opening in the side of the cone.

"We've got company," Grayshard said when they'd penetrated a little over a meter.

Rikard and Droagn turned to look behind them. There were six floaters coming toward them, still some distance away, over the tops of the trees. Grayshard focused his image enhancers. "They're Una Tlim," he said.

"Let's keep working," Rikard suggested, and he and Droagn attacked the rock face with renewed vigor, now striving for a less capacious but deeper opening.

But even as they did so Grayshard shouted, "They're shooting," and they could hear the sounds of projectile weapons going off. The Una Tlim were too far away yet to be effective, but their intentions were clear.

"Which group are they?" Rikard asked as he stowed his cutter back in its box. Droagn kept on working. Though Rikard didn't want to fight these people, it didn't look like he was going to be given the choice.

"I don't know," Grayshard said. "I can't tell them apart."

"Let's see if we can just drive them off," Rikard suggested, so Grayshard drew his micropulse. It was a close-in weapon, not intended for long range. He waited until the floaters reached the cone and started to climb, then fired. At that distance, the multiple laser pulses were greatly attenuated, and hurt rather than damaged Grayshard's targets, which he had no difficulty hitting. It made them duck, but didn't otherwise slow them down.

Rikard drew his gun. Time slowed. The concentric rings centered on his target, but the red spot, which should indicate where a bullet would hit, was diffuse. The range was too long, and by the time the bullet got there, the target could easily have moved out of the way. He put his megatron back in its holster and took one of the heavy laser rifles from the floater instead.

Una Tlim bullets began to dig up chips and dust just

below their position. There wasn't much space in the hole for them to find cover, especially with Droagn still trying to dig through to the hollow within, but they did the best they could. Rikard took careful aim at one of the floaters and fired. The violet beam hit the engine compartment, and the floater settled to the surface of the cone and slid down toward the trees. The other five floaters kept coming.

Grayshard used his micropulse to harass the approaching Una Tlim, and their shots were for the most part way off target, but a few heavy slugs struck close enough to make Rikard fear for his life. He aimed at a second floater, and brought this one down as well. The first one had disappeared into the foliage below. The other four floaters slowed their ascent.

Then there was a brighter flash from one of the floaters, and a heavier report, which came from what looked like a cannon. The shot missed, low and to the right, and Grayshard concentrated his fire on the gunners. Rikard took new aim, but could see in the rifle's scope that the heavy gun was armored. It fired again, still low and a bit to the left, and the rock cracked under Rikard's feet, and small stuff rained down from above.

"If they don't kill us," Droagn aid, "they might break through for us."

Rikard fired, the violet beam melted a crater in the heavy gun's shielding. Grayshard's shots were still the most effective. Droagn threw down the stonecutter and grabbed the floater. The big gun fired again, the shell hit just above them, Rikard felt himself being dragged backward by Droagn's strong arm, then the rock above them gave way and slid down over the opening he and Droagn had cut, even as they fell backward into the darkness.

2

If it hadn't been for Droagn, Rikard would have been badly hurt, and Grayshard would have been completely crushed. As it was they got away with only a few bruises. Broken stone kept on falling, in the utter darkness, as they scrambled away from the slide, but it was soon over. The opening above them wasn't large enough to admit much rock.

"Is everybody all right?" Rikard asked.

"I'm here," Grayshard said.

˜I'm just fine,˜ Droagn *projected*. ˜Who's got a light?˜

"Did you get our stuff in all right?" Rikard asked.

"Just a minute," Grayshard said. There was the sound of boxes falling over, a lid opening, a muffled fumbling, then a clear white light filled the hollow. Grayshard stood by the floater with half its load tumbled off. Droagn coiled beside it, his tail half buried under the white, fallen rubble. Rikard was sitting a bit farther back, his recording helmet askew.

˜Doesn't look like we're going to get out of here very soon,˜ Droagn said. He pulled his tail out from under the heap of broken marble.

"Maybe they'll think we're dead," Rikard said. He got to his feet, brushed himself off, made sure his camera was working, and went over to the grounded floater to inspect its cargo. Though a few of the crates and boxes were dented, the contents seemed to be undamaged.

˜Is that thing going to work,˜ Droagn asked, or am I going to have to carry everything?˜

Rikard tried the floater's controls. The free end lifted up a few centimeters. He and Droagn moved the rocks aside, and the floater came up to thirty centimeters. They reloaded the equipment, got out lights for Rikard and Droagn, and set up four more on the corners of the floater. At last they were able to pay some attention to where they were.

From the outside the cone-shaped mountain had seemed to be composed of a fine-grained marble, partially decomposed, with little or no variation in texture. Inside it was different, seeming at once to be both marblelike and like natural shell. The inner surface was, however, just as hard as the exterior. It was white, and their lamps, though not intrinsically very bright, reflected off it so that the whole interior was as well lit as a living room.

They were in a chamber, some six meters square, with openings on either side near the inner wall. The fall of rubble filled the outer half of the chamber, blocking the opening that Droagn had cut, which was high in the wall and partially through the ceiling.

"You still think this place was grown?" Rikard asked Grayshard.

"It could be," Grayshard said. His fingers were just touching a wall. Concealed by his gloved hand, hundreds of red-tipped white fibers were "tasting" the surface. "It's a natural material, as near as I can tell, though not like any shell I've ever encountered before."

"It doesn't look like it was made in pieces and cemented together," Droagn commented.

"I don't think it was. It feels like it was made all of a piece."

"It would take one hell of an animal to lay down a shell like this," Rikard said, "and with a very peculiar physiology."

"More likely billions of animals, like coral. I could be wrong."

The floors were flat, and showed no signs of wear. The walls met them at a 90-degree angle, only slightly rounded. The ceiling was parallel to the floor, and showed no signs of fixtures of any kind.

"How did they see in here?" Rikard asked.

"Maybe they didn't," Grayshard said.

~Or breathe?~ Droagn added. ~No air-conditioning. Is there any plumbing?~

"That's your specialty," Rikard said. "Can you feel anything in the walls?"

~They're solid, as far as I can tell.~

They had no clue as to which way to go, so they chose the corridor on the left. Halfway down it there was a door in the outer wall, tight-fitting and nearly undetectable, so that only the sharp angle of the lamps casting a tiny shadow revealed it. It opened out from the corridor, into a room as empty as the one by which they had entered. At the end of the corridor was another room exactly like the first, with another corridor opposite the entrance. They went on.

The layout varied little. The rooms between corridors were empty. There was usually just one room off the outer side of the corridor, but sometimes two, and occasionally three. They were all empty. Most of the doors were closed. The walls, floors, and ceilings were white or creamy white, but here and there were traces of orange, rust, brown, and occasionally gray or even blue.

The corridors were not perfectly straight. There was an imperceptible arcing, which Rikard could detect only by using a laser gauge that shone a beam down the corridor in both directions. These rooms and corridors completely surrounded the cone, forming a band just beneath the surface. If there were other similar bands inside and concentric to this one, they did not find them.

They proceeded clockwise until they came to a passage parallel to the corridor, but which slanted down to a lower level. There were no stairs, but unlike the Ahmear ramps, the floor surface was perfectly smooth.

The lower level was much the same as the one above. The width of corridor and room together was never more than ten meters, sometimes less. Droagn probed the outer wall, but could not determine the thickness of the shell. The material was singularly impervious to his Prime, though he could read through metal, normal stone, and most plastics with ease.

They passed other ramps, sometimes going up, as often down, but never more than one level at a time. Sometimes two corridors connected the major chambers, or ran outside the intermediate rooms. Occasionally they encountered sections of the outer wall that had caved in, and then they had to backtrack and find another route, or turn back and go the other way, or take a ramp down. And always the rooms were empty.

They chose the down-ramps preferentially. Each level was larger in circumference than the one above. At one point they found a crack that extended through the outer wall all the way to the surface. The wall was about twenty meters thick at that point. The crack was not wide enough for Rikard to reach his hand into it, and it was not straight, but weather had come in, and where it had the material of the cone was not at all shell-like, but only marblelike. How long it had taken that change to take place they could not guess. Geologists had called the cone mountains marble since they'd been discovered more than fifteen hundred years ago, Zapetti time, and yet they were not really marble after all.

As they went deeper Rikard noted that the increased interior circumference was not commensurate with the increased outer diameter, as he calculated it should have been from the exterior slope. They began to pay more attention to the outer walls, both in the corridors and in the rooms connecting and between, and sure enough, eventually Grayshard's sensitive tendrils found a doorway opening outward into a radial corridor, about twenty meters long, which led to another band of passages and chambers concentric with the one that they had been exploring.

Rikard's excitement began to wane. Aside from the structure itself, there was nothing here to get excited about. It was at least a million years old, and possibly older, and that in itself, and its mysterious origins, would be enough to keep certain scholars happy for decades, but it wasn't enough for him. He wanted more—artifacts, the nature of the builders, some clues as to their role in the galaxy at that time.

Ironically, it was just this dull kind of thing that would do the most to convince his grandparents that he was a serious scholar and not just an adventurer. Trouble was, he *was* an adventurer. Could he spend the next twenty years writing papers on this and doing what research he could among the Ahmear texts? The thought of it made him claustrophobic. Only the desire to please his grandfather made him think of it at all.

If he did major research on this, and proved that these marblelike mini-mountains, long thought to be natural, were in fact the product of some long-vanished civilization, he would have another academic credit of no small importance. But he couldn't accept that this was all there was to it. He couldn't believe that the whole core of this place was just solid. There had to be a way in.

He estimated that the top third of the cone was missing, and they had come in about halfway up that, and had by this time come down not quite halfway to the outside ground level. If access to the inner regions was at the top, they'd have seen it from the air, some kind of sinking or depression, but there had been none, just solid metamorphosed stone. That implied that one got to whatever inner chambers there were nearer the bottom, and so they continued down.

They found another connector to yet another outer band of chambers and passages, which was not what they wanted at all, but they stopped to examine the connection from the outside, shining their lights on the white surface on either side of the open door, and on the outer surface of the door itself.

Now that they were looking for it, it was obvious. There were thin smears of bluish gray that crossed the doorway and extended across the walls on either side.

"I've seen that pattern before," Grayshard said.

Rikard played back some of his recording. "You're right. We've passed marks like that several times."

¯Do they write in color?¯ Droagn suggested.

"I think it's just a sign," Rikard said, "not true writing."

"Let's go back to the last similar mark on the inside," Grayshard suggested.

They did, and Grayshard ran his tendrils along the smooth surface, white except for the faint smears of bluish gray. "There is a door here," he told them.

"I hate to use the cutter," Rikard said.

"Let me try," Droagn suggested. He held a long prybar with a very narrow working end. Grayshard guided the thin blade to what he said was the junction between door and jamb, and Droagn pushed hard.

A tiny flake of white stone spinged out. One inner edge was perfectly flat. Droagn jammed the bar in again. The blade sunk in a full centimeter. He hit it a third time, then levered the door outward.

"It's not so hard," he said, "if you get it in just the right place."

A passage extended inward about thirty meters or so, with a door at the other end. The surfaces here were not just white, but glowed in their lights with a subtle sheen.

Now that they had an idea of what they were looking for they hurried in search of more blue-gray smears. They went through corridors and chambers arranged much as before, but now the white shell-like stone of walls, floors, ceilings was glossy and clean. Here and there they found other color smears on the walls, long, short, single, multiple, almost always only one color at a time. There was nothing else visible, so either what the colors signified was well concealed, as the doors were, or the colors were just signs and labels, such as "level six" and so on.

One of the exceptions they found was a pale yellow smear above a pale cream smear. It was two colors at once, which they had seen a few times before, but the colors were shades they had not seen. But then, they were so subdued and near to white that even had such a mark been present in the outer bands it would have faded into the general creamy whiteness of the walls.

Grayshard felt around the mark with his delicate and sensitive tendrils and found, again, an all-but-invisible seam. It was not a doorway as such, since the seam outlined a rectangle with rounded corners with the bottom edge some forty centimeters above the floor.

Once again Droagn carefully wedged the prybar into the seam, under Grayshard's guidance, and pulled open the hatch. Inside was a kind of cupboard divided into three sections. In the top section was an object.

It was made of what looked like gray metal and beige ceramic. A twisted blunt cone was connected to a sphere that was oblate at an angle to the cone. From this projected three curved, round-ended rods, each pointing in different directions.

Rikard picked it up. It seemed more like something to be held than put down on a table, but there was no obvious hand grip. Rikard handed it to Droagn, but it seemed so fragile in the Ahmear's large hands that he was afraid he might break it, so he handed it to Grayshard. In his gloved hand it was as clumsy as in Rikard's, but then he extended a bundle of fibers from between his cuff and glove and held the sphere itself, with the cone and rods projecting between groups of tendrils.

"This feels right," he said.

"So it's meant to be held by tentacles rather than hands," Rikard said.

"So it would seem, from this one sample."

"It gives us some insight about the builders," Rikard said. He put the object into a box on the floater, they closed the now-broken cupboard and went on.

Shortly after that they found a door to the next inner layer. The walls here were not only glossy but somewhat pearlescent as well. It was more compact than the two outer layers, with smaller and fewer chambers, and longer and narrower passages between.

And the rooms and chambers were no longer completely empty. In one there was a pedestal. In another they found a kind of low table. In a third were shelves. All the objects were made of metal, or metal and ceramic, and all of them felt oddly proportioned and placed. There were no chairs, nothing of wood or fabric or paper or any of the softer plastics. Rikard recorded everything.

When they came to another cabinet they opened it and found inside something like a scissors except that the blades were of unequal length and one of the handles projected at 90 degrees. There was also a flat plate with a geared knob that could be twisted. It produced no noticeable effect. And there was a piece of translucent crystal shaped like a hammer handle, with a dark streak inside it along the center around which a blue bead slid slowly from end to end. Rikard very carefully put these into the box with the first object they'd found.

In other rooms there were more of the low tables and shelves. "It begins to seem," Grayshard said, "that our now-vanished hosts had quite a low reach, as I would if I were not wearing this disguise. And yet the ceilings are high and the color signs are high."

˜Long necks? Droagn suggested. ˜Or eyestalks perhaps. ˜

They found access to another and more inward band, all pearly white with the occasional color streaks that, here, were somewhat more clearly defined, with sometimes subtle differences in shade from one end of a streak to another, or across it, and sometimes with fine hairlines of no color.

They went in farther, until the curvature of the shell became obvious in any of the longer passages. Still, it was hard to estimate how close to the center they were, and Rikard was sure that eventually they would come either to an open or solid core, probably the latter to provide support for the massive structure. But it made sense to keep on going down as well. If this place were a million years old, who knew how much of it was buried.

As they explored they learned that a particular color—a thin long streak of yellow with one pointed end—was associated with ramps, which were on the outer edge of the upper band of corridors and chambers, and hence on the inner edge of the lower band. But it was the blunt end of the mark that pointed in the direction the ramp could be found. It wasn't really much help, since as they continued around each band they would inevitably find each ramp anyway, but it was something. And so they went lower, level after level, each level with a larger circumference than the one above.

After a while they found that the walls were now somewhat translucent, more pearly, and the color streaks, embedded in the outer layers of the surface and opaque, were now quite readable. The air became more humid, and somewhat musty smelling, or stale.

At last they could go down no farther. They found portals to the outer bands, and passed through eleven of them before they were stopped at the outer wall. They went around again, through larger rooms and halls, looking for the blue-gray signs for a door.

They didn't find them but they did find other signs in the outer walls, in three shades of blue. There were doors there, but Droagn could not open them. Somehow, they had all been locked or sealed.

"We're probably below ground level anyway," Grayshard said.

They returned to the core and started to circumnavigate it. There were none of the blue-gray smears that signified normal doors, but they did find one place where there was a small triple band of turquoise. It was a doorway, but it was locked. Droagn couldn't force it so they got out the stone-cutter and broke it open easily. There was a narrow passage beyond, but it narrowed as it went inward and ended abruptly. There were no marks on the walls at all that, here, were not so much white as colorless.

They returned to the innermost band and went on around. They found another triple turquoise mark, and beyond it the same kind of dead-end passage.

"Why would they put a door on waste space," Rikard wondered, "unless it was used as a closet?"

"But then why was it locked?" Droagn asked.

There were no more blue-gray marks here, and the turquoise marks didn't lead them where they wanted to go.

Rikard played back some of his recordings on a small monitor so they all could see them. The turquoise mark was three bands, the blue mark was three shades, and the thin blue-gray smear was—three shades superimposed? blue on gray on white?

"I think that's our clue," Rikard said. "Let's look for marks that are bluish and somehow composed of three parts."

But the only thing else they could find that was in three parts was russet—actually thin black, red, and white superimposed on each other. They broke it open, and there was a chamber beyond.

Beyond that were several more chambers of a much more restricted nature, but nothing else. Disappointed, they returned to the corridor.

"Let's stop a minute," Rikard said, "and try to figure out what's going on here. That mark had three components, and it was a door, but why the color change?"

"Perhaps," Droagn suggested, "blue signifies a passage, and a red mark means rooms."

"Easy enough to verify," Grayshard said.

They looked around and found another russet mark like the first. Beyond it, as before, were a sequence of small chambers becoming ever more cramped toward the center of the cone.

"At least they're consistent," Rikard said. "What else can we find in threes?"

They examined each color smear they saw, more closely this time as they looked for superimpositions and subtle distinctions. Most of the marks, whatever their color, were single smears, but there was a yellow smear that was pale canary at one end, darkening toward the middle, and nearly amber at the other end.

"How many colors does that count as?" Droagn asked.

"Maybe just one," Grayshard said. "There are no seams."

"So," Rikard said, "let's look for three horizontal bands, vertically arranged or superimposed."

They found a green smear that, on closer inspection, proved to be blue and yellow superimposed. They passed it by. Then there was a sky-blue smear, composed of blue and white, and above it a second white smear, which made three altogether. Grayshard found the seams of a door, and beyond the portal was a much larger chamber with several side passages, but again, that was all there was.

¨Maybe that's all there is altogether,¨ Droagn said.

"Could be," Rikard said, "but I don't believe it."

"We've come all the way around," Grayshard said. He pointed to a smudge on the pearly floor, a mark made by Rikard's boot heel.

They went up the nearest ramp, started around, and at last, in a larger chamber, came to a smear composed of two shades of blue and one of thin black. They had to break the portal open, and beyond was a passage that did not narrow, and that penetrated deeper than the ones below to a very much inner band of very small rooms and passages. It was very near the center, the circumferential walls were visibly curved. The passage was in the outside of the band, and the rooms were nearly wedges. It was very humid in there, and the walls were almost pinkish.

In the fourth room from the connecting passage they found things on the floor. There was a metal shape, obviously representing something organic, on little wheels. Nearby were several blocks of unusual shape, like pieces of a 3D jigsaw puzzle. Against the wall was a sequence of beads on a now-decomposed string.

Two rooms later they discovered a cabinet with an open shelf on the bottom, three shallow drawers, and a concave surface at the top with wings extending up at an angle at the sides and a mirror, now dark, at the back. In another room they found a shell-stone board inlaid with hexagons in red, cream, and olive stone, in a black frame, six hexes on a side. It looked like a game board, but there were no pieces.

Later they came on a disk on the floor one meter in diameter, divided into six segments, each of which could be pushed apart, though they were spring-loaded. Halfway around the shell of rooms and hallways they came to a large chamber with rods set into bases on the floor, each with a double sphere atop, the lower one with semirecessed buttons, the upper with a pattern of grills and vents, all arranged in a semicircle around a crystal hemisphere projecting from the wall.

"How about it?" Rikard said to Grayshard. "Does this make any sense to you?"

"Not a bit of it."

As they came back nearly to where they had entered they found yet another triple mark, in pale and dark yellow and red. Grayshard found the seams, but before Droagn could start to break it in Grayshard said, "I think I can open it. It's not latched." And with only the strength of his fragile tendrils, he slowly pulled it toward him.

3

The passage on the other side led down gently toward what had to be the very core of the structure. The pearly surface of its walls was ornamented with compression sculpture in finely detailed flowing abstract patterns, and stained with many colors in streaks, smears, splotches, dots, and arcs. The walls were almost damp, and the light of the lamps glittered off the moisture on the complex surface, which here was translucent, and seemed to glow.

Rikard recorded the walls as completely as he could. As they proceeded slowly down the passage they tried to make sense of the patterns in shape and color, though each area of decoration seemed to bear no relationship to any other. A real-time playback wouldn't be very comprehensible, but stills could be taken showing every square meter of these complex walls.

"And there are two other cones just like this one," Grayshard said. He seemed to be as impressed by this place as Rikard.

˜Maybe we're just lucky,˜ Droagn said, ˜and picked the only cone that has a place like this.˜

"That's very unlikely," Rikard said. "And there are other cones elsewhere in this world, though they're not as well preserved, or as exposed as these three. Every one of them is a potential treasure trove."

They came at last to the end of the passage, closed by an ornamented portal that opened at their touch. Beyond, only dimly illuminated by their strong lights, was a huge chamber. The floor dished down toward the center, and there were other portals all around the periphery. The floor was divided into areas separated by low walls and differences in level, and passways proceeded from the portals to the center. In each of the areas was an object of some sort. Some of them were utterly ruined, some were almost pristine in appearance.

They worked their way toward the center, moving from one display to another, marveling at what they found. One object had a heavy base, a flexible neck, on the end of which was a sphere with a drill bit. A smaller item was a flat-bottomed box with a projecting blade and a vertical rod handle. There was something like a set of dumbbells connected by electrical cables to what might have been a generator box. There were machines of heavy iron or steel, shaped like a very thick X, with valves, rods, and levers sticking out, stained apertures, and a shaft that projected from the intersection. Another machine had a heavy base, a flexible neck ending in a sphere that had a C-shaped protrusion with a hole in the lower part of the C and a needle in the upper part. On a pedestal was a small object consisting of a sharp spike, which rested in a socket, with a branched armature that had a sharp-edged tube on one side and a rosette of sharp blades on the other, connected by gears to a crank.

There were sculptures. One was composed of three large rectangles that intersected each other at right angles, each with a small disk at right angles to itself at the outer edge, all supported at an angle by a spike. There was something like broad limp noodles with feathery edges knotted at the end of an inverted fishhook. One sculpture represented a humanoid shape but with exaggerated feet and arms, tiny mouth and eyes, bulging body—possibly a Zapeth? Others were in the form of an octopus standing on four legs and manipulating batons and balls with another four legs.

In one place was a base plate with two A-frames that supported a crossbar from which hung a triple trapeze, the bars connected by soft cords. Another large object had a hollow base the size of a dining-room table with an upright at one end that supported an identical base at a height of one and a half meters. There was a circular tabletop on a pedestal with drawers all around, each drawer wedge-shaped and tracked on the left side.

And there were other things that were even less identifiable, such as an irregularly stacked pile of tetrahedral plates; a collection of small objects consisting of spheres piled on top of one another, no two the same; a wire frame outlining a hemisphere supporting a column supporting a smaller sphere with four long wires extending below the smaller sphere; and something that looked like a wet blanket except that it was made of crystal.

Anything that was small and intact they took and put into Rikard's 4D case. That still left ninety percent of the undamaged objects still in their places, not counting those in the areas they hadn't visited yet. But when they got near the center of the chamber, they found more sculptures, and these took all their attention.

They were of molluskoid beings, with a large snailfoot surmounted by a sacklike body with a pouch mouth in front and above that a tapering stalk up to about two meters with two pairs of strong tentacles and a single huge cyclopean eye. Rikard glanced back at the wire frame sculpture. The number and realism of these sculptures indicated that they were of more than just casual importance.

Most of the cyclopean molluskoids presented a front and a back with symmetrical right and left sides, but other examples showed that that was merely a convention, that these beings could be completely radial with the eye central on a pedestal foot and with the tentacles around the perimeter, or they could be asymmetrical, with a front and back but with all limbs on one side and the mouth on the other, and so on. Their bodies were amorphous, though with a single sacklike shape instead of a bundle of fibers the way Grayshard's was, but they were almost as variable as Grayshard, in their own way.

Singles, groups, in a variety of postures but mostly simply presented, here were the people of this place. Some were miniatures, made of a material so dense that only Droagn could lift them. A few were oversize, in more natural materials, but effectively unmovable. Some they deduced to be at normal scale, judging by other objects represented in the sculpture that corresponded to objects they had seen elsewhere. But none of them would fit in the case. Rikard and his companions lost all interest in the rest as they examined and discussed this new find.

"Precursor races are my specialty," Rikard said once, "but I've never run across anything like this in any text I've ever read."

"They disappeared an awful long time ago," Droagn said.

"So did your people, but we knew about them. And the Tschagan, they were nowhere near as important, but we had records and representations of them too. Have you seen their like before?"

˜No, but then I'm not a scholar. But no, in my time and place there was nobody like this, not even vaguely. ˜

Rikard turned to Grayshard, but the Vaashka stood motionless.

"They are completely unfamiliar to me," he said. "I know other molluskoid species—and they are rare—but not this one."

"We've got an awful lot of questions to answer here," Rikard said, "but I'm afraid now is not the time to do it. We'll have to make sure this place is protected, then we can start to try to find out who they were, where they came from, where they are now, and what happened to them." He felt large, as if the wonder of this discovery were inflating him like a balloon.

"And until then?" Grayshard asked.

"We take what we can and get out of here."

Reluctantly they left the sculptures near the center and worked their way up another radius toward the perimeter, collecting as they went. It didn't matter where they came out, since all exits would take them to the same circumferential corridor and from there they could find their way back to the surface.

They chose what to take with them more carefully, now that they knew what the creators of this place looked like, but even so they had about as much stuff as they could carry, even in Rikard's 4D case.

Which was frustrating since the items on this side of the central chamber were somewhat different from those where they had entered. They saw a basket suspended between two wheels with a short T-bar extending from each side. There was a set of knives but with handles like stars set at ninety degrees to the blades at their centers. On one pedestal was a set of square plates a couple millimeters thick in four distinct shades of orange associated with very thin and springy hexagons of foil with a pattern on one side and progressive symbols on the other in three colors. On another low platform was a sphere on a pedestal with five round holes in the top, below and between each hole a small screen, and below each screen a short spout, and a plate at the top that could be depressed. And in one place they found a board inlaid with irregular shapes connected by branching and curving lines, on which were tiny figures in six colors, along with a rack with six wires and three beads on each wire, and four black cubes, all the same but with a different symbol on each face. Some of these figures were strange, but some represented the cyclopean builders of this place. Rikard took one of each type, and a pair of the dice, and put them in his jacket pocket instead of the case. He wanted these for himself until such time as a more formal investigation into the nature and history of this species had been initiated.

· They left the chamber by a similar though narrower sculpted passage that, instead of opening into the band of chambers and passages from which they had entered, curved around and joined the main passage at a door marked, on the outside, by three horizontal smears of pale green—a long, a short, and a long.

"This is going to make my reputation," Rikard said as they worked their way back the way they had come. "Even if these people existed nowhere else but on this planet, I'll prove my thesis."

⁻And how will you do that?⁻ Droagn asked.

"Because, no intelligent species exists in isolation. It has to have collateral forms, and be the result of extensive evolution. There is absolutely nothing like these cyclopeans on this world, so they aren't native to here. They were obviously not as important as the Ahmear, but they are definitely a precursor species, and the existence of just one such proves my thesis."

"Aren't the Ahmear precursors also?" Grayshard asked.

"They are, but because their existence was known, they don't count. I've tried that argument before."

⁻But you discovered the Taarshome too, didn't you?⁻

"Yes, but they claim that was an accident—which it was."

˜But they existed long before anything. Surely they are as precursor as you can get.˜

"I agree, but the claim is that they were unique, and predated all other sentient species by far too long, and had no influence on any culture extant or historic."

"What about the Tathas?" Grayshard asked.

"You don't have to convince me," Rikard said. "You have to convince the academic community. My thesis is that civilization extends backward in time, more or less unbroken, to about the time of the formation of the first terrestrial planets. Other scholars claim that the Tathas were an exception, uncivilized, of no cultural importance, and don't fit in with their theories."

"That doesn't make much sense."

"It doesn't. But now they've got this to look at, even if it's not as old as the species that gave rise to both you and the Tathas."

˜Your colleagues don't like you much, do they?˜

"They don't. They spend their time at universities, writing papers, while I'm out in the field, finding things. I think they're envious."

It was a thought that hurt him. In the academic community Rikard was considered a rogue, more of a grave robber than an historian, though he always documented the sites he uncovered. Subsequent scholars had made their reputations based on some of his finds, and they couldn't argue with the fact that he'd always made sure that the lesser things he'd discovered, such as the desert ruins of the Atreef home world, or the lost library of the Neugar university on Filchin, got into the right hands—even if he did keep a trophy or two for himself. His colleagues criticized him for his unorthodox methods, and then took every advantage of what he'd found. He hoped that this discovery would make a difference.

And in the back of his mind, there was something else—maybe his mother's family might begin to perceive him as somebody worthy of their attention after all.

They continued up and up until, according to the record in his helmet camera, they reached the level at which they had entered, but apparently deeper in by two bands. But from the inside it was easy to find the doors outward, and as they passed through each doorway they saw that the symbolism marking them was consistent.

The outermost band of corridors and chambers was, by comparison with that deep within, pale and uninteresting, the material nearly marblelike in texture, the colors faded and sometimes completely obscured.

They moved around until they came to a pile of rubble blocking their way. The place where they had fallen in should have been just a bit farther on, and should not be hard to open up again, but more tons of rubble had now piled in, blocking the passage completely.

And there was a faint aroma in the air, Rikard and Droagn both noted it, something charred and chemical.

¨It smells like explosives.¨

"It is," Grayshard said, "poly-phylo-triptine."

"And all our tools are at the bottom of the cone," Rikard said, "except the cutter you used to get us in."

¨And that,¨ Droagn said, ¨is right where I left it, about thirty meters farther on, under all that rock.¨

"It would seem," Grayshard said, "that the Una Tlim have had their revenge."

They backtracked, looking for another way out, but there seemed to be no exits up here. After all, they'd come in pretty high up on the cone. Maybe all the exits were now blocked at the base. Perhaps if they went higher, they'd come to where the wall was weak with weathering and they would be able to break out. So they went up, and as they went Droagn probed the thick, marblelike material with his Prime.

Ten levels up they went around the entire cone, but found nothing. They went around again three levels higher, but still no door, and no place thin enough for them to break through. By this time they were all beginning to tire.

Then Grayshard detected fresh air, coming from some-where ahead, and he led them to a ramp going down. They descended five levels and went out one band and there they saw the telltale signs of weathering, where the material of the cone had turned completely into what might otherwise be called marble.

Now Rikard and Droagn could feel the fresh air too, coming from an outer chamber. There appeared to be a crack in the outer wall, but it was now night outside. They set to work and enlarged the opening. It was hard going with only a couple of prybars, a maul, and the lightweight stonecutter, but they broke through at last and were able to bring their equipment out too, onto the weathered slope of the cone.

Two moons were in the sky, both very small, both very bright. By their light they could see that they were in the space between the three cones. They could see the trees down in the hollow as a darkness against the ghostly white of the cones. It would be tricky to get the floater around to the other side, and they contemplated just resting till morn-ing so they could see better what they were doing, when suddenly bright lights shone at them from all around, above and below, blinding them.

"Just freeze where you are," Karyl Toerson's amplified voice called out to them. Then several of the gravity cars carrying the heavy-duty spotlights hummed closer and touched the cone. Heavily armed minions, men and women, jumped out, covered by others still on the craft and on the other gravity cars, and made Rikard, Droagn, and Grayshard move away from the opening.

Then they took all the equipment and the 4D case, leaving Rikard and his companions with only his camera helmet and gun.

"Thanks again," Toerson said as her people moved away.

Darkness returned. And all Rikard had, unless he wanted to go back into the cone in the dark, were the few things he carried in his pockets.

Malvrone

The government of the Federation was primarily representational, though the M'Kade was the principal figure and had been for over a thousand years. Most of the worlds and multiworld political units within the Federation were also federations, democracies, republics, and the like. But not all.

Some few worlds and systems indulged in other forms of government. They were the products of long political and social evolution, and so were very different from superficially similar experiments familiar to twentieth- and twenty-first-century Earth.

One of these different worlds was Malvrone, which operated something like a cross between a hereditary monarchy and a board-directed corporation. Roughly. In spite of this it was a staunch member of the Federation, supported it in most interplanetary affairs, and recognized its laws, when it had to, even when those laws were in conflict with its own.

As for the Federation, they tolerated Malvrone's differences. The world did not cause trouble, and paid an immense tax bill. It was, on the whole, an amicable coexistence.

Booking passage to Malvrone was easy. The jumpslot

station was superb, the planetary orbital station large and well equipped, and the surface shuttles were easily able to accommodate Endark Droagn. He did, however, have to use a different exit, simply by virtue of his size, not his uniqueness, and Rikard Braeth and Grayshard accompanied him. Along with them in the special connector between the shuttle and the spaceport surface installation were two other oversize people.

Degurnian Shambo was a Fahree, a centauroid being nearly three meters tall, with a heavy body like a rhinoceros and a hairy torso every bit as large as Droagn's, with arms that came down almost to his knees. He was dark gray, nearly violet in color, and wore no clothes though, unlike Droagn, there was absolutely no doubt about his gender. He did, however, wear considerable ornamentation in the form of gems and plates of metal embedded in his thick skin, especially over his beetling brows, along his spine, and on the top of his flat head.

The other was Chan viTablor, a Triezel. He was almost completely humanoid, except that he was closer to four meters tall than to three, and correspondingly bulky. From a distance one might have mistaken him for a solidly built Human, but up close there were other differences, such as the silver eyes, the long-lobed ears, the absolute hairlessness of face, and the hands that had thumbs on both sides. He was dressed quite conservatively, in a muted gray-brown suit, pale pink shirt, hematite throat clutch, and chrome-black shoes. He seemed far more comfortable in his immensity than either Droagn or Shambo.

The oversize ramp led them to the same main lounge where the rest of the passengers had disembarked, and where other passengers were waiting to board.

"This is better than Kelian," Shambo said as they got into one of the lines. His voice was low and surprisingly smooth. "There, you wound up in a kind of warehouse, and had to do business through a doorway."

"Malvrone's too sophisticated for that kind of nonsense,"

Chan said. He sounded like underwater rocks clashing together. "But if you think you have troubles, you should see the indignity a poor Mintor has to go through."

˜And how big are they?˜ Droagn asked wryly. Ahead of them were a series of doors, through which the incoming passengers were passing one by one.

"About sixty centimeters in diameter," Chan said. "They're shaped like a discus, with lots of spindly legs only thirty centimeters long and a cluster of sensory organs sprouting from the center of their top. They get stepped on, sat on, overlooked, misplaced. They usually have to hire someone of, say, Human size to accompany them, or their lives are really at risk.

"And then there are the Savanyan, have you heard of them?"

"I have," Rikard said. "The word I'd use to describe them is rats."

"Yes, that would be good, or finta, or chakoblau. Each one is between twenty-five and thirty centimeters long, including tail, and it takes at least six to pool their minds to produce self-awareness."

"They're telepathic?" Shambo said.

"Only with themselves. Personalities change as the individuals in each group change. More than twenty and they overload and start to regress again. Isolated, they're not much more intelligent than the animals they resemble. There are a lot of places where they're not even allowed, or are inadvertently 'exterminated' as pests. I've talked to a few, and ironically, they can, as an optimum collective, be more intelligent than any other single being. But boy do they get lost in the shuffle."

"Speaking of which," Rikard said, "I think we got in the wrong line." The passengers waiting to go through immigration elsewhere were being processed at about two a minute, while their line had come to a dead halt.

"Some things never change," Shambo said. He stomped one hind hoof restlessly.

"We are in the wrong line," Grayshard said. He pointed to the signs over the doors. RETURNING RESIDENTS, they read.

"So where do visitors go?" Droagn asked.

"That way," Grayshard said, and pointed to a broad corridor angling off to the right from the corner of the lounge. The sign over it read, VISITORS AND IMMIGRATION. They all left the line with relief and headed down the corridor.

At the other end was another lobby area, with many cubicles opposite the entrance. There was a higher percentage of non-Humans here, and the lines were just as long.

But before they could join the crowd a Human in uniform, with curly ruddy hair and amber skin, came up to them. "Excuse me," he said, "are you Msr. Rikard Braeth?"

"Yes, I am."

"And these are your companions." He gestured to Grayshard and Droagn, and effectively ignored Chan and Shambo.

"They are."

"My name is Ishito. Msr. Gawin sent me to help you through Immigration. I'm afraid we're rather more strict and officious here than you might be used to elsewhere, and he thought you'd appreciate some extra attention."

"We certainly would," Rikard said.

"So would we," Shambo said, leaning his upper body forward so that his apelike face was level with Ishito's.

"I wish I could be of service," Ishito said. He was not in the least flustered. "However, my instructions concern only these three. Unless," he said, turning back to Rikard, "they are also in your party?"

"I'm afraid not," Rikard said. Chan chuckled.

"If you will come with me, then," Ishito said.

He led them to a door where there was no line waiting, and into an office with the agent sitting behind a large desk in the middle of the room, and a recording witness at a small desk off to the left. The agent rose to her feet as they came in.

"Msr. Sali Carlson," Ishito said. He gestured to Rikard.

"This is Msr. Rikard Braeth, Msr. Endark Droagn, and Msr. Grayshard."

"Thank you, Ishito," Carlson said. She looked at the three travelers in turn, then smiled professionally at Rikard. "You are expected."

Meanwhile Ishito had produced a bundle of documents that he handed to Carlson. She opened it, took out a letter from the inside flap, looked at it briefly, put it back in the flap, and handed the whole bundle back to Ishito. "This way, please," she said, and gestured to a door behind her.

Ishito nodded formally and stepped to one side so Rikard could precede him. The door opened as he approached. They passed through an antechamber to another office like the first but larger, more cluttered, and with two recording secretaries, both on the right of the main desk.

The agent, a man, was expecting them and already on his feet as they entered. He smiled at Rikard, nodded at his companions, and did not look at Ishito but put out his hand so that the uniformed servant could put the documents into it. There was no introduction this time. The agent glanced at the documents, turned a couple pages, nodded once or twice, handed them back to Ishito, smiled at Rikard once again, and with a broad sweep of his left hand directed them out the door behind him.

They went through the whole process a third time. But in the fourth office the agent, a Msr. Avram Mikalsonne, took the documents and this time actually spent some time looking through them. He stamped here, punched there, inserted cards into various slots in machines on his desk, spoke tersely and cryptically to the single recording witness, then bundled the documents up again, handed them back to Ishito, smiled at Rikard, and said, "We're glad to have you with us, Msr. Braeth. We hope you enjoy your stay."

A door to one side opened.

"Your luggage has been taken care of," Mikalsonne went on. "There will be no need for inspection."

"Thank you," Rikard said, and wondered what kind of

influence his uncle had, to have gotten him and his companions through so quickly, and with virtually no hassle.

They went out the door to a small, luxurious lounge.
There were few other people present. They did not pause,
but followed Ishito to an enclosed beltway with seats.
Droagn had to ride in the aisle. The beltway took them out
to a private parking deck where a large and comfortable
wheeled van was waiting for them.

Ishito opened the van and they all got in. There was
plenty of room for Droagn. Then Ishito got in the driver's
compartment, which was cut off from the rest of the van by
glass panels. He pushed a button on the dash and a speaker
came on. He said, "Your luggage is being sent on to the
house. Would you like to stop anywhere along the way?"

"I can't think of any place today," Rikard said. He was
having trouble thinking of anything at all. He knew his
uncle did very well for himself, in the legitimate art trade as
well, apparently, as in the black market, but it took more
than just money to manage service like this.

Ishito turned off the speaker, started the engine, and they
left the small parking lot. They drove past large parking
areas—not decks—where there were other wheeled and floated
vehicles, and out to a main road that headed toward town.

"Looks like your uncle thought of everything," Droagn
said. He was coiled on a cushion, and there was plenty of
room under the raised roof of the van for his head.

"And on such short notice too." Rikard had let Gawin
know, only ten standard days ago, that he was coming.

"It would seem," Grayshard said, "that your family's
titles are not meaningless after all."

They drove through a very neat if small city and out into
the countryside. There was no bypass. There were a few
immaculate suburbs, and then they were in farming country.
The fields were yellow and orange, there were groves of
trees, stands of timber, occasional small houses of a rather
simple and rustic design. It seemed they were to be going
quite some distance, and yet they went by ground and not

by air. Of course, the roads were perfect, and the van did most of the driving.

An hour later they passed through some hilly prairie with rock outcrops. They went down a steep slope after that, with a distant glimpse of water to the left and more farms on the right, to a forested valley at the bottom. A half hour later the road entered the forest, with peculiar trees, and an occasional clearing in which they saw a couple of animals Rikard could not name. Then they crossed a river, climbed the slope on the other side, and, far ahead, caught a glimpse of something bright at the top of a far bluff. They lost sight of it again as they neared the hills. The road doubled back once through forest, climbed still higher, then went through open land again and when they reached the shoulder of the hills they saw that the bright thing was a huge building, glinting in the afternoon sun, with what looked like a small village surrounding it. As they neared they saw that the "village" was just the outbuildings.

They passed through a gate, slowed as they drove between well-trimmed lawns, entered a huge courtyard, with arches on the right and left leading to subsidiary courts. The van stopped in front of the main entrance. The building, at the front, was about six floors tall.

As they got out of the van the entrance doors opened and a man came out. He was in his middle years, and dressed quite conservatively. Rikard approached him but stopped halfway to the front door and let the man meet him there.

"Msr. Rikard," the man said. "Welcome. Will you come with me please."

It was not a question. He preceded them to the front door, and as they went another vehicle, a truck, came into the courtyard even as the van went into a side court. The truck turned into the other secondary court, and all was quiet.

The servant led them in through a foyer as large as the main lounge at the shuttleport, with stairs at the far end, two sets of large double doors on each side wall and another set on either side of the stairs, and through the first doors on the right into a parlor, as big as an average home, furnished simply but perfectly. "Msr. Gawin will be with you shortly," the man said. "Please make yourselves comfortable." Then he left.

The floors were of polished wood that almost glowed. So were the walls, of a slightly lighter color. The window frames were wood, the picture frames were wood, the doorways and doors were all of precious wood, some warm, some pale, some grained, some translucent.

There were carpets, the feel of which could only be attributed to natural animal fibers, natural plant fibers, not synthetics. The pictures were gallery quality; the chandeliers, lamps, and sconces were crystal; the furniture was perfectly proportioned and positioned so that the room was divided into four central areas and a surrounding area for communication. The textiles were all natural fibers, the finishes looked hand-rubbed, the seats were comfortable when Rikard sat down, and there was a stack of cushions that could only have been meant for Droagn.

⁓Your uncle must be very wealthy indeed,⁓ Droagn said.

"I guess the art business pays a lot better than I thought."

"Or maybe he just invests his money wisely," Grayshard said.

"I don't remember him being this rich when he came to Mother's funeral. And he couldn't have been wealthy back when Dad rescued Mom or he'd have paid the fee even if Grandfather couldn't."

⁓There's more to this than just wealth,⁓ Droagn said. ⁓Whoever set this place up is used to luxury. Very used to it indeed.⁓

"That's the part I don't understand," Rikard said.

There was a bar on one side of the room, obviously intended for self-service, even in a house like this one. Rikard felt in the need of a little refreshment. The counter was a solid block of wood, the panels in front were polished black wood, the stools were padded with leather, the glassware behind was not glass, it was crystal.

"Can I get you anything," he called over his shoulder as he checked out the stock. There were a variety of beers and ales and related brews that he'd heard of but never tried.

"Is there any fruit juice," Droagn called.

Rikard opened a cooler. "Lots." There were bottles of at least forty or fifty different kinds. "Maybe you'd better come over and choose something."

Droagn did so.

And so did Grayshard, who found, much to his surprise, what looked like professionally bottled containers of mineral-spiked animal ferment. "I am most impressed," he said as he read a label. "Private bottling. Gawin seems to have done his homework."

A door on the far side of the room, opposite the foyer, opened, and Gawin Malvrone strode into the room. He was casually dressed, in black slacks and a loose-fitting white shirt, and he had a broad smile on his face. "Rikard," he said. "Good to see you again."

Rikard put down his beer. "How are you, Uncle Gawin?" He felt inordinately pleased that his uncle should be so glad to see him.

Gawin came up to him, with his arms out, and they embraced. "Now we can get comfortable," he said, "and maybe make up for some lost time."

"I can stay as long as I'm welcome," Rikard said.

"Good." Gawin turned to Grayshard, who was holding the opened mouth of his bottle under the palm of his gloved hand, so that the bundle of fibers extending down into it was not easily noticeable. "Good to see you again, Grayshard," he said. He did not offer to shake hands. "I am honored to have the only Vaashka in the Federation as my guest. Please feel free to make yourself comfortable however you wish."

"Thank you," Grayshard said. He raised the bottle. "May I compliment your brewer."

"I will tell him. And, Droagn," he said as he reached up to shake a huge hand, "I hope you'll be comfortable here."

"I am so far."

"Good. Would you like to participate in the evaluation of those artifacts and books that you brought me?"

˜Not really. Finding them is one thing, scholarly work is another.˜

"Just let me know if you get curious." He turned to the bar and fetched himself a beer. "Let's sit down," he said.

They made themselves comfortable, but Rikard kept feeling like he'd forgotten something. "Ah, how's the rest of the family?" he asked at last.

Gawin took a pull at his beer. "I haven't seen them since, oh, some time before I went to Mensenear. But that's not unusual. We go our own ways. They're just fine I'm sure."

"You know," Rikard said, "I've never met any of them. Do they all feel the same way about me that Grandfather does?"

"I'm sorry to say that they don't think about you at all. My brother and sister rather missed your mother after she went off with your father, but not very much, and not for long."

"Is there a chance that I could meet them?"

Gawin sighed. "I'll see what I can do, but don't get your hopes up. My parents are, ah, very busy people, and Braice and Bevry each live their own lives. Braice takes after Father I'm afraid."

"Does Grandfather know I'm here?"

"I haven't told him, or had a chance to, but he knows what goes on, even here."

That struck Rikard as a little curious, but before he could ask what his uncle had meant, a servant appeared at an inner door and stood silently. Gawin glanced at him, then said, "Your rooms are ready." He put down his drink and stood, and Rikard and his companions did likewise, or the equivalent. They all went to the door where the servant stood waiting, and he preceded them into a cross passage with doors opposite and at either end.

They went to the right and through the door into an elevator. It was very smooth. They went up, Rikard couldn't tell how far, one floor or six, and when they got out they entered a large common room, with two doors in each of the four walls. Gawin pointed to the doors on the right. "You'll have the north suite," he said, and showed them in.

There was a foyer, a parlor, a dining room with a small kitchen, a private lounge, three bedrooms including one set up for Droagn—their luggage had been brought in and distributed correctly—a back office, two bathrooms, balconies looking over the back of the house and the terraced properties, beyond which were fields of something growing.

"What is that?" Rikard asked.

"It's just for appearance," Gawin said. "Those trees are date palms. And over there, those are grapes. There are seven different kinds of melons in those fields. They're all good, but I have them just because they look good. Now, why don't you take your time and settle in, make sure all your luggage is in good order, and call me when you're ready." He gave Rikard's upper arms a squeeze and left them to themselves.

They unpacked. Everything was in order. Droagn discovered the sauna and decided to take advantage of it. Grayshard got out of his harness and slithered around in the kitchen where, to his surprise, he found a special pantry with his kind of food in it. Rikard, out of habit, checked out the entire suite with his security monitor, including the kitchen, which was remarkably equipped, and especially the windows and the two exits. He tried all switches and traced the circuitry as far as he could, to make sure that the apartment was secure, not so much from outsiders as from, well, from Gawin perhaps, or other family.

As far as he could tell the place was completely tight. He wasn't sure that he could actually trust his examination, after seeing what kind of security Gawin had of his own, but there was nothing he could do about it, so he might as well behave as if it were actually clean.

The last thing to check was the comcon. There was a rather large center in the parlor and terminals in every room. Besides regular communications the system offered local sound and picture broadcasts, standard news services, planetary communications with full directory, and in-house communications with either a live or AI operator, Rikard couldn't tell which. In either case, it was very expensive, and he wondered how Gawin had acquired such tastes.

Droagn came out of the sauna, rubbing his scales with a fragrant oil that smelled something like cedar, and something like butter. "I could use a bit of refreshment," he said.

"Me too," Rikard agreed. He went into the kitchen where Grayshard was sampling a variety of food items that were every bit as fragrant as Droagn's body oil but far less pleasant to Rikard's nose. "Shall we join my uncle for a drink?" he asked.

"By all means," Grayshard said.

Rikard punched on the comcon and asked for his uncle. The operator smiled and made the connection.

"How would you like some company?" Rikard asked.

"I'd like it very much," Gawin said. *"Why don't you come down for a drink?"*

"We'd love to. Where shall we meet you, and how do we get there?"

Gawin chuckled and said, *"Just come on out into the foyer, someone will meet you."*

"Be there in a minute," Rikard said, and disconnected.

"I'm going to take him at his word," Grayshard said from the doorway. His vocalizer was buried deep in the mass of his white tendrils. Without it, he could not communicate at all, since his people had a strong chemical component in their speech, which served only to produce hallucinations in other species.

"I'm sure Gawin won't mind," Rikard said, "but he may be optimistic about his staff."

They left the suite, and found a servant waiting for them in the foyer. She smiled at them, as if she had seen a naked Vaashka many times before, and said, "This way please."

They got into the elevator and went to some floor or other. From there they took a powered walkway through a well-lit corridor. There were a few other people on the walkway, but they paid no attention to either Droagn or Grayshard. After a while they got off the walkway at another lounge, where again those present were unaffected by the two non-Humans. Grayshard moved in a rather flamboyant way as if he somehow enjoyed showing off his bizarre physiology, though Rikard had never known him to express any recognizable emotion before.

From the lounge they went through a door into a corridor with a glass roof, at the end of which was a large foyer, and off that was a large room, which was a kind of study or library. There the young woman smiled again and left them.

Gawin was sitting in a large overstuffed chair when they came in, and stood up to greet them. He, too, seemed unperturbed by Grayshard's appearance. "Please feel free to fix whatever you like to drink." He gestured to a large and well-stocked portable bar.

They availed themselves of his hospitality and sat down.

"So what have you been up to lately," Gawin said to Rikard when they were all comfortable. "I'm glad you could come by so soon."

"I followed up on that picture we looked at." Rikard told his uncle briefly what they had found in the core of the alien cone on Dannon's Keep.

Gawin got more and more excited, occasionally muttered something about this university and that museum, with a grin on his face that had little to do with avarice.

"When can I see some of this stuff?" he asked when Rikard finished.

Rikard, with chagrin, reached into his jacket pocket and took out a set of four square orange plates, each a distinct shade, and the black dice with different symbols on each face. He held them out to his uncle.

Even as Gawin reached for them he said, with dismay, "You didn't actually bring the stuff here?"

"Not all of it," Rikard said.

Gawin took the objects and looked at them, turning them over and over in his hands. "Even this," he said, "could get me into a lot of trouble. This stuff isn't legal, you know, and if anybody found out that I deal in black market art, the police would shut me down."

"From what I've seen at the spaceport," Rikard said, "you seem to be pretty well connected. If you have enough influence to get me through customs without inspection, how could something like this be any danger?"

"You walked through immigration with this in your pocket?"

"I did."

"It scares me just thinking about it." He put the four orange squares down on a table in front of him, but kept the dice, and juggled them as he talked. "I'm not as powerful as it seems. It, ah, is really Father's connections that make the difference."

"Well, then, can't he give you any protection?"

"It's not that simple," Gawin said. "Father doesn't really know about my business, let alone the black market side of it. He hates the idea of commerce in the first place, and if he ever found out there was anything the least bit shady about it—not to say strictly illegal by Federal statute—he'd throw me to the wolves."

"Not really?"

"Remember what he did to your mother. He hired Arin to rescue her because it made *Father* look bad, not really because he was concerned for Sigra. Then he kicked her out when she married your father because, again, it was a smirch on *his* image, *his* reputation."

"I thought she left of her own accord."

"That was because she was in love with your father, and she had to make a choice. Father never forgave her for that. He kept on hoping she'd acknowledge his dominance and authority and beg his forgiveness. But she never did. He shut her out of his life, out of his mind, completely. When Sigra finally died, it hardly made any difference to him anymore."

"It's difficult to believe that he could be so hard."

"It's the way the family is. Not all of us, but . . . If Father finds out about this''——he juggled the black dice——''if he finds out about 'Nevile Beneking,' he'll have no compunction about turning me in. I don't want to go to jail.''

''Just for these few little things?''

''No, for all the other stuff I've done. Do you have anything more?''

From his other jacket pocket Rikard took two small objects consisting of spheres piled on top of one another; a set of the very thin and springy hexagons of foil with a pattern on one side and progressive symbols on the other in three colors; and a set of the tiny game figures in six colors representing cyclopeans and other strange creatures, and handed them to Gawin. Grayshard and Droagn watched quietly as Gawin looked them over.

''I can't believe,'' Rikard said, ''that they'd put you in jail for running cultural artifacts. Even if Grandfather disowned you, you still have connections of your own, and you're still a part of this family, which seems pretty important even if they aren't well off. And if you really own this estate, you shouldn't have any difficulty paying any fine and restitution. And if this is all just for show, I could help out.''

Gawin's expression became ever odder as Rikard spoke. He looked up at the last, as if surprised. ''How could you help me?''

Rikard took a dangly bauble from his pocket and tossed it to Gawin. The metal was simply silver and gold. The stones were three large, polished, and faceted spheroids, each about the size of his thumb. They were transparent, and had hearts of pale iridescent fire.

Gawin at first didn't recognize the stones. After all, one never expected to see dialithite, commonly called dragongems, outside a carefully guarded museum display. But as they warmed in his hand, and began to exert their peculiar hypnotic effect, he knew what they were and gaped. For a moment it seemed as though he would fall under their spell, carried away by colors beyond human vision into realms of power and peace, so that Rikard started to reach for the stones. But before he could touch them Gawin tore his eyes away from them and looked at Rikard. If he just held the stones without looking at them, or looked at them without touching, he would feel no effect, though now, holding them as he did, the temptation to gaze and lose himself in their spell was obvious. He did not yield.

"Where in the hell did you get this?" he demanded.

"My father's legacy," Rikard said bitterly. "I have a few of these, I know how and where to sell them."

"So what do you do with the money from that stuff you brought me?"

"That's my public money, what I declare on my taxes. I set up a fund, keep the cash in various accounts, it doesn't matter. So don't sweat the artifacts, Uncle Gawin. Or your fortune either."

Gawin glanced down at the dragongems. Their colors were, if anything, brighter and more intense as they warmed in his hand. "It isn't just the money," he said. "Here, and under my own name, I live an exemplary life. You don't know how well I was covered when we met on Mensenear, and the trouble I went to afterward to cover up our relation. You know my reputation as a dealer. I can't afford to lose that, and if the connection between Gawin Malvrone and Nevile Beneking were known, we'd 'both' suffer." He handed the bauble back to Rikard. "And if there were any proof of black marketeering, the police would have to look into it, not only for its own sake but because of and in spite of my family and connections, and they'd find out, ah, about one other thing that I don't want to talk about." Rikard put the bauble back in his pocket. "So please, in the future, be more careful. We can always meet at Mensenear, the place is secure."

Gawin looked now at the few cyclopean objects resting on the table in front of him. The dragongems were forgotten, and in spite of his anxiety, he was obviously excited. "I've never seen anything like these before," he said.

"You're right," Rikard said, "since this is a newly discovered species."

"Of course there are lots of lost sentient species," Gawin said, "but few of them ever achieve any degree of culture or technology."

"These people did."

"So it would seem, if this is any evidence. I know plenty of good markets for material like this. The universities for whom I collect will be more than eager to buy these, and they will be in a place where they can be seen and studied, rather than hidden away in private collections or lost or destroyed by those who don't appreciate them. Getting permission to work on Dannon's Keep will be tricky though. Where is the rest of the stuff, not here I hope?"

"No," Rikard said, "it's not. I don't have it anymore." He felt his voice weaken, and cleared his throat. He had a hard time meeting Gawin's eyes, though his uncle said nothing. "It's damn embarrassing," he said at last, "but you remember Karyl Toerson?"

"Yes," Gawin said. He didn't like the memory.

"She got the drop on us when we came out of the cone and took everything except what I had in my pockets." Rikard waved at the few things on the low table.

"I was afraid of something like this," Gawin said. He stood and turned away from Rikard and his companions. "I was hoping she had died on Trokarion."

"I felt so stupid when she caught us like that," Rikard said. "It was as if she knew even before we did where we would have to come out of the cone."

Gawin turned back and looked at him sharply. Rikard returned the stare, then told briefly about the cave-in and their search for another exit.

"I think you were set up," Gawin said. "But what I don't like is how she knew you were on Dannon's Keep at all."

"I wasn't being overly cautious," Rikard said.

"I still think she's following you too closely. If she's

gotten to you the last two times, you'd better take precautions to prevent a third time.''

"I intend to—if there is a third time. But I know a few things too, Uncle Gawin, and if I don't want her to find me, she won't.''

"Don't be so sure. She's got more resources than we know about. I knew her a long time ago, and she was more than a match for most adventurers then. She's just gotten better, that's all, and she's had a lot more experience than you have. She's bad, Rikard, very bad, and the fact that she hit you twice implies that she's watching you, in particular, and picking on you on purpose. And getting good stuff isn't the only reason.''

"What other reason could there be?''

"Personal vengeance. Against me, perhaps.'' His thoughts seemed to turn inward. "You would be well advised to just assume that whatever your next exploit, Toerson will be there too, and be prepared to deal with her.'' He looked at Rikard again, and his voice became harsh. "But don't kill her, for God's sake, or there will be worse hell to pay.''

Rikard was surprised at this display of anger and hatred. It kept him from asking what his uncle had meant. All he said was, "Whatever you say, Uncle Gawin.''

Gawin closed his eyes for a moment and took several deep breaths, then he gestured at the objects on the table and Rikard put them back in his pockets. Then Gawin rose, shook himself as if shaking off a mood, and said, "I think it's time for dinner. Will you join me?'' He smiled at Grayshard and Droagn.

"We would be delighted," Droagn said for all three.

Rikard woke up late the next morning, feeling somewhat the worse for the evening's festivities. Fortunately, there was Kerotone in the medical dispenser. He took one of the antihangover pills, showered, dressed, and went out into the parlor. His companions were both already up.

"Can you eat?" Droagn asked.

"I think so."

"Good. Your uncle has called up twice already. Let's have breakfast."

Their guide from yesterday met them in the lobby again. But instead of just leading them, this time she showed them how to get to the breakfast room, so that they wouldn't need her in the future. Rikard paid close attention, in case he wanted to do a little exploring on his own later.

Gawin was away on business, so they breakfasted alone. Human staff took care of their needs, appropriate food according to each taste was brought, and though it was a pleasant enough hour, Rikard was disappointed that he hadn't come down in time to see his uncle. Of course, it was his own fault.

As they were finishing up, a woman named Andrefs came in to suggest that they spend some time in the pool. Even Grayshard agreed, to Rikard's surprise. Andrefs took them to the pool area, explaining as they went how they could find it from anywhere in the estate.

It proved to be an elaborate enclosed place, with a glass ceiling and rather warm air. There were private lockers where Rikard found a suit that fit and pleased him. Droagn, of course, just removed his harness and hung it over a chaise, and Grayshard took out his vocalizer.

The water was quite hot at one end, quite cool at the other, and graded between. One side of the pool was only ten centimeters deep, but the other side was ten meters deep, with a variety of diving boards. In the very middle was a constant slow whirlpool.

After a bit a servant came with a tray of drinks and snacks. They lounged around, soaked some more, and then Andrefs came to tell them that it was time for lunch. When they had put themselves together she took them to the balcony where, today, the meal was being served. Gawin was waiting for them.

They had a light but perfect late lunch, accompanied by

light and comfortable conversation. At one point Rikard asked if he could make use of Gawin's comcon system.

"Certainly, that's what it's there for."

"You don't mind if I tap into the central system?"

Gawin smiled. "Whatever you can figure out how to do, you may do—and don't worry about long-distance charges."

Rikard stared at him blankly for a moment, then felt his face redden.

After lunch Gawin had more business, so Rikard and his companions returned to their suite. Droagn selected a book of poems and went to his room to nap. Grayshard bundled himself into a very large chair in the parlor where he could spread his fibers out and just sat there. Rikard sat down at the main comcon and familiarized himself with the keyboard.

Rikard was an historian by training and profession, no matter how he actually spent his time. Specifically, he was a local historian, duly licensed and accredited, one of those who specialized in learning in depth about specific places, rather than in breadth about larger segments of the Federation, or about the Federation as a whole. He had all the credentials he needed to gain access to governmental documents, university archives, public depositories, and even the right to pursue private libraries if he could demonstrate a true need. Adventurer he might be, rogue and Gesta in fact, but the secrets of the past were what truly fascinated him, though he seldom admitted it, even when he struggled to gain some degree of acceptance in the academic community.

And the part of the past that interested him now was that of this particular world, which bore the same name as his mother's family.

He first had to establish his presence legally. It was a formality, but one in which he indulged, just in case there were questions later. That done he identified the probable location of the largest history database, and found that rather than in a university, it was a part of the government records office. He connected through.

Grayshard, in his chair, seemed to roil slowly for a

moment, like noodles in boiling water. Rikard did not ask what he was doing.

A large part of the government records were not public. Rikard could gain access to much of them if he wished, but first he looked for history synopses. These he found—military, economic, extraplanetary, and so on. He wanted dates, the earliest records available. A bibliography gave him what he needed.

There were several conspicuous breaks in the record. Everything before a certain date was represented only by later publications, and there was a long interregnum during which nothing was published at all. There were other minor gaps, times when few books were printed, and once a year of absolutely nothing though there were plenty of later books referring to that time.

He located a child's text covering the earliest history of Malvrone, written some half century after the commencement of publications. As it turned out, Malvrone was nearly a thousand years older than that, had been colonized from Humankind's home world, had been a secondary colony, and had suffered a complete social collapse following separation from the home world. This hiatus had lasted three generations, during which much was destroyed. When calmer minds regained control and began reconstruction, a man named Victor Malvrone had been chairman of the committee to reestablish connection with the rest of the civilized worlds, and had helped to establish the interplanetary nature of his world's government. On his death, he was honored by naming the planet after him. Before that it had been called "Earth," and as a colony had been known as Greenleigh.

Following the record from there was more difficult. The information was available, but a proper search would take several months. Rikard wanted only a sketch at this time. By examining the indices of various texts and encyclopedias he was able to learn that the Malvrone family remained prominent, though not necessarily in power, at least up to the time of the next major hiatus in the record. And while there could have been other families with the same name, he found no immediate reference to them, so pending further research and confirmation, he felt it safe to assume that his mother's family was at least descended from the original Victor Malvrone. Quite something to be proud of.

He was roused from his studies by the arrival of his uncle. There was some time before dinner yet, so Gawin took them to see some of the artworks he kept for himself, in his personal gallery.

Which proved to be the equivalent of any well-endowed civic museum, with paintings, sculptures, fiber pieces, holography and photography, sensory daises, and so on. It covered maybe a hectare on three levels. There was too much to see at once, so they just looked at what caught their interest at the moment, and Gawin provided them with comments about the various cultures, species, and star nations that produced them, and how each item had been acquired and from whom.

Dinner was somewhat more formal than it had been the day before. There were two other guests, associates of Gawin's who had come on business. Ben Shadan and Ainette Delacroy were both legitimate dealers who were interested in purchasing some of the works of the Federation's hottest new graphic artist, Lei Ffraab, for whom Gawin was the primary agent. They were somewhat taken aback at the appearance of the Ahmear and the Vaashka, much to Gawin's amusement, and the first part of the meal went by with no more business than getting acquainted. Grayshard, out of consideration for the Humans present, consumed his meal from an enclosed container, but Droagn insisted on his large chunks of raw meat, and when Delacroy muttered something about it, he mentioned that the shellfish that she was eating had been boiled alive, which fact bothered him.

Ben Shadan and Ainette Delacroy represented different galleries, and each was looking for recent examples of Ffraab's work to offer for sale. The prices her works were bringing more than justified the expense of a personal visit to Gawin, her agent, rather than an impersonal interplanetary call. After all, though others could arrange for showings, only Gawin Malvrone could mediate any sale of Ffraab's work, first or subsequent, for which, of course, he got a considerable commission. Ffraab's most recent graphics were being auctioned on Kelgar, and Gawin was committed to that, but he knew of several pieces she had produced last year that might be available. This was interesting to the dealers, if not exactly what they were looking for, and they worked out a deal.

The negotiations made dinner run late, but Gawin's staff seemed more than ready for the consequences, and kept the meal going with additional little courses Rikard had no experience with, but which kept everybody eating and drinking for as long as the conversation continued.

After dinner and the deal were both finished it was quite late, but nobody was in the mood to move very far or very fast for a few moments. Then Ainette Delacroy seemed to think of something, and asked Gawin about his stellar model of the Federation, created by the late Mathis Evanrood.

"Yes," Gawin said, "I still have that."

"There's not another one like it that I know of," Ben Shadan said. "Do you suppose we could see it?"

"I'd be more than happy to show it to you," Gawin said and cast a querying glance at Rikard.

"Why not?" Rikard said, and Droagn and Grayshard expressed interest as well.

As it turned out, it was the most spectacular thing Rikard had yet seen in this house of spectacular art and architecture. The model was fully ten meters in diameter, contained in a large dark chamber with galleries around it at three levels. Each star was represented by a tiny light, in perfect size and color scale. One could move around the whole display, and by merely speaking the name of a star, or a planet, have the system in question highlighted by an ultraviolet sphere. If two stars were named in sequence, they were both highlighted and common star routes were displayed as red hairlines. At the appropriate command, a star's system of planets could be expanded so that each world was visible in its current position. On the floor and on each of the galleries was a station from which one's view could be projected into the model, as if one were flying as a giant among the stars. It was a spectacle unlike any Rikard had ever experienced. Only his conversations five years ago with the Taarshome, the energy beings that had been the first sentients in the galaxy, had anything to compare.

The next day Gawin was again busy in the morning, and Andrefs suggested that Rikard and his companions look over the formal gardens, which they did, finding them quite extensive, complex, and bizarre.

But as they walked among the flowering shrubs, miniature trees, beds of meter-wide flowers or millimeter blooms, animated bushes, and ornamental grasses, Rikard couldn't help but wonder more about his family's connections with the planet. Droagn was curious too, and even Grayshard expressed some interest. They cut their tour short, and since there was some time yet before lunch, they returned to their suite to pursue the subject further.

Rikard connected through to the comcon center and, instead of going back into the history section, looked up Malvrone's government directly. There was plenty of public information, though it took Rikard's special knowledge of how to search the data in order to find anything particular.

Like most worlds, local representatives were elected by the people living in a particular area, but unlike other systems, the representatives in turn elected their directors according to function rather than location, and the directors, who made up the general board, appointed the Planetary Board, of one hundred people, who were the administration of the corporation that was the planet Malvrone.

But the officers of the Planetary Board were hereditary. There were ten of them, plus the executives of the Corporation itself, who were also hereditary. Rikard's grandfather, Artos Lord Malvrone, was the current chairman, and Rikard's grandmother, Vikaria Lady Malvrone, was the president.

In other words, his mother's family's titles were not empty, as his mother had always maintained, nor were they now nor ever had they been poor. In essence, Artos and Vikaria owned and operated the planet and all its wealth and influence in the Federation.

There was no confusion about it, no ambiguity. Rikard read over the texts four or five times, and it always came out the same. He had nothing to say, and neither did Droagn nor Grayshard.

They met Gawin for lunch in a small, cozy room decorated with prints and flowers. Rikard did his best to keep up simple conversation, and did not bring up the topic of his discovery, not sure just where Gawin, who held a corporate yet nonvoting title, fit into the scheme of things. Yet in all the time Rikard had known him, in the years before his mother had died, and since, Gawin had never said anything about it, had never disillusioned Rikard or contradicted what Sigra had told him.

"You seem to be a bit distracted," Gawin said at one point.

"I'm sorry," Rikard said as he tried to remember what his uncle had been talking about. "I guess I'm just not used to having nothing to do."

"I have no obligations after lunch," Gawin said. "Would you like to see my library?"

"I would indeed," Rikard said, though he didn't really fell that enthusiastic.

But once in the library, his enthusiasm didn't have to be feigned, and he was grateful for a distraction to take his mind off his discovery. Here were all kinds of books, including several of those he had brought back from the Ahmear city under New Darkon. There were paper books, leather books (but no illuminated manuscripts, which were kept elsewhere), card books, disks, and tapes. There were electronic books similar to the Ahmear texts, scrolls, accordion folds, and replicas of masterpieces or items too fragile or valuable to be touched.

There were a lot of books on architecture, even more on art, and technology of all sorts. There were science texts and popular texts and social sciences and psychology. There were novels, plays, poems, whatever one might want, all catalogued according to the Larson System that had been designed to facilitate retrieval of specialized topics as well as being all inclusive and infinitely expansible, and the catalogue was available on dedicated screens located at the end of each aisle and on swing-up decks attached to each table or easy chair.

And while a lot of the books were for show, or because Gawin was a natural collector, he had actually read a lot of them. Reading was his preferred form of solitary entertainment, and he knew his way around his library.

When they had seen enough of that, Gawin took them to a series of chambers high in a distant part of the house where he kept his secret pride. This was a collection of miniature castles, all built at a scale of one to one hundred. Each was from a different culture, from a variety of species, from a broad range of ages, but all were medieval in terms of their builders. Each was an authentic reproduction of a castle that had once existed, and could open in several ways to reveal the interior. Gawin had a staff of twenty craftsmen working on new models and maintenance and repair at all times.

Rikard was impressed, and would have been more than fascinated, except for what he had found out that morning about his family's position in this world's affairs. And at last he decided he had to admit to his uncle what he had discovered.

"I was wondering when you'd find out about that," Gawin said. They were standing beside a meter-tall model of a castle from the second medieval period of Far Cantroe, a simple circular tower that opened to reveal a succession of floors and cellars stacked within walls that were half the radius of the tower in thickness.

"Mother never said anything about it," Rikard said.

"She tried to divorce herself from her past as much as possible. She was cut out of the line of inheritance, and so she rejected her family the way we rejected her."

"*You* didn't reject her."

"No. But I didn't do anything to help either. Nor did I have the courage to do so. Your grandfather is used to absolute power. As a planetary ruler, he's better than most, but he carries his prerogatives over into his personal relationships. He's not an easy man to live with. Fortunately for your grandmother, she's just like him."

"And all this time, I thought Mother was poor."

"She was. When she left, she took nothing with her. She was planning on coming back to get some personal things, but Father forbade it. The jewelry she wore wasn't all that valuable. Your father was her sole provider."

"Until the money ran out. But why did she keep such a secret?"

"She was ashamed, I think. Think about how you feel about my father casting his youngest child out the way he did."

"I don't like to think about it."

"Neither did Sigra. And she had more reason than you. She'd been kidnapped for ransom, and they were about to start sending body parts back to Father to prove they meant business. Father never even considered paying the ransom. It would have made him feel weak. And then I suggested your father might be able to do something, and Father agreed to it, and I was right. And Father reneged. So how does Sigra feel. Father wouldn't pay her ransom, or pay her rescuer. I don't say she married your father because of that, they were truly in love I think. But it surely made it easy for her to forget her past, to be ashamed of it, and to ask me to never speak of it, especially after you were born. She preferred that you never knew about her shame."

"I guess I can't blame her." He closed the tower model

and turned to another, with battlemented walls and spires, only half a meter tall but nearly a square meter in extent. "You knew I'd find out, didn't you?"

"I figured you would."

Grayshard stood a couple meters away to Rikard's right. His face was turned toward a gray stone model. His attention was who knew where. Droagn hung farther back, watching and listening but tactfully removed from the discussion.

"Is that why you invited me here?" Rikard asked after a long pause.

"I invited you here because when you were a child I enjoyed your company, and when you were a young man, and when I met you again on Mensenear I was proud to think that someone like you was my nephew. Most of my family aren't very nice people. I thought we might pick up where we left off."

Rikard looked his uncle in the eye. "And you took the chance that I'd find out the truth about Mother and not hate you for it."

"I did."

"Well. I'm glad you did."

Rikard and Gawin embraced, and then let the subject lie. They looked at a few more castles, in which Droagn was very interested, though Grayshard just politely followed along until they came to one that was tall and airy and almost fairylike, which captured the Vaashka's attention completely.

But at last it was time to get ready for dinner, which this evening was held in a large, dark hall, lit by torches that actually burned. Once again there was company for dinner, just one guest this time, a friend of Gawin's named Isakar Mendoza, from Total Foam. He had just stopped by to visit on his way to Higginsplanet, and provided the party with plenty of distractions from both family secrets and the business of art dealing. Rikard was grateful for this, though it couldn't stop him from thinking about it.

After dinner they looked at a selection of sculpture that Gawin kept in a separate wing. Most of it was erotic in nature. Rikard's personal thoughts continued to distract him, though some of the sculptures were quite surprising, in subject, representation, medium, or execution. It got him through until bedtime.

Next morning Rikard and his friends and Isakar Mendoza were on their own again, and Andrefs directed them to the game room where they tried out a few of the better known and some of the more obscure entertainments. Here there was billiards in a variety of forms, single and double combat simulators, a tabletop orbital simulator contest, as well as poker, chess, backgammon, fleece, mah choi, go, and a variety of manual board games and computerized strategy games. Rikard did his best to be sociable.

They had lunch with Gawin, after which he showed them his collection of succulent plants from many worlds. This was what Mendoza had come for. He wanted to trade a few examples he had picked up on Lucerne for cuttings of some of Gawin's prize specimens.

It took a good part of the afternoon to go through the six hectares or so of greenhouse, and then Gawin had to go off again, and his four guests retreated to the pool.

Mendoza, as it turned out, was the publisher of Ruehlmann Press, one of the largest specialty publishers in the Federation, and was rather cautiously curious about Rikard in particular and Gestae in general. Rikard kept on protesting his scholarship as an historian, and countered with questions about Mendoza's selection of books. They kept up the friendly bantering until dinnertime.

Three other guests showed up for dinner, which this evening was held on an open balcony under a crystal-clear sky. Two of these were personal friends of Gawin's, Lyle Green and Stuart Saparretti, from Kernig, a distant city on Malvrone, and the third was Marcella Diangello, a representative of the Clark University on Doyle. Green and

Saparetti were there purely to be social, but Diangello wanted Gawin to handle the university's excess collections to see what he could get. Business and small talk mingled easily and it was a very pleasant evening.

But later, while everybody was occupied in one of Gawin's media centers, Rikard took his uncle to one side. "I've been thinking about this all day long," he said.

"I'd be surprised if you hadn't," Gawin told him gently.

"It's such an obvious thing, and yet it took me until just a few minutes ago to realize that when Grandfather refused to pay my father for rescuing Mother, it wasn't because he didn't have the money."

The three-dimensional images went through their motions in the stage. It was a recently popular film that Rikard had not yet seen. Somehow Gawin had gotten a copy before its home release.

"You're right," Gawin said. "It was because he sort of felt that people owed it to him to do things for him, and besides, since the deal hadn't gone down the way it had been arranged, Father didn't feel obliged to pay."

"But he had made the deal," Rikard said. "Half the ransom if Dad got Mom back alive. And he did it. So he single-handedly killed all the kidnappers in the process, how did that relieve Grandfather from his responsibility?"

"It didn't, but Father felt that way. I'm not making excuses, Rikard, I'm just trying to explain."

"I'm sorry."

"Your mother felt bad about that too, as I told you before. Especially since she and Arin sort of hit it off from the start. They had two weeks to get back here from Emblethon, and I guess they got to know each other pretty well during that time. I think Sigra had been planning on your father coming around to call in the usual way, and on Father being very grateful and all. And when that didn't happen, she got hold of Arin and arranged discreetly to meet him. Father found out and threatened to disown her, but she married Arin anyway.

"Father kept track of her for a long time after that. I came to visit whenever I could, but it wasn't easy getting away from Father without his knowing where I was going. He caught me once and I'm not going to tell you what he did to me when I got back. And then Sigra died, and Father took me aside and told me and expressly forbade me from going to the funeral."

"But you did."

"And that was when Nevile Beneking was first created."

Rikard sat quietly for a moment, watching the adventure unfolding in the stage. "So," he said at last, "I guess there's not much chance that Grandfather will ever approve of me."

"I guess not," Gawin said.

Isakar Mendoza was there for breakfast the next morning, though he had to leave immediately after. Gawin did not mention the subject of Rikard's parents during the meal, and neither did Rikard. Afterward, as he had only light business that morning, he took Rikard, Grayshard, and Droagn to his office.

"Father doesn't like his children to work," Gawin explained, "unless it's the business of running Malvrone. I have absolutely no interest in that. Braice wants the job and he can have it. None of us was trained to make any use of our lives else, so I'm rather proud of my reputation in the art world, and the fact that I can bring it off in spite of Father's disapproval. And here is where I do most of the work."

He then proceeded to show off how he could establish market connections anywhere in the Federation and on a number of worlds outside. He had a powerful and complex comcon setup, with multiple screens, printers, direct interstellar communications, powerful computers both dedicated and general, and a huge database.

As his three guests watched he found a buyer for one of the Clark University's excesses. As that was concluding he got a want for Andaluthian sand sculpture. Then he found a buyer for some of Lei Ffraab's early works, which had come back on the market on the death of their owner. He was just playing at being a dealer this morning, nothing very serious. He located a collection of rare stamps and bid on it. While waiting for the next round he found a sand sculpture and got back to the party that wanted it. He arranged for a three-way trade of various items between two universities and a municipal museum to their mutual benefit and his. The request for the sculpture got back and said they wanted something different. His bid for the stamps was topped and he bid again. It was, he explained somewhat smugly, practically a morning off.

Neither Droagn nor Grayshard had any personal or professional interest in dealing in art, but Rikard became more and more intrigued as each transaction showed off something more about the huge database. "You've got an awful lot of information in there," he said. "This system is far more sophisticated than what I'm familiar with, and I've seen quite a bit on various worlds."

"You're not going to find one like this anywhere else," Gawin said, "except at my place on Tarantor. I've taken advantage of what the Vadime of Soler Prikus have to offer. Perhaps you've heard of them."

"I'm afraid I haven't."

"They're a minor member of the Federation. They don't travel much. Quite interesting, really, an arthropod race that nonetheless superficially resemble Humans, the way your friend Grayshard does—as long as they have their clothes on. They're established on only their home system and two others. Most of their technology is on a low par with the rest of the Federation, but their computer and communications systems are maybe half a century in advance of the best of anything else we have. They control their exports but, well, I managed to obtain a functional prototype."

Rikard's attention was no longer on the data retrieval system, and there was something in his face that made his uncle pause. "Mother always told me," Rikard said at last, "that her family had more titles than money."

"Was that the way she put it?" Gawin asked apprehensively.

"She lied to me all those years," Rikard said softly.

"That's the logical conclusion one must come to, considering what we've said so far about the subject. What are you getting at?"

"Dad went broke, and went off looking for one last treasure, and never came back. But he didn't have to go off, did he? Could Mom have asked Grandfather for money?"

Gawin sat back in his chair. He didn't like the direction this conversation was taking. "I don't know, but I think that probably she could have."

"Would he have given it to her?"

"If he'd thought her asking for money was a way of admitting her error, yes, I think he would have."

"So she was too proud?"

"In many ways your mother was as much of a misfit in this family as I am, but she shared one thing with Father, and that was her pride. Father kept track of Sigra until then. But when Arin went off without your mother coming to him, he broke off the connection for good."

"Did my father know Mom could have gotten money?"

Gawin sighed. "You're a lot more like your mother than your father, in some ways," he said. "Your father was basically a happy man, restless, but content with whatever the world handed him, and not afraid to take a chance to improve his position. He didn't care who had money, who had power, who had position, he treated them all the same. I don't think he really knew or cared what kind of wealth my father had, only that he didn't keep his word. If he could have gone on living in the kind of comfort to which he liked Sigra to be accustomed, he wouldn't have minded where the money came from."

"So Mom could have bailed them out if she'd wanted to."

"She could have."

"But she didn't, and because of that Dad went off, and didn't come back, and Mom died of a broken heart . . ."

"Yes," Gawin said gently, "compounded by guilt."

Rikard sat silently for a long moment, then said, "How much can this database tell us about those cyclopean cones?"

"I'm not sure," Gawin said, "I hadn't thought about it."

"Like, are the cones on Dannon's Keep the only ones? Are there cones on other worlds? Does this database have any information on the cyclopeans at all? Can you query it by showing it the few things I brought back with me?"

Rikard may have intended the change of subject as merely a diversion, but the questions were legitimate, and now it was Gawin's turn to be interested. "I've tapped into every art, anthropological, sociological, archaeological, and historical database I could," he said. "I know of nobody else with a base as extensive as mine. And I'll have to tell you, there might be things in there nobody would think to look for, until now."

They started to ask the system questions, beginning with the obvious, for which they got only tantalizing hints. They scanned in images of Rikard's trophies and asked more questions. Still the answers were only suggestions of possibilities. But Droagn and Grayshard began to pay attention.

Gawin had someone bring them the archaeology text Rikard had retrieved from the buried Ahmear city, found the seven pictures that showed the cones, and scanned those in. The system chuckled a bit, and when it started answering— it was still only hints, though now they were becoming a bit more positive.

Then Grayshard said, "Why don't you feed it the recording you made?" and he handed Rikard his helmet, which a servant had just brought to him. "I thought you might want it," he said.

Rikard plugged it into Gawin's system and they looked through some of the recordings and fed them into the database.

Now their questions brought more elaborate responses, though still mostly cryptical, incomplete, and nonspecific. But these hints clued them in to better questions. During the next few hours they sifted through terabytes of information and at last started to get the kind of answers they were looking for.

It turned out that there were records of several dozen worlds with eroded cones of marble, all of which were assumed to have been natural. They were distributed on worlds in an irregular arc through the Federation, with no indication as to the origin. But the world with the most structures was called Tsikashka.

"Then that's where we have to go," Rikard said.

"I would think so," Grayshard agreed, "assuming that we want to find out more about those people."

"You think he could let it alone?" Droagn asked.

"And what happens when you get there?" Gawin asked. "You look for more artifacts?"

"Of course," Rikard said. "Anything that will help me discover who those people were, and that I can present to the academic community as proof of my discovery."

"You're forgetting one thing," Gawin said. "Karyl Toerson got to you twice before, and she seemed to have a pretty good idea of what you were after. She may try to ambush you again."

"She won't get away with it this time," Rikard said.

"Look," Gawin said, "I want you to be careful. Toerson is bad business. I know. Be careful. If you can bring stuff out without her interfering, that's fine, bring it to Mensenear. I'll instruct the people there to accommodate you when and if you show up. Don't bring it here.

"But Toerson may get to you no matter what you do. She's been at this a lot longer than you have. If she does, let it go. It's not worth your life if you push her too hard.

"And whatever happens, come visit me again. It's great having family that I can actually talk to."

"It is that," Rikard said with a grin.

Tsikashka

1

Many worlds produce life, and some of these living worlds produce intelligent life. A few intelligent species develop a technology, and in potential at least could become starfaring. It has happened many times.

The scope of space is such that in the Federation, by no means the largest of star nations, there are dozens of these starfaring species, though Humans are the most numerous by far. And in the scope of time, from the first sentient Taarshome—whose origins are so far back toward the beginning of the cosmos that their age can hardly be counted—until today, there have been many more starfaring nations than presently exist. It is a truism that more species of life are extinct than survive. Time is so long and space so large.

Tsikashka was a world on which a sparse life had evolved, but it produced no forms above the relative level of arthropod, though some of those species might seem quite advanced by comparison with similar forms on other worlds. And yet Tsikashka had been home, from time to time, of several starfaring species of people, though none of those who existed in the Federation today. Indeed, none of them had survived more than a few thousands of years after learning how to travel between the stars. In some cases, the home worlds of these species were known. In more cases the long dead colonies on Tsikashka were the only remaining examples.

If Rikard's surmise was correct, there was at least one other interstellar people to add to the record, though as yet without name—the cyclopeans first hinted at in the Ahmear archaeology text.

Rikard and his companions arrived at the Tsikashka system on a small, privately chartered flickership. It was Rikard's preferred mode of transportation, and since there was no regular starship service to Tsikashka anyway, that was just as well. He did take the precaution of not divulging his destination until they were under way, just in case Karyl Toerson had access to the company's records.

All travel to and from the Tsikashka system was by demand only, on the part of universities, research academies, planetary governments, Federal conservation services, and so on. And so the bare-bones jumpslot station was used to dealing with flickerships of all types. They were *not* used to dealing with private individuals. For this reason, Rikard had more difficulty than he had anticipated in getting permission just to dock at the tiny station, with a staff of under six thousand, and most of them clerical.

Rikard knew how to deal with the red tape, however, and had his credentials, but his reputation had preceded him. The whole system was run more like a university than a civilian government, and those in charge were not that happy having someone who, on the one hand, had made four or five major and a dozen or so minor archaeological discoveries that were changing the development of the history of the Federation, on the other hand was known to frequently keep good archaeological examples for himself, to disfavor monopolistic development and research, and to occasionally leave a swath of destruction behind him.

Their apprehensions were all well founded, of course, but they were people too, and the liberal application of money—administered according to his uncle Gawin's careful instructions—was strangely reassuring to those in charge, and after a delay that was more cosmetic than actually necessary, he was given his permits and allowed to proceed to the orbital station, where he brought his equipment down by shuttle to one of the larger spaceports, known simply as Port KB-7.

There were only twenty-three shuttleports on Tsikashka altogether, most of them with nothing more than a landing field, a planetary office, residential facilities for a few hundred visitors, a general service and supply store, and a preservatory research lab. Port KB-7 was one of the four ports that actually had a civilian population, some fifty thousand people of a mix of species, who with the other three major stations, XR-1, DD-14, and LA-23, provided all the amenities for everybody there on research grants.

All the ports, regardless of size or location, were enclosed in protective domes. Tsikashka was an old world and the environment was deteriorating and most people needed special equipment to remain comfortable, if not to survive. All ports also had facilities for providing surface transportation and life support outside the ports as needed.

Rikard and his companions arrived at their surface accommodations, and for once had no problems with Endark Droagn's size, or Grayshard's peculiar dietary requirements. The amenities were minimal, but space was ample, with plenty of facilities for storage, and the directory of community services listed everything a researcher might want, whether to study artifacts and reports at the port or to go afield.

As soon as they were settled in, Rikard plugged into a geographical database and checked out the locations of what they knew as the remains of the cyclopean cones. There proved to be many such remains indeed, some of them mere stumps, others broken piles, a few still-standing cones. They were scattered all around the globe, more than two hundred of them, and all of them were assumed to be natural if bizarre geological features. After all, each appeared to be a solid mass of unworked marble.

It was their good fortune that the largest and perhaps best preserved examples were a reasonable distance from Port KB-7. Rikard inquired as to how to get there, and discovered that there was no regular transport of any kind, and no air transport to speak of except between the four major ports, all else being handled by heavy floater. He arranged for one of these, which could not be delivered for three days, along with a trailer and floater carts for artifacts, and environment suits for all three. Droagn's would have to be custom-made, but the company that provided the suits was used to that kind of thing. Grayshard didn't actually need one, as his disguise was perfectly adequate for that purpose as well, but if he didn't get one it would arouse more attention than Rikard wanted.

They spent the rest of the afternoon and evening looking around the port, which was a cross between a logging camp, an academic coffee room, and an outcast bar. Rikard remembered his experiences at the Troishla years ago, on Kohltri, and was not impressed.

For the next two days, without having to leave their accommodations except for a change of view, they researched all that was known about the cones, getting physical data on each one where available, plotting their distribution around the globe, collecting theories as to their nature, all of which were plausible, uninspired, and bore no hint of the truth. Rikard did not actually expect to learn much, but he was trying to give the impression of legitimate research, which was believable since even if these cones were natural formations, their existence on several distinct worlds was sufficient cause for academic curiosity.

At last the morning of the delivery came, and they checked out their equipment. The heavy floater was really a portable living quarters, and the trailer, which floated but without power, was plenty big enough for the smaller floaters on which they hoped to haul out whatever treasures and artifacts they might find. They carried only minimal weapons—which for Rikard meant his heavy wired-in pistol, of course—since they did not expect to run into any trouble here. They had purchased standard excavation equipment, but had some special devices of their own as well. They packed everything, boarded the floater, drove to the dome exit, registered their clearance with the academic authorities, and were ready to go.

The heavy floater was completely sealed, of course, and consisted primarily of a cabin large enough for all three, with pull-down bunks, cooking and sanitary alcoves, a driver's control console, and access to the rear portions, which could be separately sealed, where they carried most of their equipment. Designed for six Human-sized explorers, it was big enough, though they'd had to modify one set of bunks for Droagn's use.

They departed the port at midday, pulling their nearly empty trailer behind them, and moved across a landscape that was rocky and damp, with sparse, coarse vegetation, under perpetually overcast skies. The air was thin and caustic. There was occasional lightning off over the horizon. They were not moving as quickly as Rikard would like, but the floater was built for power, not speed.

After only half an hour at the driver's console Rikard set the floater on automatic. It would head toward the cones in as straight a line as possible, accommodating obstructions and variations in terrain. If nothing went wrong they would reach the cones by noon of the next day.

With the guidance equipment on board, and the destination locked in, there was nothing for them to do but wait out the ride. Fortunately, the cabin's windows were large, temperature and humidity well controlled, and they had brought plenty of food and beverages along, though they'd had to make some compromises with Grayshard's ferments, and Droagn wouldn't be getting any really fresh meat.

As the afternoon wore on the level of the land rose and became drier. Ahead of them, many kilometers away, was the crest of the ridge, a black line against the gray sky. The vegetation grew more sparsely here, and there were fewer and fewer rocks sticking up from the finely tumbled gray ground.

And then, in the middle of the afternoon, Droagn saw something ahead and to the left of their line of travel. Spikes and spires stuck up out of the ground, with smaller spikes projecting from them at right angles. The ground, which elsewhere was grayish, was pinkish around the spikes, with long curving lines of a darker color that crossed their line of travel and headed toward the structures.

As they neared them they could make out more details. Some of the spikes were flat plates, others were rectangular prisms, still others were irregular columns. Their surfaces were marked with annular projections, stepped sections, grooved ridges, and other shapes. All of them were a pale amber or beige color. They looked somewhat like sand-eroded tree trunks, something like broken skyscrapers—except for those long spikes that projected at ninety degrees, high up on the sides. How they kept from falling, none of them cared to hazard a guess.

As the floater came closer they could see that there were domes at the bases of the spikes, more of them on the side nearest their line of travel than on the side facing their approach. Some of the domes were round, some ovoid, some with sloping flat faces, all with circular depressions, or radial grooves, or annular projections, or smaller spikes sticking up from the center or the side, and with what looked like doors near the ground. One dome was longer and taller than the rest, and a dull red.

The whole conglomeration was some two kilometers to the left, so as they progressed they passed around its end and got some idea of its dimensions.

Now a plate with a hole stuck up among the spikes, then a tower much smaller than the spikes, then more broken skyscrapers on the far side came into view. The clustering domes, denser on this side, they could now see rose to a height of maybe fifty or sixty meters. That meant that the spikes were something like half a kilometer high—not much by contemporary Federation standards, but then this place had not been built by any contemporary Federation race.

As they passed the end of the reach of ruins they saw larger buildings, arches and bridges, hidden by the first, simpler spikes. All were the same pale beige color, with only one or two exceptions—red, or yellow, or deep amber, once black.

And here and there, between them and the main stretch of ruins, strange objects floated above the pinkish ground, flat on top and domed below, with little igloos off to one side on some of them, and spikes that projected downward from the middle of their bottoms. Some of these objects had fallen over and were now resting canted on the soil that was as alien as the structures.

The forest of spikes continued for a long way into the distance, at right angles to their line of travel, with three or four kilometers off what looked like permanent banks of haze and fog halfway between the base and tips of the spikes. One spike was yellow, and another was black, and on this side they had more but shorter projections.

As the ruins dwindled in the distance Rikard began to doubt whether his evaluation of the uniqueness of the cyclopeans had indeed been a valid judgment. He'd guessed that because he'd never seen anything like them, in any text, they were unknown to everybody. But he'd never seen anything like these ruins either. Had he been fooled by his own ignorance?

An hour after the last of the spikes disappeared into the distance they came to the crest of the ridge, then descended to a rather more vegetated area, prairie or savanna or steppe, with a few trees with slender leaning trunks and flattened clouds of leaves high above the ground.

Later they passed through fields that might once have been cultivated, where stones stuck up out of the ground, most just a meter high or so but others up to six meters tall. All of them were slender and angular in section and gray and otherwise unmarked. Here and there among them were the trenches of archaeological digs. There had been a lot of activity here in the past, though nobody was present this afternoon. Those who had made the trenches did not seem to be concerned about intruders, as all their equipment had been left unprotected. There were tractors and power shovels and trenchers and sifters and water wagons and hand tools of all kinds, and boxes—stacks and stacks of boxes. It was impossible to say, without stopping, how long it had lain there.

They ate their supper on the floater as it carried them across a broad valley, and toward nightfall they passed, nearby on the right, an anachronistic and impossibly large structure something like a medieval castle, and yet unlike anything Rikard had seen in his uncle's collection of miniatures. It consisted of clusters of tapered cylinders, half organic, half artificial in appearance. There were few cylinders in the clusters at the side facing them, but many more farther back, so that they seemed to be forming the face of a cliff that surrounded a plateau instead of being a collection of buildings.

From a steep and smooth base carved from grayish white stone, the cylinder walls curved upward, narrowing and straightening as they rose meter after meter until, maybe two hundred meters up, they reached their narrowest and began to arch outward again. The gentle outward sweep was occasionally stepped abruptly by machicolations, from which the walls rose straighter for a while before curving outward again. Each cylinder, or tower, rose four or five hundred meters altogether before ending with battlements, bulging casements, steep roofs, or flat tops.

There were no windows in the lower part of the cylinders, but there were, above the bands of machicolations, and sometimes higher in the cylinders too, in straight rows around the curving walls. There were no doors, though there were sometimes ramps that wound slowly up the lower walls and disappeared between the white columns.

The ground around the base was littered with gray rock, darker gravel, and here and there something moved among the stones, like a snake. The full extent of these buildings was maybe twenty hectares. And this time they were something Rikard recognized from his texts, though he could not name or date their builders.

Their floater easily climbed the heavily eroded mountains on the other side of the broad valley, but they had to deviate from their course, in order to take advantage of the passes between the mountaintops. This was not difficult for the floater to manage unattended. The sun set with a spectacular glow, with shades of magenta and even green. Rikard, Droagn, and Grayshard occupied themselves as best they could. The floater would keep going the whole night without their attention. But they decided that though they didn't really need to, they would keep watches, and keep the floater's outer lights on so they could see whatever they might pass.

Grayshard drew the first watch, but before Rikard and Droagn retired they came upon maybe a dozen large creatures, like crabs, or scorpions, as big as cattle, pressing closely around something that they kept picking at with long, slender claws. Rikard shone a spotlight on the scene, and the arthropods turned but did not back off from their kill, which looked something like an elephant or a gorvalon, except that it had too many legs.

At first they thought the arthropods, with bulging eyes and eight or ten splayed legs, were scavengers, but as they passed, several of the creatures leapt after the floater, waving two sets of claws each, threatening the floater now that any threat of danger was past. They moved quickly enough that they might actually have been the predators that had brought the creature down.

Nothing happened during Grayshard's watch, or at least he reported nothing. It was Rikard's turn next, and he gazed serenely out into the night as the floater came out of the passes and started down the other side of the mountains.

Once they overtook another of the large arthropods, alone, moving parallel to them some twenty or thirty meters away. The floater passed it, and it sped up to keep pace with them for a while, and then angled away again. Rikard's watch came to an end with no further incident.

But once, during Droagn's watch, he was roused when the floater stopped. He looked out the broad window beside his bunk and saw that their vehicle was surrounded by hundreds of creatures, as big as the floater itself, moving slowly across their trail. Their humped bodies glistened wetly in the lights of the floater, long and dark gray, and whether they moved like slugs, or had lots of small feet, Rikard couldn't tell. It took twenty minutes for them to pass.

He went back to sleep after that, but toward morning Droagn roused him and Grayshard again—though of course Grayshard didn't sleep the same way Droagn and Rikard did. They were at the foot of the mountains now, going across a broad flatland, and though the sky was lightening it was still dark on the ground. Droagn pointed and off to the right they saw some lights, small white lights, but an occasional yellow or amber light, and one or two green ones. Some of them were moving from side to side. A red light came on for a moment and went out. They couldn't see any structures, though it was still dark enough that small buildings could be missed. They heard no sounds of machinery. Eventually the lights disappeared behind a shoulder of land.

They had breakfast, such as it was, as the sun came up. The flatland stretched on ahead of them, but an hour or so after sunrise they came to low rolling hills. Instead of climbing straight across they set the floater to take advantage of the valleys that cut through them, rising higher and higher.

At midmorning they passed an isolated fragment of a complex road structure. It had multiple levels supported by columns, extended for several kilometers in a perfectly straight line diagonally across their direction of travel, and competely disregarded hill shoulders or changes of level, though now it was slightly tilted up and canted to one side, and each end ended abruptly in a clean break with no ruins or other remains to indicate any larger system of which it might once have been a part, or any destination or origin. It was just as if this piece of road had been dropped down onto the ground, though there was no compression of the soil underneath it.

Higher in the valleys they came to a plateau, with badlands channeled through it, and had to slow so that the floater could find the best route, both immediate and long-range. They descended to a shallow but fast river, rose to the other side, crossed a ridge and as they did saw, on the other side of the badlands, just barely peeking up beyond the slope of the far side of the plateau, the white tips of what they thought were the cones.

2

As the floater came up out of the badlands and over the edge of the plateau they could see, some ten kilometers off, that it was not the cones that they had been traveling toward, but instead the white concrete and steel remains of gigantic pyramidal arcologies. Rikard checked the guidance system on the floater, but it indicated that they were indeed within ten kilometers of the site. It was just concealed by these crumbling structures.

Rikard switched off the automatic and angled the floater to the left, so as to be able to see between the towering white ruins. The one nearest them was in a bad state of disrepair, with gaps in the walls that revealed the interior floors, but the next one to the left was in much better condition. It was over a thousand stories tall, and even the tower on its apex was intact.

By the time they got to within five kilometers they could

see, between the arcologies, other ruins and structures, of different kinds, and at last got glimpses, in the spaces between those, of the white marble cones. They were not very tall, and apparently located in the center of this complex of ruins, as if the arcologies and other structures had been built up around them, for they could see, beyond the cones, more of the inner rings of ruins, and a broken fragment of an arcological pyramid sticking up beyond that.

Rikard headed for the gap between the two arcologies, which once had had connections between them partway up, arches and arcades and bridges. But while they were still a kilometer off they saw that the whole complex was surrounded by a fence, and then they saw the occasional watch stations a kilometer or so apart along the fence, and farther around to the left what looked like a main gate or entrance post.

˜Should we try to sneak by?˜ Droagn asked.

"They've probably already seen us," Rikard said. "Let's pay them a visit, as if that were our intention."

He slowed the floater and turned it directly toward the entrance post, so that they drove up parallel to the fence at the last. That gave him a chance to look it over. It was made of high-tensile mesh, was fully five meters high, and was apparently carrying some kind of field or charge. As they neared the entrance post several people, dressed in protective clothing with the insignia and patterns of the Federal police, came out to meet them. Four of them carried light rifles slung over their shoulders, and the fifth had a holstered pistol on his hip. Rikard pulled up to within ten meters and stopped the floater. The guards stood waiting. Rikard and his companions got into their outdoor gear and went out to meet them.

The man with the pistol was wearing the insignia of a sergeant. He came up to them as they stood beside their floater. His mouth moved, but nothing came over Rikard's radio. The sergeant tapped the side of his helmet, and Rikard turned on his external phones.

"How may I help you?" the sergeant asked again.

Rikard turned on his speaker. "Why not radio?" he asked.

"It's a good idea to be aware of what's going on around you. Changes in wind, sometimes there are animals. Are you just looking around?"

"Not really." Rikard took a sealed folder from his belt and handed it to the sergeant. "It *is* our first time here, but we've come to examine those marble cones in the middle."

The sergeant opened the folder and looked at the credentials inside, in their own protective pockets. Rikard had taken pains to obtain legitimate licenses this time, and they gave him and his companions permission to look at any cones he wanted to, not just these in particular.

The sergeant handed back the folder and smiled. "Everything's in order," he said, "but I'm afraid I can't let you into the compound."

"Why not? If everything's in order . . ."

"It's not the cones, it's where they are. This whole area is off-limits. It has nothing to do with the ruins, but everything here is standing on a bed of low-grade balktapline ore. You can't go in without proper shielding, and you can't get that unless you specifically ask for it and prove need."

"You've got to be kidding," Rikard exclaimed.

"What are you talking about?" Droagn asked. The *projected* question surprised the sergeant and the guards.

"Balktapline," Rikard explained, "is an ore from which we extract some stuff that is essential to our flicker drives. I don't pretend to understand it, but star travel would be only about half as efficient without it. But I thought"—he turned back to the sergeant—"that balktapline was found only on Kohltri."

The sergeant sighed. "That's why this place is off-limits. Kohltri is the main supplier, but there are other deposits elsewhere. There aren't many, they're usually small and rather low grade, and nobody knows how or why they exist at all. And they're all under Federal protection, just in case the Kohltri sources become unavailable for, ah, whatever reason.''

"I see,'' Rikard said. He had a pretty good idea of what those reasons might be and couldn't argue with the restriction. Balktapline ore was the most commercially important resource in the Federation, and gave it a small but significant advantage over their neighboring star nations. He could appreciate the government wanting to keep any other sources, however small and poor, for a backup.

"Is there any way,'' he said, "that you could maybe escort us to the cones? I've had some experience with balktapline and would just as soon not mess with it.''

"I don't have the authority to do that,'' the sergeant said. "But it shouldn't be difficult for you to get the proper clearances. It's just a formality, really. If you check at the Federal Mines Offices back at Port KB-7, I'm sure they'll give you the permits you want, which is the only way you'll get the proper shielding, and then you won't need an escort. The people who want to explore these ruins usually get those permits before coming out.''

Rikard saw no irony in the man's expression. "That's what comes,'' he said in disgust, "from not doing your homework. Is there anything specific I should ask for at the Mines Office?''

"Just ask for a clearance to get through Federal Zone 26653, and then you can go anywhere you want to in there.'' He jerked his head toward the fence. "But make sure the shielding has Federal approval stamps, or I won't be able to allow you anywhere near the balktapline fields regardless of permits. That stuff is nasty.''

"I'm aware of that,'' Rikard said. "Thanks for your time.'' He turned back to his companions and they got into the floater. "Keep your gear on,'' Rikard said when the door had closed. He got behind the controls and drove off back the way they had come.

They drove away in silence for a while. Then Rikard said to Grayshard, "What do you know about balktapline?''

"If you mean its origins," Grayshard answered, "I know that it is a metamorphosed residue of Tathas architectural materials, laid down when the Tathas were a spacefaring race."

The Tathas were a people accidentally created by the near-mythic Taarshome, and had passed from the galaxy before natural planetary life had come into existence. One branch had remained and degenerated and changed, on the world known as Kohltri. But another had evolved, far away, into the ancestors of the Vaashka.

"I was hoping," Rikard said, "that you might have some inside information."

"I'm sorry. Everything I know about it I learned since I joined with you. I know that reserpine and anthrace are associated with balktapline."

"That's correct," Rikard said. "And if they're also present, that means that the Tathas were once here too, and in sufficient numbers to leave a residue. I find that very interesting."

"You would," Droagn said. "Show you an obscure race that nobody knows anything about, and you get all excited."

By this time they were out of sight of the post, and out of range of any detecting equipment it might have. Rikard started to circle around to the left. An hour later he turned back toward the fence again, floating down into a depression that was well below ground level. He stopped and they sat for a long moment, to see if they were subject to any probes, but there was nothing that could be detected by the equipment on the floater, so they got out to examine the fence.

And it was a formidable fence. It was not just that it was a high tensile fence, but they confirmed that it was carrying a field that effectively kept all life forms away. They determined this by the simple expedient of trying to get close enough to cut the wires, which they were unable to do. Rikard and Droagn then unpacked a couple of sophisticated detectors that they used to scan the fence, and the field it generated.

Though the fence was only about five meters high, that was higher than their heavy floater could go—no vehicle they could rent could get more than two meters altitude. Rikard's scanner showed that the field around the fence extended above it for maybe a kilometer or more. Even if they could get over the fence some way, they still couldn't fly through the field. And yet, as Rikard examined the readouts on the field detector, he began to see a way around the problem. "I think I might be able to devise a shield," he said.

"There should be no difficulty at all," Grayshard agreed.

¯Oh, yes, there will.¯ Droagn was moving the two long probes that extended from his detector over the surface of the fence, being careful to not actually touch it. ¯This thing's got alarms all over it. Cut the fence, breach the shield, and our friends back at the gate will know just exactly where and when.¯

"Not if I can help it." Rikard put his detector away and got out another device. "I thought this might come in handy." He put the heavy box down next to the fence, as close as he could get to it, and opened it up. From inside it he extended a long, telescoping gooseneck. He held the middle of the neck over his head, and switched on the machine, then touched the fence.

¯You've just told them where we are,¯ Droagn said.

"Not at all. I didn't penetrate the field, I just turned it back on itself." He hooked a section of the gooseneck to the fence, right above the box, as high as he could reach, then stretched it along the fence, above the ground until the arch it formed was wide enough for the floater to go through. He fastened it to the fence along the way, then led the end down to the ground and back to the box again.

"That was the easy part," he said. "Physical fencing is another thing." He got another box from the trailer, a larger one, and from it took a bundle of several dozen paired cables, with clips at the ends, which he fastened, side by side, to each strand of the fence. When he turned on the power in the box to which the cables were connected, the material of the fence became soft and elastic. He stretched it aside, out nearly to the field-distorting gooseneck, and held it in place with more clips. Then he got in the floater and drove it and the trailer through the gap.

Droagn and Grayshard walked through, and started taking the fence spreader down. Ten minutes later they were done, and there was no sign of their penetration. They got into the floater and Rikard drove toward the arcologies towering above them.

The bare ground became rubble-strewn as they neared the white ruins, stuff that had fallen down the pyramidal slopes of the long-abandoned structures. As the rubble got deeper, the floater, which could handle rough ground elsewhere, even in the badlands, began to have trouble. The pieces were too big to go over, too close together to go around, and they reluctantly came to the conclusion that they would have to go the rest of the way on foot, and once again would have to leave lots of their equipment behind. Rikard found a place where they could hide the floater and trailer in the rubble, and they covered it with optical tarps so that it looked just like the ground. Unless someone literally stumbled on it by accident, it could be found only by following the coded beacon on board, which was set so that only the receivers that each of them carried would get the signal.

Before they set out Rikard went back inside the floater and put on his recording helmet. He got his holster out of the dashboard compartment, and strapped on his gun. He'd had his environment suit modified so that he could still make the connection between the circuits in the gun, his special glove, and his hand. Then they loaded four small floater carts with what they could in the way of excavation equipment, leaving room for a large gray case with black reinforcements and fastenings.

They set off on foot, towing the small floaters, and

worked their way between the larger chunks of fallen rubble. There was an arcological structure immediately in front of them, so they angled to the right in order to pass between it and its neighbor. But as they neared the corner of the pyramid the ground became even worse, and it began to look as if they might have to leave even the carts behind.

They struggled on, even so. Outlying buttresses that had collapsed added to the debris, and the easiest route was directly toward the structure itself. They could see what looked like several entrances at the lowest level, and one that was not too badly blocked by rubble. They went toward it.

When they got inside they found that the going was almost as bad as outside. The floor was covered with broken stone and concrete, rusted chunks of steel, and drifts of dust, mostly from the ceiling above, and from several floors above that, all the way to the slanting outer wall, through which they could see the gray, always overcast sky. Some interior walls had fallen, but others were still standing. They started to go through to the other side when Droagn paused. He reached up to touch the Prime, which he wore under his protective head covering. "There's life all around us," he said.

Rikard turned up the gain on his external mikes. Now he appreciated the sergeant's policy. He heard occasional slithers, like snakes or lizards, off in the darker places.

They went on, and kept to where it was light. Grayshard kept his micropulse drawn. Droagn's weapon of choice was, as usual, something he could swing. It looked like a two-meter staff, but it was made of superhard metal and contained inertial enhancers that worked with either a swing or a thrust. They passed through the ground floor of the arcology.

"I recognize this place now," Rikard said. "It was built by a people called Griem. They were a species of arachnoids. They had a stellar civilization some forty thousand years ago, and it lasted about three thousand years before they destroyed themselves in some kind of internal conflict.''

As they went through now open places on the far side of the ruin they still heard the slithering—more like centipedes than snakes—back in the remoter regions, but saw nothing. They got to the inner edge of the arcology complex, passed through a hole in the wall, and saw a rubble-strewn parkway below them. They were about a hundred meters up the side of the structure. The next ring of ruins, a wall of gray and amber columns, concealed the cyclopean cones from them.

The slope down to the parkway was actually easier to traverse than the flat ground outside the ruins, since much of the rubble had here rolled down and dispersed itself across a broader area. As they neared the bottom something large flew overhead and circled, on four long, translucent wings, like a dragonfly, then flew away.

They crossed the parkway toward the ring of ruined columns. Halfway there they frightened some small furry things that hurried away among the weathered rubble.

"Now that is unusual," Rikard said. "Native life is all exoskeletal, so those have to be the descendants of some pets somebody left behind."

The ring of ruins was composed of triangular columns joined together at their edges and rather broken near the top, though there was a lot less rubble here than near the arcologies. There were opaque window recesses in all the column walls, starting about thirty meters up. Half concealed by piles of gravel-sized rubble were several doorways.

As they approached the doorway most exposed Rikard got the feeling that something was watching them, or following them, but Droagn could detect no intelligence. They cleared the doorway as much as they needed to, and entered the ruins.

There were no floors above the ground in the first column, it just went right up to the now-open sky. The outer wall had only the one door, and the windows higher up, with no evidence that there ever were any floors above. In this column there were two inner walls, and each had a broad door at ground level and no openings above at all.

They passed through the nearest door, into another triangular column, like the first with no floors for its entire height, but with openings about halfway up into the nearest adjacent columns.

They went on to the next column. The walls between were only a centimeter thick, though strong enough to have supported their full height for all this time—however long it was. Rikard tried to think of who the builders might have been, but though he could remember having read something about them when he was in school, he couldn't bring anything more to mind.

The interiors of the next few columns were strange and tall, with tall doorways between them, and occasionally stairways that climbed the inside walls to other doorways high above, sometimes two or three above each other.

As they progressed they found that farther in there had been considerable damage, though the way was fairly easy since the rubble took much less space than that of the arcologies. They kept to their course, even though they had to go by angles.

After a while Rikard became aware that he was feeling a bit strange, and when he thought about it he realized that he'd begun to feel like this some time back. He wanted to slow down. He felt like his friends were a bit too close to him. It seemed as though, even in here with only the overcast sky far overhead, it was a bit too bright.

It was not an unfamiliar feeling, though he'd experienced it only twice before. At this moment it was so subtle that he might not have drawn the inevitable conclusion, but since he knew there was balktapline under the ruins here, he immediately recognized it as the Tathas effect, that bizarre psychosis induced by the residuum of their construction materials, which had been created to support and reinforce their psychic presence, and which had become insane even as they had, so long ago, when they had lost their purpose and begun the long descent into nonsentience.

"We're going to wish we had that shielding," he said.

The sensation got stronger as they went until Rikard began to feel, rather than see, a dark landscape, just out of the edges of his perception, superimposed on the dim walls of the triangular columns through which they walked.

Grayshard began to feel it too. "I'm surprised," he said. "I would have thought that I was immune." He was fascinated by the experience. "It rather resembles the Vaashka combat *projection*, but it is much different in flavor. It's more a constant static instead of a transient dynamic. And it is insane."

˜I don't feel a thing,˜ Droagn said.

As they came to the inner edge of this second ring of ruins Rikard felt ever more as though he were being crowded by his companions, and ever more comfortable with the closeness of the walls, and ever more disturbed by the immense height of the columns and the light at their top, and could almost see the dark shadows of the imaginary landscape on the walls around him.

˜Now wait a minute,˜ Droagn said at one point. ˜I'm beginning to feel weird. It's not much, and it's not like what you said, it's more like having a fuzzy brain, or itchy nerves. It's not much, but I don't like it.˜

Rikard, by now, had to concentrate on his objective in order to proceed and bear the company of his companions. He kept on wanting to look for a way down underground, and he felt shadows behind him that weren't there.

˜Does it get worse?˜ Droagn asked him.

"This is nothing yet."

They suddenly came to a door, beyond which was the outside, and it was all Rikard could do to force himself to go out under the gray sky. They were at ground level, in what had once been another parkway but was now a jungle. The vegetation was much more lush here than it had been elsewhere, probably due to the efforts of the vanished people who had built the triangular towers. The trees and other foliage were high enough and close enough that they could not see the cones from where they stood, or what was left of them, or even the other side of this ring of ruins.

They entered the jungle, the floor of which eventually became strewn with small pebbles, then larger rocks, then eventually rubble covered the ground and they left the jungle. Here and there, in the low spots, were more trees, and here and there in the high spots something artificial but now unrecognizable still stood upright. And now they could see the stub of one of the cyclopean cones, and beyond it another rising higher, and maybe a third off to the left behind the first, and maybe another off to the right behind the second.

It was hard for Rikard to keep a clear head. He wanted to go back under the trees, or better still down into the hollows and find a hole and lie down, and not move, and get away from Grayshard and Droagn, and wait for the dark night and the stars and whatever they might eventually bring. It was all part of the Tathas effect, but knowing it was of little help. The dark landscape, another facet of the effect, was not yet truly visible, though he could feel it around him, black and metallic and plastic and artificial. Even Grayshard was acting nervous and twitchy. Droagn was dour and grim.

As they proceeded the way got rougher. Most of the rock—really ceramics and plastics—was grayish-whitish-brownish stuff, but here and there they saw darker lumps, metallically iridescent in a subtle sort of way, here a piece of glossy black, there one of iridescent blue, and occasionally a piece that was pearly white. This was the telltale sign that the "ore" containing the balktapline and related substances was near the surface.

Now Rikard had to deal with new forms of the superimposed though subtle Tathas hallucinations. It was not quite the same as he'd felt before, but there were still the oddly apertured piles of irregularly shaped rocks, the strangely familiar monoliths, the things like small trees of bent wires and bolted-on plates, and a much-too-near horizon—none of it real, all of it only in his mind. The sky, when he looked at it, was still gray overcast and so bright it made him hurt, but when he looked away it felt black, with greasy metallic multicolored stars much too near and all connected somehow one to the other. The ground, if he looked at it, was gray soil with rocks and coarse brush, but when he looked away it felt black and waxy and always somehow concave and the rocks were black and the piles of stones like hives were black with doorways that he dared not look into.

He forced himself to pay attention to his real surroundings and now could see that there was an end to the ring of rubble, but they were not halfway there yet. And then Droagn called out.

At first Rikard thought that Droagn was just suffering hallucinations, but after a moment he heard that there really was something moving among the rubble. And then the noisemakers came into view, like giant lizards with eight legs. They were moving not that quickly but with considerable determination toward them. Rikard found it hard to be frightened by them, though their intent was all too obvious. He was numbed by the Tathas effect, and kept slipping back into the darkness and aching need for enclosure and solitude.

"*Kitah bley!*" Droagn shouted at him, but Rikard couldn't bring himself to care even that his friend had actually vocalized. Then he felt the dim edges of the psychic blast that Droagn *projected* against the creatures. They had marvelously carnivorous teeth, but they weren't intelligent enough to be affected by this mental attack.

Rikard finally became aware that he was in personal danger. He drew his gun and gripped it firmly so that he closed the connection between it and the circuitry implanted in his hand, arm, and brain. But the effect of the time dilation thus produced, combined with the Tathas effect, was bizarre, dreamlike, nightmarish. The world around him seemed to slow down by a factor of ten, which satisfied the Tathas need to slow, but in fact his perceptions were speeded up by that amount, which was contrary, and was incredibly uncomfortable, a crinkly rushing feeling along the inside of the back of his head and neck going both up and down at the same time.

He was able to see the real world more clearly now, however. There was nothing superimposed in the darkness, and yet because he was moving faster the world had actually become darker, a phenomenon that must have occurred every time he used his gun though he had never noticed it before, and it made his skin feel remote and fuzzy.

The monsters were closing dangerously, and he shot two of them even though he was severely distracted. As he took aim at a third, Grayshard tried his Vaashka attack, a combination of psychic and chemical *projection*. Rikard felt an odd kind of tickling not at all like what he would feel without the Tathas interference, but it was enough to make him miss his shot. He was dumbfounded. He had never missed before when he was wired into his built-in range finder. He fired again, and missed again.

He did notice that the creatures, though habituated to the Tathas effect, were not completely impervious to Grayshard's form of attack and that they were all as distracted as he. He realized that under the circumstances, he was really not all that accelerated, and managed to focus his attention at last and dropped two more of the creatures with his last two shots. He fumbled to reload, and then the predators turned and ran away. Rikard pulled himself together, and felt Droagn's *projection* that there was a retreat of animal consciousness in a broad area around them.

Still dazed, they crossed the rubble field toward the stumps of the cones. To Rikard it seemed as if he were going through a place that was singularly amorphous and asymmetric, superimposed on the reality of the stone-littered ground with the white cones just ahead. There were shapes within this overlying darkness, and zones. Everything was darkly metallic, with an iridescent sheen that was sinisterly comforting. Rikard tried to warn his companions about it, but it took too much effort to speak, and it made him aware that he had companions when what he wanted was to be alone. He tried to stay away from the fragments of surface material, but that didn't help. The deposits of balktapline, reserpine, and anthrace, all the metamorphosed remains of Tathas architectural materials, must have been larger and stronger than the government assay had estimated, if it could have this much affect from underground.

Grayshard was shielded by his own clothes, but he too was subject to the material. "I can't believe it," he said, and in Rikard's ears his voice sounded like dull metal squeaking over smooth stone. "What must they have been like, to have left this madness behind them?"

"They were totally insane," Rikard grated. His voice felt like sand under a hard-soled shoe. He described what he felt as they stumbled onward.

"I don't feel that at all," Grayshard said. "It's more like I'm large and diffuse. It's a subtle thing, or I would say so, except that it's almost overwhelming. How can it be both at the same time?"

Rikard couldn't bring himself to respond. He hated the sound of Grayshard's voice, and his nearness, though he was thirty meters away.

"There's one thing," Grayshard said. "I seem to be comforted by the tightness of my disguise. It makes me think that the Tathas, before they disappeared from here, did not spend much time on the surface, but interpenetrated the ground, flowed through the soil, and did not move around in open spaces unless they had to."

˜What the hell are you talking about,˜ Droagn *projected*. His communication felt to Rikard like something unpleasantly slick brushing across the top of his mind.

"What do you feel?" Rikard grated, crunched, rasped.

˜Darkness. Everything is artificial. I want to lie still all alone.˜

"That's like me," Rikard said. "What else?"

˜Why?˜

"It will help you get across this place. Don't fight it, go with it as much as you can. I've been under this influence before. What do you see?"

ˉI don't actually see them, but there are monoliths out there, and domes of stones, and wire trees. But the material all seems slightly translucent, and there are, ah, sparks inside, and the colors are all dark and unfamiliar.ˉ

"Where do you get that?" Grayshard demanded. "It's nothing like that at all."

"We get it," Rikard said, "from being exothermic animal-protein beings, unlike yourself."

He went on at length, and Grayshard responded, and Droagn did too, and so they talked themselves across the rubble to the base of the nearest cone stub. And there the Tathas effect was somewhat diminished, as if the white detritus that had fallen from the slopes above were some kind of shield.

ˉThat feels better,ˉ Droagn said. He paused a moment, his face twisted with effort. ˉI don't feel any life at all in this area.ˉ

The cone was not very tall, and its top, and the top of the other cone they could see from there, had been eroded away, which was what had produced the marblelike detritus covering the ground.

"What I want to know," Rikard said, "is why anybody would build here in the first place. The Tathas stuff has been underground since before this world produced its own life. It has to affect anybody who comes near."

"Maybe," Grayshard said, "our cyclopeans were naturally protected by their own building material."

"Could be, but what about the people who built whatever was in that ring of rubble out there?"

ˉWho knows what they were like?ˉ Droagn said. ˉAnd I don't really care.ˉ

They left the floater carts, four of which they'd miraculously managed to keep hold of during the crossing, and started up the white marble slope. The hallucinations continued, though with somewhat diminished impact, and became more precise and lucid though less intrusive as they went. The sense of oppression diminished, but now Rikard could actually see the dark empty plain on which the cones stood, see the dark and greasy sky overhead, with dim auroras to the north and south.

They got to the flat top of the stub without finding a way in. The Tathas effects were further diminished as they moved away from the outer edge of the cone top, so that the overcast sky became visible, the light was no longer painful, just unpleasant, and they could now bear each other's company. But the rubble fallen from the destroyed upper levels had blocked off any entrances that might have been exposed.

Beyond this stub they could see now that there were four other cone stubs, of varying heights. But as they looked around, and regained some control of their thoughts, they finally came to the conclusion that they were standing either on the base of a small cone, or were near the top of a large cone that had been deeply buried. The top of the stub was not that big around, but the other stubs were quite a way off, and if the remains on Dannon's Keep were any example, the cone bases should have been quite close together, so the latter explanation seemed more likely. If that were true, they might yet be in luck.

Where they stood, at the center of the stub top, the cone looked like slightly porous rock with striations of sedimentary layering. True marble decomposes into powder and blows or washes away, but this stuff, whatever it was originally, turned into marble, or what looked like it, though even it had broken down a lot over the millennia.

Though the surface was covered with rubble, they knew what to look for and could see where chambers and passages had been exposed and filled in. It looked like the effects of volcanic gases in lava, or water erosion through limestone, which was more accurate. Droagn, with his Prime, could not feel through the depth of rubble to empty chambers below. If they hadn't known better, they wouldn't look any further here. There was no hint that this place was in the least artificial. And there was no way to go in.

Having been shielded from the Tathas effect for a while, it was doubly unpleasant when they had to go back down to where they had left the two small floater carts. But that was what they had to do, if they were going to try to find a way in through the side wall. At least this close to the cone the detritus on the ground kept the hallucinations from being overwhelming.

They looked for signs that the outer shell had broken off, and found irregularities, now grossly weathered, that indicated that that had indeed happened. One hollow looked like it might have been a chamber long exposed to the elements, though there were no signs of the colored markings they had seen in the cone on Dannon's Keep. Still, from what they remembered of that place, they guessed as to where a door might be, took excavation tools from their floater carts, and started to work.

The material was brittle, and it wasn't long before they broke through. It was not a doorway, but they now had access to an inner corridor. They gathered up their equipment and went in.

The Tathas effect was much diminished as they went around the outer shell of the cone, so that they were comforted by the closeness of the walls, were not discomfited if they used only minimum lights, and could bear to be within a meter or so of each other. There was none of the dark landscape sensation.

The corridor they were in looked much like the outer shell of the cone on Dannon's Keep, with only the faintest trace of colored markings. As far as they could tell they were indeed high rather than low. They looked for a way down but didn't immediately find one. When they came to the third door leading inward they opened it and as they passed through the Tathas effects disappeared completely.

From then on their descent was much the same as it had

been on Dannon's Keep, except that, this cone being better preserved, the walls were more luminous, the color codings more easily seen—and there were more artifacts. The objects were incomprehensible, such as the metal remains of a strange vehicle, a low platform with two large wheels, one on either side, and smaller wheels on gimbals, one each at front and back, with a rusted pile that might have once been an engine, and trails of rust where a drive chain might have been. Or a flat box with several arching rows of push buttons, mostly white but some red or black or green and what looked like grills at the back. Or an arching metal rod rising from a hexagonal base of black to an inverted cone of white in the apex of which was some kind of electrical connection. Mostly they left the things alone.

They kept on, going deeper and ever more inward, until at last they found a section of passage that seemed more like the museum quality surface, semitranslucent and almost damp, and found another door inward. But this one was marked with a diagonal yellow smear behind the two shades of blue and one of thin black.

"Now this is intriguing," Rikard said. "Let's go in here."

"Sounds good to me," Grayshard said, and Droagn pulled out a long prybar from one of the carts.

He put the working end against the seam, pushed, chipped out tiny pieces of the shell-like material, levered back, and the door popped open. And beyond it were flashing lights and sirens.

3

Droagn jerked back and dropped the prybar, barely missing Grayshard. And if Rikard's camera hadn't been helmeted to his head, it would surely have fallen.

They all drew their guns, though Rikard managed to keep them out of the camera's view, but after a moment, as nothing else happened and the slanting corridor beyond the doorway remained empty, they put away their weapons and went through.

Grayshard found a colored patch adjacent to the doorjamb and stroked it with his gloved hand. The siren suddenly cut off, and the lights in the ceiling stopped flashing and now burned steadily, slightly violet.

˜They must have had a fantastic power system,˜ Droagn said. He lifted himself up on his coils till he could just touch the light in the ceiling. ˜No batteries I know of could last as long as this place has been abandoned.˜

"And even if they could," Grayshard said, "think about the switch I just triggered. No moving parts. And still it functions, after two million years."

"I can't understand," Rikard said, "how people who could produce something like this place could have just been forgotten."

˜Whoever they were, they were protégés of the Lambeza. And yet I've never heard anything about them, not even hints.˜

"Nor has anybody else," Rikard said. "I've run index checks and subject searches wherever I could, looking for just this kind of thing."

"It's the power supplies that intrigue me," Grayshard said. "How many instances of truly superior lost technology do you run across?"

"Not that many," Rikard agreed. "And what we do find is usually inapplicable to us. Like Droagn's Prime. But if we can learn how these people made such long-lasting switches and power supplies, the whole Federation will benefit."

"Exactly my point," Grayshard said. "And if I were to take such knowledge back to my people, I'd be not only rich but forgiven."

They descended the corridor until it teed into a circumferential one, and then they proceeded downward and inward, through chambers now better preserved, and still lit, though here and there the lamps had failed. Rikard recorded everything as they passed from room to hallway, past alcove and side chamber, but they didn't pause to examine the numerous items still remaining, even though here and there were some objects made of more perishable materials. They only paused when they came to those doors marked with the yellow smear, and then only to see if they could learn how to disable the alarms before opening them. They did not.

They went down, and in, until at last they reached the core. There they found and entered the museum, in much the way they had before. The only difference was that the museum was lit this time, and was quite a bit larger.

And more of the museum's collection was preserved. They proceeded slowly down a radius toward the center, trying to see everything at once. Rikard recorded as much as he could, with both close-ups and telephoto shots.

"Let's go around this way," Droagn suggested. He pointed to the far side of the chamber as he started along one of the circumferential aisles. All the smaller things were over there. Rikard and Grayshard followed.

As they went they passed through an area where there were fragmentary remains of things made of wood, leather, fabric, and other organic materials. Some of these were just dust, while others were fragile husks, and a few others were nearly solid enough to touch. But none of them was intact enough to identify, even had they known the cyclopean psychology.

When they got to the area where all the small items stood, each on its own base, they started back down a radius toward the center. But this time they paused to each take a number of items—tiny sculptures, or maybe game pieces, representing cyclopeans and other beings, including once an Ahmear; small cylindrical items that might be pens or pencils except that there were no writing points and some of them had dials or sliders that no longer functioned; once a collection of seven rings, each of a slightly different size, all made of gold or something similar, and with three gems in each inset equilaterally in the band that was cast or carved in a variety of abstract shapes; and another time what might have been a book except that the pages were folded funny and made of a kind of plastic/metallic foil with embossed dots.

They took as many of these as they could easily secrete about their persons, though they fully intended to get as much of the other stuff as they could load on their four empty carriers when they came back.

The center of the museum was plain and unadorned, a slightly elevated circular area about five meters in diameter with no stands, no objects, no decorations in the floor. Nor were there any signs of a portal in the floor, or hookups for equipment, or anything at all. It was just a bare circular stage. And yet, it was elevated.

Any city of this size, regardless of the nature of the species that built it, would have to have central communications and information systems, especially if the species was technologically advanced enough to be starfaring, which the cyclopeans must have been. It was Rikard's contention, supported by Grayshard and Droagn, that if the nexus of this system was not at the museum, then at least an important terminal should be. But there was nothing there.

They went back up another radius to the outer wall and examined the area beside each of the radial portals. But they found no clues. Then they went out into the circumferential passage surrounding, looking for some other inward access, but though they found a few closets, there were no signs of a communication center, studio, or remote station.

They returned to the museum, and proceeded slowly toward the center again, where they were all sure the com center should be. After all, the museum was at the center of the cone, which was a series of concentric shells, and the heart of the communications and data storage should be there too. As they went down the aisle between the ancient relics on their pedestals, Droagn focused all his attention on his Prime, and got a distinct though dim impression of hollows both above and below, but not a single clue as to how to get to them.

Rikard stood in the center of the low dais in the middle of the museum and tried, in his own way, to tune in on this place, to empathize with it. He looked around, saw his companions, looked up at the ceiling, at the lights. The only thing that struck him was that there were no lights directly overhead, though there were spotlights that especially illuminated the dais. And that cast the ceiling directly overhead into deep shadow.

Where small details, such as the seam of a trapdoor, might easily be hidden. "Come here," he said to Droagn. "Stand right in the middle here, or whatever it is you do, and reach Grayshard up as high as you can."

Droagn did as he was bid, coiling his tail onto a strong base and lifting himself up with Grayshard in his upper arms. It was not easy to lift his own weight on only the very end of his tail, but he and Grayshard knew exactly what was expected. When Droagn was sure he had his balance, he lifted Grayshard up in his arms as high as he could reach. He was still three meters short of the ceiling. Grayshard took off one glove and stretched a bundle of red-tipped tendrils up, thinning as he reached, until only a strand of five or six tendrils at last touched the ceiling. It feathered across the dark surface a moment.

"Got it," he said at last. "Just a seam." The strand bunched up, thickened as more fibers followed, then it split at the ceiling and the secondary strand drifted across and around.

From below, Rikard watched as Grayshard gripped the invisible gap with more and more tendrils, and then slowly pulled more and more of himself up, leaving his clothes and even his vocalizer behind, until, hanging from the ceiling, he was able to work some of the finest of his tendril ends into the jamb all the way around.

Then he must have found the latch, for he suddenly dropped down to Droagn, who slumped down to the dais. Grayshard grabbed his vocalizer and said, "Look out," but Rikard and Droagn could already see a circular section of the ceiling begin to drop toward them. They moved out of the way and watched as a circular column descended slowly from the ceiling and touched the dais with a soft thump. At that instant, arched openings appeared all around it at floor level.

There was nothing within the arches, it was just an empty chamber. Grayshard got dressed, and then cautiously they entered. The floor underneath them rose, as they had expected it would, without the need to push buttons or select a destination. A light came on above them as they rose into the hollow above the museum. The elevator stopped when its floor was level with that surrounding, and for a long moment they stood in the open cage, looking around them in all directions.

The place was lit from overhead, more dimly than in the elevator, but along the distant walls, and from stations scattered across the floor were many other lights of different colors. It took a moment for their vision to adjust to the low level of illumination.

They moved out into the semidark chamber. The lights not in the ceiling were set into consoles, some wall mounted, some standing alone. Some of these had glowing surfaces like viewscreens. Others made Rikard think of printers, because a white foil, with fading colors, protruded from slots at the top. There were what he assumed to be "keyboards," some of them associated with the "printers."

There were other forms of readout—dials with black ticks but no needles; vertical tubes with ticks and some with a kind of fluid at various levels; small domes that might have been lights. Some of the consoles had analogue input devices, such as a long lever that was free moving where it met the console, or a pentastar with each point flexible, a track ball, or a set of three elastic cords that stretched—or once used to. There were no chairs.

On a few of the consoles were loose objects, such as six-centimeter disks with colored smears; more of the penlike cylinders; a semicircular spring with pads at the ends and connected to a cable that jacked into the console, rather like earphones; pentastars attached to finger-thick rods covered with crumbling foam, which made Rikard think of microphones; and a lot of shallow dishes with a blackened green stain at the bottom.

There was ample room between the floor stations. There were dividers between sections of the wall consoles. And there was other furniture, crescent-shaped desks with drawers on the inside curve and a second level of drawers set back from the work surface; writing tables that were crescents without drawers but that were littered with papers with fading colored marks. But there were no pens or inks. On one side of the chamber was a communications console, with a viewscreen and a goose-necked mike that angled down instead of up.

And as they looked around they became aware of the soft sound of air-conditioning.

Physical, psychological, and cultural differences could not conceal the fact that this was the cone's central "computer" —or that it was still functional despite the gap of years. Rikard and his companions moved among the stations and consoles, but didn't touch anything. They didn't know what input devices might still be active, nor could they always tell the differences between input and output, or what might be just decoration.

They went around the upper chamber once, then returned

to the center near the elevator and looked the whole place over, especially the stations near the wall.

The communications area was typified by those things that they thought of as microphones, earphones or the equivalent, larger viewscreens, and in some cases speaker grills, and the lack of most of the other kinds of devices. Another section was densely arrayed with a variety of output devices, such as printers, extruders of knobbed string, a variety of viewscreens, and something like an exposed tape drive. And there was another section where there was nothing other than a simple post with a textured sphere on top freely rotating in a socket, probably the command console, or something like. But none of those was really what they were looking for.

But those three stations were arranged on three sides of a square in the circular chamber. On the fourth side . . .

The station in that position had no visible outputs at all. There were trackballs, scribble-screens, joysticks, and lots of empty jacks. Now jacks for electronic equipment was something Rikard could understand. It was the main input station, and feedback would be provided by . . . headsets or the equivalent. Grayshard went over to a console in the middle of the floor and brought back a mike and an earphone.

Rikard took them. "We could be wrong," he said. But each had a cord, which ended in a plug, which fit perfectly into one of the empty jacks on the console. "But we might as well give it a try."

Droagn had gone back to the elevator, and now returned with the large gray case with the black reinforcements and fastenings. He took it from its floater cart and set it down in front of the console. Rikard opened it and took out tools from one of the side drawers. He took apart the cyclopean plug, which consisted of a central conductor and a conducting ring, studied its internal connections for a moment, then built a new one from parts in the gray case, and plugged it in between the case and the console. The simple sensor attached to the cord showed that the power was on, and what the current and flow was. He took out a keyboard, made for large fingers, and jacked it in and handed it to Droagn.

Droagn fiddled with it for a while. A small screen on the case showed characters in his own alphabet, figures and graphs, occasional diagrams that were meaningless to Rikard and Grayshard. Then he stopped and sat back.

"I have no idea what's going on in there," he said. "But silicon and copper and glass are what they are after all, and binary is binary, and a data bank is not the same as a register, and an adder is not the same as a bus, and there seem to be no internal security devices, so I think we can get a dump."

Rikard ran a lead from his recording helmet to Droagn's console, and Droagn initiated the dump. The sheer size of the computer center indicated that the cyclopean's recording medium was relatively bulky compared to the wafers Rikard used in his helmet.

They had no idea of what they were getting. It could be a city directory, a cultural library, insurance records, long-distance phone bills, or important research information. It might take years, if not centuries, to make any sense of it all. Rikard would leave that to the scholars, he just wanted to bring it back to them.

After ten recording wafers were filled, Droagn said, "How many of those do you have left?"

"Twenty. Why?"

"It's not going to be enough. I think we got about five percent of what's here. It doesn't help that I can't tell data from programs."

"Then we'll have to do like we did at the Lambeza library. Can you indicate in some way what portion of the data space you've taken so far and what your samples are?"

"Sure, but I'll have to translate it later."

Droagn sampled widely through the remainder of the data space, but at last they were finished. Rikard disconnected and packed everything away in the big gray case.

They returned to the center, entered the elevator that,

after a moment, began to descend to the museum. When they got off the elevator it returned to the ceiling.

They loaded all their equipment, including Droagn's portable console, onto one of the carriers, and then, each of them taking one of the four empty floaters and leaving Droagn to pull the loaded one, they separated to go through the museum and each pick out what intrigued them most. That way they would be sure to get a broad range of objects.

But before they could begin to start collecting, several doors opened around the perimeter. Humans, armed and armored, entered, weapons at the ready. Then, at each door, a second person entered, this time a Federal police officer. And then, on one side, a party of people came in, civilians by appearances, who came down the radial to where Rikard and his companions were standing. As they neared, Rikard could begin to make out faces behind the protective helmets. The person in the lead of the party was Karyl Toerson. His precautions had gone for nothing.

The man who walked beside her seemed angry and resentful. "Are you Rikard Braeth?" he asked, using acoustical communication instead of radio.

"I am," Rikard said. He looked at Toerson, who was quietly exultant.

"My name is Igori Oflynn, Deputy Director of Mines, and it's my duty to inform you that you are trespassing on Federally regulated property, and you will have to leave immediately."

"Maybe there's some mistake," Rikard said. "It's my understanding that Federal regulations on this planet concern only the balktapline ore, and there is none at this site." As he spoke he carefully withdrew his folder of passes and documents from its pouch on his protective suit and offered it to Deputy Oflynn. It included his credentials as a duly licensed local historian, which technically should allow him to do research here, whatever other regulations might apply.

Oflynn opened the folder and looked at it unhappily. Toerson just grinned while her minions and the Federal

police watched on. Oflynn cursorily flipped through the
credentials without really paying them much attention and
said, "That's as may be but you crossed the balktapline
fields without a permit, and either went over or through the
barricade that surrounds this site, which constitutes illegal
entry, and this site is an archaeological site not a history
base, and your credentials don't cover that."

Toerson kept on smiling. Rikard began to feel that he
could truly hate her.

Rikard took off his recorder, tucked the helmet under his
arm, and said, "This site represents an entirely new race,
one hitherto unknown to the Federation. It is an important
discovery, and one that cannot be passed over lightly. I am
here on my own authority, it is true, but I have association
with several universities that are very interested in seeing
my recordings of this place."

"I'm sure you do," Oflynn said. "What have you recorded
so far?"

"Hardly anything, really," Rikard said. Grayshard and
Droagn just stayed still and silent behind him. "We haven't
been here long enough." He flipped a monitor down out of
the side of his helmet, held it so Oflynn could see it, and
started to play back their passage through the upper levels.
"As you can see, we entered," he ran fast forward to when
they found the first of the artifacts in the upper and outer
layers, "came in and down in as direct a route as we could
find," fast forwarded again to scenes of them looking at
later samples, "and then came in here." He showed them
entering the museum, and played the disk at real time as
they first checked it out.

"That's enough," Oflynn said, just before the recording
got to where Rikard and his companions had begun to take
some of the smaller items. Rikard did not express the sigh
he felt as he turned off the playback and closed up the little
monitor.

Oflynn made a gesture, and the police came down the
radials. Toerson's minions stayed at the doorways. The

police went through the equipment on the loaded carrier, but apparently found nothing they were concerned with.

"Okay then," Oflynn said, "but you'll have to leave now, and take nothing with you but what's on that carrier. Technically I could charge you with trespass, and damaging indigenous artifacts—"

"What did I damage?" Rikard demanded.

"You broke the outer shell of this structure, and several doors coming in. But Msr. Toerson does not wish to press charges."

Toerson smiled.

"And what the hell does she have to do with it?" Rikard demanded.

Karyl Toerson continued to smile as she brought out her own folder of credentials, and took from them papers that she handed to Rikard. As she did so Oflynn glared angrily at her. So it was she, not Rikard, who had aroused his resentment.

"They're all perfectly legal," he grated, and Toerson kept on smiling.

Rikard looked at the documents with a sinking feeling. Though they didn't say so explicitly, they gave her permission to salvage here, and effectively gave her the right to loot the whole cone.

He looked up from the papers and around at the wealth of art objects present. He wanted to protest, but if he did, he would be searched, and the few things he had taken would be found.

"I'm sorry," Oflynn said. The police stood at attention. It was time for Rikard and his companions to depart.

Pulling their three empty floater carts behind them, and the one full of only their own equipment, they left the chamber and started their way back up to the surface of the cone. They did not speak as they retraced their steps. Indeed, Rikard could not have spoken had anyone addressed him. His thoughts were black and his anger and frustration a knotted pain in the back of his head and the center of his chest. His only consolation was that he was sure that Karyl Toerson would not be bright enough to find the computer.

Tarantor

Of seven planets in the Tarantor system, six were developed to some degree. The only world without sentient inhabitants was Vista, the outermost ice world, which, besides being permanently frozen, had no resources not more easily obtainable elsewhere.

The whole system was densely populated: Earth-like Tarantor, desert Mishka, hothouse Merteth, and the moons of Galagos and Vermain, the gas giants. Even Trilipi, hot and close to the sun, had domes and an underground system.

Unlike most planetary systems in the Federation, Tarantor was not dominated by a single species, but was shared almost equally by three. Experiments of bi- and multispecies worlds had been conducted in the past, as on Kohltri, Venn, Seber Tsrebe, and Lothar, and none of them had worked. No such experiment had been tried on Tarantor; it had just happened.

There were Humans, of course, as there were almost everywhere, except on those worlds that were the homes of nonspacefaring peoples. They represented about a third of the population, and were a variety of subspecies or races. They dominated on Tarantor itself and on Merteth, and existed in lesser numbers on the other four developed worlds.

The second species of importance were the Senola, whose home world was Natimarie, but who extended throughout much of the Federation as well. They were a centauroid people, with slender but deep-chested lower bodies and narrow upper torsos. Their four legs were long and slender, though they stood no taller than an average Human. Their faces were narrow and long, with small batlike ears and very large purple, almost red eyes. Their arms were long enough to reach the ground when they stood, and their feet were doubly cloven hooves. Their skins were ivory-colored, shading to ocher, hairless except for full manes of dark, rich brown hair. They dominated Mishka and the moons of Galagos, and were second on Merteth, and in fewer numbers elsewhere.

The third species was the Grelsh. These were pseudo-humanoid arthropoids whose exoskeletons were reduced to external "bones." Otherwise they had a hard "skin" of a semiglossy light brown. They had four legs in pairs set very closely together, and were functionally bipedal. They had only two arms but each had an extra joint. Their hands were composed of two central thumbs and two pairs of opposing fingers. Their faces were round and flat, with a mouth like that of a grasshopper, four small eyes, and no feelers or visible ears. They dominated where the Humans and the Senola didn't, though they shared the other worlds with them too.

Thus, when Rikard, Endark Droagn, and Grayshard arrived at the jumpslot station, they were met by these three equally important species, who held posts in all positions and levels. Other species were definitely in the minority, and yet nobody seemed to take any special notice of either Grayshard or Droagn, as they passed through first immigration.

Rikard had been hoping to take his own ship to Tarantor

itself, but this was not permitted. He put his ship in dock, gave the crew leave, and with his companions and equipment boarded the shuttle. This was a huge, free-form vessel, almost like a space-going city. The reason for this became apparent when, an hour or so after leaving the jumpslot station, Rikard learned that the trip would take two standard days. He tried not to be impatient with the delay.

But at last they parked at the main orbital station—there were three others of nearly equal size—and then had to go through an immigration inspection again.

They did not have Gawin's protection, as they had on Malvrone, and this time their luggage was examined. They were politely but firmly informed that a number of the items they had with them would be put into safekeeping for them pending their departure. As this was not a place where threats, connections, or bribery could accomplish anything more than further hassle and possibly criminal prosecution, Rikard had to put up with it. Most of the items—tools of various sorts, surveillance equipment, and the weapons—he didn't mind doing without. He did feel rather naked without his megatron, leathers, and meshmail armor, but since they could have been confiscated instead of just locked away, he felt it wise not to argue.

And one other thing surprised him. They also took the dragongem he wore on a chain around his neck, and the bauble he carried in his pocket. The agent recognized them at once, and knew very well how to handle them without falling under their hypnotic spell. A license, he explained, was needed to import such items, and a heavy duty was exacted, and since these were purportedly personal jewelry, it would be easier just to leave them here until Rikard's departure. Once again, Rikard thought it better not to argue.

From the station they took a drop-shuttle to the surface. It was a relatively small craft, carrying only three thousand passengers. Their destination was the Alanorn sector of the city that covered that whole quarter of the continent, where megatowers crowded the shore of a huge lake. The shuttle came down silently on gravity floats, and landed at a subport nestled among the three-kilometer tall towers.

Once again they had to pass an inspection, but this one was to ensure that they had sufficient credit to cover their visit. Rikard, fortunately, had a number of open accounts on a number of planets—plus, of course, some private, closed, or secret accounts on many more—and thus was given an unrestricted pass. Others with fewer resources or wealth were given limited tickets, after which time they either had to depart or initiate immigration proceedings, which latter were difficult unless you had something the sector, the city, or the planet wanted. One or two people were turned back at the port, as Droagn and Grayshard would have been had not Rikard guaranteed their credit for the duration of the visit.

They went by aircar to the hotel that the Tarantor Tourist Bureau recommended to them, in light of Droagn's and Grayshard's special needs. This proved to be not a separate building, but merely one section of one wing of one of the taller towers—nearly five kilometers high—near the center of the Alanorn sector, and right on the edge of the lake. The aircar deposited them and their luggage on a balcony halfway up, where they were taken charge of by the hotel staff, mostly mechanicals under a Senola supervisor.

Neither Grayshard nor Droagn caused any stir. The hotel was very modern, rather overequipped with electromechanicals but with a good number of live staff of all three major species, and their quarters were large and spacious and well stocked. Rikard found it rather impersonal and depressing. Droagn was glad for the room to move and the lack of attention. Grayshard didn't care.

There was nothing Rikard could do to guarantee the security of his quarters this time, but given the procedure he'd just gone through, and considering there was nothing he could do about it anyway, he had to trust that in fact he was not being scanned, recorded, or otherwise spied on. As soon as the three of them were established, and had a good night's rest, Rikard looked up Nevile Beneking in the sector directory. He was there, in bold face, with a cross-reference to his entry in the classified directory. Rikard called up that screen, and found that the art dealer had a discreet ad that took up the whole screen, simply name, profession, comcon number and address, and office hours. Rikard punched the call button.

The screen blinked. For a moment a simple cartouche bearing only the name Nevile Beneking appeared on the screen, and then a Human face. Rikard wondered if, had he been a Senola or a Grelsh, he would have been greeted by one of his own species.

"May I help you?" the young man said. His inflection was perfect, helpful yet not to be trifled with.

"My name is Rikard Braeth. I'd like to make an appointment with Msr. Beneking."

"Certainly, Msr. Braeth. Msr. Beneking is on Tarantor at this time and is expecting you. When would be most convenient?"

"How about right now?"

The young man smiled. *"We will be awaiting your arrival,"* he said. Then his image was replaced by the cartouche for a moment, then the screen went blank.

They took a small case, containing the few things they'd liberated from the cyclopean museum, and the disks from Rikard's recording helmet, with them to "Beneking's" offices, which were in another tower, some ten kilometers from their hotel. Transportation was by underground tube, by private car. The trip took five minutes. Then it was another three minutes by elevator.

Nevile Beneking, as the business was known, occupied the entire floor at the two-and-a-half-kilometer level, except for the outlying wings, which were given over to public services of various sorts. The reception area, off the elevator, was spacious but simple, with comfortable couches, low tables, a self-service bar in one corner, and a trio of live receptionists at a broad desk. As Rikard and his companions approached, the Grelsh and Senola subtly turned away so that he was, without any effort, directed to the Human, a handsome woman of middle age, say one hundred ten or so.

"Msr. Braeth," she said. "Msr. Droagn. Msr. Grayshard." She smiled as she stood and came around the desk. "Please come with me." She gestured to a doorway behind and to one side of the desk.

They went through into a short, wide corridor, with a door on either side and a double door at the far end. This the receptionist opened by hand when they got to it and waved them through.

The office on the other side was cozy by the standards Rikard had observed so far since coming to Tarantor, no more than twenty by twenty meters. There was a large black desk in front of another door, two comfortable chairs in front of it, a couch facing it behind the chairs, and lots of art on the walls, sculpture on pedestals, and his uncle Gawin just rising to meet them.

"Rikard," Gawin said as he came around the desk. "How are you?" His smile was warm and genuine. He shook hands with all three of them. "Please make yourselves comfortable." He gestured to the chairs, and did something at the arm of the couch so that it folded out into the kind of cushion Droagn preferred.

They sat. He offered refreshments, which they accepted. "So how was your trip?" he asked them as a Senola came in, pushing a small cart.

"It takes a hell of a long time to get here from your jumpslot station," Rikard said. The Senola served Rikard a whisky on the rocks, Grayshard some kind of ugly ferment in a closed container, and Droagn a huge mug of what looked like fresh-squeezed juice.

"It does that," Gawin said, "but I mean, how was Tsikashka?"

Rikard took a sip of his drink, put down the glass, and lifted his case up to his lap. He opened it and turned it around so Gawin could see inside. "This is all we were able to bring back."

Gawin looked at the few items without touching them, and the good humor faded from his face. He looked back up at Rikard. "What went wrong?"

"Karyl Toerson was there, and she had the locals and the Feds on her side."

Gawin stared at Rikard for a moment. "But how could that be?"

"I don't know, but there it is and the Federal agent she had doing her work for her didn't seem to like it, but I guess he didn't have any choice. Just what kind of influence does she wield, anyway?"

"Apparently a lot more than I had thought," Gawin said. "And considering that I thought she was dead just a short while ago, it doesn't bode well for any of us. And what's worse, if what you have there in the case is all you were able to get away with, then it's all we're likely to see. Toerson has been selling to the black market, to people who keep their stuff to themselves. And before I lost track of her she had a reputation of taking only the best and destroying the rest to improve the value of what she took. I don't think she's likely to change that now."

"What do you mean," Rikard demanded, "'destroying the rest'?"

"Just what I said. She'll pick out about ten percent of whatever is most likely to sell for the best prices, not necessarily the best art or the most important, and then she'll smash, or burn, or otherwise ruin everything else. If you have ten Van Eyck's at a million apiece, that's one thing. If there's only one, it's worth more than ten million, and is a lot easier to carry around."

"My God, you don't mean it!"

"I do."

"But there was an awful lot of stuff down there."

"You're using the correct tense, I'm afraid. I wish there were something we could do about it, but as far as I know there isn't."

"You seem to know a lot about her," Grayshard said.

"What I know," Gawin said reluctantly, "was from a long time ago. I haven't seen her for maybe forty years."

Rikard took a longer pull at his drink. "So what about this stuff?"

"The people I dealt with before," Gawin said, "are eager for more, and they've been doing some research on their own as to its origins, although I haven't heard that they've uncovered anything."

"Well, get them over to Tsikashka as soon as possible. Maybe they can do something before Toerson loots the place."

"I will give instructions to that effect today."

"It is too much of a coincidence," Grayshard said, "for Toerson to have come on us three times by chance. Maybe you ought to tell us what you know about her."

"Perhaps you're right," Gawin said, but he was reluctant to speak. Rikard closed up the case and put it down on the floor beside his chair. Gawin looked at it a moment, and then said, "How about we have some lunch?"

"That sounds like an excellent idea," Rikard said. This was, he knew, just his uncle's way of buying time to think about what he was going to say. Droagn and Grayshard agreed, and they all left their seats.

Gawin led them through the door behind his desk into a slightly smaller antechamber, which like the office was filled with paintings, sculptures, and constructs, with just enough room for another smaller desk, three side chairs, a sofa, and two low tables. There were also comcon screens on the walls, and one of them showed the office they had just left.

Gawin took them through a side door to a broad hall, with more art of all forms alternating with decorative furniture of all kinds. At the far end a figure appeared, a man formally dressed, who simply bowed when they neared, and who led them through stained-glass doors into a roomy dining room meant for only four or five people. Here, too, art was everywhere, including the table settings.

They sat, Droagn at the place with the low cushions, and the servant offered Gawin a menu, much to Rikard's surprise. Gawin studied it for a moment, murmured something that Rikard couldn't hear, and handed it back to the servant, who bowed and left.

"What was that all about?" Rikard asked.

"What? The menu? Just a list of what was best and freshest today. I took the liberty of ordering," he said to all three of his guests.

"You've not disappointed me before," Droagn said.

Grayshard said nothing.

Gawin turned to one side in his chair, and a Grelsh servant came from behind a decorative screen pushing an elaborate cart. Gawin offered his guests refreshments, which they accepted. The servant prepared the drinks, served them, then departed, leaving the cart.

"May I offer a toast." Gawin raised his glass. "To Rikard."

Rikard was surprised, but was saved any further embarrassment by the arrival of the meal, which was served by two Senola. When the servants left, Rikard said gently, "Tell me about it, Uncle Gawin."

"You'll be the first people I've shared this with since it happened," Gawin said. "I hope you'll understand why I've kept it to myself for so long.

"It happened back when I was in my early twenties, when my grandfather was still Lord Malvrone and my father was just the oldest son. Grandfather thought my father ought to have something to do, so he put him in charge of exploiting a planet. That was Murchison, which is doing pretty well now I understand. Bevry, Braice, and Sigra stayed with Mother on Malvrone, but I went along for the experience—after all, I was the odd one and a troublemaker and this way Father thought I could work things out of my system without embarrassing the family.

"Father was ostensibly in charge of the operation, but a professional exploiter named Howvar Toerson was really in charge, and he had his daughter Karyl with him. I think her mother was dead. One of Toerson's primary agents was a young man named Arin Braeth.''

"My father."

''Yes, Rikard. He was far too capable for his years. He was in charge of everything that Howvar didn't take charge of himself, and he had a way about him that made people want to do what he asked them to.

''The three of us, Karyl and Arin and I, quickly came to know each other, and we preferred each other's company, though aside from age we had little in common. I quickly learned that I didn't have the courage or genius of your father, Rikard, nor the recklessness nor obsessive drive of Karyl Toerson.

''Arin had his professional responsibilities, I was kept at home a lot in spite of my being there for 'experience,' and Karyl was frequently just gone, God knows where, out in the wilderness. But we spent time together whenever we could, and we'd go off together on adventures. I collected stuff, Arin explored, and Karyl did whatever she wanted and caused mischief and stole.

''One time we found something, I won't tell you what it was, but we decided to keep it for ourselves. We had to be sneaky about it, because it was on site and legally part of the resources we were developing. So while Arin and I removed it from the matrix, Karyl kept guard, and then we all took it away.

''But later at the site a workman and guard were found dead, and the fact of the theft was obvious. Your father and I knew Karyl had killed the two men, but we didn't say anything, in order to protect her, and ourselves.

''But since the site was directly under Arin's supervision, and the crime went unsolved, it became obvious that he was covering up. And so he was shipped out. I was known to be a frequent associate of his, and was confined to the family camp. But somehow Karyl got off scot-free.

''That didn't seem right to me. She'd committed the

murders, and Arin and I had gotten punished. As well as I could, I checked into things, and that was when I discovered that Karyl was my father's secret mistress. And that explained a lot, you'd better believe. But like before, I kept quiet about it, but I decided to give up adventuring altogether, and when I got back home I did my best to fly straight. But I was always afraid Father would find out that I knew about him and Karyl. And if he was the kind of person to let her get off with murdering two people, then what might he do to protect his secret? I didn't want to find out.

"Karyl went her own way after that, and got into trouble more than once, and appeared on Malvrone more than once, and then disappeared altogether. I suspected that Karyl and my father resumed their relationship on her visits to Malvrone, and perhaps on his visits elsewhere, but I never again found any proof.

"Arin was blackballed from exploiting, though nothing was ever proved, and dropped out of sight for a while, then showed up again as a Gesta, and established his reputation, and collected stories about his exploits, most of which he could never have accomplished.

"After a while I began to establish my art dealership networks, both the legitimate one and the black market, and came to make the acquaintance of several Gestae, including, to my surprise, Arin one time. We met a few times after that, always on the best of terms, always with utmost discretion.

"Then, when Sigra was kidnapped, and nothing Father could do seemed to do any good, I suggested that Arin Braeth might be of help.

"At first Father refused, but when it became desperate he yielded, and I got hold of your father, and that's how that happened.

"I visited your folks on Pelgrane whenever I could after they got married and Father kicked Sigra out. Arin didn't hold it against Father that he reneged on his deal to pay for

Sigra's rescue, though he did for disinheriting her—for her sake, not his—but I always felt guilty about that.

"And that's how I know Karyl Toerson."

By this time they had finished their meal, and for a moment sat in silence. Without a signal that Rikard could detect, the Grelsh servant came in, served them a desert and after-dinner drink from the cart that this time he—she?—took away.

"I suspect," Gawin said to Rikard, "that part of the reason my father is so down on you and your father is because Arin knew about the infidelity with Karyl, as I did, and Father is protecting a guilty conscience."

"That's a hell of a story," Rikard said.

When he'd known his father, he'd just been that, a father, with enough money so he didn't have to work. It had only been long after he'd disappeared that Rikard had discovered that Arin Braeth had once been known as the most daring Gesta in the Federation. Neither his father nor his mother had talked about the past much, and he was beginning to realize now that there was indeed a past, and a lot of it. "And what you tell me about Karyl Toerson," he went on, "doesn't make me any happier about the cyclopeans and their ruins."

"I think you can just scratch that set of ruins off completely," Gawin said. "She was the one who messed up the old Human site on Venerian, from the days when we were just developing starflight."

Rikard could only stare at him in shocked amazement.

"And she destroyed the Belshpaer ruins on Turbidos," Gawin went on, "and looted the temple of Ikarion on Sigmund. That was all before she dropped out of sight, of course, but I've often wondered how many other places, which were found desolate, were her doing, especially if one or two especially good pieces did get into the black market. If she's got her hooks into the cyclopeans, and if she's getting any help from my father, then we don't have much time to spare. If there's another site out there somewhere, we'll have to get to it before she finishes with this one, and make sure she can't do anything to it."

"But aren't we wasting our time?" Grayshard said.

"No," Gawin said even as he rose from the table. "I've been running preliminary searches since I got here twelve days ago. My data banks here are more extensive than at Malvrone, and the computer is more powerful, and the connections are more extensive. Let me show you."

He led them out another way through a series of large rooms, each beautifully furnished and filled with art of all forms. His computer center, on the other hand, was a very simple place, with very little art. There was just the one major console, built into the wall, with a rather large chair in front of it, two chairs and a heap of cushions for Droagn around a low table with repeating screens so they all could see what Gawin might call up, and a self-service bar in the corner.

"I'm sorry," Gawin apologized. "In spite of having a system like this I'm really not an expert at either computers, or historical research, and so I don't feel that I've been able to do much until now. I'm hoping that your expertise, Rikard, and your computer knowledge, Droagn, and your differing perspective, Grayshard, will come in handy."

"Maybe you'd like to look at these," Rikard said, and showed him the disks from the cyclopean computer.

"You're damn straight I would," Gawin said.

He took the disks from Rikard, and first made a copy of all thirty on his system's internal memory, then gave Rikard back the originals. Then, with Droagn looking over his shoulder, he tried to access the data, which proved completely unintelligible. "Oh, well," he said, "I guess you've got to start somewhere."

They worked on the problem of the cyclopean data during the next two and a half days. At first Droagn just offered advice on how to probe the files, but he quickly took over the task, while Gawin told him what his software could do and how.

They tried out a variety of analyzers on several parts of the data simultaneously, looking for graphics, tables, text. Because the cyclopean language was color dependent, and they had no idea how it was encoded, they could not at first tell which was which, though the analyzers did identify several different types of data structures, which could have been almost anything.

Eventually, under Droagn's hands, the analyzers were able to find pictorial graphics, which were easily decoded, since they used a digital format practically identical to that used in the Federation to produce a two-dimensional on-screen representation. After all, a picture is a picture, and bits are bits, and once the ratio of vertical to horizontal pixels was found, the rest was easy.

Some of the pictures were meaningless, though Rikard and his companions were certain that they were shown as intended and were not just coincidental constructs. But some of the pictures were strictly representational, for whatever reason, and among other things, they showed cyclopeans against planetary and city backgrounds, with other species, specifically the centaurian Charvon, the arachnoid Ratash, both extinct; the extant miklewboid Kelrins; and the humanoid Thembeär, and the serpentine Ahmear, both now departed. Some of the "photos" were taken in what could only have been spaceships.

It was not unusual for a planet-bound species to disappear altogether, but starfaring species usually left some record, and aside from the cones, which had been uniformly misinterpreted, the cyclopeans had left nothing, and unless they had just departed this part of the galaxy, as the Ahmear had done, there was no explanation for that.

The pictures were not useful in themselves, but their computer structures gave the investigators some clues as to how to interpret other graphics, more diagrammatic in nature, and the computer then could begin to identify what parts of those images were captions, and from that figure out some of the nature of the more preponderant text files.

They did determine that the written language was probably ideographic and not alphabetic, which meant that it would take a very long time indeed to translate the text, certainly not within their lifetimes. The computers, however, seemed to indicate that there were several languages, and that would be of help to scholars more capable of dealing with that particular problem, by enabling them to make comparisons. But for the moment the computer restricted its searches for illustrated text, and thus they stumbled on a section of astronomical data.

Gawin's special knowledge of the Federation and the worlds within it came in handy here, and though the charts embedded in the cyclopean text were strange, the computer was able to make a comparison between current data and that of the cyclopeans. The stars had moved considerably since the cyclopean text was recorded, two million years ago according to the analysis. But the pictures in the Ahmear text could have been no older than one and a half million years, for the same reason. So it followed that the cyclopeans had been active for half a million years or so, a very long cultural lifetime indeed, taken on the average. But this only deepened the mystery—how could they have left so little when they had been around for so long?

Gawin's data included a chart of those planets with cyclopean ruins. The arrangement of those worlds, compensating and correcting for the passage of time, corresponded with other charts in the cyclopean text. And one world in that text was specially marked, with simple graphics that could easily be interpreted. It was the most important world in their star nation. The corresponding system was in the academic database. It was not far off, but a system with no regular transport. But that was all they needed to know.

They spent another day recovering from their labors, then Rikard made his good-byes, and he and his companions left for what he hoped was the cyclopean home world.

DRG-17.iv

The Federation is only one star nation in civilized space, though a moderately large and important one. Long established and well organized, almost all of its component stars and systems are identified and registered in one index or another.

Most stars have no planetary systems and so are only given catalogue numbers. Of those systems with planets, most are lifeless, and they too are merely numbered, though in a different catalogue. Those systems with life have names if they are visited by a starfaring nation or species, or are utilized in some way by them, but they and the others less frequented are more usually known by a special number, one component of which indicates the relative life level in the system. The remaining systems and worlds—a relatively small fraction of the whole, of course—are in fact catalogued by their names, which are meaningful to the inhabitants, the owners, or to history.

Some few worlds, however, have ceased to matter to the rest of the Federation, and their names are forgotten. They are entered into a very small catalogue, which mentions only briefly their forgotten history. Such was the world that was Rikard's destination. The system, identifiable also by relative star position, had, according to the catalogue, once held a civilization, and was now known only as DRG-17.iv. The code number indicated that it once had been inhabited at a certain level, had been destroyed to a certain extent by war, was now to a certain degree uninhabitable, was number seventeen of that kind, and was fourth from the sun. About the previous inhabitants, their civilization, the cause or origin of the war, or its outcome, nothing was mentioned. Indeed, nothing was known.

Though DRG-17.iv was not very far from Tarantor, Rikard did not go there directly. Instead he had his charter ship take him to Novo Boskva, one of the worlds in the Federation where ships were manufactured. There was no jumpslot station at DRG-17.iv, no shuttleport, and if he was going to investigate that world, he needed a ship that could navigate from the jumpslot to planetary orbit unassisted, and which carried shuttlecraft of its own. A Federation courier could have landed on the planet directly, one of the few starships able to do so, but it wasn't big enough to carry the equipment Rikard wanted—and besides, they weren't generally for sale.

Once on Novo Boskva, it took some twenty standard days to locate the kind of ship Rikard wanted, and the kind of pilot who would serve his needs.

Otherwise, their stay on Novo Boskva was uneventful, as was their trip to DRG-17.iv. Their pilot was a competent Human woman, named Anita Bardolino, who had some previous experience with Gestae, and so was not surprised or at a loss when Rikard expressed a desire to be cautious in their approach to the system. She flickered on past, then drove in from the far side toward an arbitrary jumpslot on inertials. It added three days to the trip, but during that time she was able to utilize the extensive system of probes and detectors with which the ship was equipped, and could determine with reasonable certainty that there was indeed no jumpslot station. Nor was there any other starship above the size of courier, or anything orbiting the planet in question other than its moon. And if Karyl Toerson were somewhere out of range, waiting for Rikard to come by, she was on the wrong side of the system, and too far away to detect him. Also, it was customary to end a flicker trip at the north pole side of a system, so the pilot came in from the south, between the fourth and fifth planetary orbits. From all they could tell, they were completely alone.

From there it was two more days' slow drive toward the planet itself. Rikard was in no hurry here, he wanted to give the long-range scanners time to survey the surface, which proved indeed to be lifeless, with no atmosphere remaining. Though once life had existed there, war had obliterated it. He also scanned the large moon, of something more than one percent the mass of the parent planet, and equally lifeless though, unlike the planet, that was almost certainly its nature, and not the consequences of the war.

Optimal orbit for an unassisted shuttle drop to the surface of the planet was well within the orbit of the moon, and their trajectory brought them past that large body, close enough so that optical imagers could observe its surface. It was tidally locked to the planet, of course, and its far side, though in darkness at this time, showed signs of some kind of artificial installation. The lunar surface facing the planet, as they came past, revealed not only the normal and expected cosmic scarring, but more recent marks, made within the last one and a half million years, perhaps, damage caused by the intensity of whatever had happened on the planet itself.

On an inhabited world, orbiting craft and stations are approximately equatorial, but the pilot put the ship into a polar orbit, so that they could examine the entire surface. But though they used a full battery of sensors and scanners, they needed only their eyes to see that the planet had indeed been scorched. Much of what had once been land was now a congealed sea of glass, though there were some polar and equatorial areas that escaped total melting. There were few craters, mostly in the shallower sea bottoms. There was no water anywhere, not even at the poles. It had all boiled off with the atmosphere.

But, as the sensors and scanners proved, there were indeed remains of the civilization that had once existed here. Some of these were under some of the thinner slag areas, and there were hints of something else, perhaps, under some of the glass. But there was nothing in those polar or equatorial areas, which was almost certainly why they had escaped absolute destruction in the first place—nothing there to destroy.

While they scanned the surface of DRG-17.iv, an entirely different bank of sensors kept watch on the rest of the system. They detected no flicker drives, no inertial drives, no gravity drives during the ten days that they surveyed the dead world. What they would have done if Karyl Toerson had shown up, Rikard wasn't sure. He was just as glad he didn't have to find out.

But at last they had done all they could do from orbit. They identified the best of the ruins, at a slag margin between a glass sheet and a merely burned area, and took a shuttle to the surface there.

During their trip and approach Bardolino had acquired some knowledge of their intentions here, and being of an adventurous nature herself, she asked if she could accompany Rikard and his companions on their explorations. Having an extra perspective—and an extra gun—seemed like a good idea to Rikard, so he told her to come along.

They all had to wear full pressure suits, of course. Rikard had had his helmet specially modified to accommodate his recording equipment, which would not only take visual images, but record all voice and radio communication as well.

Thus prepared they came out of the shuttle onto the desolate surface. The ruins of the cyclopean building, half a kilometer away, was identifiable only because they had seen others before. It was only the stub of the base of a small cone, the rest had been blown away. They brought out their equipment on a series of four floaters, and went to it.

Though the material of the cyclopean structure had not eroded as it had on other worlds subject to atmosphere and water and dust, it had been partially melted by nearby blasts, and the vacuum and unimpeded solar activity for the last one and a half million years had had their own peculiar effect. The surface of the cone was semitranslucent, a dirty grayish blue, and totally dead.

The material of the stub of the cone, thus metamorphosed, was harder than what they had found elsewhere. All signs of the original color symbols were long since gone. But even without Droagn's Prime to guide them, they could see, dimly through the semitranslucent material, shadows of interior spaces. They found the one nearest the surface and cut their way through.

Here the chambers and passages were as distorted as the Ahmear ruins on Trokarion had been. It slowed their progress as they moved inward five shells and downward three levels, since they had to squeeze through some constricted places, and break through artificially sealed doorways as they went. But the walls became less translucent, less dirty gray-blue, and less distorted, though the effects of thermonuclear destruction and hard vacuum exposure persisted until, all of a sudden, the material of the cone resembled marble once again.

They could not go farther in, but only down, and as they went to the next level the material of the cone regained its pearly sheen, and below that level they found everything perfectly preserved. This was all new to Bardolino, of course, and she was fascinated.

As were the others, since this place had not been abandoned like the others they'd visited, but killed and sealed, and thus there were furnishings in the chambers, surface coverings on corridor floors, decorations on the walls, and hangings from the ceilings. There had been no erosive effects at all since the war completely sealed off the cone with the destruction of its upper levels.

Rikard recorded everything, and they were tempted to linger and examine everything, but now was not the time. Maybe when they came back out. Now they just went down another level, and along a passage past chambers with open doors, looking for the next ramp down.

In one chamber they even found the desiccated remains of some of the people themselves—fragile to the touch, and distorted by dehydration, freezing, and sudden vacuum. Here they could not help but pause.

The remains of those people were huddled at one side of the chamber, where they apparently had died all at once. Some kind of radiation must have penetrated, even where heat did not. Rikard recorded it all but did not try to take any samples. They closed the chamber behind them, to preserve what they could against future investigation.

They descended yet again, and now they knew that this cone was different in other ways from the other two they had entered. They were too close to the center, and too deep. Where the museum should have been, there was none.

They descended another level, and went inward again, and this time they came to a complex of chambers right at the center. From what they had seen in other cones, and in the database, this looked like a centralized records office, similar to the computer center but less elaborate and sophisticated. Droagn and Grayshard checked out the computer terminals, but the radiation that had killed the cyclopeans had completely destroyed the computer system.

They moved into an outer shell, looking for a further way down. They passed through chambers with their contents mostly intact, pictures on the walls, mostly artworks but in one side chamber what looked like job charts. They decided to go farther in that direction.

Whatever this community had been, it was certainly different, because at this level there were no concentric shells of chamber and passage, but instead a continuing complex of rooms, each opening onto several others. At each doorway they paused, and went toward whatever seemed more businesslike, less residential, more governmental, less civilian.

In one chamber they found, occupying an entire inner wall, a geological map of the world, in a projection not that much different from that currently in use in the Federation. Rikard got a full and detailed recording of it, and after a bit Bardolino was able to identify which were the continents and which the seas. The graphics were different from anything with which they were familiar, though they somewhat resembled some of the images Droagn had dredged up out of the data they'd brought back from Tsikashka, but Bardolino was used to seeing worlds from space, and the graphic conventions didn't confuse her as much. Also, though they had all watched their approach, only Bardolino had really paid attention to the surface of the planet, as opposed to what had been done to it, and so she was able to orient herself on this map, and found their approximate present location, though no cities were shown.

They left the map and went through the rest of this officelike section, but this area of preservation was not extensive, and a little farther on they came to the end. They turned back, but took different routes rather than just retracing their steps, with the intention of searching the whole of this level.

And then, in one large officelike area, Droagn paused to stare at a side door that the others had passed. The blue marks indicated that on the other side was something like a closet.

˘There's something different about this one,˘ Droagn said. He touched two hands lightly to the Prime, tipped his head so that the points projecting from the circlet aimed more nearly toward the door, swung his head slowly from side to side.

"So what is it?" Rikard asked.

˘It's the wrong shape, and there's something inside I can't read.˘

They opened the door, and not only was the closet far wider than usual, and much shallower, but it was also filled with things too fragile to touch.

On shelves on either side were little transparent boxes, each of which held an insect of some kind. There was a set of pots that contained soil and probably what had once been plants. On one shelf, at eye level, was a set of little multicolored plastic blocks that fit together in a variety of ways. Near the floor was a stack of papers that began to crumble even as they watched. There were several baskets woven of a natural material, which, for a while, held their attention.

Rikard recorded everything, but it was Grayshard who pointed out that there was another peculiarity to this place. "If I'm not mistaken," he said, "this is the outline of a door." It was opposite the one they had opened.

"It looks too good to pass up, doesn't it?" Bardolino said.

"It does indeed." Rikard pushed against the panel, it resisted a moment, and then it swung away from them.

Beyond it was a large office with no other doors. Rikard felt the hairs rise on the back of his neck as the others crowded through the doorway behind him.

"It doesn't look much different from the other offices we've been in," Grayshard said.

But Bardolino had gone on into the center of the room and turned back to face them. "Oh, yes it is." She was looking at the wall through which they had come. The others turned around, and there, to the left of the doorway, was another map, not geological this time but political.

Rikard recorded it all in high resolution, even as they examined it. They found their present location without difficulty this time, and now knew the symbol for a city. They found other cities at places that Bardolino remembered as having received the most damage, as well as smaller symbols that represented smaller cities, such as this one was. A simple real-time analysis of the city symbols showed that not only did they roughly represent the approximate size, but also political importance, the way Federation maps did. And once the symbols were known, the map became easy to read, and they could identify regional capitals, and one city that could only have been the planetary capital, or the equivalent.

And that, of course, was where they wanted to go. They left the map room, and hurried up and out by the most direct route. As they left the ruins, Bardolino paused to communicate with the ship, which was still in orbit. "No visitors while we were gone," she said. They hurried to the shuttle and left the surface.

They returned to orbit but when they flew over the site of the capital they found that it was utterly slagged. It was one of the few ex-land surfaces that showed signs of cratering.

"It makes sense," Rikard said. He tried to suppress his disappointment.

"Of course it does," Grayshard agreed. "Whoever wiped these people out would have made sure that the planetary capital got the heaviest attack." The destruction of the city had penetrated deep into the crust of the planet, far below the possibility of any subterranean fortress. There was no sense in even going down to look.

Nor was there any point in their remaining in the system. The kind of research to be done here was best left to academic professionals, not an opportunist like Rikard. Bardolino set a course for Novo Boskva.

But before they departed, Rikard directed her to take the ship back to the moon, so that they could look once again at whatever facilities were there, just in case any had remained intact. She complied willingly.

They orbited the moon equatorially and performed a quick probe of its surface. Though there was scarring on the sunlit planetward face, there was no evidence of slagging there, and the back side was completely untouched. Though it was night there, the physical structures at the center of the back side were plainly evident, and showed no signs of damage. How had they been missed? Rikard, Droagn,

Grayshard, and Bardolino took a shuttle down to investigate the largest surviving complex.

The dome covering the complex was intact, and they had no way to operate the ship-locks, plainly located around the perimeter near ground level, so they landed the shuttle a safe distance away and took a pressurized floater over. They circled the dome once, at fairly high speed. There were no fractures, no damage from meteor or missile. Somehow the war had passed it by, and time had left it untouched as well. In the dark and without the ship's extensive probes they couldn't see much inside, but shadowy forms were present deep within. When they had come full circle they landed the floater on the apron of the nearest ship-lock and went out in pressure suits.

It being a lock they could cut through the hatch without letting much air escape, and they put up a temporary seal when they were inside. There were several peculiar craft in the lock, including one that Rikard remembered having seen in the Tschagan space station three years ago, though whether it was a cyclopean craft or belonged to another species he couldn't tell. There were more empty slots than craft, however.

At the inner hatch they again erected a temporary seal after cutting their way through, though the pressure inside the dome was only about half what they were used to. If the cyclopeans had found the other inhabited worlds comfortable, it was half what they had been used to, too, though there was now no way to be sure.

The structures inside were not extensive. Rather than the cones they had found on other worlds, these buildings were lattices of floors and supports, lacy partitions and rampways, construction that used a minimum of material since the whole was protected by the dome. The ground surrounding the structure had once been gardened, though now nothing remained but some unidentifiable vegetable matter long since desiccated to crumbling dust.

But as they entered the structure itself they saw that it had been stripped. Unlike the lower chambers in the ruins on the planet, there was nothing left here, no furniture, no decorations. Lights had been taken out of the ceilings, other systems of unknown nature had been removed from the supports and partitions. Like the Ahmear ruins, the survivors had taken everything and run when they knew the war was going to destroy their world, or did so shortly afterward.

They went through the empty place quickly, from one side to the other, changing levels whenever possible. There were subsidiary structures off to the sides, and other domes nearby, but there was no sense in trying to visit them. In one place they found some trash in a corner, which had been preserved perfectly. It was nothing worth taking.

Rikard was crushed by disappointment. There was lots more to do regarding these people on other worlds but he'd hoped to make the big find here, especially since Karyl Toerson was, apparently, nowhere around.

"The question remains," Grayshard said. "This was their capital world, and it has been destroyed—by whom? and why?"

"That's something I would very much like to find out," Rikard said.

"And how do you propose to do that?" Bardolino asked.

"My uncle Gawin," Rikard told her. "If you're curious, you can come along."

"This is more fun than running charter trips for Secor Limited," she said. "Besides, you've already paid for the ship. Where are we going?"

"Malvrone," Rikard said.

"That Gawin?" Bardolino asked.

"Yes, do you know him?"

"Only by reputation."

"Which one, I wonder," Rikard said.

Malvrone

1

Even in the relatively utopian Federation, some people seem to accumulate personal power, while others are helpless and ineffectual. But one of the peculiarities of personal power is that there is, as yet, no good explanation for why some people have it. Not everybody who is well connected politically has power. We all know about people elected to high office who can't control their lives, their constituents, their peers. And there are those with no real political connections at all who nonetheless manage to control those in office. It's a given that those with money also have power, but that's not always true. If it were, rich people would never go broke, and poor people would never get rich. And a change of fortunes is not always due to stupidity or hard work.

The Malvrone family had immense power. They personally ruled an entire world, and were the sole owners of the corporation of which Rikard's grandfather, Artos Lord Malvrone, was the chairman, and his grandmother, Artos's wife, Vikaria Lady Malvrone, was president. Their connections with other planets in the Federation, with Federal agencies, were among the most influential. Though not as wealthy as the family of the legendary M'Kade, they were still worth the total income of at least two worlds, and could dispose of it as they wished.

And they had wielded that power, without dissent or rebellion, for generations. Their connections and money gave them power, but more than that, their personal power enabled them to keep their connections and wealth. Those who seemed likely to lose either were eased out of the inner circle, as was Gawin Malvrone. It was for this reason that while the rest of the family occupied extensive estates in the most beautiful area of Malvrone, within easy reach of all aspects of government and culture, Gawin lived in a remote part of the world in quite modest doings—relatively speaking—within easy reach of interstellar shuttleports, both public and "private."

Wealth is not enough. Arin Braeth had discovered vast wealth, and before he died he'd passed it on to his son, Rikard. If Rikard could have converted that wealth to cash, he could have purchased and controlled a significant portion of the entire Federation. He could have bought his mother's family for small change. But his personal power was far more limited than theirs. Not that he was condemned to be powerless, for he had learned a lot in the seven years since he'd first left home to go adventuring. But he lacked the background, the experience, the whatever it was that it took to handle that kind of wealth effectively, and he knew it.

And now that he was going to face that family, he was somewhat nervous about it. He was riding in the luxurious passenger space of an air-floater, a vehicle that could either follow paved roads or fly above the countryside with other air traffic, as it was doing now. It was being driven by a living person, rather than running on a self-control grid. They were approaching a huge structure set in a parklike forest, among gardens, on a plateau overlooking wilderness and rich farmland.

Rikard moved uncomfortably in his comfortable seat. He

was dressed far more elegantly than he was used to. He also did not have his gun with him, having been instructed most firmly to leave it behind, and felt a little nervous about that.

The air-floater came down to a tiny private landing field and proceeded on floaters alone above a perfect road that led toward the huge building. In spite of himself, Rikard was impressed. He could not truly gauge how big the building was, nor of what it was made, but it glittered in the light of the setting sun behind him, as if it were designed to do so. As it probably was.

The driver brought the air-floater between wings of the building into a courtyard, as if he knew which way he was going. Being Gawin's personal chauffeur, he probably did. The floater set down at a low porch, and as Rikard got out, the door to the mansion was opened by two Human servants whose job seemed to be just that, as they held the door while a third servant came out and walked directly toward Rikard.

The man did not smile as he neared. His expression was perfectly neutral. "Good evening, sir," he said when he was some three paces away. There was no questioning of identity, no sign of recognition. "Won't you please come in." He stood to one side in an unmistakable gesture of invitation. There was no feeling in it at all.

Rikard made the smallest of nods and started toward the door. He did not look at the servant again, nor at the two who were holding the door open for him, though it could probably have stood by itself. The man who had greeted him followed three paces behind.

They entered a large foyer, and as they did so Rikard stopped, turned to the man behind him, and handed him a letter from Gawin. The servant took it, and merely glanced at it. But then, instead of directing Rikard into the large and comfortable parlor through a broad open doorway opposite the entrance, he led him through a side door on the right, to a small chamber where they paused for just a moment, then out another door opposite into a most luxurious chamber where a number of people were socializing. They stood or sat, seemingly at their ease, engaged in mild conversation, dressed much as Rikard was though with some differences in style. A number of Human servants and machines moved among them, offering drinks and light foods and taking away empty glasses and napkins. There the servant who had let Rikard into the house simply bowed and left him to his own devices.

He stood for a moment, trying to size up these people. They were of all ages, though few were as young as he, and the older people, maybe as much as one hundred eighty or so, looked all very well cared for. Someone glanced his way. He smiled, broke eye contact, and the other directed his attention somewhere else.

He moved slowly into the open crowd. The people did not seem unfriendly, they smiled his way, but they didn't know him, and did not make an effort to meet him. He smiled back when he met someone's eye, nodded now and then, and once or twice said hello when it couldn't be avoided. But he did not pursue their acquaintance either.

He was uncomfortable here. His clothes were as good as theirs but he didn't wear them as well. He was too tall, and not nearly as good-looking as he would like to be. He was surrounded by strangers who all seemed to have something to say to each other, and there were no openings for him to fit into.

He did notice that an attractive woman of about his age seemed to be watching him. He paid no attention to her at all, but remained aware of her as he moved in a not completely aimless arc among the people around the room. She was more toward the center, engaged in conversation with first one person, then another, but she kept on glancing at him. He was not surprised when, after a while, she came over in his direction. Her eyes met his and held his, and she smiled in a thoroughly neutral way as she approached. "Good evening," she said. "I don't believe we've met."

"I am sure we have not," Rikard said, "as I have been to

Malvrone only once before, and I did not meet you then. My name is Rikard Braeth, and I am here at the invitation of my uncle, Gawin Malvrone.''

"Good heavens," the woman said, and her expression now showed some small real pleasure mingled with surprise and confusion. "I would never have known you. And yet you do look something like your mother. I'm your cousin Gwineth.''

Now it was Rikard's turn to be taken aback. He knew from his uncle that he had cousins, but he'd never met them. Gawin, on his few visits, had come alone, and had spoken of his family little. "Cousin Gwineth," he said, "forgive me, I guess I wasn't expecting to meet anybody here except Gawin.''

"The chances are good that you won't," Gwineth said, "and it's probably just as well.''

"Especially my grandfather," Rikard said wryly. He watched her closely for signs of aversion, and saw none.

"I'm afraid so," she said with a small sigh. "You do know how the family feels about you?''

"I do. Except for Gawin. Here's his invitation.''

She took the letter from him, and opened it with some surprise. "He went the whole length, didn't he," she said.

"I got the impression that it was indeed somewhat formal." The invitation, hand-lettered on heavy cream-colored card stock, addressed Rikard by name.

"He's issued it as a son of the host," Gwineth said, "and that means that even Grandfather can't deny you here.''

"This is Grandfather's party, he can deny whom he wishes.''

"No, he can't. I think Uncle Gawin really wanted to see you.''

"That's the impression I got. We've been on Malvrone for seven days, and he hasn't been home once.''

"He's been here. He'll be home tomorrow. I wonder why the urgency.''

"Maybe he wants me to meet the family," Rikard said

with a dry smile, "and figured they wouldn't come to see me at his place."

"That could be," Gwineth said. "They wouldn't. I'm glad you came."

"Are you really?"

"Of course I am. Uncle Gawin and I are much alike. Both of us are barely tolerated, though I get away with it better since I'm younger and I don't engage in trade. One thing the conservative element in our family always forgets is that everybody is different. And they also choose to forget that the founders of our family were a lot more like your father than they were like mine."

"You don't sound as if you like it here very much."

"Oh, I like it just fine." She flashed him a big smile. "It's the people, most of them, I'd rather do without." The smile became somewhat wistful.

"So how come you haven't gone off on your own by now?"

"It's the money and power," she said as if she wanted to change the subject. "Would you like to find Gawin?"

"Yes I would. I'm not really very comfortable here."

"Well, you'll have to put up with it for a bit," Gwineth said with a grin. "I'll show you around and we'll meet Gawin sooner or later. Just be discreet when you talk to anybody."

"You may rest assured that I'm quite used to doing that."

They worked their way through the people. Every now and then Gwineth paused to introduce Rikard to somebody, but he felt no compulsion to remember anybody's name. He told her so.

"That's okay," she said. "You'll probably not meet them again anyway. If it's somebody important, I'll let you know."

Once she stopped to join in a conversation for a moment. Rikard stood to one side as his cousin and the other couple spoke lightly and briefly about constituencies and local level representation. Gwineth broke off as quickly as she could, then took him through a doorway into a hall.

Not a corridor, but a grand hall. The room they had left was just an antechamber. "This," Gwineth explained, "is where most of the guests mix. There are various other chambers and rooms connecting here, if you have special interests."

The display of wealth was fantastic. The hall was decorated with metals, woods, gemstones, with artwork that almost rivaled Gawin's collections, with craftwork, furniture, lighting, with ornamentations of all sorts. And it was all presented as if such surroundings were appropriate for people to mingle in.

"I suspect that Uncle Gawin will be in the game room," Gwineth said, and they worked their way across the hall. There were many more people here, and it was not easy to always keep moving. And then, too, people frequently greeted her as she passed, or called to her, and then they had to pause a moment or two. Sometimes Gwineth introduced Rikard to her acquaintances, sometimes she did not. When she did, she sometimes mentioned that he was her cousin, most of the time she did not. Rikard remained polite, somewhat distant, and even when Gwineth had to participate in a conversation, he remained silent, saying no more than necessary. It apparently was the right thing to do. Only once did someone, on hearing his name, pause and say, "Are you by any chance related to Arin Braeth?"

"I am," he said, and searched the man's face for some clue.

"He and Gawin used to knock around a bit when they were younger, as I recall."

"That's what I've heard," Rikard said with as neutral a smile as he could muster.

"Well, I'm glad to meet you then." The man extended his hand, Rikard shook it, and then the man, whose name Rikard had already forgotten, turned away to someone else.

The far side of the hall was marked by great arches. "The gaming rooms are just beyond," Gwineth said.

Rikard looked but could see no doorway, just a flat surface that shimmered slightly. He was about to ask when a man called Gwineth's name as they passed the group in which he was engaged in conversation.

"Oh, dear." Gwineth looked up at Rikard pleadingly.

The man, tall and handsome and just past his first century, came up to them. "Gwineth," he said again, and smiled. There was something familiar about him.

Gwineth turned and looked up at him. "Hello, Father."

Now Rikard knew why the man looked familiar. It was his uncle Braice, likely heir to Artos's position as director of the Board of Malvrone, even though he was not eldest. According to Gawin, who was the third, Rikard's aunt Bevry had never been interested in wielding power, only in spending money, and kept her power only to protect her financial interests.

Rikard had never met Bevry, but he could see the resemblance between Braice and Gawin, and his mother too, as he remembered her. Except that where his mother, Sigra, had been gentle, Gawin was mischievous, and Braice was hard. Sigra had had a sense of humor, as Gawin did, but Braice did not show it if he shared it. He spoke with his daughter as a father would to a child, and she responded dutifully. Rikard felt a growing apprehension. He wanted to be away from here. This was his mother's brother, after all, and he had her eyes, but Rikard feared him.

At last Braice raised his glance from his daughter's face and looked at Rikard. At last this epitome of power, poise, and pride condescended to notice his daughter's companion. His eyes met Rikard's, and though his face underwent no change of expression, all warmth faded.

But strangely, even so, Rikard felt his own confidence returning, even as he felt his anger grow at his uncle's so carefully controlled but carefully expressed dislike.

"Father," Gwineth said, "this is—"

"I know who it is," Braice said to her. His voice was absolutely flat. "You are Sigra's child," he said to Rikard. It sounded as though he were accusing Rikard of being a child, and of somehow being the cause of Sigra's death and disgrace. "I think perhaps," he went on before Rikard could respond, "that you are in the wrong place."

Rikard and his uncle were nearly of a height. Rikard felt the barest twitch of a smile begin at the corner of his mouth. "Please rest assured, Uncle Braice, that I am most certainly aware of that. But Uncle Gawin has asked me to come."

Braice's face did not change except to grow a touch colder, a touch harder. "That is Gawin's error. It is not his place to invite such as you to this event."

"Such as I? I am a grandson of Artos Lord Malvrone, and the invitation was extended to me as from him. I am not about to dispute that with anyone but Lord Malvrone himself."

"You will dispute nothing," Braice started to say, but Gwineth spoke up.

"Please, Father, Rikard, this is not the time nor the place."

"Indeed it is not," Braice said. His breathing was a little deepened, and there was some color in his face now. But Rikard, though angry, was really quite calm. He had taken Braice's measure, and knew that he was in no physical danger. He was stronger than his uncle by a bit, and in better shape, and it was unlikely the other was armed. Social danger was something else, but he suspected that whatever his grandfather felt for him, he wouldn't like it if Braice overstepped his bounds.

Braice took a breath, glanced at his daughter, then glared back at Rikard. "Let me warn you," he said, and his voice was not quite as level as it might have been, "that though my little brother has issued you an invitation in our father's name, Lord Malvrone may have some quite different feelings about it."

"That is as it may be," Rikard said, "but I'm sure that he can speak for himself."

"Indeed," Braice said, looking as though Rikard had hit him in the solar plexus. "My father can very well speak for himself, but what makes you think that my parents would speak to you at all? When they learn that you are here, there will be no speaking. They will just have you removed."

"Please, Father," Gwineth said. "You're drawing attention."

Braice looked down at her, surprise penetrating his rage, then looked around the room. The people nearest were doing their best to be elsewhere, and those who thought they were at a safe distance were watching covertly.

"Why?" Rikard asked his uncle. He felt very calm now, and very in control. "Why would they do such a thing to their grandson?"

"Because," Braice said, straining to keep his voice low, "of what your father did to my little sister!"

"He rescued her," Rikard said softly. "Would it have been better if she had died at the hands of her kidnappers?"

"Better?" Braice said. "Indeed. At least she would have been spared the years of ignominy that she spent on whatever that place was. How can you imagine someone accustomed to this"—his hand swept the air to indicate the hall and the people in it—"living on some M'Kade-forsaken world where the best you could be was a *professor*?"

"Even granting," Rikard said, "that your evaluation is true, what's wrong with it?"

"Are you really such an imbecile?"

"And even if your condition here were really preferable, how is it possibly my fault what my father did?"

"I know who you are, Rikard Braeth. The news of your doings is not hard to come by. You are just like your father, and what more could be expected? As is the father, so is the son."

"I see," Rikard said. "Then you too are an oath-breaker."

Gwineth had been trying discreetly to placate them but Rikard's words surprised her as much as they did Braice.

"What the hell do you mean by that?" Braice demanded.

"The only reason my father ever got to know my mother,'' Rikard said quietly, ''is because *your* father hired him to rescue her, and then reneged on the contract and refused to pay the fee he'd offered. That's not exactly an honorable outcome. At least *my* father married my mother, and didn't just throw her away and leave her as *your* father did.''

For a moment Braice was actually speechless, and indeed Rikard thought he could see almost more shame than anger in his reaction. As why not, since the story was true.

''Perhaps,'' Rikard went on softly, ''that is why my grandfather hates me so much, because he still feels somewhat guilty for what he did to my father, *and* my mother, after the rescue.''

Braice's mouth worked as if he would say something, but he was caught in a dilemma. At last he said, ''Just be wary. My father does indeed hate you, and if word of what you've said comes back to him, he might decide to defend his honor.''

''Rikard said nothing but the truth,'' Gwineth said. ''I know the story as well as you. What is there for Grandfather to defend?''

''If I were you,'' Braice said to her, ''I'd be very careful. You are not exactly in Father's good graces, you know.''

Then Braice turned and walked off. Some of the people nearby watched curiously. Though they were not privy to the conversation, they saw all too clearly that there had been a contretemps, and it would appear that the heir to the chairmanship of Malvrone had come off second best.

Gwineth was shocked by her father's words, but she had poise, more than he, and she watched him as he strode unresponsively through the hall until he was out of sight. ''You were quite impressive,'' she said as she turned to Rikard, and then she cowered back, almost as if struck.

''What's the matter,'' he asked her. She was afraid.

''I thought you were so calm,'' she said, almost in a whisper.

''I'm sorry,'' he said, and tried to compose his face. His expression had gotten him into trouble before, for though he felt calm, he in fact had been in a rage, and one that had shown as a flicker of something behind his eyes.

"You were going to kill him," she said. "Weren't you?"

"It wasn't my intention, but I probably would have."

"You have killed before."

"I have had cause to before. Gwineth, I'm sorry. And it's ironic that one of the things that makes it worse is that I think I'd like your father if he didn't hate me so much. And honest to God, I really don't understand why he does."

As if on cue a waiter came by bearing a tray of full glasses. Gwineth stopped the man, handed Rikard a drink, and kept the waiter waiting while her cousin drank it off. She took his empty glass, put it back on the tray, and handed him another, and this time took one for herself.

They stood side by side for a moment, not saying anything. Rikard sipped at his second drink. It was not the same as the first, rather sweeter and not as potent.

"I understand," Gwineth said, "that you have two traveling companions."

"I do."

"And are they here on Malvrone?"

"They are." He recognized her ploy. She was giving him some time to calm down, and to think about something different. "They were not invited here tonight, however, and considering the formality of the invitation, I felt that they might be a bit less welcome than I, and so they stayed at Gawin's place."

"Are they really as strange as stories have made them out to be?"

"And how strange is that?"

"That the one called Grayshard likes his food well rotted."

"He's a fungus, or very much like one, except that he moves and thinks. He has no alimentary organs at all, he just absorbs organic material through his skin, as it were. He likes it highly fermented and in a liquid state. It's easier for him to take it in that way."

"I hear he looks like a huge tangle of hair."

"He does. White, with red tips. But he wears a humanoid disguise most of the time. People don't notice him much.

"Now Endark Droagn, they notice," he went on, and told her a bit about his serpentine companion. Gwineth told him one or two stories she had heard about him, which were exaggerations of the truth, or misinterpretations. He let himself be distracted as he quite honestly and sincerely set her straight as best he could. Then, when she smiled up at him—she wasn't really that much shorter than he—he knew he was calm.

"Just be glad," Gwineth said with a smile, "that your first run-in wasn't with Grandfather, because he would have had you killed on the spot. Now let's go find Gawin." She led him toward one of the arches that they'd started for so long ago.

As they neared, Rikard could see that the shimmering surface within the arch was an optical energy field, not drapes, though it looked solid enough. It served not only to make a portal through which one had to deliberately pass, but also to cut down noise and kept casual people out.

On the other side was what Gwineth had been calling the game room. It was more like a super casino, certainly bigger than anything Rikard had ever seen, not that he was generally given to gambling.

It was spacious, but filled with people between the widely spaced tables. Rikard and Gwineth slowly walked toward the center of the near end of the room, squeezing between the players and the spectators.

There were card tables, of course, for four people, or six, or eight, or sometimes more, some of them with a dealer, many without. There were billiards, roulette, craps, a variant of keeno, a simplified four-handed competitive pinball, and even circular pocket pool.

In spite of the crowding the sound level was quite muted. Everywhere there were people talking, but their conversations could be heard only when within a meter or so of the speakers. Though there was lots of liquor, and several varieties of smoke, the air was clear and smelled pretty good. The light was quite bright, and completely sourceless. They paused between a poker table and a set of pachinko machines.

"There seems to be some serious gambling here," Rikard commented.

"This is just the social room," Gwineth said. "The serious stuff is in private rooms at the other end of the casino."

As Rikard watched some money being lost, he wondered what serious gambling could be. "Why hasn't Gawin met me yet? The note with the invitation made it seem rather important."

"He has family obligations far more demanding than his business ones, if he wants to *stay* a member of the family and not be given a remittance. Grandfather just barely puts up with him as it is. If it weren't for the fact that Uncle Gawin can get Grandfather whatever he wants at a good price, he'd have been kicked out long ago."

They proceeded down the center of the room toward the other end. Once or twice they met somebody who Gwineth had to talk to. In each case, Rikard just stayed quietly in the background. As they went they passed a variety of games, many like those they'd seen before, but some different ones as well, such as mancala, shovelboard on a circle, and a kind of rotating backgammon versus the house.

At the far end of the casino were several doors that led to the back rooms. Gwineth opened the nearest one on the right and they went through to a much smaller room, only the size of a basketball court, in which were a variety of electronic arcade games with gambling features as well as enhanced skill features.

There were quite a few people in here as well, and Rikard and Gwineth quickly went through the room, looking for Gawin, but he wasn't there. Gwineth stopped one of the perfectly dressed servants and asked.

"Msr. Gawin was here early in the evening," the woman said, "but he hasn't been here for several hours."

"Do you have any idea where he went?"

"No, Msr. Gwineth, but he left with a Msr. Rafe Tomisonne."

"Thank you." Gwineth let the woman go on about her business.

"Who's Tomisonne?" Rikard asked.

"He's a family friend who keeps on trying to get Uncle Gawin interested in what he calls 'something appropriate,' that is, more in line with family business."

"And that is?"

"Governing Malvrone and making its influence felt in the Federation."

They left the gambling room and Gwineth led Rikard, with only one stop to speak, to another private room at the far front of the casino. Here they found more physical sports, such as bowling, racketball, fencing, and hurdlepuck. Gawin was not there, and when Gwineth inquired they learned that though he had been there with Rafe Tomisonne, he hadn't stayed very long.

Rikard wanted to watch a bit, but not play, and since it was far quieter here he took the opportunity to ask, "What's the reason for this party? There's so much going on there's no way our grandparents can enjoy people's company."

"They don't," Gwineth said, "but that's not the point. Four times a year they have to do this and invite anybody to whom they have social obligations, especially those they won't invite on a more intimate basis."

"They owe all these people a party?"

"About half of them. The others are come-alongs."

"But how in the world can two people incur so many social obligations?"

"I have no idea. That's just the way it's always been."

They left the physical sport room and went toward the far back of the casino. Then Gwineth turned aside and spoke to a short, dark man of middle age. "Msr. Tomisonne," she said, "have you seen my uncle Gawin?"

"Why, hello, Gwineth, how are you doing." He smiled up at her in quite an avuncular way.

"Just fine, Msr. Tomisonne. I've been looking for Uncle Gawin all evening. Someone said he was with you."

"Oh, he was, certainly. You know, I've been trying my best to get him turned around, but he just doesn't seem interested. Maybe you could put in a word now and then."

"It wouldn't do any good, Msr. Tomisonne, everybody has tried."

"But have you, my dear? If he's not careful, you know, he'll be out in the cold."

"I think Uncle Gawin can take care of himself pretty well. Do you know where he is?"

"Stubborn, just like he is, aren't you." Rafe Tomisonne smiled condescendingly up at her. "That's really a shame, I hope you make better choices than he did."

"I have you to guide me, Msr. Tomisonne. Where is my uncle, please?"

"I left him in the war room, just half an hour ago. You don't want to go in there, do you?"

"Not really, but Uncle Gawin doesn't usually go in for that kind of thing either."

"Of course not," Tomisonne said. "He's with Lupe don Virin and Samanta Joness." He didn't seem pleased. "They're the ones who want to play."

"Thank you," Gwineth said, and without introducing Rikard, much to his relief, they changed course and went up a short hall to a room even farther back.

This was quite large, quite dark around the walls though brightly lit over the one huge table, which was surrounded by people. The lower edge of the table was composed of comscreens, and there were more screens along the walls. As they delicately and politely pushed their way through the crowd Rikard could see that the table was a very sophisticated computer-controlled and -aided military miniatures simulation. He was utterly fascinated for a short while, as the figures, each only two and a half centimeters high, went through what was nearly real-time maneuvers, over carefully constructed terrain. Then he felt a tug on his arm and looked up. Gwineth was pointing across the table. There was Gawin, with a long, thin man on one side, and a short, thin woman on the other.

"Come on," Gwineth said, and they worked their way around the table.

Gawin saw Rikard coming and greeted him warmly, and Gwineth too. "It's been a while," he said to her.

"It has, Uncle Gawin, not since the last of these to-dos."

"I wish we could get together more often."

He gestured to the two people he was with, and introduced Lupe don Virin and Samanta Joness. They exchanged pleasantries and minor conversation of a trivial nature. Rikard got to practice being polite and discreet.

Then Gawin excused himself from his guests for a moment and went with Rikard and Gwineth over to the side of the room where it was quiet and where they could sit down.

"How's your father?" Gawin asked Gwineth.

"He's just fine," she told him, "but right now he's furious," and she recounted the encounter with Rikard.

Gawin was both amused and concerned. "Braice can really be a bastard at times," he said to Rikard, "and it sounds like he deserves what you gave him, but he can cause you trouble."

"I'm sorry I said anything to him," Rikard said. "But my God, he's never met me, and here he is with this self-righteous hatred. . . . What is wrong with this family, Gawin? Why do they have to blame me for something my father did thirty-five years ago? And why do they blame him, for what anyone else would call an act of heroism?"

"Because your father didn't play by their rules," Gawin said, "and you don't either. You're not like them, and for them there is only one way to be, and if you aren't that way, then you're wrong. They have no idea what it means to be different, no comprehension of what it's like.''

"It's true," Gwineth said. "You've only met a few of us, Rikard, and except for Gawin and me, we're all like that. It hasn't been easy for me, though since I've never left Malvrone I've learned the Malvrone way perfectly.''

"So how have you been?" Gawin asked Rikard.

"Just fine," Rikard said, then saw his uncle's eyes flicker. He glanced at Gwineth. She was calmly expectant. "I followed up on the data I got from you the last time we met," he went on.

Gwineth said, "I understand you discovered a previously unknown starfaring people.''

Gawin raised an eyebrow but did not try to change the subject.

Rikard turned to her and said, "Yes," and told her briefly about it, though he did not mention his visit to DRG-17.iv. Gwineth was as excited and interested as Gawin had been.

"We're going to have to talk about those cyclopeans," Gawin said when Rikard was finished. "And about some other matters too.''

"Such as?" Rikard prodded.

"Such as a certain person who's been interfering with your explorations.''

Gwineth looked at Gawin. "Are you keeping something from me?''

"Sometimes one must be discreet," Gawin said. "Please forgive me.''

"Why did you invite me to this party?" Rikard asked.

But before Gawin could answer, his company, don Virin and Joness came over to join them.

"We've missed you," Joness said.

"And something spectacular has happened on the board," don Virin added. "You should really come see." He addressed this last to Rikard and Gwineth as well.

"Let's go look," Gawin said as he stood up. Rikard thought he was relieved to not have to answer his question.

He exchanged glances with Gwineth, who made a small face of resignation, then pretended to join in the guests' enthusiasm. They returned to the table, where don Virin and Joness pointed out what had happened, and the condition that now prevailed.

Gawin knew how the system worked, though he was not knowledgeable in warfare, and explained some of it to Rikard while they watched a turn or two as the situation developed.

And this time Rikard found that he had some comprehension of the strategy and tactics being employed, though he had no formal military experience, and now was more fascinated than before.

But he noted that Gwineth was merely being polite, and really didn't like the simulation at all.

Just as things were starting to get interesting a gentle but perfectly audible tone sounded, and everybody sort of broke for half a heartbeat, then went back to their game. But Gawin and Gwineth exchanged concerned glances.

"It's your grandfather, Rikard," Gawin said. "He and Mother are on their way in."

Rikard looked around and saw that while people were paying attention to the game, many of them were casting glances at the door.

"I don't think they should meet Rikard here," Gwineth said.

"I think you're right," Gawin agreed, "but I have to remain with my guests. Can you take care of him?"

"Certainly," Gwineth said, and she led Rikard toward the back of the room, opposite the door, and opened a blank panel even as an annunciator said, "Artos, Lord Malvrone, and Vikaria, Lady Malvrone."

Rikard looked over his shoulder as they went out and saw people he could not make out clearly come in. They were tall, and not young, and the entire audience began to perform an elaborate and pretendedly spontaneous courtesy. Then the panel shut.

They went down a short passage and through a door into another hall. It was a service hall, filled with tables, each loaded with food service, drink service, other consumables and services. There were some Human servants here, but many more robots, back where the company couldn't see them. More food and drink was constantly being brought in and set out, then Human servants took it out through any of many doors to where the party was going on.

Nobody paid any attention to Gwineth and Rikard. If they were back here it was their business and the servants had their business and were answerable only to their own superiors or to Lord and Lady Malvrone, who would never think to come into the service area.

They crossed the hall. "I can't help it," Rikard said to Gwineth. "Was that my grandfather back there? My grandmother? I've never met them, and yet here I am, running from them. Why are my own grandparents so against me, just for my father's sake? And especially since it wasn't my father who did anything wrong, just what he was hired to do. If Grandfather had paid him like he'd promised, he might not have married Mother."

"I think I can understand how you feel," Gwineth said. "You and I were raised in entirely different ways, but we share a similar attitude. I understand from Uncle Gawin that Sigra was rather like that too. I've never truly understood why my father and grandfather feel the way they do. I can repeat their arguments, but I don't believe them or feel them."

They took one of the opposite doors into a relatively small parlor where a number of people were having tea and talking quietly.

Gwineth suddenly grabbed Rikard's arm. "Maybe we shouldn't go in here."

"Why not?" He looked where she was looking, at a group of people, one of whom resembled Gwineth, though she was easily thirty years older.

"That's my mother," Gwineth said. She had lowered her

voice to almost a whisper. Rikard looked around but did not
see Braice. Then the woman turned toward them. "Too
late," Gwineth said.

The woman excused herself from her companions and
came toward Rikard and Gwineth. Her expression was a
bland smile, which showed a bit more warmth when she
looked at her daughter.

"Gwineth, dear," she said. "I haven't seen you all
evening."

"We've just been looking around, Mother. I don't believe
you've met Rikard. He's Aunt Sigra's son."

The woman's face did not change as she looked at
Rikard, neither warming nor cooling, just maintaining a
neutral distance. "I have heard about you, Rikard. I'm your
aunt Vantesse." She held out a graceful hand. Rikard took it
gently, let it go. Vantesse turned back to her daughter.
"Didn't I just see you come out of a service entrance?"

"Yes, Mother. We were trying to get away from
Grandfather."

"Indeed, I should think so." She expressed no emotion at
all. "Artos has so little patience." She looked at Rikard and
presented him with a perfectly superficial smile. "Won't
you come and meet some friends of mine?"

"I'd be happy to." Rikard tried to put some warmth into
his response. Vantesse did not react at all, but turned and
walked back to the group she had left a moment ago.
Gwineth shot Rikard a glance of mixed relief, amusement,
and despair, and they followed after her.

He tried his best to follow the conversation that ensued
after the introductions, but it was about the proprieties of
performing a certain form of social behavior while employed
in the public display of ostentatious humility, and not only
did it make little sense to him, but he disagreed with what
he did understand, and saw no reason to worry about it in
the first place. He did his best to respond with neutral
murmurs.

Gwineth was watching him with an amused expression

and after he'd suffered a bit she spoke up and suggested that he might like to see more of the party.

"I'm sure he would," Vantesse said, "but I want you to stay with me for a while. I'm sure your cousin can find his own way around. I understand that he has quite a bit of experience in coping with strange cultures."

The look she gave him as she said that was so enigmatic that Rikard almost thought she might have been cracking a joke. But all he said was, "Thank you, I'll do just fine."

Vantesse smiled with perfect neutrality. "Why don't you just explore a bit?"

"I think I will." Rikard glanced at the other people one by one. "I've enjoyed meeting you." And then, to Gwineth, "I hope we'll meet again before the evening is over."

"I'm sure we will."

He left the group, and left the room by the nearest door, and found himself in the first great hall. There were as many people now as there had been before. Nothing seemed changed, though it was several hours later. He snagged a drink from a passing waiter.

He was on his own. He was really not enjoying the party, but he decided to take Vantesse at her word.

He prowled the great hall, watching not so much the people as their movements. He paid special attention to where the servants came from, and where they went, and what they carried. He found that service entrances were subtly made to be uninviting. And that there were other doors, which didn't always look like doors, through which people went only when they thought nobody was paying attention. It was these that interested him, and when he thought he knew well enough what was going on here, he went through one of these discreet doors.

Here were the back rooms. Some were just quiet parlors. Others were like the gaming rooms and gambling rooms he'd seen before. In spite of their being away from the main flow of the party, there was nothing very exciting going on in any of them. He had expected he might find some more erotic entertainments, or something political, or gambling on a scale significant to these people and their wealth, but he did not.

Sometimes people spoke to him. When they did, he responded politely and neutrally and excused himself quickly. He addressed no one himself.

After a while he began to build a map of this place in his mind. He was sure that he was seeing only the public areas, that none of this was going on in what his grandparents would consider their private rooms, but it was a start. He cycled through the rooms a second time, to confirm his knowledge, and to verify that there were large blank areas into which he had not gone, and which were probably the service areas.

Until now he had avoided going through any of the service doors, but now he decided it was time.

The staff did not try to stop him, and he paid no attention to them. The service areas were nearly half as big as the public areas, and there were people, robots, machines, tables, automatic cabinets, bars, food service, immediate laundry, everything one would need to host a party of five to six thousand people.

And still there were blanks in his mental map. He found other doors that were more discreet, less visible, and beyond them the staff's private areas. He was not welcome here, but he just grinned, and when someone spoke he mentioned that this was his first time in his grandfather's house and they let him alone.

He took a turn, and then another, and then realized that he hadn't seen anybody for the last five minutes or so. The corridors and chambers here were empty and silent, though clean and well lit. And then he went through a door into a room that had obviously been closed away for some time.

It was a kind of parlor. Adjacent to it was a sitting room with subtly different furnishings and purposes. There was a waiting room, a corridor with long benches, a breakfast room, a library, a room with more artwork than the others.

All of them were empty, all of them looked as though they hadn't been cleaned for perhaps a month or so, and one little bathroom had a definite layer of dust over everything.

This part of his grandparents' house hadn't been used for a long time. It aroused his curiosity. Once he found a book, a hard-copy volume with pages and with a bookmark still in it, on a low table beside a leather chair. On a mantel over what was actually a functioning fireplace he found a set of photos, showing his grandfather, he assumed, with a much younger version of Braice and Vantesse, and Gawin off to one side. This had once been part of his family's private apartments. And it was now abandoned.

After an hour or so exploring he decided to backtrack and discovered that he was lost. The arrangement of rooms was more complicated than he had at first thought, and he hadn't been paying attention.

He paused to get his bearings, set a course, and proceeded as if he knew where he was going. He passed through some shut-down service areas, through empty servants' living quarters, by some bedroom suites, and in one of them paused.

It was a child's room, a little girl's room. A teenager, maybe, it was hard to tell. There were clothes in the closets, the bed was neat but unmade, there were books, toys for a much younger child, a variety of things. On the desk was a photograph, an old laserprint, showing two adults who he now knew to be his grandparents and between them a young woman, not yet twenty, whom he recognized with an ache that surprised him.

He looked away, around at the rest of the room. It was his mother's, left the way it had been when she had been kidnapped. By its neglect, this room had been preserved, this whole part of the mansion was from that time, and had been shut away.

The skin of his face felt hot and tight and prickly. Something wet dropped onto his hand. His grandfather had shut this whole place off after Sigra Malvrone had gone off with Arin Braeth. He had shut off the rooms, shut off his heart, shut her out of his life.

And had shut out Rikard too. He thought about his mother the last time he'd seen her alive, when she had still been hoping for his father's return. His long absence, to seek wealth to keep her in the style to which he believed she was accustomed, had broken her heart and she was dying even then. He had watched her die.

He had seen his father die, under the gun of a madman.

And his family wouldn't have him.

He took a breath, and another. He reached up with a hand and dried his cheek. He clenched himself, as he had been in the habit of doing since his father had gone off so long ago, and left the suite. In the corridor he turned a corner, went up another corridor, went through a discreet door, and suddenly found himself in the main hall. He could see Gawin, not that far away, talking to a small group of people, and went to him.

2

Rikard woke late the next morning in his rooms in Gawin's house. He felt awful, so he took a Kerotone pill and by the time he had showered and dressed his hangover was gone.

But he was still depressed. He thought about maybe converting some of the wealth his father had left him to cash and buying his grandfather out. Then he could shut down the whole damn planet and show this idiot family how it felt to be helpless at the hands of those who were supposed to care for them.

Except that he wanted them to care for him. And after all,

that was part of what this business of finding precursor races was all about, making a reputation for himself, proving his worth so that his grandfather and grandmother would accept him. Except that they never would, not on his terms.

But he was on the verge of something so important, of such consequence to the welfare of the whole Federation, that it would boost him into fame unheard of, and then when his grandfather, or his uncle Braice, came to peddle their influence with him, he'd just shut them out.

Of course, that would make him no better than they. Maybe what he should do would be to simply claim his place in the family and prove that he could do better, be better than they. As if they'd care.

When he got down to breakfast he found Droagn and Grayshard already there. Grayshard was wearing his gray disguise for some reason, and was not eating, but Droagn had a huge plate of fresh fruit in front of him, with a side dish of raw meat. He could eat cooked, he just preferred it this way.

˜Coming down a little late this morning,˜ Droagn *projected*.

"I got in late this morning," Rikard looked at his watch. It was nearly noon. "I've had only about four hours sleep."

"I trust you were enjoying yourself," Grayshard said.

From anybody else it would have sounded sarcastic. Rikard wasn't sure that Grayshard knew what sarcasm was. "Not really. Every time I turned around I felt like an outsider." He helped himself to the eggs, sliced grilled devison, peaches, and rye toast the table offered him. "I never did meet my grandparents, though I saw them once, and maybe that's just as well."

˜Then why did you stay so long?˜

"Because I kept hoping a good chance would come up, because they're my family, because I actually like some of them, believe it or not."

˜You sound like you're beating yourself to death.˜

"Maybe I am." The food was delicious. He hadn't had much to eat the night before, just a lot of drink, and he was starved. "I've never known any of them except for Gawin. Maybe I should just give up on them. If they don't want me I won't impose myself."

"You are no imposition," Gawin said from the doorway. Gwineth was behind him. They both looked a lot better than Rikard felt.

"Good morning," Rikard greeted them. He decided to drop the topic.

"You don't look very well," Gwineth said as she and Gawin took their places at the table. She tried very hard not to stare at Droagn.

"I'm not," Rikard admitted. "But you do. When did you get in?"

"Around three. I came with Uncle Gawin. I thought I'd come for a visit as long as you were here." She selected food from the table, and cast curious glances at Rikard's companions.

"I'm flattered," Rikard said. "Forgive me," he added, and introduced her to Droagn and Grayshard.

"I'm so very pleased to meet you," Gwineth said to them. The formality over with, she was self-controlled again. Grayshard just nodded his acknowledgment, but Droagn grinned, showing all his teeth. Gwineth just giggled.

"I'm sorry we haven't had a chance to talk before now," Gawin said. "This to-do of Father's has taken all my attention. It's the one thing he expects me to attend during the year. So, what happened on DRG-17.iv?"

Rikard wasn't sure just what he should say in front of Gwineth, but both she and Gawin were looking at him expectantly, so he gave them a brief synopsis of what he'd found there.

Gawin was more than a little distressed. "And you have no clue as to who could possibly have scorched the planet?"

"None at all. Except that of course it had to have been somebody contemporary with the cyclopeans."

"That is correct," Grayshard said. "From all the evidence we were able to obtain while we were there, the planet could have been destroyed no more recently than one and one-half million years ago."

They finished their breakfast and the table cleared itself.

"I've been working on that data you brought back from Tsikashka," Gawin said. "Actually, I hired three people to do the work for me. Oh, they're trustworthy, I made sure of that. And they're very good too. There isn't much they can do about the text, of course, but they've been sorting out all the graphics, and they tell me they're making progress."

"Are you going to show it to me?" Rikard asked.

"Of course, that's why I came away last night. Father wanted me to stick around for another couple of days while the affair winds down. But there's another thing that might be even more important than the cyclopean graphics. You may not know it, Rikard, but you have quite a reputation in academic circles."

"I'll just bet I have."

"I mean besides being a cavalier upstart and renegade exploiter. I mean because of your papers, your publications. Whatever else people may say about you, they always pay attention to what you write, and you may or may not be pleased to know that several other reputations have been made by starting with something that you uncovered and just threw away."

"I see." Rikard cleared his throat. "And so?"

"And so, I've been trading on that aspect of your academic reputation, and I have been having some people trace some other things for me, related to the business at hand, specifically pre-Human cultures."

"My favorite topic," Rikard said dryly, "and the one that seems to arouse the most controversy."

"It does that," Gawin said, "but you check the references of anybody else who does any research in that area, and they always include you among their primary sources."

"I didn't know that. Ah, so who have you been dealing with?"

"Ahmed Rosala. Verjinia Dean. And Mikal Aspikov."

Rikard nodded. He knew them all, by reputation at least, and had met Dean once at a colloquium he had attended for only part of a day. "They're all pretty good," he said. "And very knowledgeable, according to what they have published. But how did you get them to cooperate?"

"By promising them first dibs on whatever we uncover about the cyclopeans. Don't worry, I was discreet. But they also did it because they value what you've uncovered before, even if they don't approve of your methods."

Rikard looked at his uncle, seeking some sign in his face or posture of sarcasm, or insincerity, but found none. "So what did you learn?"

"That something rather strange began to happen about two million years ago, and changed in a subtle but profound way about half a million years later."

In that time, he said, the centaurian Charvon and the arachnoid Ratash, both now extinct, dominated this part of the galaxy, and being significantly different from each other had little conflict of interest (except for basics like space, power, etc.) but also little desire to cooperate (except for basic trade). Each species found their most desirable worlds subtly different, so there was little conflict there, and the two mega-cultures, so different philosophically and politically (in basic premises if not in expression or resultant effect), overlapped in large part without actually sharing (except in certain unimportant ways and one or two exceptional instances).

At that time the miklewboid Kelarins were on their first rise, aggressive and ambitious, and trying to carve an empire for themselves. Basically a tolerant if somewhat violent race, they expressed little overt aggression against the two dominant peoples, though there was a lot of competition. They took what they could in their limited area, even in systems already occupied by the Charvon and Ratash.

There were other species too, of course, among them the less tolerant humanoid Thembeär, who had since gone away; the extinct humanoid Shapsis, content to share worlds with other species as long as they made a profit; the feloid Japaskoya, also gone away, who held only one system; the weird Thaapaii, now extinct, a shared-consciousness ant colony who held several systems; the extinct para-humanoid Kataash, about whom little was known; the mantisoid Fnom, ancient and on their way down even then; the serpentine Ahmear who existed in small numbers everywhere, and who left for parts unknown fifty thousand years ago; the humanoid Zapets who were at about the steam age then and on their way up, albeit slowly.

There were other beings who were not yet sentient, such as the proto-Humans, the proto-Tschagan, and so on. And another species, which would never have been detected except for the work Rikard and his friends had done, and which they knew only as the cyclopeans.

Rosala, Dean, and Aspikov realized, only since working on Rikard's new data, that there was a common cause for some things long noted but not understood, nor even considered in relation to each other. The most important was that at the present time actual space war was all but unheard of. There was plenty of conflict, but it was local, minor, held in check. If full weapons were ever unleashed, they could destroy whole worlds, whole solar systems, as had happened about seventy thousand years ago, when the Ting waged war on the Pa'aa'da, out on the other side of the Anarchy of Raas. The two interstellar cultures destroyed themselves and were now both extinct. And the point was that that happened way out there, not here in what was to become the Federation.

The Charvon and the Thembeär were generally mutually antagonistic, and there were other friction pairs and cases where the situation was worse—i.e. the Beberine subculture of Charvon and the Galtaia subculture of Thembeär, who fought to death or destruction whenever they met—and who hence avoided each other at all costs.

It was not a peaceful time, unlike the present. Surface wars were not uncommon if space conflict was rare and star war unheard of. In contrast, the Federation and other star nations of the present time were platonic ideals, models of peace, tolerance, cooperation, and interspecies brotherhood. The Federation was perhaps the exemplar, the other nations less so, and reportedly more distant nations knew more friction, conflict, and strife, but nothing like what was considered normal two million years ago. Compared to the Federation, that was a time of constant violence, conflict, minor war, and aggression.

And then, at about two million years ago, there came another influence, a sudden and not so subtle change in the behavior of those peoples in a certain group of stars that was now near the center of the Federation.

"The Legamine Influence!" Rikard interrupted.

"Exactly!" Gawin said.

"What's that?" Gwineth and Droagn asked together.

"Simply put," Rikard said, "in the neighborhood of what are now Vergreen and Semelar, people became not pacific but empathic with other people, and sympathetic."

"Do you know where those worlds are?" Gawin asked him.

"Not really."

"They are the nearest neighbors to DRG-17.iv."

"You mean," Droagn said, "it was the cyclopeans who produced this so-called Legamine Influence?

"What is this Legamine Influence, please?" Grayshard asked.

"Nobody knows for sure," Rikard said, "but one of the leading theories was that it was some kind of limited psychic effect—not telepathic, as the Ahmear were in their special and limited way, or as you Vaashka appear to be in your even more limited and specialized way, or as the Thaapaii were each within their own hive—but something similar. And my guess now is that it was produced by the cyclopeans, who radiated a similar telepathic aura, perhaps a sending only."

"That's the way it looks to me," Gawin said. "That is, that's the same conclusion my three tame historians came to. Now the point is this, that the Legamine Influence began about two million years ago, which coincides nicely with the origin, or discovery, or first interstellar travels of the cyclopeans. The influence continued to increase over time, until about a million and a half years ago.''

"When the cyclopeans dropped out," Grayshard said.

"Exactly. But during that time, people, regardless of their differences, grew to understand each other. The differences remained, and were unaffected. But hatreds based on misunderstanding, lack of sympathy, lack of feeling, did not continue. And the influence spread, farther than that crescent of stars that we now know were the cyclopean worlds. In fact," he said to Droagn, "it was Verjinia Dean who thought that the Influence and its spread coincided with the Ahmear Lambeza, who we know were associated with the cyclopeans, and who possibly took them with them wherever they went."

"But there was resistance," Rikard said. "As I remember reading about it, those peoples, and governments, and cultures that were not affected by the Influence were appalled. It seemed to them an invasion of their privacy, a perversion of their psychology. Some were more tolerant, of course, and some even thought it a good thing basically, but on the whole the reaction was negative, and some groups were violently opposed, due of course to basic intolerance, rigidity, paranoia, sense of threat, fear, and so on."

"Exactly," Gawin said. "Ahmed Rosala has told me that there are mysterious blanks in history, as if something were deliberately erased. And it seemed to him that they were all related, not isolated and independent losses as we've thought up till now."

"Centering on the crescent of cone worlds," Rikard said.

"Yes, but following the known trade routes of the Lambeza Ahmear. And one of the things the Lambeza traded were sculptures of a fine hard marble with integral color, and things like dishes and doorknobs and goblets and material for inlays."

"That implies," Grayshard said, "that the cyclopean artifacts convey the effect too."

"It makes sense," Droagn said. "Think of the effect associated with balktapline and the other Tathas residues."

"We have to remember," Gawin said, "that the effect did not eliminate differences, or natural competition for resources, or hatreds based on those differences and natural conflicts. And it had little effect on the insane, or on the criminal mind. What it did do was enable people to understand each other better, even if they didn't agree or otherwise like each other. We've known about the Influence, and how that marks the Federation off from other star nations, such as Raas, or Abogarn, or whatever. We just didn't have any clues as to what caused it—until now."

"One of the mysteries," Rikard said, "is why and how the Influence ended. But if we remember that not everybody was pleased with the Influence . . ."

"Exactly," Gawin said. "Mikal Aspikov told me that this kind of understanding is always perceived as a threat by the bigoted, greedy, and selfish. So we can imagine that once the Influence was recognized as an actual outside influence, rather than a natural internal development, someone would try to put a stop to it."

"But this had been going on for half a million years," Gwineth said, "according to the dates you've named. What took them so long to figure it out?"

"Who knows?" Rikard said. "It was a subtle thing. But think about it, this Influence is what sets us in the Federation off from all other star nations. The cyclopeans either caused it, or spread it, or were somehow otherwise associated with it. And then somebody figured it out that it was them, and they scorched the home world. But what about all the other cone worlds? They all died off at about the same time, but they weren't scorched."

"That suggests," Grayshard said, "that those other worlds were not viable breeding colonies. Suppose the cyclopeans could reproduce only on their own world, or that only a few individuals actually bred, as among social insects. Suppose those colonies were all sterile, as far as they were concerned. Kill the home world, and the others will die in a generation or so. And the other worlds were all inhabited by other species, so whoever committed genocide would have been less eager to take them out too."

"It's as good an hypothesis as any," Rikard said. "And whoever did it, they apparently did not know about the moon base."

˜You know,˜ Droagn said, ˜there's something about that place that has been bothering me ever since we were there, but I couldn't put my finger on it until Gawin suggested that the cyclopeans might have been traveling along with the Lambeza. That moon base bore no resemblance to other cyclopean architecture whatsoever. It had to be built in part with Ahmear technology. And if that is true, and if Gawin's guesses about the relationship between the Lambeza and the cyclopeans is true, then I suspect that the Lambeza were instrumental in the cyclopeans' escape to parts unknown.˜

"The ironic thing," Gawin said, "was that, according to Ahmed Rosala and Mikal Aspikov, the destruction of the home world—and the eventual demise of surviving and disbursed cyclopeans—did not halt the effect of the Legamine Influence, or indeed prevent its spread. Indeed, when Humans became ascendant long later, the effect, though now thinly spread and diluted, continued to operate, though nobody knew its origin or cause. It was detected because some worlds, such as the Earth of Humans, had never been infected, and hence did not have the effect."

"So there are people," Gwineth said, "who are actually studying this Influence."

"Yes," Rikard said. "It is known to exist, is very poorly understood, and most of the people who are knowledgeable about it, in the Federation and elsewhere, wish it could be enhanced. I mean, rational people are, on the whole, more interested in growth, understanding, knowledge, trade, and cultural development than in paranoid self-defense, isolationism, monomaniacal independence, or unnecessary proving of self-worth due to imagined inferiority.''

"We are all a part of the psychic network," Gawin said, "even a million and a half years later. The cones are of minimal importance these days, those worlds are no more Influenced than any other. There's a lot about psychic networks that nobody understands, not even psychic races.''

˜You can say that again,˜ Droagn said.

"It is unfortunately too true," Grayshard agreed.

"So the continuation of the Influence implies," Gawin said, "the continuation of something else, the survivors of the moon base. Where did they go?''

"I have recordings of the maps and things from DRG-17.iv," Rikard said, "which may give us an idea.''

"Let's do it now," Gawin said. A servant came in at that moment, and Gawin instructed him, with Rikard's permission, to go to Rikard's rooms for the recorder. Then they all left the breakfast room.

As they went to his private study, Gawin took Rikard aside and said, "This is the biggest thing anybody has ever discovered, but there's a chance we could lose it.''

"How so?''

"I know now," Gawin said as they entered the study, "how Karyl Toerson has been able to wield such influence as to get planetary government assistance in her depredations on Tsikashka. She and Father are still lovers.''

"What are you talking about?" Gwineth demanded, surprised. "Who is Karyl Toerson, and when were they ever lovers before?''

Gawin filled her in quickly. "And so," he finished, "Father is protecting her, and letting her get away with what she's doing. I'm pretty sure Mother doesn't know about it.''

"How did you find out?" Rikard asked.

"One of my agents found herself involved in the sale of a cyclopean artifact. It was just an accident, she helps me keep track of the shadier parts of the black market. Toerson was selling, and someone we don't need to name was buying, but there was someone else behind the scenes.''

"Grandfather.''

"Exactly. It was just ten days before the party last night.''

"Does he know about my involvement with that stuff?'' Rikard asked.

"If he did,'' Gawin said, "you would never have been allowed in last night. Whatever Father may feel about Toerson, he feels even more strongly about his reputation. If you do anything to jeopardize that, he will defend himself and seek retribution.

"Remember what he did to your mother. I finally figured out that part of the problem there was that Father hadn't been able to rescue her himself, and when Arin did, it put Father in a bad light, and he couldn't stand it, or the fact that Sigra loved Arin more than she did Father.''

"So it looks like I've got to stay out of Toerson's way,'' Rikard said.

"At the very least. But let's see what we can find out from the recordings you've brought.''

Gawin set up his database and computer, and Rikard took his recording helmet from the servant who discreetly appeared just then, and got out the disks. He put them into Gawin's player, which would also input to the computer, and showed the geological and the labeled political maps.

"This is fantastic. Those symbols there''—Gawin pointed to several on the map, which Rikard and his companions had figured meant city and capital—"correspond nicely with some we've been working on here,'' and he showed some of the translation work he'd had done, on a separate screen. "And now, the map symbols make some of these other things make sense.''

They examined the polychrome text files next, but there was no way they could interpret them yet, though Gawin had hopes about one or two of his contacts eventually being able to make some progress. They knew they had them transliterated correctly, however, since some of the pictures could be compared with some of the texts, so they knew they had the colors right and so on. But it was important that some of the map symbols, which could be interpreted in context, were identical with some of the text symbols. "And there you have the start of it," Gawin said.

"Exactly," Rikard echoed, "a kind of fragmentary Rosetta stone."

For the next part of their analysis Gawin displayed anything with any graphic element at all. There was a lot of stuff that was trivial, or symbolic, or otherwise uninterpretable, but there was plenty that was truly graphic and intended to convey meaning by picture alone, and this had been separated by those whom Gawin had hired to work on the project.

Now, with the new clues from the maps, they did another sort, and found other maps that they had not at first recognized as such, and other graphics in which the symbols appeared as superimposed text. At the same time Gawin set his program to similarly analyze the pictures relative to his own database.

It turned out that there were a number of relationships and correspondences between what was known about the space in which the Federation existed and the existence of the cyclopeans. There were the cone ruins, as they had previously discovered. There were other places where reports of colored marble of a particular nature might actually have been cyclopean inscriptions, though no ruins were associated with them. There was a strong association between the cyclopean ruins and the known centers of Lambeza activity between one and a half and two million years ago, although their knowledge of other Ahmear sites was very limited. There was also new evidence that DRG-17.iv was in fact the world of origin of the cyclopeans, and their dispersal from there corresponded with the presence of the Lambeza culture.

There were no hints as to who destroyed DRG-17.iv, and the question still remained, to where did the lunar colony flee to find refuge?

Gawin still had the Ahmear archaeology text that Rikard

had brought back from Trokarion, and he loaded it into the program. After it had assimilated it, the computer identified some of the pictures as having been taken on Trokarion itself, by a simple comparison of vegetation, distant mountains, sky patterns, and other labels too subtle for the untrained to appreciate. But there were no cones on Trokarion as far as the database showed.

Nonetheless, Gawin was intrigued, and Rikard was too, and together they instituted a new analysis of the archaeological book, fitting it in with the cyclopean records, and found that it was more recent by some short but unspecified time after the destruction of the home world one and a half million years ago.

Which meant that the cyclopeans pictured in the Ahmear text were survivors after the scorching of DRG-17.iv, and were the refugees from the moon colony. All other cyclopean activity had ceased when the home world was destroyed, but this group had continued for at least a few thousand years longer, and maybe a lot more, and then had disappeared from the record without any evidence of having been destroyed. Leaving no cone.

Rikard compared the dimensions of a typical cone with the size of the Ahmear ruin he had uncovered. It was much smaller. But one of the pictures in the Ahmear text showed a small cone next to a gigantic structure with towers at the four corners.

"I think," Droagn said, "that this might be the Ahmear city we explored on Trokarion."

"And if it is," Rikard said, "then the cyclopean cone in that picture is buried under the volcano along with that city."

"It makes perfect sense to me," Grayshard said. "It seems we might like to make a return trip to Trokarion."

Trokarion

1

The Federation, taken as a whole, is a utopia. There has been no large-scale internal conflict for as long as there is unbroken history, since long before the advent of the M'Kade more than a thousand standard years ago. The star nations that surround, such as the Anarchy of Raas, the Segorian Union, or the Melagid Empire, are far more interesting places to live.

Not only do local governments there, as even in the Federation, sometimes undergo upheaval, but the star nation itself sometimes must go through trying times. Indeed the Crescent was once known as the Benevolent League before the dictatorship was put down some three thousand years ago.

Scholars in the Federation and out of it have all remarked on the stability of those worlds that are known as the Federation, on the continuity of its government, even through the time of troubles when the M'Kade came into power. His advent caused only a return to stability, not a revolution, and though his power is great, his influence is seldom felt. The stability is not his doing, and existed far back into history, even before the dispersal from Home-Space, the time when

Humankind, after an interregnum of unknown duration, formed its first alliance from among the star systems they had once previously populated.

But this nearly ideal state is not caused by Humankind either, for the other nearby star nations are also predominantly Human, though in the Coryanth Cluster, so-called, they are a bare majority, and they do not share the enduring culture of the Federation. Scholars have long suspected some other cause, something to do with the stars, with that region of space, some vector transmitted from world to world. There are other evidences, though sometimes they conflict.

But even in the Federation, not all places are utopian. By its very nature, the Federation allows its member worlds considerable freedom, even if the exercise of that freedom involves civil war and bloodshed. Hence they did not interfere with Trokarion's troubles, though they kept them from spilling out into other worlds where the Kelarins of that world traveled. Keep your troubles at home was one rule the Federation enforced. And at the same time, if someone wanted to visit such a world and got caught up with its toils, no one was liable for any undue consequences other than the visitor himself.

Rikard knew that when he returned to Trokarion, to the country of Elsepreth that had been in bloody conflict with itself for two centuries, to the city of New Darkon, where there were deaths every day. His previous presence was a matter of record, his precipitous and unauthorized departure similarly. He was liable to arrest, and if not trial, at least punishment. And he could expect no outside help if he were caught. He knew that. So did Endark Droagn and Grayshard. Which was why they were so cautious.

It was night. Rikard sat at the controls of a special vehicle, which resembled a rubble clearance truck. Grayshard was beside him, Droagn was in back, along with their equipment. They moved slowly along the streets of the once-quiet Wildercroft area, and stopped now and then when they came to a damaged building. There scoopers came out from the sides of the truck and moved the rubble around a bit, but never actually cleared anything away. From outside, the truck looked as though it were nearly full. Inside, it was Droagn's compartment covered by a false top, though the rubble above it was real enough.

They passed an intersection. Suddenly armed Kelarins started shooting at each other from either side of the street. The truck hunkered down. The rebels used it for cover, but were not otherwise interested in it. After all, the rubble had to be cleared away, and those who did the job were left alone by both sides, for the most part.

Then uniformed soldiers broke into the intersection, and the rebels fled. The soldiers, too, paid the truck no attention, except as opportune cover.

The battle moved on, and after a while the truck started to move again. It turned a corner two blocks from the place where Rikard and his companions had come out of the cellars the last time they had been here.

The truck moved on, slowly. A group of civilians came out of a building, saw the truck, and quickly passed it by. A vehicle crossed the intersection but did not slow.

They crossed the intersection and saw an armored vehicle, half a block away, ready lights on, facing toward them. They drove on straight toward it, but when they came to a side street they turned up it. It was where they wanted to go anyway.

Halfway up the block they came to the entrance with the double glass door by which they had exited when they had fled the Ahmear ruins. The truck pulled up to the curb, paused, then part of its top tipped and the rubble piled there spilled out on either side of the doorway. The top settled back and waited a long moment. Then robotic scoopers came out from the front and back end of the truck, as if to retrieve the rubble, but a side shaft on one of the scoopers broke out of line. The truck shut down, with only its ready lights glowing, and looked as though it were interrupted in its business and the crew had gone off for repairs.

The truck sat silent for five minutes, then Rikard got out,

heavily laden, went to the double glass door, and opened it. Then Grayshard, followed by Droagn, who was also carrying a lot of stuff, came out of the truck and went through the door. Rikard closed the door behind them.

He paused to put on and adjust his recording helmet, then they turned into a side corridor and went through it to a back foyer. There they took the stairs down, to another corridor with branches right and left and along it to a cellar with windows high in the walls. From there they went down a shaft sunk in the floor to a plastic composite serviceway where lights still burned, along several branches of this serviceway to a manhole and down the ladder there to concrete sewers even farther below. They went along them to sewers made of brick, and to ancient underground serviceways lined with stone, to a room where stone stairs led down to ancient stone chambers with barrel arches. The floor was covered with half-damp muck, there were rotting crates and barrels in the corners and along some of the walls. The doorways were rotting and sagging. They went on to a new hole broken through the wall that opened into a narrow lava tube, which slanted down, rather steeply at first but soon more gently, rather narrow at first but soon more broadly, until they came to a bubble.

But as they went along the tube they noticed signs of Elsepreth government presence. There were lots of foot marks, and claw marks, and the sharp points on the sides of the tube had been broken off, and now and then they found bits of long Kelarine fur. As they worked deeper into the lava tubes and began to see signs of neo-Ahmear workings, the Elsepreth presence diminished. Still they were cautious. Who knew how the neo-Ahmear now felt about things, especially if they had been shot at by the government.

Then Droagn paused, and peered around in the darkness, as if he expected to see in the light of their lamps something other than black volcanic glass. The Prime, its sharp points glinting in Rikard's lamp, rested on his head as always, and it was with this that he detected the presence of the neo-

Ahmear, not that far off in the tunnels, and knew, by their cautious movements, that they in turn were aware of the three of them.

¯Shall I call them?¯ he *projected* to Rikard alone.

"By all means," Rikard said.

And so, using his special form of telepathy, augmented by the Prime, Endark Droagn did his best to get those decadent descendants of his own people to come to him. It took a while, but eventually they came.

If they were the same serpent men with whom they had dealt before, even Droagn could not tell, but one of them wore the Subordinate that he had left with them.

With guidance and suggestions from Rikard and Grayshard, Droagn tried to establish communications with these most distant cousins, but their behavior was, as before, always somewhat off the mark, not what Droagn expected, and seemingly arbitrary. He had no real control of the situation.

After a bit Rikard tried to get them to communicate with him vocally, and used a translator to help. This was only partially successful, since it appeared that the neo-Ahmear seldom used their voices except to call through the caves at long distance.

But eventually they began to make some progress. They learned that the neo-Ahmear called themselves the RoTakhh, that they had seen the Kelarine soldiers but didn't confuse them with Rikard's party, that the RoTakhh were confused instead by their discovery of an aboveground world about which they had only myths. And yes, Toerson's people had gotten away, by the simple expedient of laying down a barrage of automatic weapon fire which the RoTakhh just couldn't withstand.

Rikard had come prepared with simple pictures of a mummified cyclopean, one of their cone cities, and of a wall with its colored writing. He had also brought a small cyclopean sculpture. He showed these to the RoTakhh, who conferred among themselves before answering that the cyclopeans were mythical beings in whom they did not believe.

They had never seen a cone from the outside, of course, but they recognized the color-smeared walls as being in a space they knew underground, adjacent to but on the other side of the Ahmear ruins. But that place was cursed, taboo, blessed, or haunted—it was impossible to tell exactly which concept they had in mind or more closely described how they felt about it—and they refused to go there or discuss it further. Even though they thought of Droagn as some kind of special person, or perhaps a demi-god, or maybe a demon from the past, they wouldn't be swayed, and the more Rikard pressed, the more they threatened to become dangerous.

"I think it's about time for me to take a hand in this," Grayshard said. Rikard drew a veil of protective material across the parts of his face that were exposed by the recording helmet. Then Grayshard, one of the warrior class of the Vaashka, began to exert his peculiar influence, half-psychic, half-chemical.

The RoTakhh were not as susceptible as other people to this form of attack. They did not fall down on the floor screaming, or thrash around with their four arms wrapped around their heads. But they were not immune, either, and began to slightly sway from side to side, though one or two rose up and down on their coils instead.

Droagn *projected* at them too. They wove and now and then one of them dipped, but they did not turn away to lead them anywhere. ˜A little more,˜ Droagn said to Grayshard.

"I'll try."

Droagn winced, as if he could feel Grayshard's *projection*. He turned to face first one of the now-quivering RoTakhh, then another, but they resisted his silent importunings.

"Don't just push them," Rikard said after a moment. "Tell them you're their boss, play on their myths and superstitions."

˜Might as well.˜ Droagn's thought was a bit strained. ˜They're not going to give in to threats.˜

Whatever it was he was saying to the RoTakhh, it seemed to be working, for after a moment they all began to weave and bob in unison, and raised their arms as if in supplication. One of them began suddenly to swipe at something invisible in the air beside him, and another curled up and put his arms over his face, but the others were making gestures and postures of acceptance.

"Looks like they'll do what we want," Rikard said.

"They will. For a while."

"Let them off," Rikard said to Grayshard. And though the Vaashka had no bones, Rikard could see him visibly relax.

"The air should be clear now," Grayshard said after a moment. Rikard undid the veil across his face, and felt none of the Vaashka combat effect.

"Let's go see what their home looks like," Rikard suggested, "and we can move on from there."

Droagn nodded, gestured imperiously with his upper right hand, and the RoTakhh, drunk and hallucinating, turned away and led them through the lava tubes deep into their own realms.

When they came to the center of the neo-Ahmear caverns, worked and built and excavated from the volcanic tuff and lava, they realized that they had misjudged the snake men, or had been duped by them, because the cavern was bright, clean, well designed, well ventilated, and extensive. The warriors had no clothing, but the civilian snake men here wore harnesses similar to Droagn's, decorated with stones and with well-worked pieces of their lost technology. Though cut off for fifty thousand years and buried underground, they were a well-established culture. There were children, who had toys, and the people they saw were engaged in meaningful tasks, though most of them stopped to watch the procession with obvious apprehension.

They were taken through several passages between private and common places to a center where they found five chiefs waiting, flanked by four wise men, all wearing marks of rank, arm bands and headbands and collars. A "runner" had obviously been sent ahead with the word of Rikard's arrival.

One of the five chiefs took the Sub from the soldier who was wearing it and put it on his own head. He looked at Droagn, who looked back at him—or her—and who kept himself a full head higher than the others. There were greetings, and then the conference began. Droagn took his cues from Rikard, though he used "language" that reinforced his image as a superior and powerful being. The nine members of RoTakhh government paid practically no attention to Rikard and Grayshard, except perhaps as curiosities, but focused on Droagn.

They were the Nine. The five chiefs were symbolically the head and the four arms of the government, and the flanking wise men were priests of some kind, and represented four more arms, advisers without a competing head. Through Droagn the visitors were made to feel welcome. Other RoTakhh brought cushions to make them comfortable, and the priests started a kind of ceremonial chant in the background while the chief and his four "Arms" conferred with Droagn, who reported to Rikard as well as he could what was going on.

The RoTakhh really had no interest in the outside world, though they had legends, some of which were surprisingly accurate. Their primary concern about the invaders from above ground was that they return there, and that people leave them alone. As the "Head" and his four "Arms" spoke, the four priests went on about their business in the background, with decorative ribbons, incense, and later some younger and smaller acolytes who helped out.

That established, Rikard used Droagn as a sort of intermediary to talk with the chiefs about the cyclopeans. He showed them the pictures, the sculpture, and asked about them.

At first the "Head" and the four "Arms" reacted much as the RoTakhh soldiers had, but then, through Droagn, Rikard talked to them about their history before their seclusion, and speculated on what had happened since then, thus proving that he knew a lot more than any stranger, and asked about the cyclopeans again.

This time the chiefs' reluctance to talk had more of the feel as if they were concealing something. Meanwhile the priests went on about their business, which seemed to be centering around Droagn. They moved Rikard and Grayshard out of the way so they could decorate Droagn with ribbons and paint and other ornaments, which he let them do though with some misgivings.

Rikard, through Droagn and following some of his suggestions, probed the chiefs' reluctance, assuring them that they meant no harm, believed in the cyclopeans, and would rather find them with their assistance than without. The priests continued their business, and at last seemed done, and the chiefs stopped paying attention to the dialogue altogether and instead focused on Droagn as the center of some elaborate ceremony.

"What the hell is going on?" Rikard asked him.

¨I'm not sure,¨ Droagn said, ¨but I seem to be the direct object of their veneration.¨

"Lucky you. Can you get them back on the subject?"

¨I'm trying, but—it seems they think of me as a hero-god from the past who has come to save them—except I think that means to be their religious slave.¨

"That does not sound encouraging," Grayshard said.

¨It's not. As near as I can make it out, when this ceremony is done and I have been 'invested,' you two will just be killed and the new church will be established, or something like that.¨

"Where the hell did we go wrong?" Rikard exclaimed. The priests and the chiefs paid no attention, but continued with their chant.

¨I don't know, but I don't seem to have any control over them at all.¨

"We'll have to fight," Grayshard said.

¨Unless you just want to shoot them all, that's not a good idea. These guys are smaller than I, but they're tough, and in a fight I wouldn't stand a chance. And then there's everybody outside.¨

"Let's not get excited," Grayshard said. "I think I have an idea. Cover yourself, Rikard. And, Droagn, just follow my lead."

He moved so that he was standing right behind Droagn, and when the priests moved away to pick up a kind of robe, and the chiefs were intent on their own preparations, he slipped out of his disguise onto Droagn's back, and left his empty clothes standing by themselves. "When I'm in place," he vocalized as he climbed up onto Droagn's head, "start waving your arms around as my words suggest, and *project* to them something similar."

⁻I'm game.⁻

Before the RoTakhh chiefs and priests realized anything was going on, Grayshard had formed his body around Droagn's head into a kind of medusa mask. For his part, Droagn rose up ever higher on his coils, and raised his arms and flexed his muscles in melodramatic command. Then Grayshard *projected*, as he had before, and as soon as the RoTakhh were under the influence, Droagn commanded them all to fall back. They did, and cowered, and then Droagn and Grayshard together, after a moment's consultation, conveyed a simple message the gist of which was, "Enough of this, let's get on with business. If I'm the god, then you should be obeying me, and not the other way around."

This seemed to do the trick. The RoTakhh became completely servile and covered their faces on command so that Grayshard could slip down off Droagn's head unobserved and back into his disguise. Rikard and his companions waited a moment for the RoTakhh to regain their senses, and when they looked up at Droagn, and saw him now back to normal except for the grin that revealed teeth much larger and longer and sharper than theirs, they seemed ready to listen.

Droagn, as Rikard's mouthpiece, again stated that all they wanted was to visit the site of the cyclopeans. They promised that they would remove nothing, which seemed to reassure them. One of the "Arms" said something that Rikard could not comprehend, but Droagn included him in his reply, which was that, when they left the RoTakhh, they would convey knowledge of their presence to others of their kin on other worlds.

The chiefs at last admitted that there were indeed cyclopean chambers adjacent to the Ahmear ruins, off to the side opposite from their present dwelling. Droagn asked for guides, and the chiefs were reluctant, but he reminded them of who he was, and they agreed.

The guides arrived. The chiefs and priests seemed relieved to see Droagn depart.

The guides led the three toward the Ahmear ruins but did not enter. Instead they circled around through a passage cut through the lava, descending all the way with occasional passages cut toward the ruins as if to verify its position. The outer surface of the ruins were covered with marks of some kind.

In one place a large natural cave went off away from the ruins, and there were lots of RoTakhh there, and others farther in, it was to be assumed. There was a kind of natural luminescence there, and Droagn paused to ask questions. He used his most powerful *projecting*, and the guides complied quickly.

Down here were the farms. The heat came from far below. The light was of mineral origin and not much use, but in other parts the light, which caused sickness among the RoTakhh, provided energy for the plants. There was water—some hot, some cold, some lit. Stinking air came from some low passages, useful for certain plants though deadly to animals. There were animals, including the fathak that had been domesticated and several other natural subterranean species. There were many caves and tubes beyond the farms, but the guides knew little in particular about them.

"We'd better move on," Grayshard said. They descended still farther.

They passed by several smaller caverns, and then on around the Ahmear ruins to what Rikard estimated must be the opposite side from that by which they had approached it. A passage turned away and slanted down, and they went on until they came to a place where the nature of the RoTakhh excavations changed, becoming galleries facing a different kind of stone, the white marble shell-stone of the cyclopean cone.

There were no marks on this stone as there had been on the Ahmear ruins. The RoTakhh guides were reverent in a different way here. Rikard took the lead, in spite of the guides' uncertainty, and went up several galleries until he came to smears of color on the marbleized surface. This stone had been further changed by the molten lava that buried it, but the cyclopean colors were perfectly legible.

"If I'm not mistaken," Rikard said to his companions, "we should now be at the ground floor."

"I think you're right," Grayshard said. "Our first approach was at the foundation."

The RoTakhh excavations went up and around, and they followed these, past changes in stone both cyclopean and natural, until they came to a portal. The RoTakhh didn't want them to enter the sacred place, but Droagn offered to sacrifice one of them to assure the safety of the party and they put up no further resistance. Droagn applied a pair of suction devices to the panel, to give him something to hold on to, then pulled the door open. He offered the guides permission to enter, but they refused, and coiled down just outside the door to wait.

"Let's go," Rikard said, and he and Grayshard and Droagn went in.

2

The place was at once recognizable as cyclopean, and yet it felt strange since it was perfectly preserved, including furnishings, decorations, and objects and surfaces the nature of which they could not guess. They went up one passage and through a couple chambers, marveling at what they saw. Flat pedestals stood on once elastic feet, in shades of yellow and amber. Sheets of some gossamer material sometimes hung from the ceiling, though the space divided made no sense as separate rooms. There were crystal objects like bicycle wheels with no spokes. In one place a series of tetrahedral solids, connected like vertebrae, snaked through an open door that had a gap in its foot to allow it to be closed without disturbing the chain. And on and on.

"There's a bit of a problem of chronology here," Rikard said at one point. "Everywhere else, the cyclopeans died out about a million and a half years ago. But this city was buried only fifty thousand years ago." He paused to look at a coil of red wire with blue bristles sticking out of it, leaning up against a corner.

"I think we have to assume that this colony of cyclopeans existed until then," Grayshard said.

˜I think we do,˜ Droagn said. ˜We know that the Lambeza took the cyclopeans with them, so they would have given them shelter here.˜

"But if they could only breed on their home world," Rikard said, "how could they breed here, and for a million and a half years?"

˜I haven't the vaguest idea.˜

They came on a thing like a half an orange but a full meter across, with purple seeds dripping from the cut surface, which faced down at an angle. Passing through a door, they stepped onto a kind of rug that crumbled to gray dust under them. Where undamaged, it was a velvety pile in red and blue, with white highlights. On the far side of the chamber was a stack of crystal beads on a wire. The dust from their passage across the rug swirled around the beads, and seemed to be drawn into them. They went on into the next room.

They went more quickly now. Though there was lots to

see on their route, much of it was repetitious, and they were eager to get to the data banks. They hurried down, level after level, pausing only when they found bodies of the cyclopeans. The first one was a badly distorted corpse lying in the middle of a room next to a crescent-shaped desk. Its body was flattened by dehydration, and a stain across the floor told of body fluids leaking out long ago. What was interesting was the stylus it held in one of its tentacles. Like many of the utensils they'd seen, it had a star-shaped handle, and the tentacle was twisted around the stellations in such a way that it could apply leverage in any direction.

The second time the body was rather better preserved. It was leaning against a kind of corrugated ramp, and along one side extensive decay had set in, but most of it was intact. The snaillike foot was pale cream below and deep blue above. The body, which contained the sacklike mouth, shaded through green to a muted ochre on the shaft that supported the tentacles and the eyestalk, which was itself nearly white. The eye had lids, which were open, and it looked as though the eye had once been red. The inside of the mouth pouch was nearly black, but it could once have been a deep blue, or even purple. The tentacles were orange, tipped with black. Rikard got a full recording in several wavelengths and illuminations.

The third time it was a set of five corpses, what appeared to be two adults and three children, or at least smaller individuals of various sizes. They were all rather well preserved, though their colors were less striking than in the previous find. They were slumped more or less together against a closed door, as if they had been trying to get through when they had died. Rikard and his companions left them in peace.

At last they reached the museum floor. The museum here was much the same as the other two they had seen, except that there were perishable materials here, which were somehow preserved despite at least fifty thousand standard years of burial.

They did not bother with the artifacts. They went right to the center of the museum, where Droagn lifted Grayshard up so he could bring down the ceiling elevator. Then they went up to the communications center, where the lights, rather more bluish than usual, came on as soon as they came through the floor.

They quickly located the main output station, and Rikard set up his recording equipment. This time he was prepared with enough disks to hold everything within the computer's data banks. As soon as he was ready, Droagn set up a simple dump—he hoped—and now there was nothing to do but wait.

But here, as elsewhere in this cone, there were common things preserved, as if this place hadn't been emptied out, but had died by surprise. There was a cyclopean body over at one console, the equivalent of plates and cups and notebooks here and there, and some pieces of equipment different from what they had seen before, lying on the consoles or desks, and looking very much like output devices, not exactly headsets, since the cyclopeans didn't have heads in that way, but the equivalent perhaps, a springy coil about fifteen centimeters in diameter that stretched out to about seventy centimeters long, on the inside surface of which were a number of electrosensitive contacts.

Grayshard picked one of them up and looked it over. "Not made for a head like yours," he said, "but since I don't have a head either . . ." He peeled back his turban and goggles and extruded a dense mass of red-tipped white fibers. He lifted the coil over his shoulders and set it down on the bundle of fibers, and let it settle into place. "It would probably have gone around their 'neck,' just under the juncture of eyestalk and tentacles," he guessed. "Not actually audio output, but direct neural stimulation."

"You don't have any nerves, either," Rikard said.

"Doesn't matter." He put the jack into one of the obvious receptacles on the desk, flipped a nearby switch, jerked once, pulled the coil partially away from his recoiling tentacles, felt around on the surface of the desk and diddled with several vernier dials, and then relaxed. "As I said, direct neural input. Doesn't make any sense, of course."

"Let me try it," Rikard said. Grayshard handed the coil to him, then put his head back together. Rikard wrapped the coil around his own head and felt the input, dim and fuzzy, probably because it had to go through his skull. There seemed to be random physical sensations snapping around softly in various places in the spaces inside his head, associated with colors and tastes, but no sound. Moments of pressure might have been analogous. It was not static, but changed and rippled, and though it did not interfere with his normal perceptions, it was rather pronounced. He adjusted the coil and the overall pattern of the locations of the sensory inputs changed. It was made to fit a certain diameter body and to stimulate certain specific nerve centers. He took it off and handed it to Droagn.

But Droagn already had two other output coils. He gave one to Grayshard, put one on himself, and Rikard put the one he was holding back on. Then they all tuned in together.

It took a while, but between the three of them they began to make sense of the outputs, how to adjust the coils, how the controls on the desk worked. Though the content of the output remained elusive, they knew they were on the right track when the direct "brain" interface suddenly gave them access to each other. For a while they got lost in mutual telepathy. This was similar to the mode of communication with which Droagn was familiar, so he was able to help them figure it out. When they could "talk" to each other meaningfully, they turned their attention to whatever it was that was the "mind" of the computer.

Again, Droagn's experience was the most help here. His expertise in computer logic told him that regardless of the psychological differences between them and the cyclopeans, they still had to use the same mathematics of binary digits, and even though the technologies might differ, electricity still flowed or it didn't.

After an indefinite time they took a break for a quiet meal. Rikard's recording helmet was still downloading. Then they plugged back in again, and now they began to try to learn how to "think like cyclopeans."

Rikard had had an experience once, years ago, when he had met a race so old that its age was meaningless, the Taarshome who had shielded his father when he had been trapped underground by the Tathas, and who had been among the first three or four sentiences in the universe. Noncorporeal bundles of energy, or pure mind, or matrices of potential fields, whatever they were they were not like any other life form. They had existed, and grown, and gone away, and come back, and it had been through Rikard's auspices that they had begun to integrate themselves into corporeal society within the Federation.

And once Rikard had communicated directly with one of them. There had been other times when he had helped others learn how to "speak" with these things the natives of Kohltri called "dragons," but it had been on a more superficial level, since to touch a Taarshome was to fry to a cinder immediately.

But that one time, somehow without killing himself, Rikard had shared minds with another in a way even Droagn couldn't imagine. It had changed him in subtle ways, so that now, when he thought about the cyclopeans, and about the Taarshome, and about thinking their thoughts, something clicked inside his head, a memory came back into his mind, and with Grayshard and Droagn along with him, he began to make sense of what had been stored in the cyclopeans' computer.

It took a while. Sometimes they lost track of time. Occasionally Rikard had to load a new set of disks into his helmet recorder. They needed to eat. But mostly they experienced directly the contents of the computer. They examined random documents until they began to understand what they contained, then initiated a three-way search looking for history.

Grayshard found the first clue, a series of concepts and computer constructs that had to do with time. They turned their attention in that direction until they began to feel that they knew how to distinguish past and future in cyclopean terms.

Droagn found the second clue, simply a matter of a further refinement of the computer's indexing system, the form of the data structures, the style of addressing and memory allocation. Even Droagn had to admit that it felt strange doing this from the inside out, and Rikard could see how this one bit of cyclopean technology could revolution- ize the information industry. Too bad he had other things to think about, he could get rich that way.

And then it was his turn to find something. It wasn't history, it was biology.

Working together they examined the files, and from these they learned that the cyclopeans could propagate either by laying eggs, or by fission and cloning. And the important part was that cloning did not prolong their lives appreciably. Given a life span of five hundred years, the products of fission or cloning could expect to add only about fifty years overall, and later fissions and clones proportionately less. In time they died.

Only individuals born from eggs could live a full life, and as it worked out the only place where eggs were laid was on their home world, which was the only place where the cyclopeans could exist while not in a symbiotic condition.

A viable colony of egg-layers, long since put by on their moon, had managed to survive the holocaust visited on them for reasons they did not understand. When the destruc- tion was safely over, they left secretly, under the auspices of the Lambeza Ahmear. They came to Trokarion, of course, and built this cone, so it was just under one and a half million years old. It was the only cyclopean colony and had somehow continued to survive down to the time when it had been buried by the same volcanic catastrophe that had destroyed the Ahmear city fifty thousand years ago. But unlike the Ahmear, who had left when the volcano had begun to erupt, the cyclopeans had chosen to remain.

Here the documentation ended.

They withdrew their attentions, their minds, from the computer. Rikard made special recordings of this and related files, which he secreted on his person, while the main recorder continued to download the entire library.

They had been working for some two standards days by this time, but it would still be a while before the major recording was completed. After taking a break for rest, refreshment, and a bit of exercise, they plugged in again and looked through the files related to the cyclopeans' biology. Most of them would prove of immense interest to scholars later, but not to Rikard and his friends at the moment.

But that was how they found out that there was something else recorded that didn't show up on the directory. Droagn did some hacking and found a late-coded document that got glitched somehow, and they looked in.

It was a special note, appended to a file on egg mainte- nance, left as an afterthought, after all other files had been closed during the volcano, as if a message to whoever might come after. Much of it was unintelligible, but the gist of it was that the reason the cyclopeans hadn't left the cone when the volcano threatened was that they wanted to protect a special refuge below the cone.

They all three came out of the net.

"Only one thing makes sense," Grayshard said. Had his mechanical voice been capable of expressing emotion, it would have done so now.

"Eggs," Droagn said. "What could that special refuge possibly be but a cache of eggs?"

"It's the only answer," Rikard said. "You don't suppose they could still be viable?"

"Circumstantial evidence," Grayshard said, "indicates that they might well be."

¯You mean the power being on and all?¯

"I mean the continued attitude of empathy and tolerance as evidenced by the Federation in comparison to all other star nations."

Rikard made a special recording of this file, which he could play back on his helmet set, to which he connected remote outputs so that Droagn and Grayshard could examine the text with him. They had only examined the first few entries of the file, and there were some clues further on as to where this egg cache might be. Logically enough, when they found the information, the cache proved to be deep under the base of the cone.

"But how do we get there?" Rikard said, as they disconnected again.

There were panels in the perimeter of the computer base, which led to passages, all of which were lit. These all connected with a circumferential passage, from which descent tubes in the wall between the museum and the outside corridor went down to a lower level below the museum, and there consolidated in a chamber, at the center of which was one more spiral descent.

At the bottom they came to a large, well-lit chamber with portals going off in eight directions, and a variety of equipment mounted in the walls between. The portals were closed, and the equipment was strange, but Droagn's Prime let him sense within it, and even though the technology was alien and the design was unfamiliar, the function was obvious. This was the control and monitoring station for long-term life-support stasis-sleep chambers.

The portals were sealed but not locked. "If we open them," Grayshard said, "what about the risk of contaminants?"

"There are eight of them," Rikard said. "We'll have to take the chance and open just one."

Beyond was a corridor, its lights dim, along which on

either side were short narrow side alcoves, on either side of which were the stasis cabinets.

˜No need to worry about contaminants,˜ Droagn said. ˜Each of these cabinets is perfectly sealed.˜

Each was separately controlled as well as collectively controlled, and each contained an egg, which looked like a translucent iridescent pearl with a ruby at its center. Telltales adjacent to each cabinet, still operative after all these years, revealed that power was on inside, and the cyclopean version of needle scales showed values of four internally metered things to be in the safe zone.

This corridor was quite extensive, but that was all there was to it, just alcoves and cabinets, each with its own egg. They returned to the central chamber, closed the portal, and tried the next.

They didn't have to enter this time, they could see that it was the same as the first. And so were all the others, when they looked into them. There were no cyclopeans here, only eggs.

"This is utterly fantastic," Rikard said when they had closed the last of the portals, "but it is something far more important than what I think we want to get involved in."

˜That's putting it mildly,˜ Droagn said.

"What I propose to do," Rikard went on, "is to get the hell out of here, and let somebody else know about it. Make sure we get proper credit for the discovery, but get out from under it before they decide we're the experts and keep us working on it until retirement age."

"Besides," Grayshard said, "we're not experts, and never will be."

"Exactly. We found it, now somebody else can take over from here. These eggs have been waiting for a long time, and I think we all agree that it is important that something be done to bring these people back. What other provisions for their cultural and intellectual survival might have been made I don't know, unless it's the contents of the library and database and the museum upstairs."

It would take cautious work on the part of experts to recover what was there. Given the situation in New Darkon above ground, they decided it would be best to look for help in one of the other nations on Trokarion, who would recognize the importance of the find and have sufficient influence over Elsepreth to take care of the find even if the war continued.

They returned to the computer center above but as they approached the elevator, which they had left open, Kelarine soldiers stepped out from behind desks and cabinets and put them all under arrest. They were quickly disarmed and relieved of all equipment, though Rikard retained his recorder, pushed over to one side so he could see with both eyes. And it was still recording.

A Kelarin with silver markings on his harness came up, the equivalent of a lieutenant in the government forces. He appeared to be the commanding officer here.

"What is the charge?" Rikard asked him.

"You are aliens in a war zone," the officer said, "and no charge is needed."

"I appreciate that, but this place is too important to be left to the vagaries of war."

"And I appreciate that," the officer said, "which is why you are under arrest." The soldiers took them down the elevator to the center of the cone.

And there they saw Karyl Toerson and her henchmen, cleaning the place out.

3

"What the hell are you doing," Rikard yelled. He started to stride toward her, but strong Kelarine hands jerked him back. The movement slung his helmet around on his head so that he could see, peripherally, the monitor for his left eye. The helmet was still on and recording.

Karyl Toerson was not in the least perturbed. She looked up at Rikard with a lazy smile. "What does it look like?"

"It looks like you're trashing the place. You can't do that, Toerson, this is a special refuge, it's been here for a million and a half years, it must be left alone, as the inheritance of the eggs preserved here."

Toerson laughed and said, "They won't need it." She turned to one of her henchmen. "Go below," she told him. "Take Egar and Rowan with you. I want to know what's down there."

The man nodded, and two others, a man and a woman, went with him out one of the side portals.

And this, thought Rikard, is the woman who has been my grandfather's mistress all these years. If he thwarted her now, what would his grandfather do to him? But if he didn't stop her, what would she do to the cyclopeans?

"Maybe you don't appreciate just what we have here," Rikard said to her. "This isn't just the dead remains of a vanished species. This is the greatest archaeological and xeniological discovery ever. There are viable eggs here. They were put aside against just such a possibility that they might be discovered, and revived, and a whole species restored."

"No one can dispute my possession of this entire site," Toerson said. "I'll kill you and smash all the eggs if I have to."

"But that's genocide."

"So what? Philip! You know what I want."

The man named Philip acknowledged, and started giving orders to the other henchmen. They went through the artifacts and started tossing aside the less-than-perfect examples, tossing them hard, so that they broke and smashed on the floor.

"Excuse me, Messer," the lieutenant said. "What Braeth said was correct, this is a preservation site."

"I'm not interested in preservation," Toerson told him. "If there are too many items, the price will be lowered." The destruction continued.

Rikard had not really believed it when Gawin had told him that this was part of Toerson's habit. "Lieutenant," he said, "whatever Toerson did to get your help, it surely can't include permission to destroy irreplaceable artifacts or kill the survivors of another sentient species."

"I'm sorry," the officer said. "I was told to follow her orders, and unless I get counter orders from my superiors" —he paused as if he had to force himself to continue —"then that's what I'll do." He looked at Rikard, who looked back at him, and saw the monitor image out of the corner of his left eye. The telltales in the corners of the monitor showed it was working with full sound, date-tracked, and luckily with the editing track on so that it could be proved that this was an unaltered recording.

The man named Egar came up from below. "There's nothing down there but life-support equipment," he said.

Toerson leered at Rikard. "I want to see this for myself." She looked squarely at the lieutenant. "Bring them down."

They descended. Toerson looked the place over, and conferred with one of her henchmen as to how to open the stasis cabinets.

"Wait a minute," Rikard said, "you can't do that, the eggs will die."

"That's exactly my intent." She didn't look at him.

"But if you do that, a whole species will disappear."

"So what?"

"What is the matter with you? Will nothing I say stop you?"

"No." She merely watched as her henchmen examined the controls, and opened the doors to the eight long corridors. What could Rikard's grandfather possibly see in such a person? "What I take back," she said, "will be only the best, worth far more for the destruction of the rest, and with no one to dispute me.''

''What if those were Kelarins in there?'' Rikard said, and glanced at the lieutenant beside him.

''Makes no difference.'' Toerson's henchman came over and spoke a few words to her. She shook her head and went over to the controls. Rikard clenched himself, there were too many weapons drawn. He watched as she worked the controls to open the first set of cabinets. It took a few moments, and Rikard turned silently to the lieutenant, whose huge amber eyes were half-lidded. A tip of tongue protruded from between his lips, and his right hand stroked the leather of his harness. It was apparent that he was now not so sure that he was doing the right thing.

Rikard readjusted his helmet so that it was fully in place. Right eye saw the world, left eye saw the monitor, and he could control focus, depth of field, filters, audio. No one stopped him, though he felt the Kelarine lieutenant moving beside him. ''Toerson,'' he said. ''You must stop.''

''No.'' From down the corridor they could all hear the subtle sighing and clicking as each of the egg cabinets in each of the alcoves opened. She turned back to him, exultant. She seemed not to notice that his helmet was in place. ''I've waited a long time for this. These stupid people have no idea what this is all about''—she waved her hand at the soldiers—''and you can't stop me.'' She turned to the second set of controls.

Rikard turned again to the lieutenant. ''You're being made fools of. When word of this gets out it will be court-martial for everybody. Your officers had no idea of her intentions, their orders cannot stand. This is a Federal crime.''

''I have my orders,'' the lieutenant said, but his voice choked. The other soldiers were not happy either.

''Toerson!'' Rikard yelled. What kind of retribution would his grandfather exact? ''How are you going to keep your part in this secret? It won't do you any good once word gets out that you killed all these eggs.''

''But I didn't. You did.'' She grinned, and killed another batch.

Then Droagn casually dropped a hand on the lieutenant's shoulder and *projected* so that Rikard could hear, ¯You are witness to a falsification of evidence, destruction of a sentient species, piracy of archaeological treasures, kidnapping of a Federally licensed historian. Perhaps you should let someone who knows about this kind of thing handle the situation. ¯

''I swear,'' the lieutenant muttered, ''there's nothing in the training manuals to cover something like this.''

Grayshard went quickly to the soldier who was carrying Rikard's equipment, and without his resistance took Rikard's gun and tossed it to him. All other eyes were on Toerson, who was just finishing the opening of the second set of cabinets. Again there came the soft sounds, while from the first corridor they could detect now a faint trace of smell, of something once fresh beginning to spoil.

Rikard strapped on his holster. ''You understand,'' he called, ''this is all being recorded.''

She turned to him now. ''Won't do you any good after I destroy the record.'' She wasn't seeing the helmet, the holstered gun, the gloves he was pulling on. She was seeing only her own victory. She turned away to start on the third set of controls.

''No,'' Rikard said, ''it wouldn't. But it might do me some good after I destroy you.'' He gripped his gun. The mesh in the palm of the glove connected with the contact on the gun butt, and the circuit between the gun and the ranging and acceleration devices implanted in his brain was closed. Time seemed to slow by a factor of ten, as all his senses accelerated by the same proportion. She laughed, which to his ears was a low rumbling sound. He didn't even need his ranging device at this distance. He shot her in the back.

She staggered forward, surprised, but she was armored and not badly hurt. She turned and drew a unitron with her right hand.

But Rikard was moving too fast. He called even as she turned, "Don't make me do this," and his voice was strange in his own ears. She raised her gun and started to aim it at him. He fired, the bullet hit the gun and tore off her hand.

Around them, Toerson's henchmen were raising their weapons, but the soldiers were in the line of fire, and without thinking prepared to defend themselves.

Toerson staggered and fell to her knees, turning away from Rikard, but as she turned she drew her other gun with her other hand and turned full around and fired at him.

He could imagine his grandfather's wrath. Recordings would do him no good, when the most powerful individual in the Federation, after the M'Kade, came after him for murdering his mistress. The bullet clipped the side of his neck. Maybe it was time to leave home, he thought, and put a bullet into her left eye.

Her head exploded. He rocked the gun back in his hand and broke the time-accelerating circuits. Around him there were a few shots as the soldiers shot those of Toerson's henchmen who had tried to fight. He looked at the lieutenant, then took off his recording helmet and handed it to the Kelarin.

"You might be needing this," he said. Droagn and Grayshard by this time had recovered their own weapons. The three of them hurried away, leaving the cleanup to the soldiers.

"Your grandfather will have you flayed alive," Droagn said.

"Only if he catches me first. I've always wondered what the Anarchy of Raas was like. Want to come along?"